Sherlock Holmes
A Scandal in Japan

Keisuke Matsuoka

Translated by James Balzer

VERTICAL.

Published by Vertical, Inc., New York, 2019

This is a work of fiction.

ISBN: 978-1-947194-37-3

Manufactured in the United States of America

First Edition

Vertical, Inc.
451 Park Avenue South
7th Floor
New York, NY 10016
www.vertical-inc.com

Editor's note: Two passages from this text have been quoted directly from original *Sherlock Holmes* stories by Arthur Conan Doyle: "The Final Problem" and "The Adventure of the Empty House."

THE DEATH OF SHERLOCK HOLMES.

1

The sky overhead was a piercing blue. The snowdrifts piled on the towering mountain peaks were already half dissolved beneath the May sun. The scene, with the protruding rocks jutting out in shy intervals from the sheer cliff, almost seemed idyllic. But grim reality cast an all-encompassing shadow over the cliffs' beauty. The snow? Nothing more than crystals of ice accumulated from spray suspended in the atmosphere. Even now a thunderous roar, like a wail of lament, echoed interminably from all corners. The noise came from the swelling falls, below, where the snow that blanketed the hills south of Meiringen journeyed to its most final end.

It was the devil's own cauldron, imposing and fierce. Over the years the falls had worn away the cliff face, forming a deep chasm below, from which mist rose in a dense fog that encompassed the entire region. Leagues below, the frothing, cresting basin of the falls was visible as no more than a white haze.

And yet, the man standing at the precipice staring down into the falls displayed no sign of fear. Fear, after all, was but a sentiment. It was abundantly clear to him, from observing the vesicular flora growing from the craggy earth upon which he stood, that no avalanche or similar disaster had visited these cliffs for many years.

Professor James Moriarty was calm. As he looked down, he was conscious of the command he held over his mental facilities. The falls spanned 300 feet across, with a drop of 650 feet. The consequences of tumbling from such a height hardly required speculation. Moriarty, however, had no intention of meeting such a fate this day.

His persecutor had failed to see the truth and would soon be lured into his trap. Even now, that enemy must be confident that the infamous criminal mastermind he pursued was now at his wit's end and sought only a companion for his trip to hell. But Professor Moriarty's back was not yet to the wall. Multiple cubbyholes existed through which he might effect his escape. And ample possibility remained that those paltry records, what his persecutor referred to as evidence, could yet be overturned.

And yet…by and by, as time went on, Moriarty found he was not so free as he might wish. He could not, as it were, relax and linger over his tea. The man who hounded him was as tenacious as a cat, and clearly determined to continue his stubborn chase.

Conducting a perfect crime required considerable expense, and his pursuer was affecting the return in profits. If their return was lower than expected, this impacted their day-to-day operations. If they wished to end this untoward state of affairs it was imperative that the man hunting Moriarty be eliminated.

Due to that opponent's circumspect and premeditative nature, however, opportunities to do him mischief were less easily obtained. Moriarty had already faced the other man once, in his rooms at 221B Baker Street, though naturally he had not been able to make any attempt on his life at the time. The man's death would have to look like an accident, and preferably under circumstances in which the body should never be recovered.

Moriarty glanced upward. Though the cliff wall behind him seemed sheer, it contained several small footholds. With some scrambling one would arrive at the ledge that stretched out above.

From far overhead, a bearded face peered down at Moriarty from the summit of the cliff. Sebastian Moran. Moran was a former colonel in the Indian army, and a renowned hunter particularly notable for his skill in bagging the fiercest of big game. After suffering a string of losses at cards Colonel Moran had mired himself in debt, and it had been a simple matter for Moriarty to induce him into the criminal fold.

Professor Moriarty waved his hand in Moran's direction. In response, Moran lifted his air rifle—disguised to appear as a walking stick—high into the air before retreating again from sight.

With that custom-made weapon and Colonel Moran's unparalleled marksmanship, the devil would soon have his due. Despite his blindness, the German mechanic Von Herder had constructed a formidable weapon. Designed to fire pistol bullets silently, the gun was tremendously lethal.

The challenge, then, lay in inducing their target to stand upon the rocks. The mist stretched nearly to the precipice of the cliffs, obscuring Colonel Moran's aim. Their plan was dangerous enough that Colonel Moran had suggested placing a decoy in Moriarty's stead, but the professor could not consent to this. It had to be Moriarty himself who lured Sherlock Holmes out. Only by convincing him that Moriarty had been reduced to desperation and had nowhere left to run, would they spur him to give chase even at risk to his own life.

The roar of the falls drowned out all other noise. Still, Moriarty sensed, rather than heard, someone approach. He turned around.

A solitary gentleman walked toward him along the cliff's strangled path. One edge of the trail wound hopelessly into the waterfall's gaping basin. The man, however, showed no sign of fear. With his gaze fixed upon Moriarty, he planted his alpine-stock, which he held firmly in one hand, squarely into the earth.

He wore an Inverness coat draped over his suit. Though the coat was thinner than the Ulster coat Moriarty wore, and the man's figure was tall and gaunt, he seemed hardly affected by the chill air. Though arresting, the leanness of his figure was logically consistent. The man was proficient in boxing, fencing, and even the singlestick. Moriarty judged it wise not to approach within reach of the man's walking stick.

The man stood at over six feet tall, and was possessed of piercing eyes, a hawk-like nose and a distinctive, angular jaw. When they had last met Moriarty had mocked him, saying that he displayed less frontal lobe development than expected. At the moment, however, his lobe was hidden from view, his forehead concealed by his cap. Moriarty smiled despite himself. The man was wearing a deerstalker, exactly like the one in the illustrated memoirs about him written by his loyal friend.

Sherlock Holmes. Thirty-seven years old. Bachelor. That a mere detective could have pressed Moriarty this far!

The man called out, his voice booming over the sound of the falls. "Naturally I immediately realized that the Swiss lad that you dispatched had no experience as a guide. Even in May the guides in these areas are obliged to wear climbing irons with ten teeth. The boy's irons had only four."

"Are you so put out that anyone might think for even a moment that you had been fooled? Mr. Holmes, intellect is meant for more than vanity's sake."

"Undoubtedly." Sherlock glanced down into the chasm, his expression unchanged. "There are truths in this world that I would never engage to dispute. A fall from this height, for instance, should be certain death."

"You threaten me? Violence is the impulse of the barbaric and the weak of mind."

"I was merely giving voice to your own thoughts, Professor. Consigning oneself thus, in a pique of rage, to mutual annihilation, hardly befits a man of culture."

Moriarty struggled to contain his glee. By God, Holmes had fallen for it. He really believed he had Moriarty against the ropes! All was unfolding according to plan.

Sherlock Holmes raised his voice once more. "Professor Moriarty. You published your treatise on the Binomial Theorem at the mere age of 21. A mind as capable as your own ought to have applied its faculties to the betterment of mankind."

"You suggest my path has been mistaken?"

"You now stand at the very pinnacle of villainy, the hand that governs that foul syndicate that pervades London's lanes and shadows. Your mark can be found upon the majority of those fiendish crimes that have gone unanswered in our city. The air of London will only be sweeter for your loss."

"You are here to convict me? Is it a crime to oppose those artless assumptions that you and your ilk deem to be 'order'? I have merely provided a learning opportunity to an immature society."

"Crime cannot be justified in the name of enlightenment. How much blood have you spilled? The fire you started near Charing Cross Station left two pitiable children dead, and they were only four and six years of age."

"Society cannot progress without sacrifice. Study your history, Mr. Holmes."

"I believe I have. Revolution comes upon the overthrow of tyrants. London's future now hangs in the balance."

The falls reverberated with a deep groan, the rising wind creating a shifting mass from the mist. Sherlock's figure floated in and out of the fog, obscured one moment and visible the next.

Moriarty began to lose patience. The other man's feet remained firmly planted upon the narrow trail that fringed the cliff. He had drawn no closer to the rocks, where he might afford Colonel Moran his shot from above. Was it wariness on his part?

He sighed, venturing a glance down toward the basin. "The tallest waterfall in the world possesses a drop of 3,200 feet. Do you know where it is located? I am sure you do not."

"In your own imagination, I presume."

Moriarty snorted reflexively, leveling his gaze at the other man. "It does exist, Mr. Holmes. But it has yet to be officially discovered. It is located in the Guiana Highlands, in the northern reaches of the South American content."

"Evidently you wish to imply that your activities extend even to such lost reaches, but it would be fruitless for us to discuss such matters. I have no means of confirming them."

"Your world is a small one, Mr. Holmes. I imagine you are entirely ignorant of recent events in the Far East."

"Trivializing London by comparing it to the world at large will do nothing to alleviate the weight of your crimes, Professor."

"Upon observing the Guiana Highland falls, I calculated its height using triangulation. There is no doubt that it is the greatest waterfall in the world, but it strikes rock first after a plunge of 2,648 feet. How deep, do you suppose, is the basin?"

It was Sherlock's turn to chortle. "Do you think that by distracting me with calculations you will delay your fate? There is no basin. With a fall that great the water would be dispersed in the air before reaching the ground."

"Hmm…" Moriarty appraised Sherlock. It seemed he, too, was in command of his more rational faculties. "You speak as if you have seen the falls for yourself."

"I believe only what I witness directly, but when one subscribes to the principles of deduction, reason operates automatically."

"We are alike in that regard. When you departed Strasbourg with Dr. Watson and crossed the Rhone Valley and Gemmi Pass, I was watching through my binoculars. You were headed for Interlaken, I presume."

"Completely correct," Sherlock replied simply.

"When the rock fell at Lake Daubensee, however, it seems you were unable to interpret that as a warning."

"If you had hoped to hamper our progress, you might have made a grander show of your presence. I suppose you were so fearful of police notice that you felt compelled to hide."

"Ask another, Mr. Holmes. Documentation of my history of co-operation with the police, as an instructor in England and beyond, dates back 20 years or more. Naturally, I never once attended upon the police in person, if you take my meaning?"

"That is well played." Sherlock narrowed his eyes. "Should Scotland Yard inquire after the name Moriarty, the account received would differ station by station. The resultant confusion would dispense with any immediate necessity for a consistent alibi."

"It is not only my own lieutenants who have assumed the name of Moriarty. My younger brother's given name is also James, and he resembles me in outward appearance. This has proved convenient on several occasions."

"You have devised everything most cunningly. I already esteemed you as a criminal of the first order and this has only further convinced me."

Suddenly Moriarty was gripped with a sense of alarm. He pursed his lips, tightly. His aim was to come across as a desperate old man who had been backed into a corner. Perhaps he was being too much of a church-bell now.

Sherlock set his alpine-stock against the rocks. His expression suddenly took on new resolve. "If you would be good enough to allow me to leave a few lines for my friend."

"By all means. We are fast reaching the final stages of the discussion of those questions that lie between us. An interlude appears in order."

The discussion of which Moriarty spoke would be a mere formality. It was clear at this stage they were beyond reconciliation. Sherlock, too, was surely aware of that fact. He displayed no signs of agitation, however, as he drew a notebook from his pocket, opened its pages, and began writing with the tip of his pencil.

"Will you be attaching the date?" asked Moriarty. "It is the fourth of May, 1891."

"That will not be necessary," Sherlock said, without looking up. "My friend will return shortly."

It appeared his mind had been settled. His implacable purpose was to eradicate the criminal mastermind Moriarty from the face of the Earth, even should it cost him his own life. His eyes, as they rested on his notebook, betrayed no signs of hesitation.

Moriarty ground his teeth. Still Sherlock refused to step from the narrow path skirting the cliff! Colonel Moran had no shot. Moriarty kept his distance as well. Certainly he might take his chance and attempt to dash the man into the falls, but Sherlock would surely reach for that stick of his first. He had yet to lower his guard once, not even as his pencil ran across the page. The slightest shuffle of Moriarty's feet was enough cause for him to recoil. His watchfulness bordered on paranoia.

Should the shot prove impossible, Colonel Moran had also prepared several boulders that could be dropped down the cliff. It was a proposal, however, that was less than ideal. One could hardly expect that a boulder dropped from such a height would hit only its mark. A poor stroke of luck, and one of the boulders might even strike Moriarty instead.

It was critical, however, that they eliminate Sherlock Holmes while the iron was still hot. Regardless of how they dispatched of the man, the plan afterward remained the same. Arrangements had been made for Moriarty to scale the cliff face after the deed was accomplished. Colonel Moran was to let down a rope ladder so that Moriarty could get from the shelf above to the top of the cliff.

The surface of the narrow path leading to the falls was naked dirt and remained damp in all seasons. Any footprints would be readily apparent. The genius of Moriarty's plan, however, was that it would appear as if the two men had gone to the falls, whereupon neither had returned. The police would deduce that Moriarty had tumbled into the falls along with Holmes. Once Moriarty was believed dead, he would no longer have the police hounding him. He could return to London in triumph, free to lead his organization unimpeded. And with Sherlock eliminated, his trail would be forever safe from detection.

Moriarty's prospects were in alignment, and fruition was near. This chance must not be allowed to escape.

At last, Sherlock plucked his silver cigarette-case from his pocket. He tore several pages from his notebook, placed the pages inside his cigarette-case, and set the case next to his stick.

His eyes drifted absently into the distance, but only for the briefest of moments. Immediately, his gaze regained its usual sharpness. He lifted his chin and leveled his eyes at Moriarty. "I find I am able to assure myself that my career to this point has not been in vain. If you wish to settle this by discussion I am at your convenience, though

I inform you in advance that I must accede to no proposal that does not involve your surrender to the police."

The sauce of the man! Moriarty felt his temper flare. Fortunately, the time for patience was nearly past. Sherlock Holmes approached the rocks, leaving his walking stick behind.

However, he did not stay his approach until he was nearly upon the professor.

"Why do you draw so near?" demanded Moriarty.

"So that we may better hear one another. We have agreed to settle these matters between us by discussion, have we not? A shape-up would be beneath the dignity of a man in your position, Professor, I'm sure."

"Indeed," said Moriarty, taking a step away and attempting to lure him further toward the rocks. "Come this way, so that we may discuss matters face to face."

In response, Sherlock grabbed him by the arm. "I shall stay at your very side. There can be no interference in our conversation."

This was precisely the behavior that Moriarty found so infuriating. With Sherlock so close, it was impossible for Colonel Moran to take his shot.

Then toss him from the cliffs and be done with it! The thought flashed into Moriarty's head as his pulse rose.

Moriarty was inexperienced in the savage art of fisticuffs. In his career as a criminal, his role had been only to organize and plan—the deeds themselves had always been carried out by his agents. This moment, however, only required that he force Holmes back a few paces. If he was able to place Sherlock on the rocks for even a second, Moran would secure the kill. No game, however fierce, was beyond the colonel's skill.

2

Sherlock realized immediately that Moriarty was preparing to free his arm.

Like Sherlock, Moriarty was tall and thin, but he was also far older. His face was pale and wan, and his eyes were hollow and sunken beneath a balding, protruding forehead. His face, which jutted forward due to the stoop of his back and tended to undulate with his movements, had ceased to quiver. His eyes were fixated on him.

A man accustomed to fighting would move briskly, before allowing their opponent a chance to read their intentions. Men less accustomed to such brush-ups, however, might hesitate before their courage reached its sticking point. Such men had a tendency to adopt mannerisms designed to conceal what they were planning. Moriarty was breathing quickly, obviously deliberating over his stance. He opened and closed his hands unconsciously, perhaps to test his own grip. Indeed, the professor's behavior was unmistakable.

A moment later he jostled his arm free and shoved Sherlock in the chest. He was pushed back toward the cliff. But Sherlock reacted immediately. A left jab? No, he stretched his arms toward Moriarty and grabbed his lapels in both hands. A look of surprise crossed Moriarty's face. *As it might*, Sherlock thought. In the Western imagination, grabbing at your opponent in such a manner during a fight would seem futile. One might secure one's opponent, but with both hands thus engaged there would be no opportunity to carry through with further strikes. Moriarty was likely only capable of interpreting his move as a precursor to desperation—namely, throwing himself from the cliffs with Moriarty in tow.

Such, however, was not his intention. His body moved half by instinct. Still gripping Moriarty's lapels in both hands he took a step backward and jammed his elbow tightly into the professor's side. He was in his opponent's pocket in an instant. Turning his body, he threw Moriarty backward, over his shoulder.

Moriarty's hefty mass was flung into the air, their positions instantly reversed. Landing at the edge of the cliff, Moriarty scrambled to gain his footing. His balance, however, already tilted dangerously toward the falls. He clutched at Sherlock's shoulders, but the other man only straightened his back and shook him off. Once a man's center of gravity had been destroyed, it was easy to dispatch him without further resistance. This was the foundation of jujitsu.

Moriarty's arms, flung up in the air, began flailing desperately like the wings of a bird. But one glance showed it was too late for him to regain his footing.

"Holmes!" Moriarty screamed as he fell. He plummeted down the sheer cliff face, his body macerated in the falls before it struck a rock. He rebounded upon impact and finally collided with the rolling water below. The entire process took mere seconds. The basin below continued to seethe with tremendous quantities of water, betraying no indication that anything had transpired. Moriarty was entirely lost from sight.

Sherlock breathed sharply, winded. Eventually, he realized that he stood at the very edge of the rocks. The spray surrounded him on all sides like a heavy fog. And how fortunate that it did, he thought. Though it was unlikely that anyone had been watching them, he was still grateful for the cover.

He was struck suddenly with inspiration. Perhaps this situation could be turned to his advantage.

Only two sets of footprints led to the place. If Sherlock did not return, he might fake his own death.

Once the remaining members of Moriarty's gang, laying low in London, were to learn of Sherlock Holmes' death, they would likely abandon restraint and venture out into the open. But without Moriarty to guide them they were nothing but a motley band of blundering fools. A few anonymous letters to the police, the proper hint here and there, and the remaining men should soon be placed in the docks.

But if he were simply to return to London? Then Moriarty's criminal agents would burrow even further underground, continuing to harass Sherlock with dogged attempts upon his life.

It would not stand. If he were assumed dead, his enemies might be rounded up in one fell swoop.

Ought he to meet with Watson so the two of them could get their stories straight? No, John was an honest man. Expecting him to conceal the death of his dearest friend would be too much.

Sherlock glanced furtively at his alpine-stock and cigarette-case, which still rested against the rocks. A twinge of guilt gnawed at him, but he was aware that he was only delaying the inevitable.

He turned around. He strode quickly toward the towering cliff face and hugged the rocks closely. Placing his feet against the outcroppings, he began to clamber up the rocks. His clothes would be thick with mud, but no matter. If he were to tumble backward, head over heels, it would be a hasty plunge into the waters below. To his ears, the roar of the falls sounded like Moriarty's plaintive wail. The rocks were extremely slick. He clutched at a patch of weeds only to have the roots pull free. Nearly losing his balance, by some feat of strength he managed to cling to the cliff face, persisting in his treacherous climb.

He found a rock shelf at the height of approximately two men from the ground. The shelf itself was some three feet deep, forming a naturally flat bed covered in soft green moss. He sprawled across it. Surely he was now hidden from sight from those below.

But were his actions rational? The thought only now occurred to him. He had not yet given much consideration to what view the law might take of his feigning his own death.

Sherlock recalled the case of Neville St. Clair, a man discovered alive though formerly presumed dead. *If you leave it to a court of law to clear the matter up,* he had told Neville at the time, *of course you can hardly avoid publicity. On the other hand, if you convince the police authorities that there is no possible case against you, I do not know that there is any reason that the details should find their way into the papers.*

He grimaced. He wondered how Inspector Bradstreet might react if he were assigned his case in London. Lestrade, at least, might be expected to show some sympathy.

But of course, Sherlock's situation was a touch graver than St. Clair's had been. Considering that he had been present at the time of Moriarty's fall, it would likely prove impossible for him to escape suspicion for murder. Would a court recognize self-defense? And should he be kept in custody for the entirety of the trial, Moriarty's brother might make maneuvers during that time. It admitted no question, then. Sherlock would have to remove himself from society for the present—heavy though the consequences might be.

The sound of voices began to mingle with the roar of the falls. Sherlock realized he was not imagining things. He raised himself up slightly and peered over the edge of the shelf.

Below him was a group of uniformed policemen. They stood with another gentleman—a man two years older than Sherlock was, sporting a mustache, and with a face that bespoke good nature. The living image of fidelity and faith, none other than Dr. John Watson.

His friend's state of distraction was apparent. He peered fretfully into the chasm several times, before collapsing upon one of the rocks with a groan. He seemed to have caught sight of Sherlock's alpine-stock. He took up the cigarette-case laying by its side.

A pang seized at Sherlock's chest. What an execrable wretch he must be, that the day should come that he must deceive the trust of the very dearest of friends.

Absorbed for a time in reading the letter he had left behind, Watson lifted his face at last, his expression one of baffled despair. His face stricken with grief, he shouted desperately into the falls: "Sherlock. Sherlock!"

Sherlock felt a wave of hot misery overcome him. Looking at the sky, his vision swam with tears. There were no eyes upon him now. Surely this once he might be forgiven for momentarily giving in to a little sentiment. Without this slight release, he feared he might cry out for Watson, and then all would be naught—he would only face constant designs upon his life, and his friend would be exposed to considerable danger.

Watson had been his constant companion. He had shuttered his practice for over a week already to join Sherlock in their present maneuvers. He recalled the day he had first met the doctor, at the hospital chemical laboratory, as if it were only yesterday. A man like Watson might be found anywhere, and yet Watson, the man, was possessed of a temperament unique among any Sherlock had heretofore encountered.

Friendships between men are built without words. Or so prevailing wisdom demanded. Sherlock had never believed such tripe. Indeed, the two of them engaged in frequent conversation. And while familiarity was known to breed contempt, such was never the case with them. Watson could be called upon whatever the hour, morning or night, and had never hesitated not only in sympathizing with Sherlock but even in joining him in his endeavors.

The only sound that remained now was the deep groan of the falls. He leaned over the edge a second time.

Watson was gone, along with the police. He had taken the stick and cigarette-case with him.

Sherlock turned his eyes toward the sky once more with a heavy heart.

He placed his two hands before his face. They were numb as churchyards, and he had lost feeling entirely in the fingertips. Was it from the climb? No, not the climb. They had been stiff as boards ever since he threw Moriarty. He must have clenched his hands with considerable tension.

Sherlock had executed the move instantly. His body had remembered it for him. The first time he had witnessed the move performed, he had been only ten years old…

Although Sherlock had still been a child then, he had recognized something unusual about the young man's appearance. He had worn a silk top hat and frock coat, like any common Londoner, but the articles were evidently too large for him. The man was so slender and slight that he might even have been confused for a woman dressed in men's clothing. His complexion, too, was so clear, and his features so youthful, that Sherlock almost didn't believe the man later when he revealed he was 22. Though Oriental, the man was evidently not Chinese. His movements were quick and agile, his posture strict, and he spoke English with a vaguely labored pronunciation that Sherlock found distracting.

The man's name was Shunsuke Ito, and he had travelled to London as a stowaway, he had told him, though discovery on the ship would have surely meant death…

Suddenly there was a change in the air pressure against his face. A dark shadow menaced his field of vision, quickly growing larger. A boulder! Sherlock gasped, rolling over. He pressed his body against the cliffs, hugging the rocks. A piercing whistle invaded his ear, before the boulder smashed into the ledge and crashed down the cliff.

He looked up. A bearded face peered back at him from atop the cliff. The face drew back, and immediately another boulder came rolling down. He attempted to take cover.

The third boulder hit the cliff with a shrill cry before rolling further down. For a moment, all was still. Sherlock shimmied out from the natural rock bed and latched onto the edge. If he attempted to simply jump down, the momentum would likely send him tumbling all the way into the falls. Instead he slithered, searching by inches for footholds. Another boulder whistled past his ear, rebounding off the rocky outcropping below before disappearing, spinning, into the watery chasm.

His feet finally reached solid ground below. The skin on both hands was scraped and raw. They throbbed as painfully as if they had been burned. Blood oozed from his palms. Sherlock's trials, however, were not yet over. He dashed toward the narrow trail that hugged the cliff face, putting new distance between himself and the falls.

It must have been one of Moriarty's men. He knew now that Sherlock was still alive. This meant Sherlock had lost half the benefit of playing dead, and to the very enemy against whom such advantage was needed most. What should he do? Surely his sterling intellect would hit upon a solution. At the moment, however, he need better apply his full faculties to escaping his predicament in one piece.

As of today, Sherlock Holmes was dead. A trifling ghost. There was no one he could rely on now. Not even dear Watson.

3

Properly speaking, it was the fourth year of the Bunkyu era. But as this year fell on the first of a new sexagenery cycle in the Chinese calendar, which according to ancient divination portended great political upheaval, the name of the year was instead changed to that of the first year of the Genji era. Changing the era name every few years in this way was extremely inefficient. Using the Western calendar, one could express the year in four simple numbers: The year was 1864.

At age 22, however, Shunsuke Ito was beginning to realize that Western culture was not always something to be aspired to.

In March in London, the air had begun to shed its chill and the snow that had accumulated on the streets had finally disappeared. Ito took advantage of the change in weather to escape the streets surrounding his college and stroll through a few areas he rarely visited.

Though Cheapside was bustling, there was something about the thoroughfare, tucked into a corner of the City of London district with its view of St. Mary-le-Bow Church, he felt was slightly off. True, Cheapside offered the same elegant scenery as the other high streets. The rows of stone and masonry-structure buildings were adorned with splendid classic architectural motifs. And in Cheapside, as in those other neighborhoods, the number of carriages that travelled to and fro was the same, as was the clothing worn by the pedestrians and the way the women dragged their hems as they walked. Ito had learned from a girl whose company he had briefly enjoyed that those skirts were puffed out with bustles and crinolines.

Yet despite these superficial gestures of respectability, Cheapside felt overladen with an atmosphere of cheerlessness. It was ordinary to see men smudged with faint coats of dirt, immediately identifiable as laborers. The children who ran through the streets, too, were less than kempt in appearance. Drunks squatted in the gutters. And the men who gathered around the hand-drawn two-wheeled stalls, sipping coffees, did not, for all appearances' sake, seem to hold respectable jobs.

But all the same, these men were all accompanied by young women, with whom they seemed poorly matched. Opportunities for flirtation could be found in every walk of life, Ito supposed. Spurred by curiosity, he took a seat upon one of the wooden crates that had been set out in place of chairs. The portly vendor glanced at Ito as if to take his order. "A coffee, please," he requested politely.

The rim of the cup he was handed was chipped. The aroma only barely suggested coffee. Ito had expected as much, as soon as he realized the stall had no coffee siphon. He rose slightly from his seat and peered across the stall. A rusted tin had been set upon a fire. Crushed beans were simply swept in and boiled. Any other method was probably too unprofitable.

A young woman sporting a gaudy hair ornament sat down next to Ito. "Buy us a cup?" she asked, a lilt to her voice that seemed vaguely coquettish.

Before Ito could reply, the proprietor handed the woman a coffee. The woman stroked her chest eagerly, turning to Ito with an inviting look upon her face.

Despite her heavy makeup the woman was clearly beautiful. Ito's interest was stirred, but he quickly admonished himself.

Of the five of them who had come to London from Japan, Ito had the reputation for being the biggest rake. For his own part, he was sure Kinsuke Endo was worse than he. The leader of their group, however, Yozo Yamao, had warned them both to refrain from their usual womanizing.

Of course, it was clear what trade the woman was plying. Obviously this stall was a place for laborers to spend what little money they had on the company of prostitutes. As this was central London such business was, of course, prohibited. But perhaps that explained the need for such complicated introductions.

Ito shrunk at the prospect of bluntly refusing the woman's advances. He had taken a seat at the stall without being aware of the custom. However, he could hardly break the promise he had made to his friends. His only option…

Ito reached into his pocket and retrieved a handful of coins. Four shillings and 10 pence, it marked the extent of the money currently at his disposal. He handed it all to the woman, speaking to her in English. It was a language he had only recently grown serviceable in.

"Another time. This is to help support you."

Would she find his charity presumptuous? The woman's eyes widened for a moment, but a smile immediately crossed her face. "Thanks awfully," she said in an undertone, taking the money without offense. "You're a gent, though. Where're you come from?"

"Japan."

"Eh, where's that?"

"The farthest East. Even farther than China."

"And do they all put a hand in the pocket for the ladies there?"

Ito smiled. "Maybe not all…"

"Right then," muttered the woman, placing the money in her pocketbook. "Thank the mussies for ye. With this I'll be after some bread 'stead of just currant cake and porridge. And with butter, not drippings."

"Life is hard?"

"Ain't it though. Everyone's busted around here. You'll want to keep clear of the metal hawkers. Costers, that lot, and set their wares too dear," said the woman, standing up. "That's me then. Thanks for the crack."

The woman's golden hair, which hung down her back in a braid, swayed like a horse's tail as she walked away.

The proprietor cleared away the woman's cup. She hadn't taken a single sip. The proprietor evidently considered Ito a rube. He could read it in the man's face.

Not that he was wrong. Ito stood up, feeling lighter, and walked away from the stall.

He glanced about. The fog, which a year or so earlier he had found romantic, he now knew owed half of its density to the coal burning from factories and homes. He was no longer so eager to breathe it quite as deeply as before. The walls of the buildings were also stained with soot, and the cobblestones on the street were significantly damaged. There were cracks and holes as far as the eye could see.

Half of London lived in poverty. Those living in the centrally located City and the West End were upper class. The other neighborhoods were located in the East End. Less prosperous areas, however, could also be found scattered, like the enclaves in East End, throughout the City and West End. Even the bustling commercial Strand district teemed with vagabonds in the side-alleys. Cheapside, too, was an example of such a place.

After Ito's grueling voyage, which had lasted four and a half months, his first sight of London had been like the glimpse of a promised land: a stonework capital where steam-powered locomotives raced with the wind and lofty cathedrals pierced the sky. It was such a breathtaking sight that he had wondered if he had died at sea and was seeing the afterlife.

Now, of course, he knew better. Once he had believed that England was a land of dreams—but if there was much worth emulating here, there was also much that was not.

Suddenly the air was split with the cracking of hooves. A hansom cab drew up short just as it prepared to round a corner. Directly, a boy ran in front of the cab and dashed across the street. He looked to be around ten years of age. Unlike the other children Ito had spotted along the thoroughfare, this boy was dressed in high quality clothing. His cap, jacket, vest, shirt, and boots all suggested he was middle class or higher. Although the boy was thin, his complexion was healthy. His thinness clearly wasn't due to malnutrition. There was also a maturity to his face, perhaps due to the proud jut of his hawk-like nose.

The tremulous manner in which his eyes darted about, however, as if the world was still new to him, was in better keeping with his actual age.

An older, much heavier-set boy leaned out from the carriage—closer to a man, really, than a boy, perhaps in his late teens. He shouted frantically at the other boy. "Sherlock! Oi, Sherlock. Wait!"

But the boy named Sherlock paid him no mind, slipping between passersby before dashing across Ito's path.

The older boy finished paying the cab and then alighted onto the street. He lumbered awkwardly as he moved, his bulky form nearly bursting from his frock coat. Although he gave chase, he was not very fast. The distance between the two boys only grew.

Sherlock glanced back at his pursuer several times. Not paying enough attention to where he was running, he collided directly into a stall lined with metal wares. The stall—a two-wheel pull-cart—was hurtled sideways. Pots and ladles careened across the cobblestones with a tumultuous crash.

Sherlock froze in place, a sheepish expression upon his face. The older boy finally caught up to him, now out of breath.

"Ahh…" He scowled, grabbing the young boy by the arms. "Have off. What's the point of running, Sherlock?"

Sherlock shook the boy's arm off. "If you want to go you can go without me, Mycroft."

"You promised today you'd finally see to your lessons with Master Partridge."

"I loathe Master Partridge. His lessons are a waste of time. He's a know-nothing. I don't see why anyone should sit for him."

"You're only angry that he scolded you for being disorderly."

"That's not true. He couldn't even answer a simple question. I only asked him why oysters don't cover the entire floor of the sea."

"I'm sure he thought it was a silly question."

"And what is wrong with asking a teacher to explain something I don't understand?"

The boy was rather argumentative for his age. No sooner had Ito finished the thought, however, than he saw the two boys interrupted by a brash shout. "Hoy!"

Sherlock and his brother turned around. Three brawny, thick-necked men stood behind them. All three wore their hair cropped close. Their jackets and vests were coarse, even by working-class standards.

"We ain't selling this lot now," shouted one of the men, his eyes bulging in a rage. "You're chucking up for them. It's a tenner, right."

The older brother seemed afraid. Sherlock, however, appeared unperturbed. He returned the man's gaze and answered calmly.

"Naturally. If I might convince our parents, of course? After all, you are hardly engaged in a reputable trade."

"Are you boshing us? You know how much we put down on this?"

"You put down not one shilling. The nails on the thumbs of your hands are splintered, and there are marks from bruising on the pads of your fingers, as well. This tells me that you possess not even a single pry bar, and are in the regular practice of prying open wooden cargo from the merchant ships with your bare hands. In the common parlance, I believe such acts are generally referred to as larcen—"

Sherlock was cut off mid-sentence. The man had struck him across the cheek with his fist. The boy was thrown bodily off his feet and landed on the street in a heap.

Mycroft quickly stepped between the men and his brother. "Please, you'll have to forgive my brother for being rude. His schooling has been getting on poorly of late, and I'm afraid he's begun to get in a way."

"Right so?! You lot are trussed out in fine enough clobber! Let's see if the older one ain't gonna get his own shiner, neither!"

"Enough!" shouted Ito.

The entire street fell quiet. Even the carriages stopped short as the coachmen turned to look. There wasn't a person nearby who was not now staring at Ito.

The three metal hawkers also stared at him, dumbfounded. Ito strode toward them quickly. Now that he was nearer, he could see just how large they were. Ito, meanwhile, was no taller than the two boys. The top of his silk top hat just barely reached the men's chins.

One of the hawkers stepped close, revealing a mouthful of crooked teeth. "Oy, what's this? Another godfer wants to empty his pockets, does he? Fancy I could do your coat up as a nursery jacket and turn it over for a penny. Give it over then, before—"

He reached out with both hands to grab Ito, as he spoke. Ito reacted instinctively. He grabbed the man's lapels in both hands, and took a deep step backward. He planted his elbow into the man's side, and quickly pivoted close. Turning his body, he threw the man backward, over his shoulder.

The crowd erupted in surprise. The man whistled through the air before striking the cobblestones on his back. Ito hadn't meant to throw him hard enough to cause serious injury. The man, however, lay sprawled on the ground, spread-eagled. He appeared to be unconscious.

Ito's top hat had tumbled to the ground. Retrieving it would have to wait.

The two remaining men stared at Ito with expressions of disbelief. The eyes of Sherlock and his brother were wide as well.

Finally, one of the men darted forward. "Damned Chinaman!"

Already he had closed the distance between them. Ito calculated quickly. The situation this time demanded karate, not jujitsu. He squared his arms to his chest and without dropping his shoulders delivered a lightning-fast rising punch. The man staggered backward with a groan as the punch connected squarely with his jaw. Ito pivoted the heel of his dominant foot toward the man, delivering a thrust kick with the edge of his other foot. The man doubled over, clutching at his stomach before tottering to his knees and collapsing.

Ito stared down at him. "I am not Chinese."

The remaining man reached into the push-cart, prying free an iron bar. It was at least four feet long. He began inching toward Ito, brandishing the bar in both hands. His eyes were bloodshot with anger.

Just then, a woman's voice called out to him. "Hoy, Mr. Japan!"

Ito glanced over only to see the prostitute from earlier. She tossed him a length of wood. It was merely a squared wooden plank, but it was as long as his opponent's weapon and appeared sturdy enough. Ito gripped it in both hands, like a katana, and settled into a stance. He held the plank with one corner facing down, thus ensuring a downward strike would deliver considerable force.

The man rushed Ito with a whoop. Ito stepped forward without hesitation, parrying his opponent's metal rod to the side and following with a full-weighted strike to the man's brow. The man froze. His eye fluttered back in his head, his body went limp, and he crumpled to the ground.

The prostitute who had thrown the stick let out a cheer and clapped her hands together. As if to squelch her enthusiasm, the shrill sound of a police whistle immediately pierced the air.

The color suddenly drained from the older brother's face. "Confound it, it's the police."

Ito helped Sherlock up, hurriedly. "Can you run?"

Sherlock nodded. Ito swiped his top hat from the ground and cut from the scene with the two boys.

While the scenery around them was for all intents identical to any street in the East End, they were in fact in Cheapside, part of the area known as the City of London. They needed only to slip through a side-alley for their surroundings to morph into those of an orderly metropolis. Ito ushered the boys into a Hamish restaurant he often went to. It was a small establishment, frequented by tourists and other foreigners. Here, even the unlikely combination of an Easterner with two English boys would not draw stares.

The restaurant was fairly quiet in this lull between peak hours. Ito sat down at the counter and ordered three lemonades from the bartender.

"Where are those four chaps you're always mucking about with?" said the waitress, Enola, teasingly. "It looks as if you've finally found yourself some English mates. They're a tender lot though, I'll grant you that."

"I thought I should make some friends my own size," Ito replied with a grimace. "Enola, may I have a damp towel?"

"Straight away," she said, dipping behind the counter.

Sherlock took the towel from her and pressed it against his cheek, which was beginning to swell. One eye was hidden behind the towel, but the other stared unblinkingly at Ito.

"Is something wrong?" asked Ito, curious.

"One of your four friends is acquainted with an English gentleman in Hakodate, but you yourself have never been introduced to the man. Your trip to England is also your first foray abroad. You have never been to America."

Ito's jaw gaped, despite himself. He stared at Sherlock. Sherlock stared back, unperturbed.

"I believe you forgot to thank the man," the older boy admonished. He turned to face Ito. "You saved us earlier. We can't begin to thank you. My name is Mycroft Holmes."

"My name is Shunsuke Ito. I am 22. How old are you, Mycroft?"

"Seventeen. My brother, here, however, is only ten."

"And very mature for his age. He is clever."

"You mean *clever*," Sherlock muttered.

"What?" Ito said.

"Your C sounds like a K, and your V sounds like a B. If you aspire to smooth communication then you should apply yourself to proper pronunciation."

A tinge of anger appeared in Mycroft's face. "Sherlock!"

Ito smiled, waving Mycroft off with one hand. "It's fine," he said, taking a sip of the lemonade Enola had brought. "He is correct. The pronunciation of C and V is difficult for Japanese people. It is also very hard for us to distinguish between L and R."

Sherlock seemed to be fast regaining his former confidence. "Like the Chinese."

"Sherlock," said Mycroft, raising his voice. "Enough."

Sherlock, however, continued to stare at Ito in fascination. "It's something, rather, that a group of stowaways should be housed under the care of Professor Alexander Williamson and his wife. However did you manage such an arrangement?"

Ito broke into a coughing fit, choking on his lemonade. "How did you know *that*?"

"Professor Williamson and his wife both work," Sherlock added, "but they take supper with you and the other Japanese men once a week."

Mycroft shook his head. "Not once a week," he said. "Once every three or four days."

A sense of alarm stole over Ito. They had taken great care to keep their daily activities a secret, and now two young boys he had just met were describing those activities in detail. Accurate detail. It was unsettling. "Forgive me, but would you mind telling me where you heard such rumors?"

"Please, forgive our rudeness," Mycroft interpolated apologetically. "There were no rumors. This is a poor habit of my brother's."

"A habit?" Ito glanced at Sherlock.

Sherlock sighed quietly, still holding the towel to his face. "You speak with a Liverpool accent. I read in the papers that the British legation at the international trading port of Hakodate was staffed largely by persons from Liverpool. Your pronunciation, however, is far from natural. Obviously you learned English from a friend who learned English from someone at the legation. From the manner in which Enola spoke of them earlier I gather that your four friends are all Japanese."

"You're awfully keen for a boy of ten," Enola said, a look of amazement on her face.

"In America," Mycroft said, suppressing a grin, "they refer to a sweetened carbonated lemon beverage as lemon squash, not lemonade. In America, lemonade refers to sweet lemon water without carbonate. I presume my brother noticed that you did not hesitate when ordering."

Ito fidgeted restlessly, reaffixing his smile. "That still doesn't explain how you knew the rest."

"You were aware of which street to take without pausing," Sherlock continued dispassionately, "which leads me to conclude that you have been in London for about a year. However, your sleeves are also stained with brill shrimp sauce and oyster soup. The fact that you are still unaccustomed to English dining manners after such a period of time tells me that you and your fellows are left to partake at your own liberty, with but few opportunities to dine with your hosts."

Mycroft seemed exasperated. "Sherlock, you are being terribly rude."

"You are also wearing the pocket watch chain that London University presents to professors upon every five years of service," continued Sherlock, his expression unperturbed. "I have read in a book that Japanese men are very proud, so I imagine the same gift was made to all five men. Even if the professor in question were appointed at the age of 30, allowing one more chain for the man himself, he would have to be over 60 now. To harbor stowaways for payment, such a professor would likely be retired and thus find himself strapped for—"

Mycroft quickly cut in. "What my brother means to say is that you appear to have received instructions in deportment, allowing us to deduce that the professor has a wife. Perhaps they are a couple with several children who have grown up and moved away, thus allowing them to furnish you with rooms."

"The professor's wife, however, works outside of the home," added Sherlock. "Your laundry is insufficient, she lacks leisure to instruct you in British English, and cannot take meals with you every day. I have an interest in chemistry, and often read articles pertaining to Professor Williamson, who was awarded the Royal Medal. I couldn't help but notice that the particulars of his career, his level of comfort, his domestic situation, and even the working habits of his wife coincide with these particulars."

Ito leaned forward. "One more point. How did—"

"How did I know you were a stowaway? The scars on your palms have not yet fully healed. They show you had repeatedly wrapped rope around your hands. You were in charge of hoisting the sails for your entire journey, work which is usually relegated to the lowest members of a ship crew. The oil in the detergent used to polish the decks causes the hands to blister. There would be no reason for a mere impoverished laborer to stay with the professor and his wife. However…"

"There is more?"

"Despite your status as a stowaway, I presume you found your passage quite agreeable. After all, even after remunerating the captain and Professor and Mrs. Williamson, your funds were more than adequate to provide for yourselves in comfortable circumstances, were they not?"

Ito's spirits had sunk with each new statement, but here at last a smile escaped his lips. "You are wrong about one thing," he murmured, his emotions conflicted. "Our funds were not that great. And it was not an agreeable journey. The moment we left our country, we knew we were committing a capital offense."

A look of shock appeared on the faces of both brothers. Sherlock stared at Ito, his eyes particularly wide. "A capital offense? You mean execution? Does Japan's government prohibit people from travelling overseas? Since Professor Williamson agreed to lodge you, I assumed that some high-ranking official must have been involved…"

"The Choshu Domain went to great lengths to sponsor us. We were given the equivalent of 350 pounds each, in Japanese money. But the Bakufu does not support us."

"Bakufu?" asked Sherlock, furrowing his brow. "Choshu?"

"Japan is a complicated country."

Just then a man rushed into the establishment and approached them. He was dressed in a frock coat, identical to Ito's. It was Monta Shiji, yet another of the Choshu Five.

Monta seemed ruffled. He spoke to Ito in Japanese. "Here you are. I've been looking for you."

"What's wrong?" asked Ito, also in Japanese.

In response Monta drew forth an English newspaper. It was the *Times*. "Look at this."

He glanced at the page, where Monta's finger indicated a small article. Shock ran down Ito's spine. According to the headline, Britain had entered into retaliations against the Choshu Domain.

He read the article in disbelief. In May of last year, Choshu had blockaded the Bakan Strait[1], and without warning was attacking American, French, and Dutch trading ships that attempted to pass through. A few weeks later American and French warships had attacked the Choshu fleet stationed in the straits, dealing a devastating blow to Choshu's maritime capabilities. Choshu, however, continued the blockade, refortifying its remaining batteries and occupying a portion of the Kokura Domain on the opposite shore to build new ones. As a result, Britain, citing the economic loss it had sustained, had called on American, French and Dutch aid. The powers were now preparing for a joint strike against Choshu.

Ito raised his head, dumbstruck. "What is this?"

Monta scratched at his face. "Our time in London has blinded us. Choshu still clings to outdated notions of the domain above all. All they speak of is *joui*.[2] They think it is a matter of samurai pride to meet the foreigners with force."

"They'll never understand the overwhelming technology and logistics of the West unless they see it for themselves. At this rate, not just Choshu but all of Japan will be crushed."

Sherlock glanced at the paper. "History shows that it is often the fate of small countries, lacking in civilization, to underestimate their enemy's strength and hasten their own destruction."

Monta understood English too. He glanced at Sherlock sharply, and stepped in close. "Even a child should know when to hold his tongue…"

Ito interceded, speaking in Japanese. "Calmly! You think that was just childish impudence? Ask those adults over there, then. This is what all English people believe. They view us as a tiny Eastern country, impulsive and barbaric."

---

1 Now known as the Strait of Shimonoseki.

2 *Joui* (攘夷) is a nationalist slogan from 19th century Japan meaning "expel the barbarians."

"But the only reason we've embraced *joui* is so we can undermine the foolish Bakufu, to weaken it and overthrow it."

"That's not how it is seen overseas. They make no distinction between us and the Satsuma Clan, who carried out the Namamugi Incident. To them we are all Japanese, and all violent by nature."

Monta fell silent, anger brewing in his face. He sighed deeply, and then spoke more quietly. "I won't allow Japan to follow this path toward destruction. I will return to Choshu and convince them that this is a war that cannot be won."

Despite his initial shock, Ito immediately found his own resolve. "I will go as well."

"Don't be foolish. My presence alone will be adequate. Don't forget, Lord Mori only agreed to send us here with the promise that we'd study this country's technology and bring it back with us when we return. Yozo, Yakichi, and Endo will all stay behind in London as well. I hardly like going myself."

Ito raised his voice. "What good will learning technology do us if Japan is destroyed?" Silence descended. Ito stared at Monta. Monta stared back wordlessly.

"We should go quickly, then," he relented finally. His tone was subdued.

"Yes." Ito nodded. "We had better."

Monta turned on his heel, his face serious, and walked toward the door. Ito followed after.

In response, Sherlock ran after Ito, stepping in front of him and blocking his path. "Wait. You're making a mistake."

Though half-annoyed, Ito paused. "You don't even know what we were talking about."

"That's not true. I was able to discern enough based on the article and your expressions. You're going to return to your country, aren't you? You can't do anything about the madness happening there. Please, consider your own safety."

"It's not madness. It's *joui*."

"Joi? Who is Joi?"

"It's not a person, it's a philosophy. You wouldn't understand. Now get out of my way."

A look of distress crossed Sherlock's face. "You said that the moment you left Japan it was a capital offense. If you return to Japan, you'll be killed!"

The entire restaurant fell silent. Young Sherlock stared at Ito, his face pleading. He seemed so mature for his age, but here, at last, was an expression on his face that a child might make.

He certainly is an intelligent boy, Ito thought. No one could deny that his observations, no matter how unasked for or even unwelcome, were correct. Behind that intelligence, however, he possessed a sensitivity that surpassed the norm. Ito was happy to catch a glimpse of the boy behind the mask, even if only for a moment.

He sighed once, and then spoke quietly. "Listen, Sherlock. I've been prepared for death ever since I slipped out in the middle of the night and boarded that ship to England. Even at sea, or while here in London, I knew that the Bakufu's men might catch up with me at any moment."

"You were never at your ease."

"Not so. The five of us slept soundly every night, because we were busy with our studies during the day. What more could we ask, than to give our lives for our country? We were too busy with that mission to worry about small things."

"But what good will that be if you're killed?"

"Nothing is certain. I will try to persuade them. I may not look it, but when I was younger my sensei used to tell me I was a natural politician."

Monta interrupted, speaking in Japanese. "What Shoin-sensei said, I believe, was that you were a hopeless student."

Ito checked Monta with a glance, and then turned back toward Sherlock. "I will tell the daimyo how advanced England is. I am sure he will understand."

"Then I'll go with you," said Sherlock, a desperate expression on his face.

"Hoy," said Mycroft, startled. "Enough silly talk."

Sherlock, however, didn't even glance in his brother's direction. "I could demonstrate the British Empire's superiority through analytical reasoning," he continued, pleading with Ito.

Mycroft grabbed Sherlock by the arm. "Every time you run off you manage to get a little farther, but I'm sure Japan is a sight farther than any train ticket will take you. If you want to get a dig at Master Partridge so badly, you had better find another way."

"That isn't my motive," said Sherlock, flatly. "We owe Shunsuke our lives. It's my duty to repay him."

"If you believe you owe Mr. Ito your life, then isn't there something you ought to say to him?"

Sherlock seemed suddenly reluctant. He stammered sheepishly, his eyes wet. "Shunsuke…. I mean to say, thank you."

Mycroft sighed. "My brother is horrendous at apologies and thank yous," he said to Ito.

"I understand." Ito flashed a smile. "You are both much more observant and knowledgeable than one might expect from children. You also show deductive powers beyond your years. Adults must sometimes seem very foolish to you. But please, turn those exceptional talents to the good of your own country. Don't let those minds go to waste by throwing them away now."

Mycroft nodded in response. "I plan to enter public service."

"That is excellent."

Sherlock sulked in response. "My brother only dislikes taking exercise. His main concern is the prospect of deskwork and a stable income."

As an only child, Ito was poorly equipped to intercede in sibling rivalry. He couldn't help but feel slightly envious, though. It must take a mutual awareness of their similarities to vent one's disappointments so openly to the other.

He nevertheless tried to intervene between the brothers. "You see? The two of you are fighting, when you should be friends. That is exactly the sort of thing I am going back to Japan to stop. Do you understand now?"

Sherlock and Mycroft glanced at each other uncomfortably, and then collapsed into shamefaced silence.

"Shunsuke…?" offered Sherlock, hesitantly. "How did you manage to lay out those three men even though they were so much bigger than you?"

"*Bujutsu*. The martial arts. I used jujitsu, karate, and kenjutsu."

"If I went with you could I learn too?"

The waitress, Enola, snorted through her nose. "Are you still on about that? I wager the only way to learn that kind of stuff is by doing it. But I fancy they'd crack you in half like a walnut if you tried."

Ito shook his head, grimacing. "No warrior would strike unprovoked at a defenseless boy. Listen, Sherlock. If we meet again, I will teach you some of the basics, but you must not neglect your physical training. Please, take care."

Ito turned to leave with Monta. Before he could, Sherlock reached for his hand.

"Be safe," he said softly, gripping Ito's hand in a strong handshake.

His eyes, though glistening, were bright and unclouded. This was, without doubt, the pure expression of a ten-year-old boy. Sherlock was an enigmatic child, thought Ito. Governed entirely by reason, and yet possessing a depth of sensitivity that was greater than that of the common man.

Ito nodded to him, turned his back, and began walking toward the door, following Monta outside. The stench that hung over the Thames had drifted even this far on the wind. The rows of stonework buildings, cloaked in fog, spread out before them. Soon, he would be saying farewell to all of it.

"An unusual pair of brothers," said Monta, as they walked. "Whose children were they?"

"I haven't a clue." Ito matched the other man's pace, hiding his own mawkish feelings with a smile. "It was my first time meeting them. I couldn't tell you who they were or where they came from."

4

Shunsuke Ito was born in 1841, the 30th year of the Tenpo era. At his birth, however, he was not called Shunsuke Ito, but Risuke Hayashi.

He was born the son of a farmer in the Province of Suo. When he was twelve, his impoverished father, as was common at the time, was adopted into a samurai family, and the family name changed to Ito. Along with his father, Risuke Ito became a foot soldier for the Choshu Domain.

Although his academics were poor, at age fifteen Risuke was made a student at Shoka Sonjuku, a private school run by Shoin Yoshida. He drew Shoin's attention and received the name Shunsuke.

In July of the following year, under Shoin's recommendation, he accompanied the Choshu detachment to Kyoto for three months. When he returned, he studied in Nagasaki for close to a year. That autumn he moved to the Choshu Domain's Edo Yashiki—the Choshu Daimyo's compound in Edo—which was where he met Monta Shiji, with whom he would later travel to London.

It was at this time, in 1858, that the Chief Minister of the Edo Bakufu, Naosuke Ii, signed the Treaty of Amity and Commerce between Japan and the United States without obtaining imperial approval. The Bakufu fiercely quashed any of its opponents. As a result, Shoin Yoshida, a Bakufu dissenter, was imprisoned too.

The news struck Ito with grief and anger. In contrast to the Tokugawa Bakufu and the Satsuma Domain, who had espoused the opening of Japan since the arrival of Perry's black ships, the Choshu Domain strongly advocated for Japan to maintain its isolationism.

Joui. Expel the barbarians. Drive them from our shores.

Under this banner of *joui* the young retainers of the Choshu Domain dedicated themselves to war, seeking to overthrow the Bakufu. Though Ito would later speak of *joui* as an outdated notion to young Sherlock, at the time he too had been a soldier in its cause. He had participated in the burning of the British legation at Gotenyama, in Shinagawa. This was something he hadn't been able to bring himself to reveal. At the time, the legation was under construction and therefore uninhabited—but Sherlock and Mycroft surely would still have been horrified.

After becoming a Choshu retainer Ito changed his name once again. He still called himself "Shunsuke," but with a character meaning "spring."[3] He aspired to become the type of person who would fill people with the hopeful warmth of spring. Ito had changed—he began to question *joui* itself. Burning the foreign legation only seemed to have spread chaos and weakened the country as a whole. If they continued on the path they were on, wouldn't this only open the way for the West to invade?

He began to wonder whether it might not be better for the Choshu Domain to temporarily join with the West and learn from their more advanced technology to overthrow the Bakufu.

Then Monta Shiji concocted a plan to travel to England. Along with Shunsuke, they gathered three other likeminded individuals—Yozo Yamao, Yakichi Nomura, and Kinsuke Endo.

The five of them were granted permission by the lord of the Choshu Domain, Takachika Mori, to travel to London and study in secret to learn Western technology and bring it back with them when they returned. Initially, however, they were unable to even ascertain their form of travel. There would be a considerable amount of funds required. And not least, if the Bakufu learned of their plans they would be sentenced to death.

Eventually they were able to use the funds meant for purchasing guns as collateral to borrow 5,000 *ryo* from a merchant with ties to

---

3 He changed his name from 俊輔 to 春輔, which both read as "Shunsuke."

the Choshu Domain. A thousand ryo per head was certainly a large sum, but in terms of covering the five of them crossing the sea and living in London, it was far from extravagant.

They slipped out by boat under cover of night. At Shanghai their party divided into two ships. Thereafter, Ito's days were spent in hard, slave-like labor. The journey was long. The five were already long out to sea by the time their petition reached the daimyo in Edo.

After a grueling four-and-a-half months, they finally reached London and the house of Professor Alexander Williamson. Yakichi Nomura taught the other four conversational English—of the five he was the only one who had learned English beforehand, from a legation clerk in Hakodate.

The sights that awaited them in England were near-miraculous: the museums, the art galleries, the naval facilities, the banks, the factories. This proof of the astounding difference in strength between their nations hastened their party's sense of urgency. They could hardly sit idly by as Choshu marched to war with Britain, America, France, and the Netherlands. So Ito undertook yet another three-month passage, and somehow was able to return to Yokohama with Monta. But they were too late to negotiate for peace. Then there was the Battle for Shimonoseki. After four months of shelling by naval forces allied against them, Choshu's batteries were destroyed.

After the war Ito continued to work for peace. It was a dangerous business. Even now Choshu retainers adhered to *joui*, and plotted sabotage and assassinations. A growing rift between those in the domain who believed in deferring to the Bakufu and those who believed in pursuing *joui* promised future tensions.

When the Bakufu sent a force to subjugate Choshu, Choshu surrendered. Then Shinsaku Takasugi instigated a rebellion. Ito rushed to Takasugi's side, leading private militias against the loyalists. Joined by irregular forces, they were able to defeat the loyalists and topple the Bakufu's second Choshu expedition. With victory secured and the Bakufu's forces routed on all sides, the shogunate's influence was greatly weakened.

Thereafter, the Choshu and Satsuma domains joined forces, with Ryoma Sakamoto of the Tosa Domain mediating. This alliance overwhelmed the Bakufu forces, and Yoshinobu Tokugawa, the fifteenth shogun, was forced to finally restore imperial rule.

Finally the Edo Bakufu had fallen. The Choshu and Satsuma domains formed the core of the new Meiji government that would develop afterward.

After the Meiji Restoration, pockets of adherence to *joui* remained, with frequent assaults on French sailors by retainers from Bizen, Tosa, and other domains. Ito was constantly travelling the country, putting out new fires. In recognition of his accomplishments, he found himself appointed to a succession of posts in the Meiji Government: among them the junior council for Foreign Affairs, the first governor of Hyogo Prefecture, and the first minister of Public Works, the last post in which he worked to promote industrialization. During his stint as junior assistant minister to both the Ministry of Treasury and of Popular Affairs, he changed his first name yet again, this time to Hirobumi.

The English he had learned proved very useful. From November 1870 (3rd year of Meiji) to the following May, he travelled throughout the United States; upon returning, he helped establish Japan's first coinage law. In November of that same year he travelled to the United States once more, that time to serve as vice-envoy to the Iwakura Mission, during which he delivered a speech in San Francisco. The following spring, he received an audience in Berlin with German Emperor Wilhelm I, during which he also made the acquaintance of Chancellor Otto von Bismarck.

Throughout all of this, Ito never forgot his first impression of a train in London. Throughout his rise through the Japanese government, one of his greatest ambitions remained the construction of a railway. He pushed to include railway construction in development plans he worked on with Shigenobu Okuma, and in June 1872 finally procured provisional operation of the new Tokyo to Yokohama line, extending from Shinagawa to Yokohama. In October the entire line opened in earnest, going all the way to Shimbashi.

1881. Spurred by his encounters in Berlin he maneuvered his political rival Okuma into resigning. Okuma had supported an English-style parliamentary constitution, but Ito preferred to adopt a Prussian-style constitution which maintained the imperial prerogative. Real progress had been made toward establishing a parliament and the drafting of a constitution.

March 3, 1882 (5th year of Meiji). He travelled Europe on orders by Emperor Meiji to study the various constitutional systems of the West. He left on the 14th of March. He visited the University of Berlin and University of Vienna to study historical jurisprudence and political administration. The groundwork was laid for the creation of a cabinet system and the drafting and enactment of the Constitution of the Empire of Japan.

At this age, patches of white began to appear on Ito's head. In Europe, he realized he would soon be 41. His had been a tumultuous life. The establishment of a genuinely modern Japan was close. He was certain his goals were in reach.

On February 12, 1883, he left Berlin and travelled to Brussels, Belgium. On March 3, exactly one year after receiving his orders from Emperor Meiji, he set foot in London once again.

Ito had changed much since his first visit to the British capital. He could look at the city with much more perspective. He no longer had to scurry through the shadows, eking out a meager existence. He was surrounded by an extensive contingent of hangers-on and treated as an honored guest of state; his time was consumed with relentless royal audiences and scholarly meetings. His plan was to spend two months studying the English constitution.

However, there were two people with whom Ito wished to meet while in London, by whatever means necessary. If the older brother of that strange duo he had rescued, all those decades ago, had entered government service as he had said, Ito thought finding him would be a simple matter.

5

Hirobumi Ito's attachés were vociferously opposed to the idea of his wandering London unattended. They stared at him in affront at the mere suggestion. Japan was on the cusp of modernization—allowing one of the driving figures of that movement to walk the streets unguarded was sheer folly.

Ito, however, was far more proficient in English now than during his first time in London. So he made a personal request to the British Home Office staff, asking one of the clerks if there was a civil servant named Mycroft Holmes—of what sector, he didn't know. The clerk replied that he would look into it.

It was early in April, a typically dismal, overcast afternoon. Claiming he wanted to shut himself up for a time in one of the reference rooms at the British Library, Ito managed to detach from his group and slipped out a window. Though he was in his forties, his physique had been hardened by war. He easily passed through the garden and hopped into a carriage, giving the coachman the address he had jotted down: "221B Baker Street, please."

He'd heard Mycroft was responsible for auditing books for a variety of government departments. Ito had been able to send him a telegram, but Mycroft had politely refused to meet. The answer Ito had received was markedly reserved, and he couldn't help but feel some misgivings as he read it. But then, perhaps the other man's answer was only natural. After all, he was being contacted by a foreigner he had met only once in his teens. And, too, the Home Office had briefed Mycroft on Ito's title and situation in all its minute details. Perhaps that, too, had put Mycroft off.

But Mycroft had sent his brother's address. Sherlock apparently now worked as a private detective. As a result his place of business, which also doubled as his residence, was open to visits from the public. Ito was in high spirits as the carriage jostled him side to side. A detective! It was the perfect career for Sherlock. Though Sherlock must have improved significantly in his sociability; after all, when dealing with clients, grace and manners were vital. He would now be 29 years of age. Ito wondered what sort of man he had become.

Baker Street was a broad road stretching from north to south in the West End, running from the northeast corner of Hyde Park to the southwest corner of Regent Park.

The building the carriage slowed down in front of was one that might be found anywhere through London. Rows of sash windows, trimmed in white, lined its rich brown brick walls. It was a lodging house, and must command a considerable rent. The small entryway was crowned with an arch window bearing the inscription of 221B.

Ito rang the bell. Shortly after, the door was opened. An elderly woman in a simple dress poked her head out.

Mycroft had also confided the name of the building's landlady to Ito. He removed his top hat. "Good afternoon, my name is Hirobumi Ito. It is Mrs. Hudson, I presume?"

"Ah," said Mrs. Hudson, a smile spreading across her face. "You've come early. We had a telegram from Mr. Holmes' brother. You're quite the distinguished guest. Is your party…?"

"I am alone. My apologies for coming unannounced. Is Mr. Holmes in?"

"I'm sorry to say he's been down to Leatherhead since the sixth. We expected him back this morning, but he's yet to make an appearance. I'm afraid things can be quite sudden with Mr. Holmes. It was a young lady that came around before seven, asking that I ring him up."

"I see. Being a detective must be a very difficult job. Like a physician."

"It's Dr. Watson, that shares the lodgings, who is the physician. Will you wait inside? I'll put on the tea."

"Thank you very much," said Ito, as he was shown in. Going up the stairs, he was led through the first door.

The room he entered left him speechless.

While the fireplace, furniture, and other ornaments might appear elegant to the Japanese eye, they would hardly be counted ornate by English standards. The room was fairly spacious, with a second room off the back—likely the sleeping quarters.

The room, however, was in a state of extreme disarray. Mountains of books and papers lay toppled across the easy-chair and sofa, leaving absolutely no space to sit. A Persian slipper stuffed full of tobacco had been left lying out; there were cigars in the coal scuttle. A stack of unopened correspondence was pinned to the mantelpiece with a jack-knife, and scattered next to it was a variety of paraphernalia including a pipe, a syringe, a knife, and several bullet cartridges. One wall was the proud bearer of an assortment of bullet holes, which formed a pattern spelling out the letters "V R."

The writing desk was also covered with an array of chemical apparati and materials. This was likely the source of the strange odor that permeated the room. A mummified finger bone lay haphazardly next to the butter dish and a violin rested on the table with its case.

Mrs. Hudson withdrew, leaving Ito alone in the disorder. He approached the unlit fireplace. A crooked fire poker had been tossed upon the floor, as baffling as everything else in the room. It looked as if it had first been bent nearly double and then bent back to its original shape. It would require preternatural strength to achieve such a feat. Surely it could not have been the work of the delicate young boy Ito had once known, fully grown though he now should be.

Just then, the sound of footsteps echoed on the stairs. Ito could hear the voices of two men, engaged in friendly conversation. "Still," said one of the voices, "it was quite astounding such a powerful venom should go undiscovered during autopsy."

The other voice was deeper in tone, aloof yet also strident, exhibiting a turn of phrase that was oddly distinct. "Undoubtedly he had been schooled in his fiendish methods in the Orient," said the owner of the voice, "as only the most cunning savage would hit upon such a technique. Having pacified the serpent, he had trained it to return at the sound of his whistle."

The door opened. The first man to enter appeared to be in his thirties. He was of fairly average height with a thick neck and well-developed frame, and sported a mustache and a grey suit. A smile lingered on his lips, but when he saw Ito he stopped short. "Sherlock, you have a guest," he said.

The man who followed behind him was exceedingly tall. He must have been over six feet in height, and was thin and gaunt. His slim limbs, jutting out from his frock coat, looked almost unnaturally long.

The man seemed older than his natural years. But that had been the case even when he had been a boy. Ito recognized his hawk-life nose and sunken grey eyes. Perhaps it was the severity of his expression, or his square, jutting jaw, but Sherlock gave an impression now of being even more stubborn and unyielding than he had been before. His facial expression was exceedingly cold, accompanied by a scowl—as if he had just encountered something distasteful. His brow was knit with a heavy crease.

Ito was a swirl of conflicting emotions. "We finally meet again," he said.

The man in the grey suit reacted graciously. The same could not be said of Sherlock Holmes. He strolled past Ito without a word and took the pipe up from the mantelpiece. Persian slipper in one hand, he stuffed the pipe with tobacco. He never even made eye contact.

Ito was at a loss. The man in the suit glanced at him apologetically. "It is good to make your acquaintance. I am Sherlock's friend, John Watson."

Sherlock quickly raised a hand to restrain Watson. As his eyes remained pointed downward as he spoke, it was not entirely clear to whom he was speaking. "I am far too busy to meet anyone without an appointment."

Watson furrowed his brow. "That is news to me. I remember you allowed time for Miss Helen Stoner, though she came at a very early hour."

Had Sherlock's brother not contacted him? "I am sorry for coming unannounced," said Ito, "but I had no other chance. Today was the only day available."

Sherlock continued to avoid looking Ito in the eye. He wagged his finger like a conductor as he spoke. "A fact of which I am well aware, Shunsuke... Excuse me, *Hirobumi* Ito, as you are known now."

Ito felt a sense of relief. "You remember me, then."

"Hmph," Sherlock grunted, though the expression on his face remained distant. "I recall the mole on the right side of your nose."

"I'm pleased you also know my current name."

"Certainly, you are very well known, numbering among a very few persons now central to the Japanese government. I am in the habit of monitoring the newspapers closely, and could not help but read of you. *The red disc in the center of our national flag shall no longer appear like a wafer over a sealed empire, but henceforth be in fact what it is designed to be, the noble emblem of the rising sun, moving onward and upward amid the enlightened nations of the world.* Quite the rousing speech."

So Sherlock was familiar with his San Francisco speech! Ito was delighted, though the hint of mockery in his voice did give him pause. "I must give credit to England for introducing me in my younger days to the concept of a modernized nation."

Sherlock stuck his pipe into his mouth and lit it with a match. He rested one elbow against the mantelpiece and blew out a puff of smoke. He made no attempt to speak again.

"Perhaps you have a commission?" asked Watson.

"No," Ito answered. "Now that I am finally in London again, I simply wished to renew our acquaintance. Perhaps Sherlock has forgotten, but I made him a small promise before I left."

Sherlock finally turned his attention toward Ito. The expression in his eyes was piercing. "Call me Holmes. And if you refer to your promise to educate me in the martial arts, I have two reasons for no longer desiring your help."

A knock sounded on the door. Watson crossed the room and opened it. Mrs. Hudson stood on the other side, bearing a tray arranged with the tea things. "Mrs. Hudson, good," said Watson. "They are at it now so I will take the tea in. Which is the sugar?"

"Two reasons?" asked Ito.

"The first reason is that you are now 41 years of age, which leads me to suspect you are no longer in your physical prime. Should you wrench your back, I would rather not be petitioned by the Japanese government for compensation."

"My country would never make such demands. I am here on a private visit."

"The second reason is that a very talented Japanese master has opened a dojo on Fleet Street, and thus I have already acquired the basics of jujitsu."

"I see. But what of karate and kenjutsu…"

"They are unnecessary. The karate master I encountered two years ago was also Japanese. With his short limbs I was able to knock him down with a left straight before he could affect any true damage. The same is true of kenjutsu. A fencing lunge is more than adequate to take the throat quickly. In either instance, they are unsuited to my height."

Unexpectedly, Ito felt himself growing irritated. With 16 years as a politician under his belt, he prided himself on having cultivated a certain degree of forbearance. Sherlock's provocations, however, struck a more sensitive nerve. He couldn't help but take offense at hearing Japan's martial arts so easily derided.

Watson returned from the door. He held the tray in one hand and deftly cleared the table with the other. "So, what were we talking of?"

"Nothing in particular," Sherlock said, his pipe still stuck in his mouth. "I see there are three teacups. Mrs. Hudson might have saved herself the trouble. Our guest should be leaving shortly."

This final comment was too much to ignore. Ito fixed his eyes on Sherlock. "I have been overlooking your rudeness for the sake of old friendship, but I am surprised you find any work as a detective with manners such as this!"

"I see you are angry. Would you care to know the reason for my coldness?"

"I certainly would," said Ito.

"You burned down the British legation," Sherlock said shortly.

Ito faltered. Silence descended on the room. The awkwardness grew palpable.

"The situation in Japan was very complicated at the time," he defended himself, his voice unsure even to his own ears. "The Choshu Domain…"

The detective snorted. "*Joui*. I assume this is what you refer to? Minister Ito, when I asked you if *joui* was a person you ought to have corrected me. You burned the legation immediately before you left Japan. Surely such an example would have proved enlightening to me."

"If I had told you about the legation it would have only upset you…"

"Yes. I may have been a child, but at the very least I doubt I would have asked to go with you."

"I'm sorry. But it didn't seem like a good time to explain such things."

"And what of Professor Williamson? His wife? Had you adequately explained the meaning of *joui*, I doubt anyone would have permitted you into their home. You and your four fellows were well aware of that fact, that is why you chose to remain silent. Am I mistaken?"

"With *joui* we had taken our desire for reform too far. After coming to London, I realized our mistake."

"The only thing you realized was that you required British weapons and technologies to defeat the Bakufu. True civilization flows within the veins of British citizens. *Your people* are inveterate savages."

With each sentence the other man uttered, Ito was finding his anger harder to control. "I thought you an intelligent man, but it seems to me that you despise not just me, but all Japanese."

"Hardly," Sherlock said, his tone growing even more pettish. "My treatment of you now is motivated by disappointment. As a child I believed you to be a gentleman of distinction, but I know now that I was mistaken. The manner in which you have used your wives has been particularly egregious. You avoided the company of your first wife for many years, and even after marrying your second wife you continue to divert yourself with others."

Ito was taken aback. This was information about his private life that should not have been public. He sputtered vacantly. "How did you…"

"I didn't realize at the time, but the woman who came to your aid that day was a prostitute. The prostitutes of Cheapside are pragmatic by nature and would never trouble themselves with a client once their trade was accomplished. The only explanation is that you took an interest in the woman, made her acquaintance and paid her, but did not avail of her wares. Her actions were thus her manner of repaying you. Your fellows had blamed you for mashing, blamed you because you had a wife. Considering your age, however, you could not have been married for long before leaving her behind on an extended stay in England, which tells me there was little affection in the marriage."

"I'd thank you not to presume. Still, where did you learn of my second marriage?"

"Despite being a man of your position, you were forced to sneak away in order to meet me. Your movements are restricted. Your attendants keep a close eye upon you. The cause? The behavior you engage in upon sneaking away. Your fellows would not be in a frenzy to keep such gossip from the newspapers unless you have a wife. I find it doubtful, even with your present fortunes, that you could have maintained a relationship with the wife you neglected so poorly in your earlier career. Therefore, it is only logical to conclude that you have remarried."

Ito was bewildered. He remembered the day he first met young

Sherlock. The boy's powers of deduction had been so astounding then that it was hard not to suspect he was peering directly into one's mind.

Everything he said now was true. Ito had often been censured for his dalliances with geisha. Those who knew him best had nicknamed him "the broom," in reference to the manner in which he swept women up and discarded them later.

"I readily admit to my own faults," he finally relented, rattled. "And perhaps it was conceited to assume I could teach you anything of the martial arts. But there is one thing I beg you to take to heart. The Japanese are not, as you say, savages."

Sherlock stubbornly refused to concede the point. "I remain unconvinced."

Ito raised his voice, losing his patience again. "Then you believe we are barbaric by nature? That is what you mean to say?"

"I mean precisely what I said earlier."

"What you said earlier? Oh, about the *cunning savages*, schooled in the *fiendish methods of the Orient*?"

This finally caused the other man to glance at Ito. There was a palpable shift in his grey eyes.

"Britain's policy of colonization is not as just as the citizens of your country seem to believe," Ito snapped. "It was Britain that began sale of opium in China to cover the trade deficit from the great volumes of tea you import. The Qing Dynasty were entirely correct to confiscate and dump those 23,000 crates. And yet Britain responded with force. It was Britain that exploited China's weakness in order to force Japan to open its borders. To you the East may seem a nuisance, but to us the West are truly invaders!"

"You had better save your objections for the Honorable Mr. Gladstone," the other man said, lowering his gaze to his pipe. "I am but a common detective."

"You eschew any involvement. Your business in consulting with the public, however, is not exempt."

"Your meaning?"

"I once believed the West to be a land of science, but your people seem prone to seeing the East as a repository of mystery and the occult. During my previous trip to London, we took port in Shanghai. There, there were great numbers of snake charmers from India who had set up trade. They made their money by hoodwinking Westerners, by pretending to control the snake with the playing of their flutes. But there is no snake that responds to the sound of a flute. The snake charmers simply kick the basket in secret, exciting the snake to show its head."

Watson made an expression of surprise. "Is that how it is?" he asked Ito.

"No Easterner would be fooled by such a farce. There were similar spectacles in the Ryukyu Islands, but they quickly fell apart."

"Ho there." Watson smiled at Sherlock. "Did you hear that? If what this gentleman says is true, then there may be a fatal flaw in your earlier reasoning."

Sherlock gazed out the window resentfully. "I'm very busy. It may seem to you as if I am doing nothing, but I am currently directing the entirety of my brain toward the analysis of yet unsolved cases."

"But Sherlock..."

"Watson!" His back still turned, Sherlock waved a single hand, with a gesture akin to shooing away a dog.

The room fell silent. Watson sighed and turned toward Ito apologetically. "You will have to forgive us. Sherlock has just returned from a case, and I am afraid he is very tired."

A twinge of regret began to steal over Ito. He had let his temper get the better of him. Such behavior was inexcusable in a politician.

"Not at all," said Ito, bowing his head. "It is I who should apologize for intruding in this way. I beg your pardon. Mr. Holmes, I wish you good health. May your exceptional powers of deduction continue to bring comfort to those in need."

Sherlock did not turn around. Ito could only feel disheartened by such a turn of events. Most of all he was disappointed in his own lack of forbearance. This painful interaction was not the reunion he had hoped for.

Watson accompanied Ito to the door. He told him he'd see him out.

They descended the stairs and stepped outside. Surrounded by the bustle of Baker Street, Watson turned toward Ito. "It was a pleasure to make your acquaintance, and most edifying as well. I am certain Sherlock will find cause now to make a closer study of the habits of snakes."

A weak smile escaped Ito's lips. He felt thoroughly dejected. "Thank you, but I'm afraid this exchange has only revealed my own immaturity. Please, give my regards to Mr. Holmes."

He turned his back on Watson and walked away.

There was one thing that Sherlock had said, in particular, that Ito could not help but dwell upon. *As a child I believed you to be a gentleman of distinction, but I know now that I was mistaken.* His eyes had been sharp, accusatory, and tinged with a deep disappointment. No matter how Ito justified it, it was too much to expect Sherlock, or anyone, to dispassionately accept the burning of their own country's legation. Add that to the misgivings he had formed regarding Ito's character, and Ito ruefully felt his earlier treatment was perhaps only reasonable.

He waved down a carriage. "The British Library," he told the coachman. A piercing sadness suddenly welled up in his breast. But what could he do but endure it? When all was said and done, Ito's life had perhaps been too selfish to expect friendship in the ordinary manner of things. It was far too late now to change the past.

Sherlock Holmes stared deliberately at the fire poker—the one that had been bent out of shape by Grimesby Roylott. He resolved that Watson should find him in this exact posture when he returned to the room.

Had he turned to his books and papers immediately, it would have seemed as if Ito's comment on the snakes had rattled him. On the other hand, were he to do nothing and simply continue smoking his pipe, Watson might assume he was brooding. Which certainly was not the case.

Footsteps echoed on the stairs. Watson entered the room.

"I was mistaken in my application of force," Sherlock murmured, lifting up the poker. "Had I gripped it but three inches further to the left, I could have corrected the bend most precisely."

"Mr. Ito was formerly your hero, I gather," Watson responded lightly, as he began pouring the tea. "But however he might have disappointed you, surely there was no need for such abuse. Doubly so now, of course, if he regrets his former actions."

Sherlock's hand slipped, nearly dropping the poker. He quickly corrected himself, but not quickly enough to prevent Watson from snorting.

He did not care to think too deeply on the meaning of that snort. Tossing the poker aside, he retorted, "I spoke the truth when I said I am but a common detective. That does not alter the fact that I operate for the glory of Her Majesty and the great Empire of Britain."

"Quite so," said Watson, sipping at his cup, "but there is something to what the gentleman said. Might it not be true that the campaign in China was not waged for the sake of spreading civilization and order? Either mistaken notions have taken hold in the East, or Britain's true motivation was profit. I wonder."

Sherlock responded testily. "One might contest that the nation that has constructed a truly modern civilization is the one better equipped to make sound and objective judgments on such matters."

"Yes, one *might* suppose."

"What do you mean, Watson?"

Watson turned toward him with a somber expression. "I don't mean anything in particular. But I am reminded of my time in Afghanistan. I cannot help but feel that I somewhat understand what the gentleman was driving at."

It was true that Sherlock had no war experience. He fell silent.

Then he reached for the bottle on the corner of the mantelpiece, and removed a hypodermic needle from his Moroccan leather case. "Would you mind leaving me?" he muttered.

"Listen here now," his friend took on a severe tone. "How many times have I warned you that the feeling of mental stimulation you get from cocaine is only illusory? I am a man of medicine. Must you do that in front of me?"

"That is precisely why I asked you to leave me," Sherlock said blithely, adjusting the needle. He rolled up the sleeve of his left arm and peered at the numerous marks already there, searching for a new location in which to inject the needle.

Watson dashed his teacup back down with a sharp clatter. "Next I suppose you will take up opium. Perhaps it will give you better insight into the mysteries and occult of the East."

His footsteps grew distant. He slammed the door shut behind him as he left.

Sherlock closed his eyes with a sigh. How much easier it would be if he could abandon his own tedious pride. Unfortunately it was not in his purview to change his own nature. His deep-honed powers of observation and his unflinching deductive acumen were rooted in such mild eccentricities. His abilities were supported by this disparity: It was impossible to be both exceptional and ordinary.

6

March 10, 1891, midnight. Heavy rains showered over Western Italy. On the outskirts of the Port of Livorno, abutting the Mediterranean Sea, tall waves battered the wharf and extended to the carriageways, soaking the roads. The ocean's surface churned in ridges and hollows, and the beam of a faraway light blinked in and out in the night. Flashes of lightning split the pitch-black sky, followed by rolling thunder.

Wrapped in a blanket to ward off the cold, Sherlock Holmes sat on a wooden crate in a small cabin. He'd already been soaked to the bone by the time he made his way inside. He would have liked a fire, but was forced to content himself instead with the single candle that burned before him.

There were footsteps at the door. He rose from the crate. A man entered the cabin, folding his umbrella. He was massive—so massive that he nearly burst from the seams of his Ulster coat. His hairline fell far back along his head. Though he was even taller than Sherlock, his face was not as large as his frame. It was a long face, or would be if not for his heavy-set, portly cheeks. Their parents would have it that the two brothers shared the same grey eyes and hawk-like nose, but Sherlock himself begged to differ. He could see no similarity between his brother's features and his own.

Mycroft, now 44 years of age, carried a thick, bulging leather case in one hand. He cast a quick glance at the trunk next to Sherlock. "You are *supposed* to be dead. You should not have been wandering around the canals in the middle of the afternoon. It was too exposed."

Sherlock knew it was highly unlikely he had been followed

throughout the day, but was unsurprised to see that his brother knew of his movements. "Indeed. One would only be able to pick up a secondhand trunk at a decent price without being remembered from Serge's store, capriciously open from the hours of 1:00 to 3:00 in the afternoon. Your shrewdness has never been in question, Mycroft. You ought to have become a detective."

"What is in the trunk then, a change of clothes?"

"The trunk contains those articles minimally necessary to present myself as a gentleman. It would not do to seek an audience with the Dalai Lama while dressed in rags."

"You'll hardly be meeting the Dalai Lama."

"Why's that, now?"

"Tibet is under an isolation policy. It is closed to foreigners. The country is also under Qing Dynasty rule. As Britain's influence has seeped into China since the Opium Wars, you cannot be sure you will be safe."

"But surely the Qing Dynasty's lack of assertiveness has caused the Tibetan people to lose faith in their rulers."

"Tibet is a landlocked country. In order to reach it you would have to take port in China or India. Britain keeps close watch over the ports of China, as you can perhaps imagine. And of course, India, too, is British territory. Surely you are not ignorant of the fact that Her Majesty Queen Victoria is likewise empress of the Indian Empire."

"Naturally I would sneak in. I obviously do not intend to enter as pleasure tourist, saluting my presence like a fool."

"If you endeavor to deceive anyone by means of the false nose and chin putty that you've placed in your trunk, I beg you to develop more worldly opinions. Sherlock, you and I are but fish in a small pond."

Sherlock began to grow annoyed. "*You* may spend your days at a desk, Mycroft, but my cases have taken me across the sea many times already."

"By sea you only mean the Straits of Dover. Just because you received an official request from the French government once, don't pretend that you have a broad understanding of the world. Think, now, do you truly propose that an unidentified 37-year-old Englishman can stroll in and request a meeting with the Dalai Lama? They have long been awaiting your arrival, I'm sure."

"We cannot know unless I try."

"Nor should you underestimate Britannia. The empire on which the sun never sets has colonies scattered across the globe, and its influence extends even farther than its territories. There is no place left on Earth where a man who is by all rights dead would find safe harbor. The moment you seek food or shelter of anywhere, you would be taken into local custody and a wire will be dispatched to England. It will take less than a month for Scotland Yard to ascertain your identity using anthropometry."

"I will live away from human notice."

"You had best forget about the Dalai Lama, then. Or the Caliph in Khartoum. How do you propose to respond when they ask who you are? Tell them, 'It is I, the great Sherlock Holmes, and I have only faked my death'? In Islam, the very act of faking one's death is punishable by execution. These travel plans of yours are completely bosh."

"I was under the impression you were here to help me, Mycroft."

His brother stared at him silently. He took a folded piece of paper from his breast pocket and handed it to Sherlock.

"I take this to mean you've finally deigned to procure a letter of introduction to a ship captain for me," Sherlock observed.

"Though I am but a minor government worker responsible for auditing the books, some have recognized my talents and consult me now and then on a few trivial matters. I had to call on several favors to arrange for the ship. It is a smuggler's ship, of course."

"Dear Captain Leroy Cartlett," Sherlock read at the top of the page. After the initial pleasantries, obligations and requests, Sherlock finally arrived at the final port of call at the bottom of the letter. A cry involuntarily escaped his lips. "Yokohama?!"

"The ship will dock at Calcutta and Shanghai along the way, but

I advise you to stay fast within the hold. By no means are you to go ashore. The moment you are identified it would lead to an international incident—you would be sent to the dock, and I would certainly lose my post. Even your entrance into Italy was illegal. It is fortunate enough you were not arrested in Florence."

"I don't like it," said Sherlock, staring at Mycroft. "Why must I go to Japan?"

"Tokyo is developing into a modernized city, with a capable police force. You can expect law and order when you arrive. Once you land, you must visit the residence of Lord Hirobumi Ito."

"Ito…"

"Under no circumstances are you to approach the British legation. Remember, you are presumed dead."

"Have you contacted him already?"

"No. Even a letter is out of the question. If it were to fall into the wrong hands, the British authorities would know immediately."

"But why must it be Hirobumi Ito?"

"Are you a fool?" Mycroft's voice rose in anger. "If you want to pass yourself off as a dead man and conceal your identity, you will need a patron with enough clout to avert the eyes of justice. Japan has implemented a constitution in recent years and has introduced a Diet. Lord Ito was their first Prime Minister. And he himself was once a stowaway. It was during that period we made his acquaintance. He will certainly sympathize."

"Only a quarter century ago, Ito and his fellow countrymen were assaulting foreigners en masse in the name of *joui*. This so-called modernization may be superficial only."

"*Joui* was a tragedy, but you must allow that it was the Japanese refusal to submit to Western rule that has permitted them to maintain their independence. Not even the British Empire can interfere directly in Japan's laws and government. It is the only place where a dead man can find refuge from the British police."

"Kindly remind me as to when I earned the enmity of the British police. If you recall, I risked my own life to depose of Professor

Moriarty—a criminal of the highest order."

"Lord Ito might say something similar. He and his fellows pursued *joui* for the future of their country."

"The two are not the same. With Moriarty's death, peace has been restored to the streets of London. If it came out that I were still alive, however, his network of criminals would burrow underground. By convincing the world of my death I have arranged for justice."

"In your own mind, yes, but in the minds of the police you are a suspect in a murder investigation."

The windowpane, battered by the rain, flashed with lightning. A slice of Mycroft's face was illuminated in the stark light. A heavy rumble shook the glass.

Sherlock had already accepted his fate. He still could not stop himself from taking the truth hard. "I am a suspect?" he muttered, almost in disbelief.

"Naturally," said Mycroft. "There were no witnesses, and Moriarty now rests at the bottom of the falls. You have no recourse by which to prove self-defense. There is also the matter of the letter you left behind, which suggests murderous intent."

"I never wrote that I meant to kill him."

"*I am pleased to think that I shall be able to free society from any further effects of his presence.* I believe those were your words. As the possibility remains that you struck first, the police are duty-bound to construct a case against the deceased. Their hands are tied."

"But Moriarty was not alone. One of his confederates lay in ambush atop the cliffs."

"Then unfortunately, unless that man is apprehended, you have no hope of returning to society. I don't expect you have a mind to turn yourself in."

"Moriarty was a dangerous criminal. I included all necessary proof in the letter that I passed to Watson."

"The fact that he is a dangerous criminal does not give you the right to kill him. Sherlock, I understand that you were willing to barter your own life to dispatch this man. But you survived. In society's

60

eyes, meanwhile, you are dead. To be plain, then, though you are alive, you must consign yourself for the time to the indignities of death."

Another peal of thunder shook the cabin. Sherlock waited.

"Law and order are absolute," Mycroft intoned softly and soberly. "That, more than anything, is the meaning of civilization. And that is why you must flee to a country beyond the reach of the British police. Watson insists that your actions were heroic. Only with yourself and the deceased Moriarty do his words carry any weight. There are legal questions as well. Moriarty's younger brother has also launched a defense of the professor."

Sherlock started. "His brother?"

"He hopes to prove Professor Moriarty's innocence and restore his good name. He insists his brother was murdered, by none other than Sherlock Holmes."

"There is a brotherly resemblance, I see."

"Or perhaps he learned what occurred from the man atop the cliff."

"Until after Moriarty's fall, I had no notion that there was another man atop the cliff. I chose to hide and affect my own death under the belief that there were no witnesses."

"That was a miscalculation. Not only was there a witness, but this witness is a member of the syndicate you face." Mycroft stared off into space with a grave expression. "I must confess I myself am not entirely satisfied. Did Moriarty truly make an attempt on your life?"

Another flash. Sherlock inhaled sharply. "What do you mean?" he asked flatly.

"One of Moriarty's own agents lay waiting atop the cliffs, and even now his brother acts feverishly to restore his good name. Was this criminal Moriarty truly as isolated, as driven to desperation by your pursuit, as you say?"

"The evidence I had collected would have made things quite impossible for him. It was the gallows for him, without a doubt."

"If that is the case, then you had no need to kill him. You could have seen him put in custody, and left the courts to decide his fate."

"Had he been allowed to live, he would have used his genius to devise some elaborate means of escape. He even bragged to me that he possessed intimate knowledge of the lost reaches of the South American continent. Eventually he would have returned to London to resume his criminal endeavors."

"Perhaps, but he must not have been as pressed as you say if he had liberty still to flee. This means he might have turned his hand to crime again at a later date. Certainly this is a more consistent way to look at it. Likely Moriarty believed he could overturn whatever evidence you brought against him. He only feigned being rounded off in order to arrange a private meeting with you. In fact, it was *he* who planned to kill *you*. It may even be that it was Moriarty who first thought to pass himself off as dead."

Sherlock shook his head. "Impossible. Watch how the trial unfolds, and you will admit that Moriarty would have been convicted."

"We are of different minds. But no matter. You will have your way."

Mycroft's comment stuck in Sherlock's throat. He rounded on his brother sarcastically. "Indeed, eminent older brother, how very wise you are to see your younger brother's mistakes and yet cede the point! You were always patronizing when we were children, and I see you are still."

"Come now, Sherlock. Let's not be cross over something so minor. We do not know the truth yet, that is all."

"Minor? Indeed, the subject at hand is only my very fate. But I see you care only for appearances."

"I?"

"Yes. You are eager to see me gone from the shores of England. If your brother, a murder suspect who has faked his own death, were to be arrested in country, who knows what consequences it might have for your *auditing position*."

"Don't be unpleasant. It is for your sake that I have taken such extreme measures."

"No. I am sure what steps you have taken, you have taken for yourself."

The ensuing silence was accompanied by the incessant rain. The draft that came in through the cracks in the walls made the candle flame flutter, and the light of the cabin flickered.

Sherlock stared at his feet. Where else could he look? As an adult, he was proud of how he'd learned to respect his brother's intellect. He had believed he could face his brother as one adult to another. But perhaps this had only been true so long as he still felt an advantage in some area other than sheer intellect, to even the ground between them: Sherlock prided himself on being a man of action, whereas Mycroft detested social interaction and preferred the comforts of home. He was even a member of the Diogenes Club, which was frequented by the most solitary of men. Sherlock, on the other hand, was ceaselessly on the move. He prided himself on being the more active one, at any rate.

But recently Mycroft had changed; now he seemed to have more of a sense of the pleasures of being of use to others. Perhaps it had been after coming to the aid of the Greek interpreter. And only a few days earlier, when Sherlock had asked for Mycroft to arrange for a carriage, he had been astonished to find Mycroft had driven the carriage himself—sallying forth to meet Watson in person. It was a level of activity from his brother that would have been previously unimaginable. And now here he was, having come all the way to Italy with only a moment's notice.

Without his worldly advantages, Sherlock would once again be forced to compete with his brother on intellectual grounds. Mycroft for his own part might not have had any intention of competition, but for Sherlock this was a matter of gravest import.

To begin with, Sherlock was not particularly fond of his brother. Mycroft was seven years older and possessed a wealth of experience that Sherlock lacked. As the older brother, his parents had expected him to be the one to carry on the household. As a child, Sherlock's clothing and personal articles had of course been hand-me-downs.

Since there were no two people more alike in person and in temperament than the two brothers were, it was impossible for their egos not to clash. And they were far too similar to become playmates or confidantes.

Mycroft tossed the leather case to Sherlock. "I am returning the money you put in my care. Mostly the payments you received from the King of Scandinavia and the French government. It should be more than enough, however, for you to live in seclusion."

Sherlock placed the case into his trunk with a certain morose air. "Enough, at least, for whatever meager life I may find in the Far East."

"Be rational, Sherlock, and try to think more positively. When Lord Ito was forming his cabinet, he welcomed Piggott, the son-in-law of our own MP Jasper Wilson Johns, as a legal advisor. They may have adopted a German constitution, but there is also a degree of respect and understanding for the English style of governance there. You may rely on Lord Ito."

"Am I to spend the rest of my days as a nameless Englishman in Japan, polishing Lord Ito's boots?"

"If I am correct in my assessment, which I think I am, the trial in London shall not go as well as you plan. Of Moriarty's remaining men, I expect that two of the major players, at the very least, shall go free."

"You still insist the evidence I prepared is incomplete."

"I do. Either way, England will have need of you again. The fieldwork may prove difficult for me, but as you said, we won't know unless I try. I will contact you when things look favorable for your return."

"How long will that take?"

"Ten years? Twelve? More? Let us say, around the time when the statute of limitations should expire on those suspicions that should fall upon your head when it becomes apparent that you are still alive. That would be the most pragmatic view."

Sherlock pursed his lips. His brother's reasoning was more than valid. Though he didn't want to accept his prognostications regarding the trial, Mycroft otherwise had a point. Few figures of state other than Hirobumi Ito would likely be willing to sympathize with, much less shelter, a wanted dead man such as himself.

"The younger Moriarty deserves credit for his brotherly devotion and loyalty," muttered Sherlock, unable to stop himself. "It is certainly more than I should aspire to."

"Oh? And what of 'brotherly resemblances'?"

"In our case there is no resemblance," Sherlock returned quickly and indignantly.

"You are, as ever, thankless. If you do not agree to this plan, then you are at your liberty to tear up the letter of introduction I have provided."

A childish provocation! Sherlock seethed. Mycroft only said such things because he knew that Sherlock had no choice.

"Sherlock," Mycroft added quietly. "Thankfully you had not enrolled in a life insurance plan. Had you listed Watson or I as the beneficiary, we would have surely been charged with fraud."

"As parting words go, those were abominable."

"I thought you would prefer it to trite condolences." Mycroft withdrew his pocket watch and glanced at its face. "The boat will be leaving shortly. It is a small cargo vessel, docked at wharf number 17. Do not be late. Farewell, Sherlock. It is better if we do not write."

Sherlock was startled to sense a hint of affection behind those ironic words. It was too late now, though, to confirm that. Their conversation was over. Mycroft turned his back to Sherlock, opened his umbrella, and stepped outside.

The younger Holmes remained rooted. The claps of lightning that pierced the window were diminishing. Distant thunder reached his ears. He could see the puffs of his own breath. Finally the weight of realization fell upon him. He and his brother, too, were now separated. It was lonely being a ghost with no place left in the world.

7

During the interminable days of the hellish sea voyage, the same thought occupied Sherlock's mind: *He should have just fallen from that cliff.*

His circumstances onboard were far from dignified. He had no cabin, only a corner of the decrepit cargo ship's hold by the sails and steam engine. Rather than there being a proper partition, his space was corralled off on four sides by barrels. He shared the hold with a throng of Asian passengers, all of who were likely stowaways. Sherlock suspected they were Chinese rather than Japanese, but as he did not speak their language there was no avenue for communication. He was laid up for days on end in a stupor of seasickness. The most he could stomach was a few crumbs of bread and a bit of soup.

Not that he was idle. From the first day on deck one of the swabs succeeded in shoving a bucket and mop into his hands. He also helped with hoisting the sails. On windy days the rope would be wound so tightly around his hands that he worried his fingers would be torn off.

Even the grueling physical labor, however, was nothing compared to the terror at night, as the boat pitched violently in the waves. For several days in July they were lashed by hurricanes, and the hold started filling with water. Several Chinese passengers were ordered to rush to rein in the sails, but fell from the mast and were injured. Sherlock could hardly stand by and watch. He spent his waking hours frantically scooping water from the ship with buckets; every hand beside the captain's was likewise busy in bailing out the ship.

The troubles continued. In August, as they approached the

Indian Ocean, a cyclone reared its head and the boat was blown off course. Every night they could hear angry shouts from the captain's chamber.

Sherlock approached the captain several times to discuss improving the working conditions, but his efforts were for naught. Every day Captain Cartlett drank like a fish. He was constantly inebriated. When he learned of the captain's proclivity for drink, Sherlock began to genuinely fear for his and the other passengers' lives. He considered attempting to orchestrate a mutiny, but as he was unable to communicate with the other passengers there was no opportunity for him to enlist any allies. The sailors were all Spanish or Italian, and the stowaways were all Chinese.

He had no idea what course they were charting, but their progress seemed exceedingly slow. Even the slowest would have arrived in Yokohama within fifty days, but theirs continued to flounder in the Indian Ocean even after three months.

Sherlock's strength and spirits waned. Above deck or in the hold he spent his days in a listless haze. His hair grew wild, and he found no leisure even to shave his beard. Being on board was like working on a slave ship. And yet it was precisely because this ship was not fit for long journeys that they were so easily able to falsify their route and evade inspections in each country. It was only after visiting several ports and seeing how deftly they passed, unimpeded, between the warships, that Sherlock realized this.

His head ached and spun. His reality grew phantasmal. He was wracked with nausea, hunger, and dehydration. Then, one day, as Sherlock lay barely conscious, a flurry of footsteps descended into the hold. The captain made an announcement. They had arrived!

He staggered up the stairs along with the Chinese stowaways. They emerged like the defeated remnants of a tattered army. On deck, the sky above was tinged in blue. Judging by the crispness and slight chill of the air, it was early morning. The Chinese passengers lined up along the starboard. Everyone shouted in excitement.

He shuffled toward the balustrade on unsteady legs. He cast his eyes down at the waves and gasped instinctively.

Countless flat barges and tiny fishing boats floated upon the water. Stout, half-naked fishermen, as small in stature as, yet clearly distinguishable from, the Chinese men surrounding Sherlock, swayed to and fro as they pushed their long oars through the water. The scene was just like that of woodblock prints.

Day had broken. Beyond the port rose a range of mountains, and a hazy, cone-shaped silhouette floated far in the distance. As the sun rose, the clouds that hung about the skirt of the mountain were bathed in red. The peak towered high above those clouds, limpid and glassy. Mount Fuji.

Sherlock's weariness vanished in a heartbeat. They had arrived in Japan, the fabled country of the Far East.

The ship docked in Yokohama port. Captain Cartlett ushered the group onto the pier without offering even a word of farewell. No one was there to meet Sherlock. He teetered off the ship with his heavy trunk in his hands, and alighted onto an empty dock.

But even so he had to stop a moment, awestruck. Rows of Western-style buildings lined the docks. Their architecture was similar to the British colonial style, as might be seen in India or another of the empire's territories.

This made him set off cautiously. No sooner did he maneuver down one of the side streets than the scenery around him changed. There were lines of wooden houses with tiled roofs in close profusion. Men and women dressed in kimonos bustled to and fro across a bare earthen road. A two-wheeled cart, pulled by a man instead of a horse, passed. The inhabitants were shorter, and likewise everything else— the façades of the buildings to the size of the vehicles—was designed more compactly. The signs on the storefronts were covered in letters he could not read. In addition to recognizably Chinese characters, there were other symbols that resembled squiggling worms. As far as the eye could see the whole street was full of loud confusion, and yet one glance was enough to see that the streets were hygienic. Unlike in London, there were no puddles of sewage by the side of the road.

Everywhere was clean.

Sherlock opened the case Mycroft had given him. In addition to English currency, it was stuffed with notes, maps, and other papers. He had already checked its contents while on the boat.

The English-language maps were a priceless commodity. From them, he learned that the ship had not docked at a wharf for foreign vessels, but at a district reserved for passages to the outlying islands. This had allowed the passengers to enter without going through immigration procedures. Despite the harsh trials he had faced at sea, he was forced to admit that Mycroft's judgment had been correct.

By now Sherlock had been wearing the same soiled blazer for far too long. And with his unkempt hair and current ragged appearance, there was no telling when the police might stop him. His attention was caught by a narrow alleyway, in which half-naked fishermen drew well-water up in pails and upended them over their heads. Apparently they had just finished their labor. The fishermen glanced oddly when Sherlock approached, but made no move to stop him. It seemed the well was accessible to any who wished to use it.

He stripped down and began washing himself off. He would never have behaved so immodestly in London, but in this place it seemed of little consequence. The men surrounding him were already in varying states of undress.

Finished, Sherlock re-attired himself in a white shirt and ascot, a frock coat, brightly colored trousers, and leather shoes. He tucked his long hair underneath his silk top hat. His beard had, too, become prodigious in volume, but perhaps in Japan they might assume he was from some country where such beards were customary.

As he changed, several children rushed toward him and surrounded him. Had they come to steal his luggage? But no, they didn't make any moves to do so. Even after he finished changing and started walking away from the alleyway, the children followed, smiling. Were they beggars? They didn't seem to be beggars.

He realized they were simply marveling at his strangeness. Eventually the children ran back in the direction from which they had come, to a group of women who appeared to be their mothers. The children pointed at Sherlock and jabbered to the women, who craned their heads upward to stare at him. Judging from their expressions, they were flabbergasted by his height.

Such naïvete. Could this truly be the country that some 20 years prior had been loudly crying for *joui*?

But then Sherlock spotted a group of what appeared to be French citizens. According to his map, he was now in a neighborhood known as Motomachi. There was a so-called "foreign settlement" nearby with embassies and trading companies. It was far too dangerous to approach that area. He headed toward the railway station instead.

At the side of the road he found a money changer. The Japanese bank notes were machine-printed and resembled Qing currency. Sherlock couldn't be sure which bills were worth what. He thrust forward one of the less valuable-looking bills as a tip, but the clerk thrust it back with a smile, refusing to take it. Apparently tipping was not the custom.

The money changer's calculations were also extremely fast. Sherlock glanced at the rate written on the board several times to be sure the amount returned to him was right. It was. The clerk moved his fingers over the empty counter as he worked the sum, almost as if he were operating an invisible abacus. Were all money changers in Japan like this? So skilled at arithmetic they could rival mathematics professors?

As he continued on, Sherlock glanced back and forth between his surroundings and the map he held. The two bridges spanning the river were the Bentenbashi and Oebashi. The station he was looking for was just beyond.

The street leading up to the railway station was lined with gas lamps. The station itself was a brick building in the American style. It was surprisingly modern, fully Westernized even. In contrast to the British colonies, here in Japan, technologies from several countries were mingled together. It was incredible to think that all of this had been accomplished in the mere two decades that had passed since the

Meiji Restoration.

Sherlock was forced to ask passersby for directions to his platform. To his surprise, the people he spoke with were very friendly. They all smiled, concierge-like in their hospitality, and nearly all spoke English, if only in broken fragments. His height also seemed to be a matter of fascination to the Japanese—who stared as if he were an outlandish beast. Children and young women, in particular, approached him curiously. He faced no shortage of helpers as a result. As he went, Sherlock stopped to ask for directions several times. Each person responded with evident good will, answering his questions in their own stilted English. Not one demanded any gratuity in return.

At this point, Sherlock couldn't help but feel obligated to the kindness of strangers. He also was starting to realize just how difficult it was to get around in a country when one could not communicate. When he'd been invited by the French government to visit their country, on the other hand, he'd been provided with a translator. He had no prior notion that travelling through a foreign country on one's own should prove this difficult. As galling as it was to admit, once again his brother's judgment had been correct. If Sherlock had gone around the British colonies accosting strangers left and right as he was doing here, he would have attracted police attention in very short fashion.

In Japan, however, he was even free to ask the police themselves for guidance. Next to the train station there was a small building like a guard hut with uniformed police officers constantly garrisoned inside. At first glance, they stood stiff and upright like the most unbending of sentries. And yet, when Sherlock approached to speak with them they removed their hats and smiled, eagerly giving him directions in their broken English. He couldn't help but feel that the salaried thieves of London—the policemen in name only—might learn a thing or two by their example.

Finally he boarded his train. Sherlock stared out the window as the motion of the vehicle jostled him to and fro. Of the people outside, he couldn't see a single sword-wielding samurai or top-knot. The men's haircuts were no different than those in the West. The women, meanwhile, wore their long hair in braids that hung down their backs and were tied off with ribbons. About half the people were clothed in suits and dresses, and the other half in kimonos, although to his eye there were slightly more wooden Japanese-style buildings than Western-style buildings.

Everything he saw was bustling and lively, but orderly and safe. At one point he saw fragile-looking pottery dishes on display outside of one shop. This, too, would have been unthinkable in London— simply asking for destruction or theft. Nor did he see any children attempting to filch fruit from the various grocers. The houses of the commoners he saw were small, and from the outside their lives hardly looked affluent, but perhaps that was only how it appeared to his English perspective. Indeed, Sherlock saw no dissatisfaction on the faces of the citizens strolling along the streets. Only quiet enjoyment at the arrival of autumn.

For by now it was September. He couldn't be sure of the exact date: it was probably the first or second week of the month, or so the captain had said. Four months had passed since his death had become common knowledge throughout London. He wondered how the trial had progressed. Had Watson recovered at all from his friend's passing?

The train ride passed with Sherlock absorbed in such thoughts. An hour later, they at last arrived at Shimbashi. Descending from the train, Sherlock found this area was truly metropolitan. There was a stately three-story brick building, apparently the Imperial Hotel, which had been completed just the previous year. A number of foreigners could be seen coming and going through its doors. He slipped quietly away from the high street and onto a quieter, residential avenue.

He followed the map as he walked. On either side of him were impressive mansions. Ito's home was located at number 36, Takanawa Minamimachi. He headed there now.

It proved to be a Western-style building, with an unusually spacious garden for Japan. But Sherlock felt a sense of misgiving at the sight of the nameplate affixed to the gate. They did not look quite right. He didn't think they were the characters used to write *Ito*.

An elderly woman passing by caught his attention. He stopped her and pointed to the nameplate. "Ito?" he asked.

"*Iwasaki*," replied the woman with a smile, before walking away.

This was not good. The building was brand new. It looked as if it had replaced whatever stood there before. Had Ito ceded the land and moved elsewhere?

The excitement Sherlock had felt at his first visit to Japan was steadily fading, and his underlying exhaustion rushed back in. He found himself tottering. Now would have been the time for cocaine, but he hadn't brought any on his journey—it seemed unwise to carry narcotics, especially considering he might have been arrested at sea. Would he be able to refill his supply here?

Sherlock shook off his tiredness and began canvassing the area, asking passersby for help. Unfortunately, it seemed Ito was a popular surname in Japan. Perhaps not as common as Smith and Jones were in England, but at least the equivalent of a Taylor or Davis, it seemed.

While there was no one unfamiliar with the name of Hirobumi Ito, first Prime Minster of Japan, that brought Holmes no closer to Ito's new address. In the end, he found himself making the rounds of several neighborhoods.

While he walked, the sun rose high and then, as he continued to look, began to set. The streets began to grow dark. Sherlock hardly had the energy to be impatient; he was struggling to put even one foot in front of the other by now. The trunk he dragged behind him felt heavy as lead.

Twilight was settling in by the time he finally arrived at a traditional, Japanese-style house. Though only a single story, the building was quite large in scale, with an expansive Japanese-style garden waiting beyond the gates. The nameplate read *Ito*. He had now seen the same characters on several other houses he had passed. There was no guarantee this was, at last, the right house, but Sherlock had reached his limit and could no longer care.

There was no door on the gate, nothing to stop him from entering the property. In the garden, he found koi fish swimming in a small stream. He only took one glance at them, but found that after looking down he was no longer capable of lifting his head up again. His body suddenly felt impossibly heavy.

He fell forward and landed face down in the grass.

Later, he heard the sound of footsteps, but muffled, as though coming through a thick fog. How much time had passed? He lifted his eyes ever so slightly, and spotted a slender young girl in a white dress. She was Japanese, perhaps around 14 or 15. Her expression was innocent, her eyes wide with surprise. Frozen, she stared down at Sherlock.

He attempted to speak, but only a groan escaped. The girl's face changed to show her fright, and she stumbled back and ran into the house.

Before long, he saw her returning with an older woman, who looked to be in her early forties. She was as slender as the girl, and dressed in Western clothes. The girl's mother, perhaps? Her pastel-colored dress was simple and unostentatious, but evidently order-made. This was clearly a well-to-do family.

Seeing Sherlock prostrate on the grass, the older woman looked astonished. She spoke in Japanese. She took the girl by the hand and pulled her into the house again.

Stay, thought Sherlock hazily. *I need but a moment.* They were treating him like they'd just found a fox in the henhouse. How would he ever tell them the reason for his arrival if they did not stay?

By the time the two women returned, this time with a man in tow, Holmes' mind had grown distant once more. The man appeared to be around 50 years old and he was dressed in a hakama—the only one of the three dressed in Japanese clothing. He carried a wooden sword. Sherlock wondered if he had been in the middle of fencing practice. His expression was severe—it was clear he'd rushed outside as soon as he'd heard of the intruder. There was a mole on the right side of his nose.

Sherlock recognized him. It was Hirobumi Ito. Ito, however, did not appear to immediately recognize Sherlock. Perhaps it was his overgrown beard that made him look like a stranger?

But the Japanese man's eyes soon grew wide. "Sherlock? Can it be you?" he asked in English. "Mr. Holmes, I should say! But what are you doing here?"

At this, Sherlock was overcome with a flood of emotion. A bitter laugh escaped his lips, and tears welled into his eyes. The confusion only lasted a moment, however, before the world began hurtling away. The last bit of strength left him, perhaps because he knew he was finally safe, and his vision grew dark.

8

Sherlock returned to consciousness in spurts. First, he appeared to be leaning on someone's shoulder. At some point he had been lifted onto his feet and was shuffling forward. Then he had the impression that the household kept multiple servants. Several men and women in a chaotic jumble were propping him up as they attempted to carry him into the house. The servants were all much smaller than he. It was like an episode from *Gulliver's Travels*, he thought vaguely.

He lost consciousness again. Eventually, his eyes fully opened. He was lying on his back. The wooden slatted ceiling above him clearly belonged to a Japanese-style room. The wallpaper, however, was Western in style. And lifting his head, he could see that the furniture and appointments were German in make. He was also lying on a bed rather than on the floor. The room was decorated with items gathered from throughout Europe, and yet it retained a sense of Japanese style.

Sherlock sat up and put both feet on the floor. He felt carpeting. His feet were bare, without shoes. He stood up slowly, bracing himself against the dizziness. Through the window, it was dark outside. The Japanese garden drifted dimly beneath the pale light of the moon.

He must be inside the Ito estate. Opening the door, he was greeted by a Western-style bathroom. It had both a shower and a bathtub. He turned on the faucet, and hot water instantly poured from the tap.

Sherlock felt grateful. This had to be a Western room for guests. He removed his clothes and washed himself thoroughly. His earlier bath in well-water had been far from adequate in removing the filth that had adhered to his body over his grueling four months at sea. There was nothing in the world he wanted more than a bath.

Afterwards, he returned to the room and dried himself with a towel, and realized his trunk was missing. His shaving things and other clothing were in that trunk.

But there was a shallow wooden chest. He opened it and found a kimono. He draped it over his body, and further confirmed his earlier assessment: The kimono had certainly been provided for foreign guests. The sleeves were sufficiently long, and the hem reached his ankles. Sherlock had to rely on memory in tying the sash, trying to recall the knots on the kimonos he'd seen in town. He stood in front of the looking glass, peering at his reflection. It would have to do.

He was interrupted by a woman's voice, speaking in English. "Excuse me."

A portion of what Holmes had thought was a wall slid open, revealing a kneeling woman dressed in Japanese clothes. No, not kneeling. It was a sitting posture, known as *seiza*. She was the older woman he'd seen in the garden earlier. She delicately placed the fingers of both hands against the floor and bowed her head. She spoke again in English. "Thank you for coming so far to visit us. My name is Umeko. I am Ito's wife."

Abashed, Sherlock attempted to imitate how she sat on the floor. He prostrated himself in the Moslem fashion he had once learned. A quiet, restrained laugh escaped Umeko's lips. It seemed his pose was incorrect.

Sherlock lifted his gaze and attempted to regain his composure. "I should be thanking you. You are very kind to welcome me in this manner, despite my abrupt arrival."

Umeko smiled at him. "My husband hopes you will join him for supper."

"It would be my honor."

"Please." Umeko stood up gracefully. Her movements were like a dancer's.

Sherlock rose to his feet as well. She must have heard the bath running and timed her appearance to coincide with when he would finish dressing. Almost like a detective. What impressive sensibilities. He couldn't help but mark the contrast with Mrs. Hudson, who made a habit of barging into his rooms while he was still asleep in order to prepare breakfast.

They came onto a wooden slatted hallway facing onto the garden. According to a book he had once read on Japanese architecture, this area was called the *engawa*. It was a type of veranda, or exterior hallway. On the engawa, Umeko assumed the seiza posture once more. She muttered something in Japanese, before opening another sliding door at the end.

She gestured for him to enter the room. Sherlock stepped through the door and immediately hit his head against the beam.

When he recovered, he saw a girl dressed in Japanese clothing, sitting in seiza on the tatami. She giggled. It was the young girl from the garden. Another young girl, also dressed in Japanese clothing, sat beside her. This second girl looked to be in her early twenties, and resembled Umeko in appearance. She whispered to the first girl, reprovingly: "*Asako!*"

So the first girl's name was Asako. The two girls sat side by side, close to the wall. Hirobumi Ito was sitting near the front of the room, with his back to the sliding door Sherlock had entered from, rather than further in where he might be expected. In front of him there was a *zen*—a small, tray-like dining table which Sherlock had also read about, on which all courses in a meal were compactly arrayed.

Deeper in the room there was a second zen, below an alcove hung with a decorative scroll. A sitting cushion had been placed before it. Apparently this was to be his seat. But in the West, such a prominent place was reserved for the head of the house. Was this where guests sat in Japan? Sherlock made his way to the table and attempted a seiza position in imitation of Ito.

"Please, relax," his host smiled. "You must find it painful to sit in that manner."

"Hardly. As they say, when in Rome, do as the Romans." Sherlock bent his legs underneath his hips and sat upon his calves.

"Well! You are very flexible, but you will lose feeling in your legs if you sit like that for long. If you will excuse me..." Ito shifted his position and sat cross-legged.

True, Sherlock was already beginning to lose feeling in the tips of his toes. It wasn't painful to the point of being unbearable, but if the master of the house had suspended with formalities then it was pointless for him to suffer in pride. He crossed his legs as well.

The girls, though, remained in seiza, and were shortly joined by Umeko, who took a seat next to Asako. The three showed no signs of discomfort. With some sense of obligation, Sherlock attempted to return to seiza as well.

Ito held up a hand. "Please, stay as you are, Mr. Holmes. We Japanese are accustomed to the position. The ladies take no great pains, I assure you."

Sherlock re-crossed his legs. "I see. Then if you do not mind."

"I believe you have already met my wife. These are my daughters, Ikuko and Asako."

So the second young woman's name was Ikuko. She and Asako bowed their heads deeply. "Welcome to our home," Ikuko said in English. "It is an honor to meet you, Mr. Holmes."

Her pronunciation was impeccable. "Can you speak English as well, Asako?" Sherlock asked.

"I can," the girl returned, smiling. "I have heard many rumors about you from my father."

"Oh? Rumors of what kind?"

"Well," Asako began softly, and a mischievous grin lit up her features. "What can you deduce about us merely by looking?"

"Asako," Umeko cut in, frowning at the girl.

"It's quite all right," Sherlock reassured her. "I won't say anything rude. It is fortunate, though, that you remain here even after your recent move. If you had been at your other house, near the springs outside the city, I should have lost the pleasure of your acquaintance."

Asako glanced at Ikuko, a twinkle in her eye.

Ikuko stared, as if she could not believe what she had just heard. "We were told never to speak of our other home in Odawara. How could you know of it?"

Sherlock smiled. "A simple observation. I see as well that your mother is an exemplary woman. Generous of heart, tolerant, and—"

Suddenly Ito interrupted, as though he had realized something. "That is enough for today," he told his wife and children. "You may leave."

Asako balked. "I want to hear more about London…"

"Asako," Umeko restrained her daughter again. "Enough."

The dissatisfaction was apparent on Asako's face. "Now, now," Ito started in an appeasing manner, "you can speak to Mr. Holmes tomorrow morning. That is, if Mr. Holmes is willing."

Sherlock gently lifted his shoulders and lowered them again. "Naturally."

Asako lost her glum expression. The three women bowed deeply, rose solemnly, and disappeared through the sliding door.

Once they were gone, Ito released a heavy sigh. "I didn't realize it was you at first, with that beard."

"You agree with me, I assume, that your wife is very generous-hearted. I gathered as soon as I observed your daughters' noses. Ikuko is your wife's legitimate daughter, yes. But Asako is not. You may dote on her, but your wife displays considerable patience in enduring such a situation."

Ito grimaced. "From whom did you learn of our house in Odawara?" he whispered.

"From Umeko and Ikuko. By observing their faces I could discern they have been in poor health these many years. As a politician of great stature, it would hardly do for your family to take the waters at a public inn. The most suitable solution would be the springs close to Tokyo."

"You are correct—as always. It seems the people in my family are fated to poor constitutions. I am the rare exception. My father did not manage to have any other children besides myself, and my first daughter with Umeko died when she was only two and a half years old."

"My sympathies. But surely a lack of sons is no cause to sport with other women."

"I believe I told you once that I admit to my own faults. Despite appearances, Umeko, too, was formerly a geisha."

"Then she is a wife of many talents. Indispensable, I should think, to a household with such complicated affairs."

"Mr. Holmes," Ito said abruptly, and his face grew serious. "You will forgive my rudeness but I have inspected your belongings. Our residence in this house is temporary, and our presence here is not public knowledge. Though you may be an acquaintance, for a foreigner to suddenly appear at our door… It was necessary that I ensure you brought with you nothing dangerous. I hope you understand."

Sherlock started. "Surely you did not report my presence—" he said, staring at Ito.

"No," Ito shook his head. "There was a letter in your bag from Mycroft…from your brother. I have grasped the situation."

His heart sank. "As Prime Minister of an entire nation, of course you are under no obligation to shelter a dead man."

Here Ito stopped him. "I am no longer the Prime Minister. I abdicated my position to draft our constitution. I now head the Privy Council."

"The Privy Council are the Emperor's closest advisors. You are a man of position, after all. I am but a common citizen. And assumed dead, at that."

"We are the same. If the Bakufu had found me when I had come to London I would have been put to death. It was thanks to Professor Alexander Williamson and his wife, whom I know you respect, that I and my four comrades survived. I am only grateful that I can now repay my debt to England."

Sherlock openly stared, only to meet the other man's calm gaze.

His chest swelled. He was at a loss for words. He had never been very good at handling emotion. "I can't thank you enough," he murmured.

"Nor I, you," said Ito, taking a small vessel from his zen and lifting it into the air. "Shall we toast?"

Sherlock recognized the vessel. It was a cup used for drinking rice wine. He lifted his own. In response Ito tipped the saké bottle over in his hand, filling his cup with a clear liquid.

Ito glanced down at Sherlock's hands as he poured. The scars from where the ropes had been wound about his hands were still obvious. It would be some time before they faded. And Sherlock had not forgotten that Ito had sported those same scars while in London.

A look of sympathy crossed Ito's face, now that he had perhaps inferred how difficult Sherlock's journey had been.

They were silent for a moment. Ito filled his own cup with saké and raised it into the air. "To second lives."

Awash in emotion, Sherlock raised his own cup in response. As he brought it close to his lips he detected an exuberant, banana-like aroma. He tipped the cup back and swallowed. It was warm, he thought, near body temperature. As a result, it diffused readily through his stomach. The drink had an attractive profile, with a smooth sweetness accompanied by refreshing acidity. A mellow richness, different from wine, spread over his tongue.

At last, here was a meal fit for human consumption. Just the thought was enough to bring tears to his eyes. He spoke unguardedly. "I thought I should never actually find you."

"This villa belongs to the Arisugawa-no-miya household, but I was given free use of it. It has been some time since I have been able to enjoy such a traditional Japanese lifestyle. It is impressive that you managed to find this place."

"The search gave me an opportunity to familiarize myself to some extent with the geography of the prefecture and city of Tokyo. I have the safety and orderliness of the streets, as well as the kindness of the people, to thank for my success. The design of the city is quite efficient. The gas lamps in Yokohama reminded me of London."

"I arranged for those lamps."

"You did?"

"My time in London left a deep impression on me. If we are to have trains, I thought, we must have gas lamps fronting the station. It was foolish of me, perhaps."

"Certainly not." Sherlock laughed, but there was a tightness in his chest. "The truth is…you were right."

Ito's face twisted up in confusion. "About what?"

"On the way here, our boat passed through Shanghai. My brother had told me not to leave the boat, but I could not resist being curious."

"Ah," Ito smiled. "There were a great number of Indian street performers, I presume?"

"It was just as you said. Snakes have no eardrums, only an internal sound organ known as the inner ear. While not entirely insensible to sound, it is doubtful they could distinguish the notes of a flute as a mammal could. And on top of that, they are carnivorous. They do not drink milk."

"I remember that Dr. Watson was worried you may have been entirely mistaken in your conclusions…"

"No. The long and short of the case held. Roylott believed he was controlling the snake with his flute and milk. What actually happened is likely that he thrust the snake into the vent headfirst, so it could only crawl forward. As Roylott's room was moist and dark due to the other animals he kept, the snake returned readily to it in search of its nest. Indeed, his assumption that the snake was under his control likely caused him to be careless and thus fall victim to the creature's fangs himself."

Ito listened to this explanation blankly, but once Sherlock was finished he smiled. "I do not know the particulars of what you are speaking of, but I am glad that you arrived at the truth."

The detective could only shrug his shoulders. "It is my brother who placed the treatise on snakes in my bag. I suppose he had read Watson's story and wished to point out my mistake."

"You are lucky to have a brother who is so astute."

This pricked his ire. Ito didn't know about his antagonism towards Mycroft. Sherlock sipped from his cup. "Speaking purely in my own capacity, the significance of my individual existence is greatly injured by the existence of a brother. I may be unique, but the presence of a brother, identical in blood and greater in experience and years, cuts my own value down by half."

"I'm sure that isn't so."

"You do not have brothers and would not know."

"I have children. They are brothers and sisters."

"Perhaps then with different mothers there is no desire to compete. They may be brothers, but they are also half strangers."

"Mr. Holmes. As collected and rational as you may be, you can be possessed of the strangest notions. Did your brother not help you to escape the country? He seems very dedicated to you."

At this, Sherlock could only fall silent. He would have liked to agree with what Ito said, but could not shake his feelings of distrust. He was inclined to cynicism. Mycroft was likely only feigning solicitude as an excuse to better parade his own problem-solving skills before his younger brother.

He had to admit, at the end of the day perhaps it was petty jealousy on his part. But if Mycroft felt himself to be even slightly superior to him, that then was reason enough for him to be irritated. In the end, Sherlock was simply incapable of seeing eye to eye with his brother. He simply could not accept him.

Ito grasped his chopsticks. "Shall we?" He indicated a small bowl. "That, Mr. Holmes, is stewed warabi."

Sherlock lifted the small bowl. It was difficult for him to manage the chopsticks. He immediately recognized the stuff in the dish, however, as the same bracken-root that grew in the highlands of Scotland. Wasn't bracken a weed? No one ever ate it in England, of course.

Once he had taken a mouthful, however, he found the texture pleasant—soft but with enough bite. The overlay of sweet and sour in the broth was likewise exquisite.

Ito seemed to guess his thoughts. "When we adhere to preconceptions, we miss the opportunity to enjoy very many delicious things. Don't you agree?"

This made Sherlock frown. He was beginning to worry that if he agreed too readily with everything that Ito said his own dignity might suffer in consequence.

But of course, this was Hirobumi Ito's country. The culture, the affability of the people… Sherlock was forced to admit that he had met with much to defy his expectations.

He placed his chopsticks on the tray and glanced down. "What am I to do now?"

"There is no need to worry," Ito reassured him gently. "As long as you accompany me all will be fine."

"I am afraid that might lead to a spectacle. I drew the attention of quite a many Japanese as I made my way here. A lanky Englishman earns many stares in this country. People will think it strange to see me always in the company of the head of the Privy Council."

"No, so long as you are at my side all will be fine. When Piggott Wilson Johns came to Japan to advise on constitutional matters, we could be found in discussion nearly every hour of the day."

"Ah, the son-in-law of MP Jasper Wilson Johns."

"Yes. Our lords of parliament do not speak English very fluently, and so they tend to keep their distance when foreigners are concerned. I doubt there will be any problems while the two of us are together."

"Is that so… It's possible that I might meet other foreigners here as well, is it not? Even other Englishmen?"

"If that should happen, all you need to do is play along and make conversation. Mr. Holmes, I understand your misgivings. When I was first in London I felt the same. As time passes, you will grow more bold. Perhaps as bold as I was, when we met in Cheapside!"

Sherlock had to laugh, despite himself. "I do not know that I am quite as brave as you," he murmured. His voice sounded lifeless to his own ears.

"But of course you are. And a good deal more clever." Ito raised his cup once again. "So then, welcome to Japan, Sherlock Holmes."

9

Sherlock had never been so grateful for a bed that didn't rock. He slept soundly for the first night in four months, awaking most agreeably in the morning. When his eyes un-shuttered themselves, he found himself gazing upon neither the ever-looming ship hold nor his rooms in Baker Street, but at less recognizable settings. He soon remembered, however, that he was currently a guest at Hirobumi Ito's estate.

Shortly a servant entered and led Holmes to another room, in which a barber was waiting—one in the service of Ito and his family, it seemed. Once Sherlock's hair had been cut and his beard shaved, he finally recognized his familiar, dapper self in the mirror again.

Back in his bedroom, he noticed that his trunk and leather case had been restored. His clothes, too, had been removed and hung up in the closet.

His hosts were very thorough in their attention. One couldn't call anything less than this a civilized life. Sherlock dressed himself in a shirt with starched collar and his morning jacket. He put on his silk top hat. Then he stopped. His leather shoes were nowhere to be found. But one did not wear shoes indoors in Japan.

In the mirror, other than his bare feet, his reflection matched how he had looked on Baker Street down to the last detail.

The bedroom's furnishings included a low table, upon which his breakfast had been laid out. He sat down at the table alone, cross-legged. The table had been arranged with a great number of small bowls, each filled with a minute portion of something different. He saw fish, he saw mountain vegetables, but everything else was alien.

"Excuse me," a girl's voice called. The sliding door opened, and Asako showed her head. She was wearing a brightly colored dress, likely one of her finer articles. Her hair had been tied up neatly as well. She held a newspaper in her hand.

The girl looked upon Sherlock with evident happiness. He didn't understand its cause, but perhaps she was reacting to his change in appearance after his haircut. She approached and sat down next to him.

"Good morning. Would you care to take the morning paper?"

"Thank you." Sherlock took the paper from her, but found himself perplexed on the front page. It was written entirely in Japanese. "While I possess considerable powers of deduction, I suspect it will take several months until I am able to read the language. I know, of course, that kanji are a type of pictograph."

Asako leaned over him. "Here, look at this character. This is *ki*. It means tree."

"Ah, I can see how it would mean that." The character did look somewhat like a simplified tree.

"And now look at this one." She pointed to a character that looked like two *ki* side by side, and then to another character that looked like three *ki* in a bunch. "This means forest. And that one is *mori*. It means woods."

Sherlock smiled. "Quite straightforward. There are more and more trees."

"And this character is *hi*. It means fire. It sort of looks like it is burning, doesn't it? Two *hi* lined up vertically makes the character for *honou*. It's like a bigger, hotter fire. A blaze. And you can even use the two characters together to spell *kaen*. The more *hi* you use, the hotter it looks."

"Undoubtedly. This article, then, is about an arson case that occurred near a station in Tokyo?"

Surprise flashed on his tutor's face. "Can you read it already?"

"No, but considering the frequency with which the character for fire is used, and the placement of the article, I assumed it must be a fairly serious incident. And yesterday I became quite familiar with the characters for Tokyo and station."

"So that's what it is! You are very perceptive."

"The article on this page must be about some accident or crime. The headline is very large. What does it say?"

"Hmm… Thefts of miscellaneous articles continue. A string of cat burglaries have struck homes throughout Kanto, targeting items such as pottery, dolls, and woodblock prints. Over 100 cases have already been reported, and police are in a heightened state of alert."

"Pottery, dolls, and woodblock prints. Are these items of value?"

"No. They were all hina and ichimatsu dolls, which are worth almost nothing. The rest were amateur prints and things like common flower vases used to decorate the alcoves in people's homes. It's all pretty worthless. A pawnshop probably wouldn't even take them."

"Most interesting. None of the items were rare, then?"

"You can find them in almost any home. The kind of junk that gets left over in open-air markets."

The sliding door opened once more. This time Ikuko bowed, sitting in strict seiza. She wore an even finer dress than Asako, and a glossy ornament in her hair. Her makeup had been carefully applied.

Upon raising her head, Ikuko seemed to notice Asako's presence for the first time. "What are you doing in here?" she said in English, her expression severe. "You shouldn't bother our guest."

Asako stood up. "Well, what about you? Why are you bothering Mr. Holmes?"

Before Sherlock could stop them, the two began arguing in Japanese. Then their mother, Umeko, appeared. Like the two younger girls, her dress was fit for high tea. Her hair was tied up neatly, and her makeup was meticulous. By London standards her attire would have been slightly behind season, but here in Japan, Sherlock recognized, it represented a level of sophistication only available to the most privileged classes.

Umeko furrowed her brow. "Why are you both here? Your father is ready to go. Outside now, hurry."

Asako, who had been putting on ladylike airs earlier for Sherlock's sake, made a face at her sister. Ikuko immediately retreated to the hallway, her own expression unamused. Asako ran after her. Umeko gave an embarrassed smile and lowered her head. Sherlock stood as well. It seemed he had missed his chance to take breakfast.

Approaching the front entrance, he saw that the servants had lined up in the garden. Umeko was waiting as well, along with Ikuko and a fidgeting Asako. In all their finery, it looked almost as if they were preparing to leave for a ball.

Ito appeared next, dressed dapperly in a frock coat and bow tie. Sherlock donned his shoes, which had been laid out for him, and joined him in the garden. A bellows camera had been set up on a tripod on the lawn. The lens was pointed toward them. Behind it, the photographer was busy making preparations.

Sherlock glanced at Ito uneasily. "What is all this?"

"I hoped you might take a commemorative photo with us."

"That is a problem. I am supposed to be dead."

"Believe me, I had my own misgivings on the matter, but my daughters were quite insistent."

Asako had sidled up close to Sherlock at some point while he was talking to Ito, and was now staring up into his face. Her expression broke into one of pleasure. Though less obvious than her sister, Ikuko also glanced at him several times out of the corners of her eyes, while fussing over her bangs.

"I will take care that the photographs do not leave this house," Ito whispered into Sherlock's ear. "It is rare that I have the family together like this. It would be a great favor to me."

Sherlock was taken aback. "You are not regularly together?"

"We live under the same roof, of course, but I'm afraid that since Asako's arrival Umeko has grown cold."

"That is understandable."

"And Asako is rebellious. She has been a handful for the servants. I cannot remember the last time I saw her so well-behaved. We seem like a family today."

"If your eldest son also lived with you I imagine the situation would be even more challenging. He is around five, I believe? I should congratulate you on having a son, but as the boy is not Umeko's the situation must be complicated. Your second son is not Umeko's, either, but as he is still a babe perhaps you have not yet reconciled yourself to his presence."

"How do you know about Bunkichi and Shinichi?"

"Last night you referred to your children—brothers and sisters. And I noticed a photograph in your study in passing. Both of the boys resembled you. As neither bore a particular resemblance to Umeko, however, I assume that their mother…"

"Enough, I understand. But please, will you take the photo? For the sake of our domestic peace?"

At the photographer's request they formed a line in front of the entrance to the house. Umeko inclined her head to Sherlock, her lips curving upward gently. She seemed quite agreeable to the prospect of the photograph, too. Perhaps she also was pleased to see her family together like this.

Then Asako fastened onto Sherlock's arm, and Umeko reproached her. She released him, her face momentarily twisted in dissatisfaction, but then stood by his side instead. Ikuko stood close on his other side. Each time he turned his attention her way she dropped her eyes in confused embarrassment.

After all the fussing, the family was finally in position. Sherlock stood up straight, posing. At the photographer's word, Sherlock Holmes and the Ito family were immortalized in photographic record.

It was just as they finished that a carriage pulled up in front of the gate. The servants bowed their heads. Sherlock and Ito boarded the carriage together; Asako watched them go, smiling broadly and waving her hand. Ito looked pleased, but Sherlock was left feeling discombobulated. Pleasantries did not come easily or naturally to him.

The carriage took them to the Emperor's palace. The area—a sprawling tract of green surrounded by a moat—had once been known as Edo Castle. The building itself, which lay beyond a double-arched bridge, had been completely refurbished, although its exterior was an exact double of the Kyoto Imperial Palace which Sherlock had once seen in a photograph. It was a Japanese-style structure, made of wood, with a tiled roof.

Ito told Sherlock that this building was known as Meiji Palace. It measured 5,800 *tsubo* in area, which was some 4.7 acres in British measurements. The palace consisted of three sections—the main hall, for courtly functions; the inner rooms where the Emperor engaged in government matters; and the Imperial Residences, which served as the Emperor's home. Each section was connected to the next. A separate building, joined to the palace by a covered corridor, was reserved for the Imperial Household Agency.

Near the entrance Sherlock saw an opulent carriage porch, with a traditional Japanese gabled roof. Their carriage, however, came to a halt to the right of the door, rather than directly in front of the entrance. Ito explained that the porch was reserved for guests of state and diplomatic envoys.

Once they alighted, a contingent of servants, ranging from guards to what must have been staff, bowed toward them in perfect unison. Sherlock and Ito began walking forward. The carriage porch was a detached building, the interior of which was exquisitely decorated with Western ornamentations. Once through the carriage porch was an inner courtyard, across which awaited the massive main palace building.

When they entered the palace, Sherlock observed that though it, too, was traditionally Japanese in style, it housed a huge Western hall painted in brilliant dizzying colors, with a raised, two-story ceiling. Though it was as splendid as the Palace of Versailles itself, the ceiling mural was in fact designed in Japanese patterns. The hall had wooden floors and the fixtures were Western in style, but the interior was decorated with an eclectic mix of Japanese and Western ornaments. Even the chandelier had an Oriental charm. The space was very exotic.

Even when describing Western rooms, the Japanese calculated

floor space according to how many tatami mats might fit inside. The audience chamber, Sherlock heard, was 160 mats in size. The Eastern and Western *tomari-no-ma*—or waiting chambers—each measured 175 mats in size.

Around two dozen men in frock coats and tails stood in conversation inside the Eastern waiting chamber. They all looked to be in at least their forties. As Ito entered, they immediately turned their heads to attention and bowed deeply. Ito spoke to them in Japanese and the men resumed their conversation. No one paid Sherlock any special notice, just as Ito had predicted. He could not help but remark to himself that Ito had certainly become a man of stature.

"Are they the other lords of the Privy Council?" Sherlock inquired.

"Yes," Ito answered him in English. "Though it would be more accurate to refer to them as counselors. In addition to the counselors there is a vice-chairman, a chief secretary, and three additional secretaries. The council was formed to deliberate on the drafting of the constitution. It has immense influence in the government."

"Then in a sense perhaps the head of the Privy Council is even more powerful than the Prime Minister."

"No. I sit third at court. That is one place lower than when I was Prime Minister. But now that the constitution has been successfully announced, I hope to return to my former glory."

But something seemed off. If the council was in session surely a table would have been prepared. Still, this was no mere social gathering. None of the counselors were smiling. They were engaged in what seemed to be an earnest discussion.

"Mr. Ito," he whispered. "Has something happened?"

"Nothing in particular. It has already been dealt with. Do not worry yourself."

Just then a man, who appeared to be a member of the staff, rushed into the room, his face pale. He shouted something in Japanese and the room went silent. The expressions on the men's faces grew stony. The air grew thick.

Ito sighed, and called out to several men in Japanese. The men he picked out were quick to shout, "*Hai!*" and gather around Ito. He turned back toward the main hall and they marched with him. There were five men in total, likely the vice-chairman, chief secretary, and secretaries of the Privy Council whom Ito had mentioned earlier. Sherlock accompanied them.

The group exited into the courtyard. Two Western men were walking toward them. One was in his fifties, with grey hair and a round face that sported a beard even fuller than Ito's. He wore a frock coat with a stiff collar and gold buttons. The other man was a Russian officer, dressed in a white military uniform. He looked to be a few years younger than the man in the frock coat. Both men had their mouths set in hard lines.

The vice-chairman and other council members stood to the side in a row, their presences visibly subdued. Sherlock joined them. Ito alone walked forward to meet the two guests.

As soon as the man in the frock coat caught sight of Ito he began haranguing him in heavily accented English. "Chairman Ito! How long must we wait before you answer us in good faith?"

Ito replied in conciliatory tones. "My deepest apologies, but we ask that you please give us a little while longer. It is taking longer than expected to reach our opinion."

The officer snorted. "As soon as that foolish judgment was handed down you should have begun an immediate retrial. Surely such a serious incident between our two countries demands an *immediate* response."

"Of course," Ito began agreeing. "You are absolutely correct. However, in our constitution, the judiciary is a separate branch from the Privy Council—"

The man in the frock coat broke in. "Chairman, did you not agree with us that Sanzo Tsuda should be executed? You say that the judiciary is a separate branch, but Japan remains an imperfect nation. We know that the legislature is at least swayed by the Privy Council. Do not tell me that you cannot exert that same influence over the judiciary."

What was this? For the first time in many ages Sherlock sensed a game afoot. The council vice-chairman and his four colleagues only looked on in silence. It seemed they did not understand English. Ito had been left to deal with the two Russians alone. Two against one hardly seemed fair play. Perhaps he might be of assistance…

"Ambassador Shevich Dmitry Yegorovich, good morning. It is an honor to meet you."

Ito turned toward Sherlock, his eyes wide. The two Russian men also seemed taken aback.

Shevich stared. "An Englishman? Who are you? How do you know me?"

"You are generally well known, but in truth I only know of you from what I have read in the papers. It is clear from your deportment that you come from nobility, and in addition to Russian I also detected an Italian and Swedish accent in your English. The Shevich line is a long and distinguished one. And as a diplomat, I am certain that you have served in Rome and Naples, as well as Sweden."

"What's this?" said Shevich, his expression growing increasingly stern. "You speak as if this is something you have only now surmised, but as you are accompanying Prime Minster Ito I wonder if you are not a spy from the British legation. The Japanese government has gone crying for help and Ambassador Hugh Fraser sent you, hasn't he!"

In a panic, Ito attempted to reason with the ambassador. "This is a misunderstanding. This gentleman is here to advise me on a completely separate matter."

"Taking advantage of your breakfast appointment with Prime Minister Masayoshi Matsukata in order to assault Chairman Ito with these questions is hardly becoming conduct for a man of nobility such as yourself," Sherlock reproved Shevich. "Nor do I commend your bringing Lieutenant Colonel Kanevsky with you like a guard dog, to intimidate your hosts. Japan had no military men present at the meal. Using a show of force to personally intimidate the Prime

Minister of another nation does seem uncouth, does it not?"

The faces of the two Russian men flushed red. Shevich launched into an immediate slew of invective. "I knew it, Japan thinks it can cling to Britain's skirts! Only the Prime Minister and a few of his closest advisors were present at today's breakfast. How else would the British legation know this so soon?"

Sherlock promptly lifted a forefinger to silence Shevich. "Please, lower your voice. Remember, we are in the Emperor's home. No one has reported your meeting to me. I discerned all this upon first seeing you."

"What is this?"

"You are unaccustomed to Japanese food—there are traces of miso soup in your beard and on your sleeve. That you were compelled to take Japanese food while in state dress tells me that you had a breakfast appointment. A man of your high position, overbearing as you are, might request a change in menu—unless of course your partner was a figure of considerable importance in the Japanese government. Then, you seem to be disappointed in the results of some trial. I gather discussions did not go as you had hoped. However, if your breakfast had been with a member of the judiciary your next port of call would undoubtedly have been a member of the legislature. And had your meeting been with a mere cabinet member your next target would have been His Prime Minister. You would have had no cause yet to harangue the head of the Privy Council here."

"From this you conclude that my meeting was with Prime Minister Matsukata? Still, someone must have told you there were no military men present on Japan's side. You even knew the name of my companion, Kanevsky. How do you explain that?"

"The names of Russian military officers are engraved on the edge of their buckles. Additionally, Lt. Colonel Kanevsky is wearing his full badges and honors. The rank of major has now been abolished in the Russian military, yet the lt. colonel wears a silver major's badge. It is usually worn on the cap. I can only imagine that by including even his eliminated badges the lt. colonel endeavored to cut a more awe-inspiring presence. Had other military been present, however, such a display would have come off as ludicrous."

Kanevsky flinched awkwardly, glancing at Shevich out of the corner of his eyes.

Shevich's own eyes widened in surprise, before turning indignantly toward Ito. "I do not know what this man advises you on, but I expect you to take full responsibility for his insolence."

Sherlock rested his gaze on Shevich. "Chairman Ito is blameless. I spoke to you of my own volition. Your comments were unbefitting to a man of your nobility. However slight, you might attempt some compunction when—"

Ito turned his gaze to Sherlock, in warning. "Mr. Holm..."

He froze mid-sentence, blanching at his mistake. Sherlock, too, was momentarily taken aback, but he soon smiled sheepishly at Ito. As soon as he stuck his neck into an argument between the head of Japan's Privy Council and the ambassador from Russia, he knew any hope of continuing to pass as a nameless Englishman had been lost. He certainly did not care to compound his crimes further with a series of false names and assumed identities.

Shevich blinked. "It cannot be. Sherlock Holmes?"

A look of disbelief crossed Kanevsky's face. "Your death was reported in the papers some months back."

Ito broke in, his expression pinched. "The articles were a misunderstanding. The truth is that I invited Mr. Holmes here to advise the Privy Council. To avoid difficulties, however, until a correction is run I ask that you please keep knowledge of his presence here to yourselves."

Shevich furrowed his brow. "To avoid difficulties? What is really motivating you? You say advisor, but Sherlock Holmes is a detective by trade. There is but one matter on which he could be advising you. You have invited him here to train spies!"

Anger flashed in Kanevsky's eyes. "You have struck a secret bargain with the British. Behind our backs!"

Ito shook his head. "Certainly not. We would never—"

Sherlock interrupted. "You have hit the nail on the head, gentlemen. Japan has already refashioned itself as a modern nation. It is only natural they should have their own intelligence branch."

"Russia will not allow you to train spies behind our back!" Shevich roared.

"But of course," Sherlock said innocently. "As you see, nothing is being done in secret, nothing is behind your backs. All has just been laid bare, has it not? Japan may establish an intelligence agency under my advice, but they would certainly never release spies in Russia. Your being informed, now, should give you cause enough to trust their motives."

"The reports of Holmes' death can only be subterfuge," Kanevsky exhorted Shevich. "He must have faked his death on secret orders. The British are contriving to insinuate themselves into Japan's intelligence network."

Shevich stared at Ito, incredulously. "You are playing a dangerous game, Chairman. Do realize of course that this is Britain's first step toward colonization. You will soon find yourself a puppet government to their queen. Japan will soon be beset with internal strife, just as it was with China. Be on your guard, lest you become a nation full of opium addicts."

"Worry not," Ito said, soothingly. "Opium has been outlawed in Japan ever since the Edo Bakufu."

"It was outlawed in China as well. The English imported it by force." Shevich turned on Sherlock fiercely. "I plan to consult with my own country, and inquire directly with the English authorities as to the truth of reports of your death. I expect no answers from the British legation. Undoubtedly they have been instructed to deny all knowledge. May you be prepared, when the time comes."

"There can be no crime in killing a man who is already dead," Kanevsky added menacingly.

"Undoubtedly," Sherlock replied drily, secretly amused at how the ambassador and his lt. colonel were so unsparing in their threats. "But now that we have made each other's acquaintance, I hope we

97

may enjoy the pleasure of each other's company until you receive your answer from England. I promise that I shall neither run nor hide."

Shevich drew close. "Mr. Holmes. The deplorable attempt on the life of His Imperial Highness and Successor to the Throne, Tsarevich Nicholas, has thrown this tiny Eastern nation into crisis. If Britain thinks to use that crisis as an opportunity to interfere, however, you will be disappointed. Russia will not cede Japan."

Finished speaking, Shevich turned on his heel. Kanevsky glared a moment longer before following.

His Imperial Highness, the Crown Prince? Sherlock turned toward Ito. "Has something befallen Tsarevich Nicholas?"

Ito sullenly returned Sherlock's gaze. He sighed deeply, stroking his long beard with the tips of his fingers.

10

At the rear of the courtyard was the state banquet hall, known as the *houmeiden*. It was spacious and elegantly decorated. At the moment, however, there was no one inside.

Ito led him inside and closed the door behind them. Once they were alone, he let his anger fly. "What were you thinking! After all the trouble we took to conceal your identity!"

Sherlock sauntered about the hall casually. "You mustn't be so angry," he said lightly. "After all, was it not you who let my name slip?"

"Well yes," Ito had to admit. "But that could have been papered over. After all you said, however, there is no going back. You faked your death and entered this country illegally. And I harbored you. Knowingly!"

"Irrelevant, and furthermore it will take a month at the least for the truth to come out. You certainly display a politician's resourcefulness, telling Ambassador Shevich that the reports of my death in the *Times* were mistaken. So long as Shevich and his man believe I am here to advise on spycraft they will raise no questions with the British legation. And even if they should, they will assume the legation is lying."

"This is also true," Ito conceded. "Ambassador Shevich said he plans to inquire directly with England, but Scotland Yard believes you dead. With you here, the only way the English authorities could ascertain the truth would be to dispatch a letter to the legation in Japan."

The detective smiled. "The legation, however, is entirely oblivious to the situation. There would be considerable confusion, and all correspondence would be at cross purposes. Until such matters are resolved, Russian hands will be tied and I shall be at liberty to travel freely."

"But after a month my culpability in the matter will still come into question."

"Fear not," Sherlock said calmly, his face serene. "You must only insist that I told you the reports were mistaken, and that you had no reason to doubt me. Say that I insisted there was no better proof of what I said than that I arrived by ferry."

"But after that you will be arrested! The authorities will think you acted alone in your deception."

"What is the problem in that?"

"The problem! Do you truly think I could stand by silently and watch as you are treated as a criminal?"

"But I have committed a crime," Sherlock murmured. He stood still and stared off into space. "I cannot escape suspicion in Moriarty's death. Now that I have thought things over at length, I must admit to myself I did have murderous intent when I went to face him. It was perhaps my only recourse, but still one I arrived at in disregard of the law. The fact that I was prepared to die with Moriarty does not pardon my crime."

"Then you accept guilt?"

"There is no telling how things will play out. But I am inclined to surrender myself to the courts. On a previous case I chose to let the man who stole the Blue Carbuncle go free. That responsibility, too, still follows me."

Ito looked shocked. "Why, you are serious. But in his letter, your brother wrote that some of Moriarty's men still remain. And what of the younger Moriarty's efforts against you? If you allow for things to be decided at trial you may find yourself in prison."

"Then I shall find myself in prison. Had I died I should have been equally helpless. It is a stroke of providence, perhaps, that I have even this opportunity to observe which direction the winds of judgment blow."

Ito groaned involuntarily. "Mr. Holmes, are you sure your current resignation is wise?"

"My original plan was undermined the moment that Moriarty's man concealed himself above the Reichenbach cliffs. Surrendering to justice and serving my penance should allow me to return to society an honorable man. Should Moriarty's gang remain at large, I could then return to confront and confound them."

"I am surprised at your change of heart, considering that you endured four months at sea to come here."

"I was weak." A shadow crossed the detective's face. "I thought such concerns could wait until my survival was assured. Thanks to you, I have found safety at last in Japan. My gratitude knows no bounds. But here in this great land, in the lap of Mt Fuji, all I do *is* survive. A mere conduit to convert oxygen into carbon dioxide."

"There is no telling what the future will bring, Mr. Holmes. You should await your opportunity. It is how I have managed things."

"Our situations differ. I am a detective by profession. So long as there is life in me I cannot bear to allow my brain to go to waste. Your circumstances must be dire, seeing that they demand the presence of the full Privy Council, seeing as the pressure of drafting a constitution has passed. I imagine the Diet and the courts are likewise in a state of panic. If there is a case to be solved between Russia and Japan, pray allow my intellect to be of service in the matter."

"It's true… Japan's position these four months has been precarious," Ito offered hesitantly. "Our relations with Russia are strained, and the future of the nation is in peril. If we do not handle things carefully now, there may be war."

"I was under the impression that Japan and Russia enjoyed mostly friendly terms. When did such a drastic change occur?"

"It is a matter of government at the highest levels. I am sorry, but I simply cannot consult with a private detective on such—"

"You deny me the opportunity to repay your kindness?" Sherlock broke in forcefully.

"Repay my kindness?" Ito looked as though he'd never heard of such a phrase. "What need is there for you to repay my kindness? I told you yesterday, it is I who am repaying my own debt to England."

"It may seem trifling to you, but I owe you my life. Those ruffians in Cheapside would not have treated me kindly, child that I was or not. There has not been a day since that I have forgotten your bravery at that time."

Sherlock's voice lingered in the stillness that followed, resounding in Ito's ears.

To the chairman, his actions that long-ago day in Cheapside had been of small import. Only a few short years earlier his life had been a vicious existence of kill or be killed. But for a ten-year-old boy living in London the incidents of that day must have left a considerably more vivid impression: vivid enough to permanently alter his life.

Ito sighed. "I appreciate your sentiments, but this is not some petty quarrel between the good people of London…"

"I beg you not to underestimate my profession. Two years prior a very important bundle of documents went missing that were definitive to the Britain-Italy relationship. It was I who recovered them."

"So you fought Russian and French spies?"

"No. But there was a risk that the documents would be sold into the hands of one of those two countries. So you see, I am not one to balk simply because matters of a national scale are involved."

"I have no doubt of that." Ito's voice was sure, and he realized he was beginning to feel a sense of relief. The truth was that he had wished for someone to rely on in these matters. "There is one thing I would like to ask, however, Mr. Holmes."

"I am at your full disposal."

"Since that tussle earlier with Ambassador Shevich, you suddenly seem in much better cheer. I might even think that the prospect of a case has given you a new sense of purpose and gratification. Are you honestly motivated by repaying some debt to me, or do you simply wish to work?"

Sherlock narrowed his eyes, and sniffed in an over-affected

manner. "Perhaps both," he snapped. "But if you insist on keeping me uninvolved, Chairman, perhaps I shall inquire if *Mrs.* Ito has any matters that require consultation."

"What case could my wife possibly have that would?"

"I'm sure she would be interested in better knowing your whereabouts. Perhaps I shall visit the geisha quarters this afternoon and inspect the soil, so that I may tell her if I find any on your shoes."

"Are you threatening me? I was already inclined to accept your help!"

"Quite so then!" Sherlock closed the discussion. He moved to the back of the room and pulled out one of the dining chairs that had been stacked to the side. He sat down. Leaning forward, he laced his fingers into a steeple. "Now then. What has happened to Tsarevich Nicholas?"

Ito walked over to a rack of shelves placed against the wall. "This space is also used as a reception area for envoys from other countries. Newspapers are provided at breakfast. The English ones should be somewhere in here."

They had archived past newspapers. Ito searched through the stack for May, pulling out a small section. He unfolded a paper and handed it over. "Your journey must have been confined, indeed. The entire world has already heard reports of the incident."

Sherlock took the paper from Ito.

"He was attacked?" he whispered immediately, staring at a front-page article. "And while in Japan!"

"It happened near Lake Biwa, the largest lake in our country. It was just last year we received a visit from Prince Arthur, the third son of your Queen Victoria, and we believed we would have no trouble hosting dignitaries from other countries as well."

"The days of *joui* are over, yes." Sherlock folded the paper. "Tell me everything that occurred, in its entirety."

"The gist of it is there in the paper."

"No, I wish to hear it from you. Your perspective on the matter will have advantages that an English reporter lacks." He closed his eyes, as if he were about to appreciate a fine concerto. "Begin."

Ito hesitated, but he had no choice. He sighed. "The incident occurred on May 1, one week after you disappeared from the Reichenbach Falls."

11

The Russian Empire was a gigantic nation, occupying the northern half of the entire Eurasian continent. For the past century they had been at war with the Ottoman Empire, aiming to expand their territory along the Mediterranean Sea, but British pressure had halted those plans.

So Russia turned its attention to the south. Its aim was to expand its control from China to Japan. In the winter, the seas adjacent to Russia froze over from the extreme cold, preventing them from launching ships; it was imperative that the nation have access to a warm-water port. And as Britain's reach now stretched to China as well, a battle for influence between Britain and Russia was sparked in the Far East as well as in the Mediterranean.

When Emperor Alexander III ordered the 22-year-old Tsarevich Nicholas to attend the groundbreaking ceremony for the Trans-Siberian Railway in Vladivostok, Nicholas had been spending the previous year travelling through Asia with his younger brother and cousin. They would end their journey at Vladivostok, attend the ceremony and then return to Saint Petersburg.

Though they had been travelling, theirs was no mere pleasure journey: Their trips were taken on massive, newly developed warships—part of a foreign policy of military display.

Nicholas and his companions began in Europe, travelling from Vienna to Greece. From there they visited Egypt, British India and Ceylon, then proceeded to Singapore, French Indochina, the Dutch East Indies, Siam, British Hong Kong, and finally Shanghai and

Canton in China. Before returning to Vladivostok, they gave word that they would also make a stop in Japan.

It was only twenty years since the Reformation. For Japan, as a newly modernized and rather poor country, a visit from the crown prince of the great Russian Empire was a matter of no small importance. To complicate matters, Tsarevich Nicholas indicated that he wished to disembark from his warship and tour the country.

Just the previous year, Prince Arthur of Britain had visited Japan and purchased a painting by Shouen Uemura, *The Beauty of Four Seasons*. Perhaps the Tsarevich did not wish to be outdone. Japan was thorough in its preparations, knowing that any faux pas against the Tsarevich could lead to an international incident.

They chose Prince Takehito Arisugawa, a full colonel in the Japanese army, to head the Tsarevich's escort. Lieutenant General Soroku Kawakami was to assist him. And Naohide Madenokoji, who had spent ten years in Russia as a foreign exchange student as part of the Iwakura Mission, served as interpreter.

Joui was a thing of the past. As a country governed by law, any acts of *joui* were treated as a criminal matter. But it was by no means true that such sentiments no longer held any sway. More than a few people in the country resented Russia vaunting its military strength at northern Japan. They were fearful of what might happen. The escort arranged for the Tsarevich decided that security should be on full alert during his visit. They stationed both uniformed and plain-clothes policemen along all roads.

Finally, on April 27, three advanced Russian warships were deployed to Kagoshima, while four more made port in Kobe. The *Pami-at Azova*, the flagship which bore Nicholas, docked in Nagasaki. The contingent's size was nearly what you might expect of an invasion.

Nicholas' younger brother had taken ill during their tour of Asia and been forced to return home early. Therefore, only Nicholas and his cousin, Prince George of Greece, visited Japan. The Japanese government received them as guests of state.

Nicholas began his tour dressed unofficially, in a suit and necktie.

Easter was approaching, as was his birthday. His itinerary remained uncertain, as Japan was anxious to make appropriate arrangements for both. Before the trip could progress, however, Nicholas began sneaking away to explore the streets of Nagasaki.

It seemed that the Tsarevich—influenced by *Madame Chrysanthème*, by Pierre Loti, a French writer known for his romantic novels—hoped to find himself a Japanese wife. Indeed, many Russian officers had taken Japanese wives—a fact that seems to have only inflamed Nicholas' passion for Japanese women. He held sumptuous parties nearly every day and lavished invitations on geisha.

Nicholas also actively visited the homes of ordinary Japanese people. The interpreter, Madenokoji, said the Tsarevich found the Japanese people friendly and welcoming—a marked contrast to the Chinese.

Nicholas was apparently so taken with Japanese culture that he even got a tattoo of a dragon on his right arm. On May 4, around the time Holmes pushed Moriarty over the Reichenbach Falls, the governor of Nagasaki Prefecture threw the Tsarevich a welcoming party. He was shown Arita porcelain and toured Suwa Shrine.

On the 6th he went to Kagoshima. Though Duke Tadayoshi Shimazu—the last daimyo of the Satsuma Domain—was known to dislike foreigners, he entertained Nicholas warmly. One hundred and seventy elderly warriors performed a samurai dance in his honor, and Shimazu himself even engaged in a dog-shooting exercise. (According to several accounts Prince Ukhtomsky, who accompanied Tsarevich Nicholas, seemed offended by this second display. Nicholas himself, however, was delighted.)

On the 9th Nicholas arrived in Kobe via the Inland Sea, and from there travelled to Kyoto by train. They even held the Kyoto mountain bonfire festival, Gozan no Okuribi, out of season, in his honor. On the 10th he visited Fukiage Omiya Palace, Kyoto Imperial Palace, Higashi Hongon-ji Temple, Nishi Hongon-ji Temple, Nijo Imperial Villa, and Kamowakeikazuchi Shrine. He watched a traditional match of kemari at the Asukai Estate, and then horse races at

Kamo Shrine. Nicholas seemed particularly taken with Kyoto. Once he was told it had been the old capital, he referred to it as the Moscow of Japan.

The 11th was the day of the incident. It was a little past noon. Nicholas had taken a day trip to Lake Biwa to see the sights, and had stopped for lunch in Shiga Prefecture.

On the way back, Nicholas led the rickshaw procession, followed by Prince George, with Prince Takehito behind. Many more rickshaws followed behind carrying attendants, military officers, luggage and so forth. The road leading back to Kyoto through the town of Otsu was lined with a swarm of people who had come out to welcome the Tsarevich, but all had been ordered to keep their heads bowed, just as though the Emperor were passing through. The guards and police performed the deepest ceremonial bows of all. There were no cheers of greeting. The entire crowd waited in solemn silence as the Tsarevich passed. The rickshaw wheels creaked, and the national flags hoisted over the streets flapped in the wind. There were no other sounds.

It was then that a member of the Shiga police force—responsible for Nicholas' safe passage—drew his sabre and swung at the Tsarevich. The policeman's name was Sanzo Tsuda. He was 36 years old.

The sabre struck Nicholas above his right ear. In addition to the cut, the sabre was heavy enough to damage his skull. Nicholas jumped from the rickshaw and fled to the side of the road.

Tsuda chased after Nicholas and attempted to strike again. Prince George managed to hit Tsuda on the back with a bamboo cane. He flinched at the blow but did not stop his pursuit. But the puller of Nicholas' rickshaw, Jizaburo Mukohata, took this chance to tackle Tsuda by the legs. Meanwhile the puller of Prince George's rickshaw, Ichitaro Kitagaichi, picked up the sabre and struck Tsuda on his neck.

Prince Takehito attempted to rush to their side but was blocked by the crowd. By the time he finally reached Nicholas, Tsuda had already been restrained. There was a cut on Nicholas' head a little under four inches in length. As for how deep it went, they couldn't tell.

The Prince immediately realized the gravity of the situation. Giving orders to his attendants, he soon wrote up a full summary of the event. And then a telegram was dispatched to Tokyo, to Emperor Meiji.

12

"And what did you do when this happened?" Sherlock asked, when Ito had finished his account.

"I rushed back to Tokyo."

"When was this?"

"I transferred from a rickshaw to an overnight train, and arrived at Shimbashi Station at one in the afternoon."

Sherlock pulled an exasperated face. "Chairman Ito, the Crown Prince of Russia was visiting Japan. Surely it was no time for you to slip away on one of your *excursions*."

"No!" Ito rushed forward, flustered. "What are you saying? I was at Sorokaku Villa, my second home in Odawara. I had already sold our home in Takanawa Minamimachi, and the Odawara villa will soon be our main residence. I am even planning to build a new villa in Oiso."

"Please confine yourself to only truthful statements, Chairman. I located Odawara on the map last night. It is not very far from Tokyo. Furthermore, I assume those in the Japanese government are aware of your Odawara villa. If you had been where you said you were, they would have contacted you earlier. You were not present at Sorokaku Villa when the incident occurred. This is precisely why you have now been provided with your current residence. The Arisugawa-no-miya household was compelled to provide it for you. On the day that Tsarevich Nicholas was injured, I suspect you were in the vicinity of the Hakone spas, dallying instead with the geisha who—"

Sherlock's powers of perception were formidable indeed! Ito

interrupted, raising his voice loudly. "Enough! I surrender. I was indeed at Tonosawa hot springs."

"You should have told me so from the beginning. And what did you do upon arriving at Shimbashi Station?"

"They had sent a carriage from the palace. After rushing here, I found that His Grace was asleep in his residences."

"His Grace?"

"The Emperor."

"You were unable to wake him?"

"His Grace deigned to receive me in his sleeping quarters so as to hear my opinion, still dressed in his bedclothes."

"And did His Majesty immediately begin with questions?"

Ito groaned reluctantly. "He first lectured me on moderation."

A disparaging look crossed Sherlock's face. "You give even the Emperor cause for concern."

"I regretted my actions deeply. Of course, I apologized. Fortunately, His Grace still has faith in me as a politician."

"Certainly. If not, you would have never been permitted into his sleeping chambers."

"Had you the time and money," Ito probed, "wouldn't you yourself consider paying a visit to the geisha quarters?"

"Certainly not." Sherlock's gaze was steely. "Then, tell me, what did the Emperor say?"

"His Grace stated his intention to travel to Kyoto and apologize directly to Tsarevich Nicholas… Prince Takehito recommended he do so in his report, and His Grace agreed."

"It seems it was a most serious situation."

"Indeed. Everyone was of one mind, you could see it in their eyes. An island nation of 40 million people, against a continental nation of 120 million? Japan doesn't have the strength yet to fight a great empire like Russia. The Russian navy is six times the size of our own, and their naval budget eight that. We are no match for them. If there was a war, Japan would surely lose."

"And so was the Emperor able to meet with Tsarevich Nicholas?"

Ito nodded. "His Grace boarded a morning train and arrived in Kyoto by nightfall. At the request of a Russian court physician the meeting was postponed until the following day, and His Grace slept at the Kyoto Imperial Palace that night. On the following day, the 13th, His Grace visited Tsarevich Nicholas at the Tokiwa Hotel."

"You did not accompany the Emperor?"

"First there was an emergency meeting in Tokyo to discuss our response—I certainly had no time for 'excursions' then. I left for Kyoto nine hours later, and was even permitted inside when His Grace met with Tsarevich Nicholas. This surprised me—even Prince Takehito and the interpreter had been barred entry. But I had been there when His Grace met the Tsarevich several years earlier during an official ceremony. Perhaps that was why I was allowed inside."

"It's only natural that the Russians would show such caution, seeing as how the Tsarevich had so recently been assaulted by an officer of the law."

"His Grace apologized to Tsarevich Nicholas. Originally, the Tsarevich had been scheduled to visit Tokyo as well. His Grace expressed his desire that he should still feel welcome."

"And how did Nicholas respond?"

"He stated that he would have to await his father's direction as to whether or not he would visit Tokyo. But he did add that he was grateful to the people of Japan for their warmth and concern."

"It seems unlikely that the Emperor and Empress Alexander III would allow their son to continue his tour of Japan after sustaining such a grievous injury."

"Very unlikely. In the end, the visit to Tokyo did not occur. We received notice on May 19 that the Tsarevich would be departing. His Grace had hoped to invite Tsarevich Nicholas to a supper at the Imperial Villa in Kobe, but the Russians refused this invitation as well. Instead the Russians held a luncheon upon one of their warships, indicating that they wished to invite His Grace to join them. I was adamantly opposed to this, as were the members of the cabinet."

"That is understandable. If the warship had departed with the Emperor still aboard he should have been kidnapped."

"His Grace insisted that we must trust the Russians. The luncheon occurred without incident, and His Grace returned to the palace."

"His Grace is brave."

"And then on the 20th, one day after originally scheduled, the Russian warships departed for home.

"It is what occurred after that which is the problem. Japan was gripped by panic. Rumors ran amok that the Russians were going to retaliate. Schools were closed, and people came out in mass to pray at the shrines and temples. In Yamagata Prefecture's Kaneyama Village, local officials outlawed both the last name Tsuda and the first name Sanzo. A woman even committed suicide in front of the Kyoto Prefectural Office by slitting her throat, as a means of showing contrition to Russia."

Sherlock snorted.

Ito was taken aback. "Do you laugh?"

"A drastic step, considering she was not even an acquaintance of Nicholas. Her death only further inflamed passions, I imagine."

Ito hesitated, but chose to be honest. "True, the chaos only spread. Some glorified her for what she did, but there were also those who reacted negatively. They commended Sanzo Tsuda for his attack on the Tsarevich, seemingly driven by *joui*... But regardless of which side people took, both believed war was imminent."

"And what steps did you take? Seeing as you speak English, I assume you approached Ambassador Shevich."

"Yes," Ito said, and his voice for the first time seemed despondent. "And he told me they were watching closely to see how Tsuda would be punished. According to Shevich, if Tsuda escaped execution there was no telling how it would affect relations between our two nations."

"I believe he made a similar threat this morning. Strange that he should repeat himself some four months after the incident occurred."

"Not so strange." Ito shook his head. "The matter appeared settled for a time. Then something occurred which we can't seem to
make sense of. Mr. Holmes! How relieved I would be if you could
unravel this mystery."

13

Ito firmly believed that the Meiji Restoration had allowed Japan to, however narrowly, escape Western force and colonial rule. But their nation now lacked the military strength needed to resist Russian advances. He worried that Russia would demand compensation for the incident, either in money or land.

Ambassador Shevich, in fact, had said as much. Shevich stated that if Prince Arthur had been attacked during his visit last year, England would have surely demanded either Shikoku or Kyushu in compensation. What choice can we have, he said, but to demand Hokkaido? However, if Sanzo Tsuda were to be sentenced to death, circumstances would of course be different...

Ito later learned that Foreign Minister Shuzo Aoki, acting independently, had made a secret agreement with Ambassador Shevich before Nicholas even arrived: If anything were to happen to Nicholas while in Japan, the perpetrator would be treated as if he had committed a crime against the Japanese imperial family itself.

So their options were limited. The Japanese government began approaching judges to oversee the trial. Under article 116 of the penal code, any who harmed the Emperor or his family were guilty of high treason. The death penalty, then, must also apply to Sanzo Tsuda.

Ito supported this move. He insisted decisive action—even martial law—would be required if public opinion turned against them. Prime Minister Matsukata, Minister of Internal Affairs Tsugumichi Saigo, and Minister of Justice Akiyoshi Yamada were all in agreement.

The Communications Minister, Shojiro Goto, suggested that abducting Tsuda and putting a bullet in him would be the best remedy for the situation. Ito grew angry. If the law could not punish Tsuda, then assassination was in order? Now was no time for such childishness. Such short-sighted thinking would see the return of the Bakufu! No, Tsuda must be sentenced to death in a court of law.

However, the head of the Supreme Court of Judicature, Korekata Kojima, opposed applying article 116.

He argued that the article applied only to the imperial family of Japan, and did not cover crimes committed against the imperial families of other countries. According to the law, royalty from foreign countries must be treated in the same manner as citizens. This did not permit a sentence of death for mere injury.

Goto gathered all of the judges the government had approached. He argued that a modern nation had to separate the judicial, executive, and legislative branches. The Japanese judiciary was entirely independent, and must not be subjected to any influence from the state. If not, other countries would assume Japan to be an untrustworthy nation, ready and willing to break its own laws. Could such a thing be allowed?

The judges who had originally been leaning toward the death penalty revised their stance in response to Goto's appeal. They flatly rejected a request for a meeting from Minister of Justice Yamada and Minister of Internal Affairs Saigo on grounds of impartiality.

They declared that if adhering to the law resulted in open war with Russia, the judges too would become soldiers and fight to defend Japan. But the independence of the judiciary must be preserved.

All of this occurred in May. On the 27th, Tsuda's case received an unusually swift ruling. He was convicted of the attempted murder of an ordinary citizen, under article 292 of the penal code. The penalty was life in prison. He had evaded execution.

Ito was stunned. He and Saigo cornered Goto in his office, and Ito banged his fists on his desk. "You protect the law even if it means war!" he'd shouted.

Goto answered him quietly: "Whether or not there will be war is up to the government." As with the other judges, if there was to be war he promised to join the effort.

The Meiji government was populated with people from the former Choshu and Satsuma domains. Goto, however, hailed from the Iyo-Uwajima Domain. He would not be cowed.

Immediately after the Tsuda trial, Saigo took responsibility and resigned. In June, Minister of Justice Yamada resigned as well, citing illness. Naturally Foreign Minister Aoki, who had complicated the case with his secret promise with Ambassador Shevich, had already been demoted.

Shevich was outraged when he learned that Tsuda had only been sentenced to life imprisonment, and began making preparations to leave Japan along with the other members of the Russian legation. In short, Ito thought, they were preparing for war. Undoubtedly the Russian Emperor had given orders. Alexander III had been watching the trial closely as well, and had also wished for the death penalty for Tsuda.

The Japanese Navy prepared for potential battle. Batteries were stationed along the coast, and warships were deployed to the Sea of Japan. Members of the government began suggesting, once again, that Tsuda should be assassinated. Ito was at his wit's end.

The Choshu Domain had, not so long ago, plunged foolishly into a war with Britain, America, France, and the Netherlands. It felt as if that nightmare were repeating itself. Back then, Ito had raced back from London in an attempt to negotiate peace, but he had succeeded in changing nothing. To make matters worse, it had been Shinsaku Takasugi who had fended off unreasonable demands from the Great Powers after the Choshu War. But Shinsaku Takasugi was no longer with them.

When a missive arrived from Russia, signed by both the government and the court, Ito steeled himself for a declaration of war. But when he read its contents, he sighed in relief.

The letter noted that as Tsuda's decision had been reached in accordance with Japanese law, Russia could only be satisfied with the sentence. So Russia had accepted the results of the trial. There was not even a demand for monetary compensation or land. War in the Far East had been averted, thanks to the forbearance and generosity of that formidable nation.

"Indeed," Sherlock murmured. "This is most curious."

"I have yet to reach the puzzling part of the matter," Ito said.

"No, there is something in this that does not sit well. Russia battles Britain for supremacy in the Far East. The events you describe have given them an ideal pretext by which to invade Japan. Likely Shevich did in fact receive orders to return to Russia. What could have inspired the change in the expected course?"

"Perhaps you should read the papers from the days after the attack? Directly before Tsarevich Nicholas returned to Russia, there was a huge outpouring of letters and gifts from Japanese citizens to the Russian warships. Crowds knelt in prayer at the port where ships were moored. We were told that Tsarevich Nicholas was deeply moved. You laughed earlier, but the incident of the woman who committed suicide was widely reported, and I believe helped earn international sympathy. The Tsarevich even ran a letter of thanks in the newspapers, under the name of his aide-de-camp Prince Baryatinsky."

"The Crown Prince may have taken a generous view, but I doubt his father, Alexander III, is quite so magnanimous," Sherlock refuted bluntly. "Alexander II was assassinated by a terrorist's bomb. Ascending to the throne after such violence, Alexander III has ascribed to a belief that peace is less a sentiment as it is a state to achieve through force. He has rejected the diplomatic approach of his father, who valued friendship with the Germans, and has instead adopted the same anti-German sentiments as the Slavophiles."

"The missive we received was also signed by the Emperor."

"A question—if Russia had demanded Hokkaido, would you have ceded it?"

Ito scratched at his balding pate with the tip of his finger. "It is impossible to speculate."

"Be honest."

"At present, Japan has no hope of defeating Russia… No, no, I cannot say."

"The difference in military strength speaks for itself. I find it difficult to believe that Alexander III would allow such an opportunity to escape him. He does not seem the type to take such a weak diplomatic stance. Surely there was opposition from the Russian government."

"True. Russia's foreign minister, Giers, thought that the best possible outcome would have been for Tsuda to receive the death penalty, and then for the Russian Emperor to request a reduced sentence, thus preserving Russia's honor. He was greatly dissatisfied with Tsuda's judgment."

"What of the Russian people? Was there no call for war?"

"Initially the Russian papers reported that Prince George alone had come to Tsarevich Nicholas' aid, while the Japanese people merely looked on. We heard there was much anger throughout the populace, but apparently after His Grace's visit to the Tsarevich, the Russian government implemented a ban and such stories ceased to appear."

"This is even stranger. An observer might think all of Russia trembled for fear of the Emperor of Japan. Such a reaction might be expected of a small country when dealing with a greater. It is almost as if your situations are reversed."

"His Grace is formidable."

"Perhaps to yourself and the people of Japan, but I doubt that Alexander III is intimidated by the rulers of other nations. Why should the man who invaded the Ottoman Empire and advanced fully to Constantinople dither now? Do remember, he builds the Trans-Siberian Railway precisely to delve into the Far East."

"Well, unfortunately, since then the situation has developed in a direction more consistent with your views." Ito sounded disgruntled. "In September, relations grew tense once more. Now Russian warships have all but occupied the Sea of Japan. And Ambassador

Shevich has demanded a retrial for Sanzo Tsuda."

"Surely it is a violation of international law for the Russians to attempt to renege on what they agreed to in their earlier missive."

"Yes, but they have suddenly brought forward the document they signed in secret with Foreign Minister Aoki. They claim that as a previous agreement exists in writing, that agreement should take precedence. You would almost think the Russian Emperor and government were previously unaware of its existence."

"Hmph. So Alexander III shows his true stripes, then."

"Only it is not the Emperor alone who is responsible. It seems the one calling for a tougher stance is none other than Tsarevich Nicholas himself."

"So the Crown Prince has changed his tune as well. That is interesting."

"According to reports, he now publicly refers to the Japanese as 'yellow monkeys' and insists that we cannot be trusted. He says we are savages who should be wiped from the face of the Earth."

"Such outbursts are understandable. He was injured badly enough to damage his skull. Perhaps his brain was even injured, causing the Tsarevich to grow violent in his temperament?"

Ito did not think that likely. "Tsarevich Nicholas' injury was not that severe. He seemed in excellent spirits! During His Grace's visit, he seemed more embarrassed about it than anything else. Russian government and military officials all attested at the time that the Tsarevich held no ill will against Japan. He was grateful for the reception he had received. He treated Japan with the same friendliness he had shown before the incident—just as the papers reported."

"I see. This is a puzzle, indeed. In addition to Nicholas' inexplicable behavior, we must consider that the Russian Navy has taken action. Not to mention the shifting response of the Russian court and government. Why have Nicholas and his father, Alexander III, belatedly taken such hard stances? Curious, very curious."

"Some have suggested that the crown prince may have been persuaded by his father after returning to Russia…"

"To go from pro-Japanese to referring to the people as 'yellow monkeys'? The change is too drastic, even allowing for that possibility. If the Emperor's intent had been to overthrow Japan all along, I suspect he would have disregarded his son's feelings from the outset and gone to war immediately. We have not yet explained why he would first lay the option of force aside and sign that letter, which appeared in the papers."

"Russia's fickleness has put Ambassador Shevich in a difficult position, but even more so us. Perhaps this time there will be a demand for money or land."

"And the man who attacked Nicholas, Sanzo Tsuda? Where is he being held?"

"Hokkaido. He is serving his sentence in Kushiro Prison."

"What were his motives?"

"The trial was carried out in a hurry, if you recall. The interviews were less than thorough. After a verdict was handed down, no further investigation was pursued."

"Excellent." Sherlock rose to his feet. "When the police fail to act it increases the value of consultants such as myself."

"What do you plan to do?" asked Ito.

"If I am correct, a great number of Russian warships are currently harbored in Tokyo's port."

"Yes... In fact, nine ships have gathered at Shinagawa Daiba, which is located in the Shiba Ward. All nine are medium-class vessels."

"Then I shall go there now."

"Now? But how did you know that the warships were there? Did you visit the port yesterday?"

"No. I was too busy looking for your home, and I never approached the docks." He set the newspaper down on his chair. "But you and I are to rescue Japan from war, are we not? Hurry now, we must be off!"

Sherlock's expression was animated. His voice carried across the hall. Even his posture had grown sprightly. Ito stared half in amazement. Sherlock faced concerns enough of his own, but at the moment he seemed entirely insensible to them. For a man supposed to be dead, he was in remarkably good spirits.

On the way out, Sherlock paused. "I almost forgot, I wish to ask you something."

"What is it?"

"It is something Ambassador Shevich said earlier, about Britain aiming to control Japan. He cautioned you to be on your guard, lest the nation become addicted to opium."

"Yes. What of it?"

"Is that the general view of things here in the East? That Britain was responsible for the Opium Wars?"

"Britain was responsible. There is no denying that."

Sherlock looked vexed. "Hmm…"

"That is not to say that I blame the British people. Britain's government and military had their own motives. The responsibility lies with those who were in power at the time, I suppose. Every country has blemishes when you explore their history."

This response did nothing to wipe the expression of dejection from Sherlock's face. He began walking once more, this time in silence. He stepped outside quickly.

Ito followed dubiously. Sherlock was a strange man. He possessed an intellect of extraordinary proportions, but his moods could be tumultuous, to say the least.

14

Sherlock bade Ito leave his advisors behind. They also travelled incognito in a plain carriage, without the imperial crest. Ito told the vice-chairman and chief secretary of the Privy Council that they were only slipping away for some amusement. From the look of discomfort on the vice-chairman's face, Sherlock judged such behavior was not uncommon. Apparently there were no matters before the council today important enough to require the chairman's presence.

Though he thought it only natural a major politician might feel uneasy travelling alone without guards, Ito exhibited no such qualms. He displayed the same boldness he had shown facing down those ruffians in Cheapside. He may have ascended to the highest rungs of government, Sherlock thought, but he had once been a feudal retainer. He exhibited a degree of courage you would expect from one who had led such an eventful life. Though of course, Ito was far from the only hard-nosed man in all of Japan.

"The Supreme Court of Judicature is equivalent to England's High Court, if I am correct." Sherlock sat next to Ito as the carriage jostled them from side to side. "The head of the court, Korekata Kojima, refused the request for a death penalty. He must be deeply devoted to the concepts of government based on the rule of law."

Ito nodded. "Few men are as formidable as Judge Kojima. But that is also what makes him reliable. He has a point. The independence of the judiciary is vital to a strong government."

"According to Mycroft, your power stretches even to the courts. I suppose even he was unaware that Japan had achieved a separation of powers."

"I became head of the Privy Council in June, but regardless of my position, so long as Kojima is in office the Supreme Court is immune to influence. Should the fact that you faked your death and entered the country illegally become a problem in the judiciary, I would be powerless to protect you from Kojima. That is why I thought you should remain at my home, in hiding." Ito added, "I hope my saying so does not make you feel apprehensive."

"Of course not. This matter is of my own making. Fortunately we are here in the Far East, as that grants a reprieve."

Ito sighed. "In truth, I feel divided on the matter. Before, I admitted that Kojima was right. But Russia is upset again, and we are back in the same predicament. I suppose I could call for Sanzo Tsuda's execution once again…"

"But your conscience prevents you?"

"Yes. If I truly value the independence of the judiciary any such course would be abominable. Doubly so, as of late."

"As of late? Explain."

"More strongly than ever, I am aware of the importance of Japan becoming a constitutional state. Certainly more so, today."

"But why more so today?"

Ito smiled. "Why indeed? You are always making inscrutable statements, I thought I might try my hand at it as well."

Sherlock snorted. He detested questions he could not answer. But it was better to remain calm.

He could not help but feel troubled, however. "Ito…" he whispered, but then hesitated. "No, it's nothing."

"What is it? Ask me anything."

"To place value on the independence of the judiciary is to place priority on the law…"

"Naturally."

"Then, do you believe that even when the blackest of scoundrels is involved, taking the law into one's own hands is inexcusable?"

"Are you asking if I think that instead of killing Moriarty, you ought to have had him arrested and brought to trial? The courts are the foundation upon which a country of law and order resides."

"I see," Sherlock said lowly.

"And yet," Ito looked hard at him, "there were no judges involved in much of what I did during the fall of the Bakufu. Still, those involved recognized the necessity of such actions."

"You refer to your clansmen in the Choshu Domain. I, however, have few such allies."

"What of Mycroft and Dr. Watson?"

"Mycroft cares only for self-preservation. Watson alone is my friend."

"Mr. Holmes," said Ito good-naturedly, "my teacher when I was younger, Shoin Yoshida, once told me to take pride not in avoiding mistakes, but rather in correcting them."

"But even if you believe you are correcting your mistakes, who is to say if you are in the right?"

"I suppose you have only your own judgment to rely on. But you are clever. I am sure that that alone is adequate."

Though he had faltered earlier, Sherlock felt his equilibrium return. "Well, thank you," he said softly.

"And thank you." Ito smiled, suddenly. "Of course, I suppose such words are premature. I still expect you to save us from the brink of war."

Sherlock could not stop himself from losing a bitter laugh. "Naturally. Leave it to me."

The view outside the carriage window suddenly broadened to show a harbor spread across the horizon. It was not like the port he'd seen in Yokohama, but possessed a charm all its own.

The ocean sparkled beneath the muted autumn light. The waves gently lapped back and forth. Several Western-style buildings lined the beach, and the shoreline bustled with small fishing boats. Sherlock's eyes were drawn to small islands that dotted the waters further out, each encircled by stone walls, and equipped with piers and docks for berthing.

"This area is known as Daiba," said Ito. "Daiba means fort. The name comes from the batteries that once stood here. They were built in haste by the Bakufu to drive back Commodore Perry, but Perry passed by and landed at Yokohama instead."

"I do not see any batteries now."

"The waters near the coast in this area are shallow. Large ships would run aground. The man-made islands you see there were built for the batteries offshore. They are all suitable for berthing, and so have been repurposed to that effect."

The carriage had to stop on a slightly elevated hill. Several other carriages had also lined up along the road, lending the area an impression of bustling prosperity. Sherlock alighted. The breeze carried to him the scent of the tide.

His attention was drawn out to the water. Nine relatively small armored ships equipped for steam and sail—so identical in appearance as to be indistinguishable—floated in the harbor. From their shape they appeared to be Russian. Three ships had drawn up to the artificial islands on their port side. Another three rose beyond, lined up in a similar column, and beyond those ships yet three more. The arrangement was similar to how new ships were unveiled during naval parades. Their majestic presences declared for themselves their monopoly of the ocean.

"The ships arrived about two days ago," Ito explained. "Of the three berthed at the artificial island, the one at the front is the flagship, the *Kondrat*. The ship beyond that is apparently named the *Kesar*."

"How does one distinguish between them?"

"Who can say? They are all much smaller than the *Pamiat Azova*, Tsarevich Nicholas' imperial flagship. They are destroyers, possibly, but their finer capabilities are unclear."

"What are the names of the other ships?"

"That is also unclear. The Russians are not allowing anyone near."

"That is perplexing. It is like Perry's black ships all over again."

Ito's voice was sullen. "Do you see now the danger we are in?"

Sherlock strode forward without replying. He descended the hill, before veering toward the collection of Western buildings located along the beach. Ito came after, unsure as to his intentions.

This area was rounded in by a fence, and uniformed Russian naval officers stood near the gate. When Sherlock approached, two young soldiers barred his way.

He made a brief salutation. "Please fetch someone who can speak English," he said.

One of the soldiers responded, speaking with a Russian accent. "State your business?"

The man's rank was visible on his badge: Матрóс 1-й статьй. Though Sherlock did not understand Russian, he was aware that the badge indicated a first-class seaman. He also glanced at the man's name, imprinted on his buckle. "First-Class Seaman Mitkov, I wish to speak with the commander of the *Kondrat*."

Unfortunately, Mitkov was apparently not so easily taken in with this gambit as Lt. Colonel Kanevsky was. Perhaps as a petty soldier he was only too aware of the fact that few people would know his name. Mitkov narrowed his eyes. "Only essential personnel of the Russian Navy may pass. Do you have an appointment?"

"This is my advisor from England," Ito began. "I am—"

Sherlock raised a hand to stop him. "I wish to speak with your superiors."

Mitkov was unmoved. "Do you know the names of any of the ships other than the *Kondrat*?"

"The *Kesar*."

"And the others?"

"The others…?"

"You tell me you have business here when you do not even know what ships have been anchored? Move along."

Ito's face twisted in outrage. "The insolence! Do you know who…"

Sherlock grabbed his arm. Ito trailed off mid-sentence. Mitkov continued to stubbornly block their way. Sherlock left, ushering Ito away with him.

Once they distanced themselves from the gate, Ito spoke in a dissatisfied tone. "If I had identified myself we could have gone inside."

"No. We would not have been shown inside, as the commander would have come out to greet you. As Chairman Ito, your position is *too* elevated. We can't allow for any preferential dispensation. If we are to discover any information of a private nature we must infiltrate the area by less exceptional means."

"The Russians have brought these ships to intimidate us. What do you hope to accomplish by visiting the fleet? Have you discerned something of why the ships are here? They still have not given us a clear answer."

Sherlock ignored his questions. "That sailor sounded as if he is accustomed to asking those questions. Most likely he is in a regular habit of having visitors tell him the names of the ships and deciding based on their answers whether to allow them to pass."

He stared out toward sea. He could not see any of the names of the ships on the hulls.

"Russian warships don't display their names in very large letters," Ito said, following Sherlock's gaze. "In accordance with international treaties, however, they do list the names on both port and starboard, albeit in very small English lettering. The names can be found engraved at both the bow and the stern, but you would likely have to approach quite close before you saw them."

"With a strong telescope I might be able to see the names of the ships in front, but the subsequent rows are shadowed. And the three ships in the middle row would be difficult to make out even from the offing—oh, but what do we have here?"

He thought no one was allowed to approach the waters where the Russian warships were anchored. But now he saw a small fishing boat in between the ships, heading to shore.

"Fishermen are allowed to pass through," said Ito. "It is their livelihood, after all. There are, however, restrictions in place. They must approach from the southeast, and then pass either to the north or the west. If they attempt to turn back they will be apprehended. Nor are they permitted to stop or slow down."

Sherlock pointed toward the horizon. "The sea is to the east?"

"It is. The fishermen do not put out to sea from here, they only pass through on their way home. Even if we posed as fishermen, it would be impossible to get a full circuit view."

Several fishing boats had been pulled aground on the dunes to Sherlock's left, facing the ocean. The bare-chested fishermen had finished their work and were now busy unloading their hauls, just as he had seen docking in Yokohama.

It was worth a try. Sherlock began walking in their direction. "We will ask the fishermen."

Ito matched his stride. "You mean whether they were able to read the names of the ships?"

"Fishermen have good eyes. And in Japan, I believe even the common classes receive education in English. I experienced this myself, yesterday. They may have only had glimpses, but a glimpse may be enough."

Sherlock came up to the fishermen who were still on their feet, busy at work. "Good morning. I have some questions. Did you see the names of those ships when you passed by them?"

As he'd expected, the fishermen only furrowed their eyebrows and stared. Sherlock glanced at Ito expectantly. Ito began translating, his expression reluctant.

One of the fishermen began speaking. He did not seem to realize that this white-bearded man was none other than Hirobumi Ito.

"He passed through in a zigzag," Ito explained to Sherlock, "so he does not remember which ship was which. He is unsure if he read the names correctly, but he believes he read *Kesar*, the Kondo-something-or-other, the Lasu-something-or-other, and the Kuri-something-or-other. It is unclear in what order he saw them."

"Hurm." Sherlock glanced over the fishermen. "Did anyone else see anything?"

A second man spoke. Sherlock cocked his ear towards the

chairman, and Ito interpreted: "I saw *Kesar* and the Kuri-some-thing-or-other, too. But I don't remember what route I took. And there was something like *Timur*, and another starting with a W, I think. I only passed four ships."

The third man said, "I can't remember my route either. I only saw seven ships. The *Kondrat*, something starting with 'Ya' I think, one that looked like...zori. The *Kesar*, *Arsen*, and the one starting with a W."

"That is only six ships," Sherlock said.

The fisherman looked sheepish. "I don't remember any more. I saw them all out of order, too."

The other fisherman shook their heads, helplessly. In the end, the majority had paid no attention to the names of the ships. Ito was even more perplexed than before.

But Sherlock bowed his head in thanks. "Thank you. It has been extremely enlightening."

He turned on his heel and returned in the direction they had come. Ito trotted after him. "I told you. That is the most we can expect from the fishermen."

"And yet it was enough. Do you not agree?"

"We can list the names we know, but that sailor is certain to follow with more difficult questions. Last time he chased us from the gates. This time he may attempt to apprehend us."

"Chairman, you ought endeavor to take a more positive view." Sherlock pointed to a signboard erected on one of the dunes. "I have noticed something about the kanji letters in this area since we arrived. Many of them include three dots along the left side."

"Ah, that is called the *sanzui*. It represents a spray of water. This one here, with the *sanzui*, is the character for 'sea,' and this one is the character for 'wave.'" Ito pointed to another kanji character with the same three dots. "This one means swimming. As I'm sure you've guessed, these characters all have something to do with water."

"Very edifying." Sherlock continued walking. "I learned some of the rudiments of kanji from Asako. She explains things very well, much like you. I suspect she would make an excellent teacher."

"Asako, a teacher?" Ito grimaced. "That would be fine, but I'm afraid she is only playing the cat for you."

"Playing the cat…?"

"Excuse me, it is a Japanese expression. It is like the English phrase… butter wouldn't melt in her mouth?"

"If she is difficult at home you have only yourself to blame."

"I told you, I am already well aware of that fact."

They arrived at the gate once more and saw First-Class Seaman Mitkov had just allowed an ornately dressed woman to pass through. His easy-going expression quickly disappeared when he caught sight again of Sherlock and Ito.

"What do you want now?" he asked.

"My apologies for earlier," Sherlock called, his tone suddenly booming and pompous. "I'd forgotten to ask my friend in the Russian legation for the names of the ships."

"Your friend?" Mitkov smirked condescendingly. "Fine. Then what is the name of the ship behind the flagship, to the side?"

Ito winced. There was no way he would pass the man's questioning.

But Sherlock remained calm. "I believe you are referring to the *Laskar*. Construction began at the Baltic Shipyard on February 10, 1887. The ship was launched on October 10 of the following year, and was commissioned on July 1, the year after that."

Mitkov's eyes widened. "And the ship behind the *Kesar*?" he added, his tone less certain. "The one anchored to the northeast."

"The *Timur*. It is an improved model of the *Laskar* and was commissioned on May 11, 1890. All nine ships are Vladimir Monomakh-class, but the *Timur* is the fastest. It is positioned in the northeast to lead the fleet, as one would expect."

"Ah…and the ship to the southeast…"

"Seaman Mitkov, how long do you mean to prolong this tedious game? Do tell me…that is, if you wish to make petty officer someday. The *Yakov* is anchored directly behind the *Kondrat*, but I would see to maintenance of the two ships in attendance behind the *Timur* first, those closest to the offing, the *Kliment* and the *Walery*. After all, there is not much use in having the latest ships if they are not kept in working order. Placing the *Zaur* and *Arsen* in the rear was the obvious choice.

"Seaman Mitkov, I am an Englishman, true, but in recognition of my particular advantages Ambassador Shevich and Lt. Colonel Kanevsky have requested my advice in strengthening the fleet. I would not be above recommending changes in personnel as well if there need be."

Mitkov jumped aside in a panic. "My apologies, sir! Please forgive me."

"Much better." Sherlock passed through.

Natural politician that he was, Ito betrayed no sign of surprise as he followed. Through the gates there were rows of Western buildings. Russians in uniform as well as woman and children milled about. There were very few non-Russian foreigners visible. It seemed the port was under partial Russian occupation. It was no wonder, Sherlock thought, that Ito feared war.

So far Ito had remained nonchalant. As soon as they turned the corner, however, he could no longer conceal his curiosity. "How did you know the names and positions of the ships? And the dates of construction and commission, as well?"

Sherlock placed a finger to his lips, urging quiet. "It was elementary, Chairman. I thought I would give our seaman friend a showing, considering how impertinent he had been. I was already somewhat familiar with the Vladimir Monomakh-class ships from what I have read in the papers. The 'kuri-something-or-other' was obviously the *Kliment*. The ship beginning with 'ya' must have been the *Yakov*. Lasu would be *Laskar*, and the ship starting with W was obviously the *Walery*. Naturally 'zori' could only be *Zaur*. I had seen no diagrams or photographs, however, and could not be sure which ship was which."

"But surely you could not have worked out their positions only from what the fishermen said?"

"Chairman, surely I could. The fishermen were headed toward the northern tip of the beach, meaning they would approach from the southeast and pass through to the northwest. They would not have passed the three westernmost ships on the berth side. The first fisherman stated that he had gone in a zigzag. If he had passed between two ships in the rear that would have been impossible. First he travelled along the southeastern ship's starboard and then turned west at its bow. Next he travelled north, and then west, and then finally exited travelling north."

"But he only remembered the ships' names. He had forgotten in which order he had seen them. And the other two couldn't remember how they had passed through at all."

"Chairman Ito, having taken such pains to acquire this information it might behoove you to apply your mind to its judicious application. The second fisherman stated that he saw four ships. The only plausible route by which that would be possible would be if he had travelled starboard along the three ships furthest toward the offing and then turned west."

"Of course!"

"Furthermore, we know that the three ships toward the offing, in no clear order, are the *Kliment*, the *Timur*, and the *Walery*. But as the first fisherman witnessed the *Kliment*, we know it cannot be the northeastern ship."

"This is becoming difficult…"

"The third fisherman saw seven ship names. That means he either travelled starboard along the southeast ship, turned west at the bow, travelled straight, and then turned north after the second ship, or he began by travelling west behind two ships, and then turned north and travelled straight. No other routes are possible."

"I will take your word for it."

"He also saw the *Walery*, meaning that the northeastern ship is not the *Walery*, either. A process of elimination therefore tells us that it is the *Timur*. Then, either the *Kliment* and *Walery* must be the ship in the southeast corner, and the one before it, the *Laskar*—which the first fisherman saw—must be the middle ship. That leaves the second berthed ship, the ship behind that one, and the ship east-adjacent to that. But two rear ships face each other across the channel, and these two must be the *Zaur* and *Arsen*. So this means the third fisherman chose the latter of the two possible routes I mentioned earlier. Therefore, the second berthed ship is the *Yakov*."

"Wait… Are you saying you were not sure where all the ships are positioned? As you explain it, you still don't know which ship is the *Kliment* and which is the *Walery*. Nor the *Zaur* and *Arsen*."

Sherlock grinned. "Precisely. I predicted, however, that Seaman Metkov would first inquire as to the name of the middle ship. It is the most difficult ship to observe from all angles. Had he asked for a ship I did not know, I intended rather to see us through by using the trivia I had at my disposal to overwhelm him."

Ito's eyes twinkled in appreciation. "Mr. Holmes, you show remarkable intelligence and fortitude."

Sherlock accepted the compliment. "Thank you. Now come, let us discover what it is the Russians are up to."

As they walked, he felt lighter in step. He observed the other passersby closely.

"What do you expect to find?" asked Ito, dubiously.

"From what you told me earlier, Russia displayed aggression once before in July. Ambassador Shevich's agitation this morning seems strange, considering two months have passed since. He seemed quite intent. This leads me to believe that a person of some stature has arrived in Japan, someone important enough to intimidate even the ambassador."

"We have received no such reports. The ships in the harbor are only medium class."

"Likely the person has come in secret. He chose not to travel by imperial flagship so as to conceal his presence."

Ito looked shocked. "You believe that Tsarevich Nicholas has returned to Japan?"

"I am not certain yet, but in light of Ambassador Shevich's

behavior the possibility is significant. For obvious reasons, I highly doubt the Emperor would be in Japan. The Crown Prince, however, might…"

Suddenly Sherlock stopped short. He raised a hand to restrain Ito.

There was a brick building in front of him, by which several men dressed in both frock coats and uniforms stood conversing. He recognized two of their faces.

Lt. Colonel Kanevsky was first to notice them. His face immediately froze. He leaned over and whispered to Shevich, who was next to Kanevsky in conversation with another person. Shevich immediately turned his eyes in their direction. His expression grew stony.

Sherlock heard him speaking in Russian to the other persons present. It seemed he had directed them to leave. The group dispersed until only Shevich and Kanevsky remained.

Ito walked toward the two men, bowing his head deeply. "Ambassador, thank you for your visit this morning."

"What is this?" Shevich looked furious. "What would possess you to show your face here? I request that you leave immediately."

"Strange," Sherlock mused. "We are in Shinagawa Daiba, a section of Tokyo. Why should Chairman Ito be barred entry? Even considering that Russia has used its military force to illegitimately occupy the area."

Shevich wheeled on the detective. "No one has given you permission to enter, Sherlock Holmes. It is just like one of the Queen's rats, to slip in through a crack in the wall."

"After learning of the Tsarevich's presence, Chairman Ito and I thought to offer our greetings directly."

Kanevsky spoke through gritted teeth. "Who told you that…"

Shevich checked him quickly. The lieutenant colonel clenched his jaw in mid-sentence.

Shevich glanced back and forth between the other two. "There must have been some sort of mistake. As you see, no imperial flagship is present in the harbor."

"It is very suspicious that the *Laskar* has anchored in the center, as if it is being protected. Perhaps you care to explain?"

"Dead men should not ask so many questions. Do you want to be thrown into the brig?"

"Should anything happen to me, the British Empire will be informed of what has occurred."

Shevich's jaw twitched. Kanevsky fell silent as well. He cast a glance at Shevich.

It was a bluff, of course. There were advantages to their believing him to be a British spy, at least for the moment.

"Mr. Holmes," Kanevsky grumbled at last. "The international community does not look kindly on spies who fake their death to travel overseas. As soon as we gather the requisite proof we will report you."

"I wonder how the international community might look upon the illegal occupation of one of Japan's ports."

"We have paid to rent this space," Shevich barked, evidently displeased. "The restrictions we have placed on ships moving through the harbor were also negotiated with Japan. Ask Chairman Ito."

Sherlock glared. "By negotiation, I assume you mean threats of force. Europe and America will find it difficult to notice an invasion if you do it in stages. So long as I am present, however, it will not pass. London will hear of this."

Shevich scratched his head. "Clearly we do not see eye to eye. What can we do at the moment, to end this meeting peacefully and convince you to leave the area?"

"I wish to know what actually occurred when Tsarevich Nicholas was attacked at Otsu."

"Then you should ask Chairman Ito. You are aware, I presume, that the perpetrator was captured and is being held in Japan."

"I don't understand," Ito said. "Russia was originally happy with the way events concluded. Why is the issue being brought back up?"

"Japan is to blame. The Tsarevich is outraged at your country's failure to reach an appropriate judgment in Sanzo Tsuda's case. The

Emperor shares in his displeasure."

"Has the Tsarevich's injury worsened?"

"Nothing of the sort."

"Then allow me to meet with the Tsarevich and receive his concerns in person."

"Impossible. At present he will grant no audiences, not even with your Emperor himself. He is uninterested, as he says, in hearing from 'the monkeys.'"

Sherlock laughed derisively. "Monkeys, you say. Indeed, there is something there. Why might the Tsarevich now detest the Japanese, when previously he searched the country for a wife?"

Ito also stood his ground, unconvinced. "If I cannot meet with His Highness, then I would like to speak with the Russian staff who travelled with him during his visit in May."

"To what end?"

"To learn why the Tsarevich has changed his opinion," Sherlock chimed in. "If we cannot meet with the Tsarevich himself, it is only logical that we should like to hear from those who travelled with and were close to him."

"Perhaps you would like to fly to Greece and meet with Prince George," Shevich said coldly. "As a ghost I am sure you can spirit yourself away at a moment's notice."

"I was hoping rather to impose on your good faith."

Kanevsky pressed his lips together firmly and glanced again at Shevich.

The other man finally looked wry. "Chairman Ito, were I to grant your request and set up a meeting with the Tsarevich's attendants, would you promise to keep this Englishman from sniffing about any further?"

Sherlock and Ito exchanged looks. "So be it," Ito agreed, returning his attention to Shevich.

Shevich's eyes glittered suspiciously in response. "As you know, last year, the Tsarevich began his tour of the Near East and Asia. Japan was his last port of call. His Russian attendants were chosen upon careful screening by the court. Would one of these attendants be acceptable?"

"So long as they actually travelled with the Tsarevich during his trip."

"We will confirm the details in advance in writing. Once I receive your signature and seal, I will send the attendants to wait on you."

"That will be acceptable. How long will you take?"

"We could be ready by this afternoon. You need only wait at the palace. One of my counsel will bring you the documents, and if all passes muster I will send the attendants forthwith."

"So the attendants are in Japan now," Sherlock mused, as though to himself.

Shevich turned on his heel, purposefully ignoring him. "Now. I would appreciate it if you leave this area immediately."

Kanevsky cast Sherlock a bitter look as he took after Shevich. The two didn't look back.

Ito sighed. "Let's not provoke them any further. We should leave for now."

"Yes, I suppose." Sherlock stared at the nine ships, floating upon the water. "We have made progress, however. We now know that the central figure in this drama himself, Tsarevich Nicholas, is out there, waiting."

15

Sherlock and Ito arrived at the Privy Council Chairman's office at a little past one in the afternoon. The first person to meet them was the Russian legation's legal counsel, who presented a document outlining Shevich's previous stipulations and requested Ito's signature and seal.

The counsel also brought photographs and dossiers for the two attendants they were to meet. The first was Soslan Chekhov, a collegiate assessor of the 8th rank, aged 46, a plump man with frizzy red hair and round glasses. He worked for the Ministry of State Property. Chekhov's portly stature clearly indicated that he was a civil worker, rather than in the military. Though he had served as a staff officer for some time, he had apparently been chosen as one of Nicholas' attendants primarily for his extensive ability in English, having studied overseas in England.

The second attendant was Anna Luzhkova, aged 37. She was of noble birth, proficient in both English and French, and had previously worked as a university instructor before becoming employed, like Chekhov, in the Ministry of State Property. In the photo, her face was thin and unusually severe in appearance.

Attached to the dossiers were credentials attesting that the two had been selected as attendants by the court.

Ito signed the papers, and the counsel left by carriage. Half an hour passed. A new carriage arrived, and Collegiate Assessor Chekhov and Anna Luzhkova entered Ito's office. They matched their photographs in every detail. Both were unassuming, but of the two Chekhov seemed the least reliable—at a glance, Sherlock could tell he was retiring and timid by nature.

He was gripped by a sinking feeling. He guessed that though Chekhov was surely diligent in his work, he was in all likelihood less than capable of acquitting himself deftly in the Tsarevich's presence. His role as an attendant had, therefore, probably only been secondary.

Minutes into their interview, his fears were confirmed. The two had not even accompanied Nicholas to Japan!

Chekhov and Anna were not attendants to *Nicholas* so much as they were to his younger brother *Grand Duke George*. And it was this Grand Duke George who had contracted a cold and returned to Russia early in the trip. Apparently Chekhov and Anna had left with him, and accompanied the Grand Duke on his official duties inside Russia. They knew almost nothing of the Otsu incident in Japan.

Ito leaned against the back of his chair and stared up at the ceiling. "We have been fooled. These are indeed two of the attendants chosen by the court. They satisfy all of the stipulations that I signed earlier."

Sherlock forced himself to hide his disappointment with a smile. "Shevich is very clever in his leveraging of documents, just as with his previous agreement with Foreign Minister Aoki. Of all people, I should have known better. I played right into his hands. We should have been more thorough and clearly stipulated for attendants who had followed Nicholas in Japan."

Ito leaned forward to address the two attendants. It was a slim hope but still worth a try. "I suppose you two are our only option. Have either of you met with Tsarevich Nicholas since his return from Japan?"

Chekhov and Anna glanced at each other tentatively. They turned their eyes back toward Ito, and then shook their heads in tandem.

"Humph," Sherlock snorted. He was appalled at his own foolishness. By the terms of their formal agreement, he was now forbidden from openly approaching Shevich.

"To tell the truth," Chekhov interjected, shyly—he strongly resembled a previous client from the case of The Red-Headed League—

140

"Miss Luzhkova and I were ordered to Japan only quite suddenly, last week. We were told to be off as soon as we boarded the cruiser. His Royal Highness, Grand Duke George, is vacationing in Paris, which left us both free. We were told that English speakers were required."

Ito looked at Sherlock inquiringly. "For what reason, I wonder."

"Whether there is war or a demand for land, there will be a prodigious amount of paperwork," Sherlock said frankly. "International standards demand concurrent English and French translations. Every sentence, every word must be translated without fault, necessitating as many people familiar with all the languages as possible."

Anna nodded. "We were told something similar before we came. The legal counsel at the legation would be doing a translation, and we were only to check whether or not it was correct."

Shevich had given these two only as sacrificial pawns. "The younger brother, Grand Duke George?" Sherlock asked, discouraged. "Was he concerned over his brother's injury?"

"Naturally," Anna replied. "His Royal Highness Grand Duke George recovered from his cold shortly after returning home and resumed his duties directly. When news of the incident arrived he was extremely shocked and went to speak with the Emperor and Empress on the matter."

"He was relieved to learn that Tsarevich Nicholas' injury was not severe," Chekhov tacked on. "And he was glad it had not ruined our relations with Japan."

Sherlock looked at the civil servants. "But of late, tensions seem to have increased once more."

Chekhov's and Anna's faces both grew clouded.

"To be frank, I do not know what to make of it," Chekhov confessed, eyes wide. "Tsarevich Nicholas had been so fond of the Japanese, yet now…"

"He refers to them as monkeys?"

"Yes," he whispered. "What could have caused such a change?"

Ito furrowed his brow and pounced. "I thought you hadn't met with Tsarevich Nicholas since the incident?"

Chekhov blanched. He'd clearly fumbled. He looked to Anna for help. She let her head fall forlornly.

Sherlock leaned forward with a hint of hope in his chest. "Please, the truth. You have met with His Highness, haven't you?"

"We were given strict warnings to speak of nothing outside the tour..." Anna began.

"Miss Luzhkova, you evidently wish to tell us the truth. I will ask more directly. Tsarevich Nicholas was on the ship during your recent passage, was he not? On the *Laskar*?"

Chekhov and Anna looked shocked. Chekhov withdrew a handkerchief and began dabbing the sweat from his brow. "You know so much... Chairman Ito, Mr. Holmes, will you promise to keep this between us?"

"Most certainly."

He lowered his voice. "It's true, His Imperial Highness the Tsarevich is aboard the *Laskar*. The two of us...Miss Luzhkova and I...we were told nothing of the matter. We were most astonished when we saw His Highness."

"And did you speak with Tsarevich Nicholas?"

"No. You see, we are not particularly in His Highness' favor. He is usually surrounded by his own followers, and especially during this trip he was in constant conversation with several military officers."

"Did you overhear any of what they said?"

"I did. I passed the room they were in several times. Only..." Chekhov broke off mid-sentence, and it was clear, with his apologetic side-glance at Ito, why he hesitated.

Ito was unfazed. "Do not hesitate on my account. Whatever you heard, please feel at liberty to repeat it."

"As you wish." The man sounded dubious. "Well, on the day we left Vladivostok, I was headed to the materials compartment to return a book. The door had been left ajar and I saw His Highness Tsarevich Nicholas inside. He was with the *Laskar*'s captain, Matinsky, as well as Commander Narozhilenko. The Tsarevich was shouting. He said that the 'yellow monkeys are dangerous,' and if we do not deal with them now it will soon be too late."

"I overheard His Highness as well, while in my bed in my sleeping quarters," Anna added fearfully. "He used the word 'monkeys' several times, and spoke of Japan's people as barbaric and deceitful."

Chekhov sighed. "I hardly believed it. The last time I had met the Tsarevich was during the tour, before His Highness Grand Duke George fell ill. His Highness had been most courteous and kind. While we were in Egypt and India, he even mentioned several times how much he was looking forward to visiting Japan and his hope we would leave for there soon. Then there were the letters from his trip, with the photographs he had taken with the geisha. According to his writing, he found no country as enchanting as he did Japan."

Ito groaned. "After the Otsu incident, an outpouring of concern and contrition came from our country's citizens. We heard that His Highness was grateful for the messages. Was that a lie?"

Anna shook her head. "We were not with His Highness during his trip to Japan so it is hard to say for sure, but I heard from those close to him that he greatly regretted being unable to visit Tokyo. I believe the Tsarevich's message of thanks, printed in Japan's newspapers, was genuine."

"The officers who were aboard the imperial flagship with His Highness at the time of the incident are baffled by his abrupt change, as well," Chekhov mused. He looked fearful. "I can't understand it. Why would His Highness return to Japan in secret, and why is he now waiting, hidden, at sea? It is puzzling."

Ito turned towards Sherlock. But Sherlock only looked back in silence.

Despite the two civil servants' confusion, the purpose of Tsarevich Nicholas' visit was quite clear. Shevich had already told them—he had come to demand the death penalty for Sanzo Tsuda. Why, however, did he desire revenge now, after all this time? Why draw a sword that had already been sheathed?

16

After the interview, Ito was required at an emergency meeting of the Privy Council. It was not a meeting to deliberate over the details of Japan's constitution—but now that they knew Nicholas was nearby, the council had their work more than cut out for them.

By now it was past 4:00 P.M. By Ito's request, an English translation of the Sanzo Tsuda investigation records arrived for Sherlock. Sherlock thanked the chairman and headed out alone, by carriage. He could read the report while he travelled.

The Russian attendants were not the only people to have travelled with the crown prince during his tour of Asia. Reporters sent from various newspaper offices had also followed the trip. Ito had earlier telegraphed the Japanese branch office of the French paper *Le Figaro* on Sherlock's behalf. Luckily they had reporters who spoke English, and Sherlock made his way there now.

In the carriage, Sherlock spotted a brand-new factory through the window. He recalled having seen facilities of similar construction in London.

As luck would have it, the coachman was Australian. They had no difficulty communicating in English. "An ice-making plant, I believe?" Sherlock shouted over the wheels.

"That's right," the coachman shouted back, without turning around. "The Aoyama Ice Plant, built just last year. Japan is having its own industrial revolution."

"They use highly condensed ammonia gas to create the ice."

"Yes indeed. The technology's been here since around when they ousted the Bakufu. Before that they used to have to cut ice from Mount Fuji and transport it to Tokyo."

Sherlock had mistakenly assumed that was still their method. Japan's industries were developing at a much faster pace than he had imagined. What had taken 100 years of development or more in England was being accomplished in Japan in but 20 or so years.

Everywhere he looked the people seemed productive and hard-working. He stared out the carriage window at the crude row houses that lined the street. The laborers seemed diligent despite their apparently low quality of life. They didn't loiter or cause public disturbances.

In Russia, he mused, two percent of the population were aristocracy and all of the remainder were serfs. But though Japan's total population was far less than that of Russia's, the Japanese citizenry were not to be underestimated. The Russian people worked only because they had to for tomorrow's bread. The Japanese, meanwhile, seemed to labor constantly at full potential, with nothing but a few rice balls as reward. Unlikely as it might seem, in the near future the power difference between the two countries might not be as great as the difference in their nations' land mass. Even the great British Empire, peerless the world over, was but an island nation at heart.

Sherlock shook these abstractions from his mind. He needed to skim through the Sanzo Tsuda report before his carriage arrived at the *Le Figaro* offices. He removed a packet of documents from the large envelope and began.

Sanzo Tsuda was born February 15, 1855, and was now 36 years of age. The photo included in the packet was blurry and difficult to make out; it had been poorly printed. Nevertheless, he was able to discern a young man with a Western-style haircut, standing with his arms crossed, dressed in an outfit with a stiff collar that resembled a military uniform. According to the inscription the photo had been taken 14 years earlier, during the Satsuma Rebellion. Tsuda's expression seemed stubborn.

He was the second son of a doctor in the Musashi Province.

Shortly after his brith, his family moved to Ueno in the Iga Province of Mie Prefecture. At age 15, he moved to Tokyo and joined the garrison, launching his career as a soldier in the government forces. At 17 he was transferred to the regular Nagoya garrison. At 18 he was dispatched to suppress the Echizen Buddhist riots. In July of that year he was transferred to the Kanazawa outpost.

1877, the 10th year of the Meiji Era, marked the beginning of the Satsuma Rebellion. Sherlock read that when Tsuda turned 22, he made the rank of corporal for the first battalion of the seventh infantry regiment. A month later the seventh regiment was incorporated into the detached first brigade, and they were swiftly dispatched to Hinagu to strike Saigo's[4] army from the rear. It was there that Tsuda was shot in the left hand. He was taken to the Yatsushiro dressing station in Kumamoto for treatment. He was later moved to a hospital in Nagasaki and discharged at the end of May. He returned to the main Kagoshima forces and fought numerous battles in Kagoshima and Miyazaki, before eventually being promoted to sergeant. On October 22 he returned to Kanazawa.

After the Satsuma Rebellion came to an end Tsuda fell ill several times—Sherlock deduced exhaustion had perhaps taken its toll. He was frequently in and out of hospitals. On October 9 he was awarded the 7th Order of Merit in recognition of his past deeds.

According to the investigators, Tsuda remained exceedingly proud of his Order of Merit. For someone from dissolute samurai stock, such as Tsuda, that award was likely one of his most sustaining possessions.

He left the army before turning 27, and became a policeman. He was assigned to be a patrolman at Owase Police Station in Mie Prefecture. Three years later, however, he attacked a fellow officer during a social gathering and was dismissed from his post. Perhaps owing to the Order of Merit, however, he was re-employed as a policeman before the year was out, this time hired by the Shiga Prefecture force.

---

4 Takamori Saigo was an influential samurai and one of the Three Great Nobles of the Meiji Restoration.

All that was nearly ten years ago. During investigative questioning, Tsuda had repeatedly insisted that Takamori Saigo was alive and resided in Russia.

Popular knowledge had it that Takamori Saigo had died during the Satsuma Rebellion. There were rumors, however, that he had in fact survived and had secretly travelled to Russia. To Sherlock—who was in Japan under similar circumstances, having faked his death in England—the rumors did not seem quite so fanciful as they might otherwise have appeared.

But for the most part, Saigo's so-called escape to Russia was regarded as mere fantasy. Yet Tsuda persisted in his belief. And at the time there had been another rumor—the one that Tsarevich Nicholas was visiting Japan in preparation for Russia's declaration of war. Possibly this had stoked Tsuda's worries that Takamori Saigo would reappear.

If the rebel Takamori Saigo were to suddenly return to Japan, the end of the Satsuma Rebellion might no longer seem so decisive. Investigators wrote that Tsuda seemed to be paranoid that his Order of Merit would be revoked.

So these were the morbid delusions of a man whose only point of pride in his life was a single military award. To Sherlock reading the report, it was evident that Tsuda was suffering from mental illness.

Many of those who had followed the samurai path were left adrift after giving up their swords following the Meiji Restoration. Many were forced to either dedicate themselves to the government army as soldiers, or to set out on unfamiliar lives as laborers. Tsuda believed that by becoming a policeman he had managed to preserve his dignity as a warrior. He took pride in that fact, and supported his spirits with the memory of his military honor.

Several witnesses attested that Tsuda had shouted *joui* when he attacked Nicholas. Tsuda claimed he did not remember the events of the day all that clearly. His testimony was vague, and his motives were unclear. Indeed, investigators had only conjectured that Tsuda feared Takamori Saigo was still alive. The man himself had never stated this outright.

According to the report, Tsuda had told the investigators that he "had to get one in." *One* referred to at least one strike of his sword; Tsuda's statement could therefore be interpreted as, while he had intended to injure Nicholas, he did not mean to kill him.

But then again, Tsuda's attack had been brutal, aimed at Nicholas' head. It was unlikely he had only meant to injure the crown prince.

Sherlock sighed and returned the documents to the envelope.

He had received no new answers from the information. Whatever had driven Tsuda to violence was not to be found in the report he had just read. He knew of several incidents in England of officers who had fallen into despair after leaving the army, and who had committed crimes of one sort or another. Perhaps this case was similar to those?

Still, something nagged at Sherlock.

After the incident, Tsuda's Order of Merit—the award that had brought him such comfort and solace in his otherwise empty life— was rescinded. Which was only natural. Had Tsuda truly failed to foresee that this would be the most basic repercussion of his actions?

The Japanese *Le Figaro* offices were not much different in appearance from those of a newspaper in any other country. The room was crammed with desks, and employees jostled against each other elbow-to-elbow. A curtain of tobacco smoke hung over the news floor, and the offices appeared as though they were in a hazy fog.

A challenging environment, Sherlock thought. He was sitting on a sofa for guests in the corner of the room. He began smoking the pipe he had brought with him, seeing no need to hold back here.

A man in his thirties approached, carrying an envelope, and sat across from Sherlock. This was the correspondent Loic Borloo. "The Privy Council informed me you would be coming. I was surprised to hear they plan to rebuild Meiji Palace. You are an architect, that is correct? Mr....?"

"Lionel Harding," Sherlock said smoothly. "One of the *oyatoi gaijin*, the foreign engineers. The palace was originally meant to be a stone building, designed by Josiah Conder. But due to budgetary concerns, we ended up going with a wooden building instead."

"I had heard that the Imperial Household's Bureau of Construction was opposed to this plan, at first."

"They were, but Chairman Ito was able to persuade them."

"So this is why they have decided to rebuild the palace? But tell me, why are you interested in Tsarevich Nicholas?"

"I thought we should consider the possibility that foreign leaders might take up residence in the palace…"

"*In the palace?*"

"If Russia occupies Japan," Sherlock said, briefly. "As a reporter, I'm sure you are aware that Europe's castles and palaces have tended to change hands after war. It is the way history tends to go."

Borloo looked around them and spoke again in a lowered voice. "So, you think there will be war?"

"It seems possible, certainly. Russia is occupying the harbor. There are nine Russian ships in port."

"We have been wondering about the ships, as well," Borloo said excitedly. "We've asked for interviews several times but are continually rebuffed. I even tried sneaking into the occupied Daiba district, too, but the sailors at the entrance had none of it. They wouldn't let me pass unless I gave them the names and positions of their ships. They sent me on my way quite brusquely."

"My sympathies."

Borloo grimaced. "To be honest, I cannot fathom what the Russians are up to. They seem to be all over the place. You know when Tsarevich Nicholas was travelling through the East? Well, when his brother, the Duke George, fell sick and had to go back to Russia early, they sent all the most capable attendants back with him."

This meant that Chekhov and Anna were, despite Sherlock's impression, two of the most competent retainers of the retinue. "Is it possible that this may be why the Otsu attack was later forgiven?" Sherlock asked.

"Indirectly, maybe. Essentially, the Russians mismanaged the

Tsarevich's itinerary. For instance, while in Siam, the military photographer was left aboard one of the ships, ignorant of the schedule. They failed to take even a single photograph."

"Are you saying the Russians have no documentation of their time in Siam?"

"None! At the time, we almost didn't notice, because all the international newspapers were relying on Siam's local reporters, and no one disembarked."

"So the press never entered Siam?"

"Siam is a unique situation. It is an independent country, not a European colony. We couldn't get permission for the press in time to catch up with the Tsarevich. But the local reporters agreed to take photographs and notes for us. The rest of us loafed around the waters near the coast. When the Russian military photographer saw us all aboard, he must have assumed he didn't need to disembark either."

"It sounds as if it was you and the other reporters, then, who were responsible for this lack of official documentation."

Borloo frowned. "No, it was the photographer's fault. I remember specifically, he did everything correctly in Egypt, India, and Ceylon. When they later found they had no official documentation of the Siam trip, the Russian court approached all the international newspapers, including ours, to ask for our notes and photographs."

"So they purchased newspaper records about Siam to cover for those the military had forgotten to take?"

"Yes. Both written and photographic. They only wanted a copy of the written notes, but as the photographs were to be used for imperial purposes, they asked us for the rights and film negatives. Our main office accepted. They offered us quite a sum of money."

"And what of your own firm? You didn't mind giving up your photographs?"

"At some point in the future I'm sure we'll be able to run photographs in our papers, but not with our current printing technology. The best we can do now is run tracings. So generally, the photographs are of no particular use in writing our articles either."

"Did *Le Figaro* take a great many photographs?"

Borloo nodded. "The times have changed. Photographers no longer need to carry around dry plates and toxic chemicals everywhere they go. Since three years ago, with Eastman's Kodak camera, we can take photographs wherever we please."

"Was the Russian court only interested in buying the notes and photographs from Siam? No other countries?"

Borloo shook his head. "No. After all, in Egypt, India, Ceylon, Singapore, Indonesia, Hong Kong, and Shanghai, the military photographer managed admirably enough on his own."

"And what about in Japan?"

"The exact opposite than what happened in Siam. The Tsarevich brought only the Russian military photographer with them, and all the newspapers, including ours, were left in the cold."

This struck Holmes as odd. "Why were you left behind?"

"It was almost Easter, and almost Tsarevich Nicholas' birthday. We were told his itinerary was unclear. The Tsarevich was sneaking out on his own, of course, but we didn't realize that until after the incident at Otsu."

"So the press never accompanied Tsarevich Nicholas while he was in Japan?"

"Precisely. Including the day of attack. Our newspapers, that time, had to rely on Russian records."

"Were there any photographs from the day of the incident?"

Borloo smiled wryly and withdrew two photographs from the envelope he had placed on the table. "This is all I have. I don't believe these are from the day of the incident. They were probably taken around Nagasaki or Kyoto."

One of the photographs featured a rickshaw, with Tsarevich Nicholas inside, dressed in a boiler hat, necktie and blazer. He stared at the camera with a solemn expression. His face was thin and mustached; he might almost have been a young international student. Sherlock studied the background. It looked as if they were near a temple or shrine of some sort.

The second photograph was also of a rickshaw, but from a different angle. Here, Nicholas was dressed in the same clothing as in the previous image, minus the hat, and was staring up at the sky leisurely. There was no cut on his head. Most likely the photograph had been taken before the attack.

Sherlock looked at Borloo. "There were no other photographs?"

"None. After the incident we had to hassle the Russians relentlessly before even acquiring just these. It took nearly a week for them to arrive."

"And the notes?"

"Sparse as well. They contained very few details. There was no mention of the tattoo Nicholas had received on his arm, or of the several days he had spent in the company of geisha—those were all details that we uncovered later through our own reporting. All the Russians gave us was a brief listing of the official receptions that Japan had arranged."

"And what is your impression, seeing these photographs?" Sherlock's voice took on a clinical tone.

"My impression…?" Borloo considered. "Well, he seems to be in a much better mood than he was while in Egypt and India."

"He appears to be in good spirits to you?"

"Yes. At the Nile River, for example, he scowled constantly. And in Hong Kong and Shanghai he did not like the Chinese. I suppose in Japan he was finally able to relax. Considering what happened, I can't help but feel sorry for him."

"And you were given no photographs after the Otsu incident, I presume?"

"No photographs, not even a few notes. We had to interview the Japanese government to get any details at all. Like how the Emperor visited the hotel to check on the Tsarevich, or the dispute over whether Sanzo Tsuda would be given the death penalty."

"I see." Sherlock placed the photographs on the table. "The Russians seemed set on stoking anti-Japanese sentiment. They reported that Prince George of Greece confronted Tsuda alone…"

"I don't think that that was their intention," Barloo countered earnestly. "Our first reports had it the same."

"What's that now?"

"Even though we never got any memo from the Russians, immediately after the Otsu attack we were able to speak with someone from the legation. *They* claimed that the Japanese entourage stood around doing nothing while Prince George saved Nicholas. Later the Russian court released Nicholas' diary and it, too, said the same. He wrote his entry the same night of the attack."

"Are you sure that it was Nicholas himself who wrote that?"

"Our correspondents in Russia saw the actual document. It was posted during a court press briefing. All the world's press was present, all familiar with official documents signed by the Tsarevich. It was his own handwriting, without a doubt."

Sherlock leaned forward. "Do you know what else was written in that diary entry?"

"Just a moment." Borloo stood and walked to his desk. He deftly removed a packet of papers from within a towering pile of documents. He put the papers in front of Sherlock. "This is the English translation. The original, of course, was in Russian."

He began skimming the first page.

"A great number of commoners crowded the road at the turn ahead. Just as the rickshaw turned the corner, I felt a heavy blow on my right temple. I turned and was affronted by the sight of a patrolman, with a grotesque expression, gripping a saber in both hands, poised to strike at me. 'Are you mad?' I shouted, leaping from the rickshaw. But that detestable face continued to follow me. I was in no position to stop him, and was forced instead to flee. I thought that I might take shelter among the crowd, but the Japanese had begun dashing away in a panic. As I ran, I turned to look over my shoulder, and saw George was close on the patrolman's heels. I ran what must have been another 60 feet before turning to look once more, and saw the danger had passed. George had knocked the savage down with his bamboo cane. By the time I doubled back to the rickshaw, the rickshaw drivers and the other policemen had seized the brute. One had grabbed the man by the lapels and thrust the confiscated saber at his neck. None of the Japanese commoners had come to my aid. Why were George and I left alone with that barbarian on the road? I do not understand."

"Curious," Sherlock mused. "This differs from the description of events Japan provided."

Borloo nodded. "After the Russian court released Nicholas' diary and these details were reported, the Japanese objected. We interviewed several people who were on the road that day. After piecing together several accounts, it seems the true heroes of the day were the two rickshaw drivers, who succeeded in capturing Tsuda. The first blow was from Prince George's bamboo cane, but that seemed to have been ineffective."

"Yes, I had heard as much myself."

"However, this did cause Tsuda to turn around to look at Prince George, which created an opening. That was when the rickshaw drivers entered the fray. One of them picked up the saber Tsuda had dropped and used it to strike him on the neck and back."

Sherlock returned his attention to the papers. "'One had grabbed the man by the lapels and thrust the confiscated saber at his neck.' That is written in the diary. The previous sentence mentions rickshaw drivers and policemen, but it does not state who struck Tsuda with the saber."

"We ran a correction that Prince George had not confronted Tsuda alone. The Russian papers, however, have only avoided the topic afterward. They never admitted a mistake. The truth is probably still not well known among the Russian population."

"Is it possible that Tsarevich Nicholas wished to apotheosize his cousin, Prince George, by writing this?"

Borloo shook his head. "There was no shortage of witnesses along the road. Surely he would have anticipated the lie would out. Either way, after writing his diary entry the Tsarevich himself seemed to realize the truth. On May 18, a week after the incident, he invited the two rickshaw drivers onboard one of the Russian warships. Nicholas awarded them with the Medal of St. Anna and 2,500 yen."

Sherlock quickly calculated the amount in his head. It was astounding, to say the least. "143 pounds? That is nearly three times the yearly salary of a butler in England."

"And they received pensions of 1,000 yen, as well. A tremendous windfall for two rickshaw drivers, I'm sure."

"Did they pledge those pensions on the spot? No consultation with the Japanese government beforehand?"

"I believe so. Aside from the rickshaw drivers there were no other Japanese. Japan only had people observing from the shore. After learning that the medal ceremony was to be held on deck, supposedly they telegraphed the Russians to suggest they move the two ships to the rear for a view of Mt. Fuji. I imagine they were trying to be helpful."

"The 18th. That was two days before the Russian ships left Japan, if I am not mistaken. It was after that, then, that the court released Nicholas' diary?"

"Yes. The Russians paid the rickshaw drivers all that money without ever mentioning a word of it to the newspapers, and all the while they were backing a story in Russia that it was Prince George who saved the Tsarevich. Later, people figured out that the two rickshaw drivers had become wealthy from their extravagant spending habits. After the truth came out, the Japanese government awarded both of them with the 8th Order of Merit White Paulownia Leaves Medal, not to mention pensions of 36 yen."

"Those two must be quite famous now."

"In Japan, at least. For a while people even called them 'the great decorated rickshaw drivers.' Their names are Jizaburo Mukohata and Ichitaro Kitagaichi. But recently…"

"Their reputations have taken a fall?"

"Imagine if two London hansom drivers suddenly came into 200 pounds! The rickshaw drivers have acted as you would expect. Mukohata had a criminal record, and now he spends his days gambling and whoring. I heard he got flimflammed into some strange business venture, and has already used up his money. And Kitagaichi has supposedly purchased a huge plot of land in the town in which he was born."

"Yes, economic prudence can certainly be a challenge." Sherlock stood up. He had gotten all the most important information and there was no point in staying further. "Thank you, this has been most informative."

"Yes. And Mr. Harding," Borloo said, standing as well. "Please contact me as soon as a schedule is set for the palace reconstruction. We would like to be the first to break the story."

"Without question," Sherlock smiled. "Until then, I hope you will see fit to keep my visit private."

17

He walked down an avenue lined with crude street stalls that vaguely reminded him of London's East End. As the sun began to set and evening approached, Sherlock was seized by a melancholy feeling.

He had been gallivanting around all day but with little to show for it. Having fallen for Shevich's amateurish trap, he was now legally proscribed from approaching the man. In London he might be able to determine someone's location by investigating details of the soil, but in Japan, he was at a loss. What good would it do him to uncover a discarded tobacco butt if he was unfamiliar with the domestic brands? Once, Sherlock had written a monograph on the 140 different varieties of ash, from pipe, cigar, and rolling tobacco—but none of those varieties were Japanese. Sherlock was now at a significant disadvantage. He needed to relearn the entire world.

In his dejected state, he passed a stack of familiar-looking small boxes at one of the stalls. They were labeled in English. Fortuitous. This was exactly what he needed, perhaps, to banish this despondency. Sherlock paid the man at the stall and flagged down a carriage, cradling a box in his arm.

There remained only a trace of the pearly grey of twilight in the sky when he finally arrived at Ito's estate. He passed through the dimly lit garden and headed for the main door.

Before he got there, Ito appeared at the entrance. He was even dressed in a yukata. He must have returned much earlier.

"Your business kept you quite late," Ito greeted him inquisitively. "Were you able to meet with the correspondent?"

"I finished at *Le Figaro* some time ago. I was merely taking in the sights."

"I see." Ito glanced down at Sherlock's box. "What is that?"

"It is nothing."

"Show me."

"It is a personal article that I purchased in my own time. There is no reason for you to meddle with it."

"There is if you are bringing it into *my* house." Ito's expression grew severe. "Does that say cocaine?"

"It is only a 7 percent solution, quite mild."

"Give it to me." Ito reached for the box.

Sherlock held it away. "Cocaine is legal even in England, a nation that is developed and civilized. I do not believe it is restricted in Japan."

"But it is a narcotic."

"Nonsense. It merely stimulates activity in the central nervous system."

"It leads to progressive deterioration and morbidity of spirit."

"That's an old wives' tale." Sherlock hid the box behind his back. "It refreshes the mind and clarifies thought. It is as indispensable to me as rice is to the Japanese."

"Cocaine—and rice?!" Ito made a grab for the cocaine, the veins on his face and neck protruding. "Give it! You will not bring that in here! I will see that stuff outlawed soon enough."

"I thought you had no influence over the judiciary?" Sherlock struggled against Ito with all his strength, attempting to knock the other man's hands away. "It is not your concern, leave me be."

"Leave you be? To ruin yourself?"

"I might say the same of you and your geisha habit!"

"I returned home directly today. Your disappointment in me had hit home."

"And if your *forbearance* lasts until tomorrow, I might find it more persuasive." Sherlock's voice dripped with sarcasm. "One day, however, is not much to boast about."

"Give me the box!" Ito shouted. "Give me the box—or you won't be allowed through this door!"

Umeko appeared in the doorway—at a glance, took in the struggle and froze, her hand flying to her mouth.

Sherlock was distracted by Umeko's appearance, and Ito grabbed his chance to jerk the box away.

He immediately dashed it to the ground. The box broke, the glass implements inside shattered, and fragments went flying. Small packets filled with dried leaves were scattered across the dirt. Ito began ferociously grinding the pouches into the ground with his wooden sandals.

"Stop that!" Sherlock leapt forward and grabbed Ito by the collar.

"Let go." Ito grabbed the other man's collar in return.

The jujitsu techniques Sherlock had learned from the London dojo had saved his life at the Reichenbach Falls. But Ito did not so much as budge from Sherlock's attempts to throw off his opponent's center of gravity. Rather, the Japanese man continuously shifted this very center, skillfully redirecting the force of Sherlock's attacks. That Ito's reflexes were still so sharp was surprising for a man of fifty. Their struggle grew even more heated as both desperately competed to prove their superior strength.

A shriek rent the air. Ikuko and Asako had rushed outside to intercede. Both were shouting in Japanese. Clearly, however, they were imploring the men to stop. Asako's face looked wild, ready to break into tears at any moment. Ikuko's expression, too, was beseeching.

Seeing the two girls, the fight in Sherlock instantly withered. He relaxed his arms and Ito fell back, short of breath. Sherlock could only stand, at a loss as to what to do. At some point Ikuko had latched on to him, full-bodied. And Asako was holding back Ito. The girls had thrown themselves into harm's way together to stop the two men's fight.

His anger apparently still unspent, Ito dumped out the remaining contents of the box and tore apart the packets. He ground the leaves beneath his sandals. Only once they had been thoroughly pulverized and contaminated did he stop, straightening himself with a sigh. Sherlock leveled a glare at him. Asako, however, stared at her father imploringly. Ito wheeled about in a rage and began walking back toward the door.

"Umeko," he shouted angrily. "Clean this up. Do not leave even a *speck* of a leaf, do you hear me!"

He disappeared through the door. The garden grew quiet once more.

Ikuko stared up into Sherlock's face, seeming no less troubled than before. But seeing that the detective had already calmed down, she hurriedly released him. "Excuse me," she murmured, flustered.

The silence grew uncomfortable. Asako stared at him with wet eyes. Sherlock realized that it was he who was responsible for this deplorable situation. He had done this.

"Forgive me," he muttered. "My behavior was unacceptable."

"Mr. Holmes," whispered Umeko. "Please, talk to him…"

He nodded. He walked toward the entrance. His pace quickened. Only once he was racing into the house did he realize that he had forgotten to remove his shoes. He plucked them off in a rush before hurrying down the hall.

Sherlock spotted Ito through a half-open door. The other man was in his study, standing in an absent daze. Sherlock stepped inside. "Ito…you were right. This is your home. It is only right that I follow the example set by the master of the house."

Ito slowly turned to face him. His gaze was piercing. "Not just in my house. I want you to refrain from it entirely while you are in Japan. Indeed, I wish you would swear to never take up the habit again."

Sherlock fell silent. Ito possessed a gaze that could unsettle even the most steely of fortitudes. And what could he say in return? After all, Ito was right.

Ito vacillated for a moment, and then spoke once more. He seemed determined. "Until you return to England, I promise to refrain from my gallivanting as well."

Sherlock stared at Ito, openmouthed. Ito returned his gaze.

It seemed incumbent that he say something. "I understand how great a commitment that is from you," he said softly. "I promise, then."

Ito nodded quietly, breaking his stare. He continued to linger, staring down at his desk.

Something else seemed wrong. "Ito, what is it?"

Ito lifted a single sheet of paper and sighed deeply. "This is a section of the unequal treaty we signed with the British. Here, read the column under supplement B."

Sherlock saw it was in English. He read the section out loud. "In the event that Japan offers, surrenders, cedes, loans, leases, or sells any national properties to Russia, Britain shall reserve the right to demand a trade of at least equal value with Japan."

Ito groaned. "This supplement is not commonly known. In short, anything that Japan gives to Russia we must give to Britain as well."

"These are abysmal terms." Sherlock put the paper back on the desk. "I cannot believe it was signed."

"Western countries with constitutions already in place formed a great number of treaties with the *less advanced* countries that were designed to impose rule—designed to force barbaric, closed nations like ours to listen to their more knowledgeable, more powerful betters. Terms included recognizing extraterritorial rights for foreign residents, ceding territory, leasing territory, and so on and so forth. Some countries even lost tariff autonomy. The Treaty of Nanking, which the British imposed on the Qing Dynasty after the Opium War, was the first of these unequal treaties."

Sherlock chose his words delicately. "I imagine you were reluctant to agree to such terms."

"It is true, feudal Japan lacked basic legal principles. Torture and other cruel punishments existed, trade was unregulated, and contracts were unprotected. Perhaps that was why the West believed they needed to resort to controlling Japan through treaties."

"Our perspective was somewhat different. After being closed

off for so long, many believed that Japan would not understand the rules of international society. If a foreigner broke the law in Japan we had no idea by what standards he would be judged. It also seemed possible you might not understand the concept of tariffs. From our perspective, Britain was simply helping Japan manage its affairs in a more modern manner. The same interpretation had been applied to China, earlier."

Ito laughed mirthlessly. "After the attack on Tsarevich Nicholas, Russia is likely as convinced as ever of our barbarism. And yet it is precisely at this juncture that we show our concern for *the rule of law* by choosing to not execute Sanzo Tsuda. It must seem like very impertinent behavior from such an *uncivilized* nation."

"Britain does not see Japan in that way."

"Perhaps *you* do not, but the British Empire might disagree. Five years ago a merchant vessel sank off the coast of Japan. The English captain and the 26 Western crewman used lifeboats to escape. The 25 Japanese passengers, however, were all left onboard. None were saved."

"If you are referring to the sinking of the *Normanton*, I read of it in the papers. It was a tragedy."

"It was clear the Japanese passengers had been abandoned. The captain, however, insisted that they were forced to leave them behind because they did not understand English and had retreated to the hold rather than board the lifeboats. The entire crew was found innocent in the ensuing investigation."

"But the captain was later charged with murder. He was found guilty, I believe."

"Imprisoned for only three months, and that was the end of that." Ito gave Sherlock a morose stare. "Things were easier when I was younger. I thought I could do anything in the name of *joui*. I meted out punishment, cutting down those who angered me where they stood. Law and order is a much more difficult affair. That became painfully clear to me after the *Normanton* incident. The captain and his men ought to have paid with their lives, and yet I was powerless to lift a finger against them."

An image suddenly flashed before Sherlock's eyes. It was of Moriarty, waving his arms frantically and shouting his adversary's name just as he was about to tumble to his death. What had he hoped to communicate in that moment? Did he wish to plead for a fair trial? To say violence was only the purview of the barbaric? Moriarty's own misdeeds, of course, withstanding.

"The greatest villains take sanctuary in the protection of the law," Sherlock said, voicing his own thoughts.

Ito did not retreat. "And yet the law remains paramount. If we allow people to be killed without trial, merely because they are criminals, we would be left with an entire nation of vigilantes. We would recede into the past, when we must progress into the future."

Images of the Reichenbach Falls grew more vivid in Sherlock's imagination. Moriarty, falling. His body receding, growing smaller and smaller, plummeting down the sheer cliffs before dashing against a rock. His body rebounding into the air, before finally colliding with the frothy surface of the water below.

"You are an admirable people," he murmured. "You especially, Mr. Ito."

"Me? What do you mean?"

"With your jujutsu you can toss people about like sticks, but instead you are patient and follow the law."

Ito's expression softened. "It was for the future of my country," he whispered, and looked down again.

They were silent for a moment. Sherlock wondered how Ito had felt upon hearing the verdict that Sanzo Tsuda would be imprisoned for life.

The sheet of paper from the unequal treaty was still lying on the desk. Ito stared at it. "This was brought up in this afternoon's meeting of the Privy Council. I had completely forgotten about this article. Considering this agreement, if we were to cede Hokkaido to Russia we would likely be forced to give Kyushu to the British."

"It will not come to that, Chairman," Sherlock assured him. "We shall chart a course through these straits."

Ito turned his attention back to the English detective and sighed. The expression in his eyes was gentle. "There is a man I'd like you to meet tomorrow."

"I am categorically alone in this country. I appreciate every new acquaintance I can make."

Ito finally smiled. "I am sorry to disappoint you, but you have already met him before."

18

The following morning, the sky above Tokyo was clear. The two men travelled to a Western-style building located not far from Ito's home. It was constructed in the Beaux Arts style, its exterior built of stone, with colonnades. The building was grand in scale and expensive in appearance, even compared to the houses Sherlock had seen in Tokyo's upscale residential areas. At a glance, he might have assumed it belonged to a foreign minister. But Ito said the owner of this residence was Japanese.

Although the building was Western, Ito and Holmes still removed their shoes in the foyer. In this home, there were many more servants than there had been at Ito's estate. The two were led into a spacious reception hall. The hall, too, was Western in design. Its dusky natural stone walls were decorated with antiquated weaponry from around the world. There was a boomerang used by Aboriginal hunters, as well as an Aztec atlatl. There was also a bola—three round stones connected by cords—a throwing weapon originating in Southeast Asia, but also used by groups such as the Eskimos, and by the Pampas Indians of South America to hunt ostrich. It was the Inca Empire's weapon of choice for long-range warfare.

Ito pointed to the bola. "There is a similar weapon in Japan. It is called the *mijin*, a type of chain and flail."

Many collectors in London held similar tastes. From a European point of view, none of these items were particularly rare. But such a collection was likely quite uncommon in the Far East. Holmes was most intrigued by the descriptive plaques affixed beneath each weapon, rather than by the weapons themselves. "I see these plaques are quite unsparing with this one particular kanji."

"Ah, *furu*." Ito nodded. "It means 'old.' The plaques include words such as 'antiquity,' 'ancient,' 'archaeology,' 'discovered in old geological strata'… With so many ancient items decorating the walls, it is only natural that this character would come up so often."

"Fascinating. I must admit that I am greatly intrigued by the Eastern alphabets."

"Intrigued? All of these items from around the world, and it is the plaques that draw your attention."

"I must confess to being quite familiar with varied weapons of antiquity. I'm afraid this display offers little new to rouse my interest."

"Then tell me, what is this?" Ito pointed to an object resembling a lanyard. The cord had been coiled, but it looked to be around six feet in total length. In the center of the cord there was an oval patch, knitted from wool.

"That is a huaraca," Sherlock replied. "A variety of sling used by the cultures of the Andes. A stone is placed into the center patch and then the rope is folded in two, held by the ends, and swung. The stone is propelled using centrifugal force. The huaraca also arrived in Japan during the Yayoi period, but never achieved significant popularity. The few that were discovered have simply been referred to as slings."

Ito peered at the plaque under the sling in amazement. "Most impressive. You are brilliant as always, Mr. Holmes."

"Nonsense. Even a pawnbroker knows a great number of things. To be useful, knowledge must serve the purpose of deduction."

"Deduction? Very well, what can you infer about the owner of these pieces?"

Sherlock looked over the displays, voicing each thought as it occurred to him. "Like you, he is originally from the Choshu Domain. He has a natural fighting spirit, but has found himself stranded and alone in tight predicaments. Again like you, he has enjoyed the frequent company of women, and was often in charge of procuring funds for dalliances—he was artful in convincing the Choshu leaders to part with such dispensations. You have frequently availed yourself of his skills."

A laugh escaped Ito's lips. "Amazing! How did you find out so much?"

"You entered this estate without greeting the master of the house, so you have likely been friends since youth. And while I'm sure the man in question has any number of comrades, the range and variety of this collection of weapons, from so many nations and times, leads me to infer they were collected through trial and error—from a desire to overcome peril through his own resourcefulness. The weapons, however, are disappointingly impractical and have since become mere decoration. Moreover, collecting all of them would have demanded significant capital."

"Indeed."

"And from the scale of the house he appears to be a man of means. Many of the highest posts in government seem to now be filled by members of the former Choshu Domain. But luxury of *this* magnitude would be impossible for a government official, unless they were colluding with conglomerates and other businessmen to misappropriate funds. What is likely then is that you recognized his ability for fundraising while together in the Choshu Domain, and this has allowed him now to involve himself with the Ministry of Finance—"

He saw Ito's expression stiffen. He glanced at something beyond.

Sherlock fell silent and turned to follow his gaze. A man dressed in kimono stood behind them. He was about five years older than Ito, with deep wrinkles creasing his brow. His hair was long, longer than Ito's, and his beard had been cut short. Also like the other Japanese man's, this man's expression was stern, but the countenance around their eyes differed. Where Ito's eyes were piercing, this man's were more bovine and obtuse, and it was more difficult to discern what he was thinking. He had an angry expression and began speaking in Japanese.

"Inoue," said Ito, speaking in English. "Please speak in English, so that your other guest may understand."

The man whom Ito had referred to as Inoue directed his gaze toward Sherlock. "It's true, I am the man who was left behind at the British legation. I do not know who you are, but if you have come now to protest you are rather late."

Ito glanced at Inoue and grimaced. "Things only went sideways that day because you forgot to bring the gunpowder."

"I hid it so well that I forgot to bring it! You were better prepared, you remembered to bring the saw. It is thanks to you that we succeeded in setting fire to the legation at all."

"Inoue," said Ito, casting an uncomfortable glance at Sherlock. "Perhaps you could avoid particulars?"

So. Inoue must be one of the men who had helped Ito burn down the British legation, before Ito first came to London. A vague memory stirred in Sherlock, who addressed himself to the man. "Are you, perhaps, the man who came running into the Hamish restaurant that day? Ito, myself, and my brother, Mycroft, were there, and you came carrying a newspaper. There was an article about a Western attack on the Choshu Domain."

Inoue furrowed his brow. He seemed to be having trouble recalling the event, which was only natural. It had been 27 years ago.

Ito, however, nodded emphatically. "You are correct. He was known as Monta Shiji at the time, but he is now known as Kaoru Inoue. You recognized me immediately, Mr. Holmes, but you did not recognize my friend so quickly."

"As might be expected. I met you a second time at Baker Street. I have not seen Mr. Inoue since I was ten years old." Sherlock approached Inoue and extended his hand. "Mr. Inoue, it is a pleasure. Sherlock Holmes, at your service."

Inoue shook his hand, but his face remained unsure. "Sherlock Holmes... I believe I have heard that name before."

"He is a renowned consulting detective," Ito provided.

"A detective?" Inoue's face grew steely. "You have brought him here because you wish to investigate me?"

Sherlock grinned. "Set your mind at ease, Mr. Inoue. I have no intention of looking into your personal accounts, or reviewing your payments and deposits. After all, I believe your corruption has already come to light and you have since accepted your share of blame."

"My blame?" Inoue frowned. "What exactly do you mean?"

"It is a weekday morning. Instead of departing for work you have fortified yourself at home, and are dressed in only a kimono. It is impressive that you possess the means to lead such an untroubled life even after having lost your position."

Inoue glared at him. "Yes, now I remember. There was an impertinent child in the restaurant that day. He talked far too much."

Ito laughed, evidently pleased. "You remember, then. No need to be so guarded, Inoue. Mr. Holmes is a friend. Mr. Holmes, Inoue has held government posts at various times over the years, just as you have surmised. Presently, he is taking a leave from government. But it is not because of finances. Inoue has been trying to revise the unequal treaties."

"Is that so?" Sherlock asked.

Inoue sank down upon one of the sofas with a groan. "After becoming Minister of Foreign Affairs I proposed appointing foreign judges. Ito betrayed me."

Ito appeared chagrined. "I wanted to avoid a divided cabinet. I thought you understood."

Inoue snorted. "I'd thank you to refrain from attributing anything nefarious to my wealth," he said, returning his attention to Sherlock and gesturing about the room. "Unlike Ito, I did not come from impoverished circumstances. I was attached to the Mori Clan, though I imagine that means little to you. Regardless, I came from noble lineage and therefore was quite comfortable to begin with."

"Noble lineage?" Ito raised his eyebrows. "A mid-level samurai at best, I would say."

Inoue grunted. "Ito, why are you here?"

"Russia is pressuring us for Tsuda's execution again. Since you worked on the construction of the Rokumeikan, I believe you've enjoyed a strong relationship with the legation. You even boasted of having close friends there."

"And you were hoping for inside information? I have a secret for you, then. Nicholas is aboard one of the warships moored in Daiba."

"We already knew that."

"You did?" Inoue seemed disappointed. "I haven't heard anything else particularly interesting."

Sherlock watched him carefully. "Do you have any idea why Nicholas has now returned in secret?"

"A pretext. They needed a port in Asia at which to dock. Nicholas' attendants are currently secretly negotiating with King Rama V, of Siam. But Siam is an independent nation, not a colony of one of the Great Powers, meaning Russia cannot approach their ports on unofficial business. Though independent, Japan is more flexible and our harbors are conveniently located."

"What are they negotiating?"

"Nothing very important. During Nicholas' visit to Siam the Russians failed to take proper records, so they wish to see what the Siamese have recorded."

"I see. I heard recently that the photographer hired by the Russian military forgot the arrangements."

Inoue nodded. "Not only the photographer. The Russian delegation made a number of embarrassing mistakes."

"After the older brother caught cold, and their most competent attendants were sent back to Russia?" Sherlock asked.

"Precisely. Their translator was inexperienced and there were a number of concerns as to whether or not Nicholas' statements had been adequately conveyed to King Rama. Since this could affect diplomatic relations in the future, the Russians are hoping to compare Nicholas' records with the Siamese and correct any inaccuracies."

"Is that all? Then why should Tsarevich Nicholas be forced to wait aboard a warship in Japan?"

Inoue sighed. "While comparing records, there was apparently disagreement over what Nicholas may or may not have said. According to the Siamese records, when King Rama expressed his dissatisfaction at France's establishment of the Kingdom of Luang Prabang as a protectorate, Nicholas agreed with him. The Russians, however, insisted that Nicholas had said nothing. There was also a disagreement over whether Nicholas had or had not said that tom yum kung was better than borscht."

Sherlock laughed through his nose. "I doubt Nicholas himself is very concerned with correcting the record on such matters."

"It does seem unlikely. Perhaps the Russian court is being overly cautious."

A look of consternation had appeared on Ito's face. "*This* is the reason that Tsarevich Nicholas has docked in our country?"

"Ostensibly. The trouble with Siam was likely just an excuse to mobilize their warships. Comparing records is hardly so important. By seizing on the blunders their delegation made in Siam, they have found an excuse to station their ships here. And they can claim, outwardly at least, they only took port here because Japan is a trustworthy country."

"Are you saying that Russia hopes to cause trouble for Japan while evading international notice and interference from other countries?"

"In all likelihood. In particular, they'd probably want to avoid any meddling from the British legation. They are rivals in the Far East, after all."

It was a persuasive theory. It would explain why Ambassador Shevich and Lt. Colonel Kanevsky had been so guarded before, and had accused Sherlock of being a spy.

This meant that after the attack on Nicholas at Otsu, Russia had already resolved to take a hard stance against Japan. But they pretended to withdraw at first in order to avoid British opposition. They accepted Sanzo Tsuda's original sentence only in order to deceive the other Western powers as they tightened the screw in secret. Was that the situation here?

But there were several witnesses on the Russian side who attested that Nicholas' initial gratitude toward Japan had not been false. At the very least, Nicholas felt an affection for Japan that had not been significantly altered immediately after the incident. To the bewilderment of even his attendants, however, he now referred to the Japanese as yellow monkeys. How much was genuine feeling on Nicholas' part, and how much a Russian conspiracy?

Ito crossed his arms. "Is there no one in our cabinet who has influence with the Russians? Someone from our side who could speak openly with someone from their side?"

Inoue leaned back against the sofa. "No one with the military. They are hostile. The only possibility I can think of is Munemitsu Mutsu, the Minister of Agriculture and Commerce."

"Mutsu has connections to the Russians?"

"There is a book that the Ministry of Agriculture and Commerce has been desperate to acquire for some time. *The Complete Work on Russian Natural Sciences*. It covers the latest research in fields from meteorology and geological science to natural philosophy, biology, earth sciences, astronomy and so on."

"Yes," Ito nodded. "I have heard of the book before. When I was Prime Minister, the Minister of Agriculture and Commerce mentioned it frequently."

"Is natural science that important?" Sherlock inquired.

"We immersed ourselves rapidly in Western technology," replied Ito. "And after technology we moved onto economic systems, and then to medicine. But we have put off developing the natural sciences."

"Why not simply invite advisors from Britain? Or from some other Western country?"

"You misunderstand. What we want are Russia's research results. Europe and America are far away from us, and their geographic conditions differ greatly. Russia possesses research facilities in China and has collected steady data from them. That data is included in *The Complete Work on Russian Natural Sciences*. Right now, Japan suffers flood damage each time a typhoon hits, and earthquakes are a serious threat. Heavy rains or droughts could endanger our food stores. It is vital that we deepen our knowledge of the natural environment."

"France for our military, Germany for our constitutional assembly," Inoue proclaimed. "Japan looks to the West for its models. If we had to begin from scratch, progress would take us many decades. For the natural sciences, Russia is our only choice. The experts all agree on this."

"Then you only need to obtain a single copy of *The Complete Work on Russian Natural Sciences*?"

Inoue shook his head. "It is not the sort of work that can be obtained through a bookseller. Genpaku Sugita's *New Text on Anatomy*—created from a translation of *Anatomische Tabellen*—was a simple enough matter. This would prove much more challenging."

Ito sucked his teeth. "There are very few copies of the *Complete Work* in existence. Each is imprinted with a serial number, and access to all copies is carefully restricted. Only research facilities approved by the Ministry of State Property are allowed to view copies of the book. Reproduction is also forbidden. In truth, requesting a copy is similar to requesting state secrets."

Sherlock shrugged lightly. "With conflict with Russia worsening, I imagine obtaining a copy should prove impossible for the immediate future."

Inoue straightened up. "Regardless, the Minister of Agriculture and Commerce has the strongest connections to Russia. His department is more concerned with matters of peace, and he has many acquaintances in the Ministry of State Property."

"This Minister Mutsu? What manner of Russians is he acquainted with, specifically?"

"One moment. Let me see my notes." Inoue rose from the sofa and retrieved a pocketbook from the bookshelf. He began flipping through the pages. "There are only a few on the Russian side who are open to reason to begin with. Ah, here it is. The Ministry of State Property. Soslan Chekhov and…. yes, Anna Luzhkova."

Ito slumped his shoulders. "Those two again. Come to think of it, they did say that they were with the Ministry of State Property."

Apparently discovering new contacts would prove more difficult than they had thought. "An earnest pair, and both naturally retiring. If we were to request a meeting with the Ministry, they would probably push it onto those two," Sherlock said to Ito.

"I see why they were chosen as attendants." Ito returned his attention to Inoue. "Isn't there anyone else? Any Japanese person you know with a strong connection to Russia?"

"None." Inoue returned his pocketbook to the bookshelf. "You know as well as I do that attempting to revise the unequal treaties is a very thorny path. Approaching a Great Power from our side gets us nowhere. Even on a personal level, it is nearly impossible to build friendships on equal terms."

Sherlock and Ito gave each other perplexed looks.

A thought suddenly seemed to occur to Inoue. "Of course. How about those two?"

"Those two?" asked Ito.

"The rickshaw drivers," said Inoue. "Jizaburo Mukohata and Ichitaro Kitagaichi. Seeing as they are receiving lifelong pensions from Russia, they must have contact information for whomever handles the payments."

"Ah, them." A look of disappointment crossed Ito's face. "Whatever contacts they have, I'm sure our people are already aware of them."

"But wait," Sherlock said excitedly. "That may indeed be a capital idea. The rickshaw drivers have received medals from Nicholas, as well as a great sum of money. It follows that the Russians may have been less guarded in their presence, or even have taken a liking to them."

Inoue smiled and nodded. "You may be on to something. When they were invited aboard the warship they were asked to come in their rickshaw uniforms rather than in formalwear. They were brought aboard just past noon but the medal ceremony didn't occur until later that evening. There was some worry that they had been invited aboard only to be made fools of, but they apparently received a warm welcome from the ship's crew."

Sherlock's confidence grew. "Russia may be willing to lower its guard if it's the two rickshaw drivers who contact them. Perhaps we will even learn some information that would have been unattainable through government channels. More to the point, Nicholas is still aboard the *Laskar*. We may manage to meet with him directly."

Ito was more dubious. "You think we should go ask the rickshaw drivers to spy for us?"

"Of course not. *I* will not be going. The rickshaw drivers will likely be found in some public house or establishment of ill repute. Even should the Russians be less guarded about two drivers, they may still be under watch. I would only draw unwelcome attention. And of course, I would be unable to communicate with them."

"How then do you propose we…" Ito trailed off mid-sentence. He stared at Sherlock in disbelief. "No, you don't mean…"

Inoue's face lit up. "There are two of them. So there should be two of us."

Ito cradled his head in both hands. "Tell me this is a nightmare," he muttered.

19

The octagonal, red-brick tower of Ryounkaku floated above the land-scape in the distance, indistinct against the clouded sky. Sprawling along the Sumida River, Asakusa, the entertainment district, already hummed with early afternoon activity, too impatient for sunset. The sukiyaki restaurants, even the public houses, overflowed with patrons. The scene here had changed little since the fall of the Bakufu, thought Ito. Groups of rough-looking men drank in front of open-faced store-fronts with boiled octopus and wild poultry hanging from the eaves.

Unfortunately, Ito was currently in no position to look down his nose at the drunkards already boozed into stupor at this early hour. At the moment he would easily have passed for one of these men, himself.

He glanced at Inoue, who was walking next to him. Inoue wore a *happi*—a livery coat—as well as a workman's apron, trousers and tabi. He looked the very image of a rickshaw driver, though one well past his physical prime. He also carried a cane. The overall effect was con-vincing: an old rickshaw man gone drinking for the day, in disgust, after his strength had given out.

Ito was less confident about his own appearance. "Is this really going to work?" he couldn't stop himself from whispering.

Inoue glanced his way. "Relax, relax. This rickshaw disguise is perfect for you. A pathetic old man with no other profession to fall back on—you've got it down to a tee."

"I doubt you'd find the leaders of any of the Great Powers pulling hijinks of this sort. If His Grace saw me now, I'd be lucky to escape with just a dressing down."

"Japan is a peculiar case. Our statesmen are from the Satsuma and Choshu domains. We are men of battle, our spirits forged in blood. Adventure is not so strange for the likes of us."

"Mr. Holmes likely realized as much when he asked us to carry out this mission."

"Possibly. He did meet us first while we were young men, after all."

Their destination was a public house. They passed through the straw curtain hung across the entrance. "Irasshai!" the proprietor shouted in welcome. The establishment was cramped, loud, and raucous, every table full. The air reeked of tobacco. The customers shouted rather than spoke.

Their information had been correct. Jizaburo Mukohata and Ichitaro Kitagaichi sat inside at a table in the corner. Rather than rickshaw uniforms, they were dressed in expensive-looking blazers. Mukohata was 37, of medium stature and build. Kitagaichi was 31, and larger in frame. With their professional clothing and ages, they might have passed off as respectably employed, but in all other aspects it was only too clear that they were a pair of slovenly drunks.

Their table was blanketed by a stunning number of saké and beer bottles. The faces of both rickshaw drivers were beet-red. Mukohata leaned forward and muttered something incoherent. Kitagaichi frowned, dropping his chin into his hands.

"Come on," Mukohata said to Kitagaichi. "It's me you're talking to. Just 30 yen. I'll pay you back in a month."

"Leave off," said Kitagaichi, not even bothering to make eye contact. "I've lent you 300 yen already as it is."

"Come on, 287 yen!" Mukohata slapped Kitagaichi on the shoulder. "You can't count what we spent together on the blink!"

"Careful! You'll spill the drink!"

"Stop being stingy. You've got plenty of cash left."

"Not after I bought that land in Ishikawa. I can't get my hands on most of it, now."

Inoue leaned over and whispered to Ito. "Shall we?"

Ito nodded slightly. "Yes, let's get this over with."

He hadn't drunk a single drop, but Inoue suddenly began stumbling about in an imitation of drunkenness. He ingratiated himself in between the two rickshaw drivers. "Ahh! The good sirs Mukohata and Kitagaichi! Just the men I hoped to see. You'll spare a fellow a drink, I'm sure!"

Kitagaichi squinted at them. "What crew are you two geezers with? I don't know you."

Inoue forced himself down into an open seat at their table. "Who's a geezer? I'm only 55. And my friend here is a strapping 50!"

It was too late to turn back now. Ito joined them, sitting down next to Inoue and fixing a smile on his face. "The great, decorated rickshaw drivers, in the flesh. It is an honor."

Inoue followed Ito's lead. "In the flesh! I bet before long they'll be replacing Sugawara no Michizane's face with yours on the five-yen note."

Mukohata snorted, and took a sip from his saké cup. He stared at Ito over the rim and spoke condescendingly from beneath hooded eyes. "That right, old man? They wouldn't put a face as old and ugly as yours on it, now would they?"

Ito's temper flared. Inoue kicked him in the leg before he had a chance to respond and continued speaking, his expression innocent. "So you got that pension for life? Do you have to meet with the Russians? How does that work?"

Kitagaichi looked annoyed. "What's it to you?"

The corner of Mukohata's lip curled. "They're probably jealous. If you geezers want a pension, find a big-shot yourselves and risk your own lives."

The proprietor made his way toward them, glancing over for their order. "A beer," said Inoue. "And another for my friend!"

"Hoy." Mukohata glared. "We're not paying for that."

Inoue turned back to him with a smile. "Don't be a curmudgeon. Tell me about when you got the medal. Was Nicholas there? Was it all big shots?"

Kitagaichi brought his cup to his lips. "What's to tell? It was on the deck of the ship. Tsarevich Nicholas and a bunch of other fancy folk were there. The rest were all sailors."

Mukohata didn't seem to mind bragging. Once his tongue had loosened he grew quite loquacious. "You chaff probably can't even picture it! There was a gorgeous sunset as they presented us the medals. Nicholas pinned the Order of the White Eagle to our chests with his own two hands. Then they filled our bamboo hats with money, 2,500 yen each, and promised us a lifelong pension to boot. We were drunk on vodka, and the sailors carried us on their shoulders. We were blessed—even Mt. Fuji appeared all clear and sharp that day, a deep, rich red. After the ceremony, we were all partying and drinking on ship late into the night."

Something wasn't right. "Mt. Fuji, you said?" Ito asked.

"Eh?" Mukohata thrust his jaw forward scornfully. "What are you, deaf, old man? Don't question me. If I say Mt. Fuji, I mean Mt. Fuji."

"Mt. Fuji was clearly visible, and it looked red?"

"What are you prattling on about!"

Ito stared. "The Russian ship had its anchor down and never left the pier. There were two other armored cruisers behind the *Pamiat Azova*. You shouldn't have been able to see Mt. Fuji from its deck."

"Eh...?" The rickshaw driver's eyes flashed with anger. "What is this nonsense?"

"It's not nonsense. Major General Soroku Kawakami was watching from the shore. He suggested advising the Russians that they would have a view of Mt. Fuji if they moved the two ships in the back."

"Major General Kawakami? Stop making up stories."

"No, I heard it from the man himself."

"Perhaps we are remembering wrong," Kitagaichi interrupted, his voice faltering. "It must have been after the ceremony that we saw Mt. Fuji. Isn't that right, Mukohata? It was after, wasn't it?"

Ito seized on his words, too. "I thought that you were celebrating

179

on board after you got medals? It was late at night by the time you left the ship."

Kitagaichi's eyes darted back and forth. He was clearly uncomfortable.

"You keep messing with us, old man, and we'll toss you in a ditch," Mukohata growled.

"I'm sorry, I didn't hear you… I must be a little deaf."

"I'll kill you!" Mukohata grabbed a beer bottle and staggered to his feet.

Ito didn't hesitate to grab Mukohata by his lapels. He lifted his hips, pivoted his body and swung his arms upward. He extended a knee and threw the rickshaw driver backward, over his shoulder. Mukohata traced a parabola in the air before crashing bottom-first against the next table. The table fell over. His body rolled across the floor like an empty bottle.

Ito had released his grip on the driver at the last possible moment, so as to soften the landing. There would be no bruising, but the mental shock would likely last some time.

The entire room instantly fell quiet. Kitagaichi stood up, panic coloring his face. Inoue, however, had already unsheathed the sword hidden in his cane in a swift horizontal slash. The blade touched the other man's throat. Kitagaichi froze in fear.

The sound of police whistles reached their ears. There was a loud clamor from outside. The public house's proprietor was nowhere to be seen. He must have run off to call the police.

Inoue sheathed the blade back in his cane. "Shake your rag!" he shouted at his friend, and with a deft turn of his heel, raced out of the shop.

Ito scrambled after him. A mob had already begun to collect at the door. He shoved his way through and burst onto the street.

The two ran as fast as they could along the Sumida River. Though lightfooted in their workmen's trousers and tabi, they quickly grew winded. Ito developed a stitch in his side.

But his friend's face betrayed evident enjoyment. "That was

something!" he shouted, the smile on his face bigger than any Ito had seen for some time. "Wasn't it, Shunsuke? Just like when we were young!"

Inoue's smile was infectious. Ito couldn't help but return it. "Without a doubt, Monta!" His voice was hearty and hale. "Just like when we were young!"

20

That evening it began to rain. But with no wind, even with the sliding doors to Ito's estate open, not a drop fell inside. Sherlock sat cross-legged on the tatami, staring out at the veranda and into the misty garden beyond. It was a sublime evening, wet and twilit.

Ito had changed into a yukata and was sitting near the low table, but his expression was far more troubled. Inoue, also in yukata, sat against one of the outdoors pillars, his knees drawn up to his chest.

After listening to their report, the detective had involuntarily snorted. "A smashing show."

Inoue furrowed his brow. "Smashing?" he said. "The only thing that's been smashed are our plans to use the rickshaw drivers to contact the Russians. All because Shunsuke... Excuse me, because *Chairman Ito* lost his temper."

Ito's expression grew a shade darker. "We would have never gotten any information from those two. Their ears have been stuffed with money."

Sherlock nodded. "Ito is right. I am more interested in the unusually lavish reception the rickshaw drivers seem to have received. As I understand, it was largely circumstance that allowed them to set on Sanzo Tsuda when they did; Prince George was the one who created the opening, moments earlier."

"That's right," Ito agreed. "The only reason the onlookers from the road didn't come to Nicholas' aid was that their heads were bowed. They could hardly notice the disturbance at first—they hadn't even seen it."

"Nicholas likely bestowed the drivers with medals because of how it would look internationally," Inoue conjectured. "Particularly to British eyes. He wanted to avert suspicion from his secret plans to take a hard stance on Japan."

"That may be so, but still, their reward remains far too large," Sherlock disagreed. "Besides, a lifelong pension is usually beyond the discretion of a crown prince. Not to mention the Russian court allowed Nicholas' diary to be published as is, even though it credits Prince George far more than it does the two drivers. This is very strange, indeed."

Inoue glared at Ito. "Perhaps if we had questioned the drivers more carefully, rather than tossing them around the room, we might have learned something. You let your temper get the better of you."

"You're the one who drew a sword."

"I was protecting you! I didn't want the other one to try anything."

"You're speaking as though our time was wasted. Mr. Holmes just said we made a smashing showing!"

Sherlock smiled. "You may not have achieved our original objective, but you did come away with something. A commendable effort. We now have testimony that they saw Mt. Fuji that day."

Ito glanced at him. "It's true that Mt. Fuji was more distinct than usual that evening. That was what prompted Major General Kawakami to make the suggestion for the better view."

"If Mt. Fuji was not visible from the ship deck, we must conclude they left the ship at some point. They must have gone to a location offering a better view of Mt. Fuji, whether at sea or on land."

"During the medal ceremony?"

"From what you described, it sounds as if the rickshaw drivers became quite distressed when you attempted to question them about Mt. Fuji. Why else would they have reacted like that?"

"The *Pamiat Azova* is a large vessel," Inoue observed. "And Major General Kawakami was on shore. So if a smaller boat had been let down the ship's starboard side, he would not have noticed. And if the boat first headed offshore before turning back, there would be no way to know who had launched it."

Sherlock agreed with this apt assessment. "No one but the Russians were aboard the ship. It would have been a simple matter to abscond with the drivers."

The door to the room slid open. Umeko bowed once, sitting in seiza in the hallway, and then stood and entered the room with a tray. "Would anyone care for some tea?"

Inoue rose and approached the low table, and sat down again. "Thank you. I will take some."

Umeko laid the table with ashtrays and Japanese teacups. Sherlock took up his pipe and went over as well. Asako and Ikuko entered the room. Ikuko struck a match and Sherlock bent the pipe in his mouth toward the flame. A graceful smile lit up Ikuko's face when he said thank you.

Asako held out an English newspaper. "Would you like the paper?"

Sherlock gave a gentle nod and took the newspaper from her. Articles from England arrived in Japan via wire with only three days' delay. Compared to how long he'd spent at sea, the speed at which information travelled was astounding.

"It's unacceptable that these two drivers are receiving their pension directly from Russia," Ito muttered, holding his cup in one hand. "The Japanese government ought to step in."

"True." Inoue took a sip of tea. "If our relationship with Russia sours any further, it is important the government be able to cut those pensions off."

"The way they conduct themselves, we should even consider revoking their Orders of Merit."

Sherlock puffed at his pipe. "Now that the rickshaw drivers are no longer a viable option, we will need to make contact with the Russians some other way."

Ito acquiesced meekly. "I will try Chekhov first; he seems amenable. I expect little will come of it, though."

"Yes. He was attached to the younger brother after all, Grand Duke George—not to the Tsarevich. He says he accompanied the Grand Duke on official duties, as well. Though I would like to know what those duties were."

Inoue glanced at the detective. "His activities are quite well known in financial circles. For the past several years he has involved himself in labor disputes at the coal mines, lending an ear to the concerns of the peasants."

"The concerns of the peasants, you say?"

"After the Emancipation Reform 30 years ago, Russian peasants began to work in factories and mines. But the woeful mining conditions have proved contentious—and of course, Russia is an absolute monarchy. For the peasants, no amount of hard work can improve their circumstances. Who would apply themselves to such grueling and dangerous work, if there were no prospect of recognition or advancement?"

"If Grand Duke George is involving himself in labor disputes, does that mean he foresees the introduction of capitalism to Russia?"

"Many businessmen in Japan thought it might, and were looking forward to new investment opportunities. However, it seems Grand Duke George is genuinely interested in the plight of the peasants, and has been petitioning his father, the Emperor, to improve their working conditions. The financial world lost interest when it learned there was no actual talk of privatizing the coal mines."

"And you have heard nothing since?"

Ito snorted. "Inoue is uninterested unless profit is involved."

"Did I not risk my life with you today for the sake of our country?!"

"You enjoyed yourself."

"Yes…" Inoue admitted. "But so did you!"

The two had to grin at each other. Umeko and the two girls smiled discreetly.

If Ito refrained from his dalliances in the future and returned home like this more frequently, Sherlock thought, he might look forward to such domestic happiness more often. And Ito, for his own part, seemed to have rediscovered the joys of family.

And Sherlock had begun to feel the promise he and Ito had made last night was for his own benefit as well. Internally, he had resolved to never try cocaine again. Though he did feel a little restless from time to time, he was already beginning to regain a sense of composure he didn't know he had lost.

He glanced absently through the English newspaper. Then one of the articles had caught his eye. As he read, Sherlock swallowed, hard.

"Is something wrong?" Asako noticed.

"No…" Sherlock said, but his dazed voice belied him. "I happened to spot my name in one of the articles, that is all."

"In an article?" Asako leaned forward. "What is it about?"

Umeko frowned. "Asako!"

Ito put on his reading glasses and extended his hand. "Let me see."

Sherlock handed him the paper with a morose face.

Ito took the paper and perused the front page, muttering as he read aloud. "The greatest point of contention in the civil suit into the cause of death of James Moriarty, who is believed to have fallen to his death from the Reichenbach Falls, Switzerland, in May, is the relationship between Moriarty and Sherlock Holmes, Esq. Mr. Holmes is believed to have fallen to his death together with Mr. Moriarty. The suit was brought forward by James the Younger, Moriarty's brother. Unconvinced by Scotland Yard's conclusion that the two men argued verbally and had tussled before falling together, Mr. Moriarty has argued before the criminal jury that Mr. Holmes murdered his brother. Opinion is also divided over whether Moriarty or Holmes initially invited the other to the scene of the incident. In related court matters, the younger James Moriarty has begun additional defamation proceedings, arguing that allegations of his brother's involvement in a myriad of crimes before his death are unfounded…"

Ito's voice trailed off. He fell silent, and removed his reading spectacles.

Sherlocks stared wordlessly at the tobacco smoke floating before his face. As far as London was concerned, Japan may as well have been the afterlife. Sherlock's reach did not extend to the world of the living—he could only watch events unfold from afar. He was powerless even to help the one true friend he had left behind.

21

The rain grew stronger as night fell. Sherlock lingered quietly on the veranda, staring out into the darkness of the garden. He crossed his arms and leaned against the pillar, remaining in that pose for a long time.

He was not currently exercising his logical capabilities. Try as he might to focus, his emotions continued to run amok, interfering with his ability to analyze the attack on Nicholas. For the moment, fruitless though it might be, he preferred to give in to melancholy and grief about London. He searched for some sense of proportion. If he gained some perspective, he might at least approach the Nicholas case better in the morning.

Though they were concerned, the members of the Ito family had since retired to their respective rooms. No one had spoken to him for some time. But now he heard footsteps approach from the hallway.

Those footsteps proved to be Ito. "Mr. Holmes," he whispered. "You should rest."

Sherlock let loose a sigh. "I'm afraid Morpheus has yet to visit me this evening. I accomplished very little today. Since I cannot sleep, I would rather absorb myself in this rain, and the darkness of the night. Perhaps I will hit upon a method by which we can meet with Tsarevich Nicholas."

"Is that really what you've been thinking about?"

The sound of raindrops could be heard bouncing off the eaves. "It is not," he admitted soberly.

Ito's tone was solicitous. "Mr. Holmes... I stopped reading partway through the article, but the second half…"

"I read." Sherlock nodded. "In both the criminal and civil cases, the only person to rebut Moriarty's brother's claim was Dr. John H. Watson. Though I have allies among the police and barristers, they do no more than their jobs demand… Watson alone insists my conduct was honorable."

"If a defamation suit is brought forward, Dr. Watson will be quite busy. Hopefully it will not interfere with his practice. You do not fear that Moriarty's brother will make designs upon his life, do you?"

"The younger Moriarty is a mere stationmaster in the West Country. He lacks his brother's cunning mind and propensity for action. Perhaps he is simple enough to even believe the elder Moriarty's innocence."

"You must be desperate to know how the trial unfolds."

"Me? No, I am but a dead man. What could I do?"

"But you worry for your friend. Am I wrong?"

Sherlock stared out into the darkness, into the garden. "I have caused him much misery."

"Come now," Ito replied gently. "Do you remember the day we first met? When I read in the paper that the Choshu Clan was on the verge of being annihilated?"

"Yes. I think I can now understand how you felt. If only I could dash over the sea and return home now, I would not care what became of me. I can think of nothing else. Did you feel the same?"

"If I were to fall before achieving my goals, I still had compatriots to carry them on. You are alone, however. I cannot imagine what you are suffering."

Sherlocks dropped his gaze, agitated. "If only my own brother were more capable."

"He helped you escape. He seems quite capable."

"Moriarty's brother shows more dedication than mine does. I see Mycroft's name nowhere in the papers. He allows Watson to expose himself like this while *he* reclines on a bureaucrat's chair."

"He supports you from the shadows."

"No. He is an opportunist by nature. I am sure he has already forgotten his dear, departed brother."

"I think, perhaps, that you yourself would rather *not* believe that."

"But I make a habit of only speaking the truth."

They were silent for a moment. Finally Ito spoke again. "There is a tanka by Shinsaku Takasugi, written when he was very ill. 'If you die, catch up to Buddha and Confucius, so that you can finally ask them the way.'"

Sherlock's laugh was without mirth. "Very witty. Now that I am dead, I suppose I had better apply myself to finding God."

Ito smiled, relieved that the detective could joke. The atmosphere lightened a little. But soon Ito's expression grew serious again.

"Mr. Holmes. If you decide you wish to return to London, by whatever means, know that I can prepare a ship at a—"

Sherlock raised a hand.

"I assure you that I have no such wish," he proclaimed. "I owe you my life, and as payment I intend to rescue this country from its crisis of war. I promised as much. I will not renege on that oath, regardless of what may come."

He turned his eyes again to the darkness outside. The raindrops seemed clearer than they had earlier, and the sound of the drops were more distinct in his ears. He felt as if his faculties had been honed back to sharpness.

He turned his back on Ito. "All the clues point to Nicholas. Our only choice is to meet with him directly. If we do not have an intermediary, then we must push through by force."

"By force? The harbor is swarming with Russian troops, and he is housed in the very middle of nine warships. It would be more than foolish to sneak onboard."

"I doubt the *Laskar* is our destination. He was only there to facilitate negotiations with Siam. Likely he has long since snuck ashore, and availed himself of more congenial surroundings."

"You believe Tsarevich Nicholas is no longer aboard the ship?"

"If the rickshaw drivers were able to abscond from the ship, there is no reason to assume Nicholas could not do so in secrecy as well. Our problem to consider now is whether he is on Japanese or Russian shores. If he has returned home then our fight is with ghosts. But luckily, the probability of that is small. Nicholas is preoccupied with Japan. Surely he has taken up lodgings somewhere nearby."

"But how can we find out where?"

"And I am forbidden to approach Ambassador Shevich," Sherlock sighed. "We will need help from some more benevolent Russians."

Just then, they heard footsteps from beyond the estate. A silhouette appeared at the gate and walked swiftly across the grounds, holding a lantern aloft in one hand.

"Who's there!" Ito shouted.

The stranger approached the veranda and stopped, raising the lantern. The light revealed a man cloaked in the mantle of what appeared to be a uniform. His face was illuminated in the weak glow, showing a man of about 30, with a mustache and a cap in the French military style.

Sherlock immediately deduced that this man felt respect and loyalty toward the master of the house. The wetness of his mantle suggested he had arrived by carriage but had parked a distance away, so as not to disturb them with the sound of hooves. And it was also apparent from the mud on his trousers that he had rushed here from the carriage as quickly as possible.

"Ah," Ito said, still in English. "Sonoda. Why have you come at this hour? Mr. Holmes, this is Yasukata Sonoda, chief of Police Services for the Ministry of Home Affairs."

So this was the man who headed Japan's police force. Sonoda, however, betrayed no reaction upon hearing Sherlock's name. He began speaking in a rapid string of Japanese.

Ito looked irritated. "In English please, Mr. Sonoda, so that Mr. Holmes may understand."

Sonoda bowed to Sherlock in apology, and then began again in English. "Excuse me. Chairman Ito, we've had a telegram from the Teshikaga sergeant's outpost. Sanzo Tsuda has died. Suddenly, while in custody at Kushiro Prison."

"What?!" Ito shouted.

Sherlock felt a chill run down his back. It was as if his arteries had frozen. The situation had just turned dire. This was no time to let emotion get the better of him—his powers of deduction were desperately needed!

22

Despite it being the middle of the night, a steady slew of visitors came one after the other to Ito's estate. The chief secretary and department heads from police headquarters all made their appearance. The Japanese they spoke to each other was unintelligible to Sherlock, but he soon recruited Ikuko to listen from the next room and translate for him.

The situation was delicate. There was a strict news blackout in place. Nothing would be reported in the morning papers. But Sanzo Tsuda was most certainly dead. The cause was under investigation, but for the time being appeared to be acute pneumonia.

They discussed the developments leading up to his death in great detail.

Kushiro Prison had been established six years ago, during a time of public instability and a spike in crime rates, and a corresponding increase in the number of incarcerations. Many prisons were built in Hokkaido, not only to make it more difficult for the criminals to flee but also to take advantage of convict labor for land development. Kabato Prison was built in 1881, Sorachi Prison the following year in 1882, and Kushiro Prison three years later in 1885. Only serious offenders with sentences of ten years or more were transferred to these new institutions. They were drafted from prison houses throughout the country.

Of the nearly 1,000 convicts at Kushiro Prison, around half were, like Tsuda, serving life sentences. The majority were assigned to construction work outside, building roads from Shibecha to Kushiro or

Atsukeshi. The work—clearing roadways through thick forests and wilderness—was grueling. The remaining convicts worked in the factories inside the prison, with duties ranging from construction and metalwork to mechanics, soy sauce processing and straw goods. Other work included farming, forestry, and woodworking.

Tsuda, however, was assigned only simple tasks such as straw making, filling out prisoner name badges, and work charts. Though reports indicated some concern over his poor health, there was, in truth, no other work he could be assigned. None of the supervisors wished to furnish him with anything that might be used as a weapon.

One might assume conditions at Kushiro were atrocious. But the complex had many features besides its cell house: There was a mess hall, baths, an infirmary, a sick ward, and even a chaplain's office where prisoners could read the Bible and take English lessons. In late May, when Tsuda received his life sentence, the Russians had even complained the prison conditions were too lenient in comparison to Siberia.

As an inmate, Tsuda made no trouble and was not prone to outbursts. But he did act and speak in odd ways, and the guards and other prisoners avoided him. He was in constant poor health, and often didn't eat. Some worried that he might be trying to starve himself to death.

In late August, a single-page "Will and Testament" was discovered in Tsuda's solitary cell. The document included a request that any money he possessed be sent to his family in Iga-Ueno, and listed his concerns over the future of Japan. Nail and hair clippings belonging to him were discovered folded inside a separate paper.

The details of the will were reported to the Hokkaido commissioner. The commissioner feared that if Tsuda committed suicide, *joui* sentiment might be rekindled. He ordered that Tsuda's watch be strengthened.

By September, Tsuda had grown thin and emaciated. His appetite was erratic—he would go three days with nothing, only to eat regularly the next. On the 7th, he complained of a severe chill and was transferred to the sick ward, where he seemed to have a slight fever. The prison doctor diagnosed him with a cold. At the time he was eating rice porridge three times a day.

But his fever did not improve and his appetite faltered. The following week he was given sugar, chestnuts, sweets, pickled plums, milk, and other delicacies, but he still could eat nothing. He grew weaker and weaker.

The previous day, Tsuda began having trouble breathing. His face grew pale and sickly, and his body was covered in sweat. He complained several times of pain in his chest. In the morning he vomited about a cup's worth of blood, and by afternoon his vomiting had increased.

As of today, Tsuda had been bedridden. He lacked the strength even to heave up blood. The doctor had been forced to use strips of paper to drain the blood that still pooled in Tsuda's mouth. As his condition grew critical, the warden, the secretary, the head of the guards, and several others assembled in the sickroom. They all looked on as Tsuda passed away.

After his death, authorities reached out to his immediate family, relatives, and even acquaintances, but no one was willing to take his body. The law stipulated that if no one came forward to claim him, he would be buried in Kushiro Prison's graveyard.

The prison was thoroughly examined down to the last screw, but no one discovered any signs of poison. At present, there was nothing to contradict the diagnosis that Tsuda had died of illness.

But the timing couldn't be worse.

The commotion Tsuda's death might cause in Japan was worrying enough, but even more concerning was how Russia would react. What if the Russians assumed Tsuda had been assassinated because he could not be executed? It might look to international eyes as if Japan had turned to cowardly, barbaric measures to avoid war or demands for compensation. International trust would etiolate, and it would be more difficult than ever to establish Japan as a nation governed by law. And any hope of revising the unequal treaties would fade to a mere pipe dream.

Police Chief Sonoda's voice grew faint, and ended in a whisper. "There is something else. As of now, the details are still unclear, but…"

Ikuko pressed her ear against the sliding door, desperate to make out what was being said. Sherlock brought out a cup and showed her how to hold her ear against the base so she could hear better.

This seemed to do the trick. Ikuko began translating again. A colleague who had worked with Tsuda at the Shiga police force had testified that before Nicholas had even visited Japan, Tsuda had already apparently met several times with some Russian personages.

Since March, Tsuda had been leaving work as soon as his shifts ended. The colleague stated he had often witnessed two men, Westerners, greet Tsuda in the streets near the police station. Both men were tall and slim, perhaps in their twenties or thirties. One spoke in what sounded like Russian, while the other translated into Japanese. The colleague had not been sure what the men were discussing. The three would usually depart together, on foot.

Kushiro Prison only permitted visits from family members, and the two Russians never visited Tsuda after he was incarcerated. The Shiga police attempted to track the two down after the incident, but had been unable to identify them.

Ito spoke very little throughout the briefings divulging all this information. Finally, the leaders of the police force began discussing how best to inform Russia of Tsuda's death.

Sherlock, meanwhile, fell to his own deliberations. He still did not fully comprehend the temperament and daily habits of the Japanese people, and yet his powers of deduction were needed for the very same. The situation was a conundrum. Although this case differed greatly in character from the crimes he'd encountered in the West, time was of the essence. The Far East faced its greatest danger yet. The situation brooked no delay.

23

Gentle afternoon light streamed over Tokyo, alighting on a stagecoach rumbling through a side street of Ginza. The buildings in the area were a mixture of Japanese-style structures with tiled roofs, and Western red brick buildings. The shop signs shared their spaces with rows of weeping willows. Sherlock was fast becoming used to such sights.

He and Ito sat at a table in a Western café, staring at the street through the open-air shop front. Although average Japanese citizens were turning out more and more to the entertainment centers, in Ginza at least the sight of a 50-year-old Japanese man in frock coat, in the company of a peculiar Englishman, was not so very out of place. Or so Ito claimed. Indeed, the ratio of foreigners passing by in this area seemed quite high. Fortunately, at this time of day it was not likely that anyone from the British legation would happen by. Sherlock wanted to avoid dealing with the authorities or having his identity called into question at all costs—particularly at this juncture.

He was still legally prohibited from approaching Ambassador Shevich, and the meeting with Chekhov and Anna had been only a one-time offer. Since the two Russians were acquaintances with Minister Mutsu, however, he and Ito had reached the two through the Ministry of Agriculture and Commerce to arrange a meeting. Naturally, they had not divulged their identities.

A portly man with red hair entered the café. He was immediately recognizable. Chekhov seemed to notice Ito first; his attention then shifted to Sherlock. His round eyes filled with apprehension.

He wiped the sweat from his face with a handkerchief as he approached. "Chairman Ito. Mr. Holmes. You put me in a very difficult position. I was told very clearly that I was not to speak with Mr. Holmes again, even if I happened to encounter him in the street."

At this point Anna entered the shop as well, and her face immediately blanched. "As…we were contacted by your Ministry of Agriculture and Commerce, I assumed it was related to *The Complete Work on Russian Natural Sciences*…"

Sherlock was unfazed. "But the two of you are here now, at any rate. Please, have a seat. It was very important we meet with someone from your side, and you two are the only ones available to us at the moment."

Chekhov and Anna sat down across from them, their expressions uneasy. Chekhov leaned forward and whispered, "The Ministry of Agriculture and Commerce has always pursued the natural sciences, and is inherently peaceful. That is why we have done everything in our power to help. To have our friendship taken advantage of in this manner…"

"Your feelings are understandable," Ito soothed him. "But in the interests of peace, Mr. Holmes and I had no other resort. None of Tsarevich Nicholas' advisors, with the exception of yourselves, are willing to meet with us."

Anna's uncertainty grew. "Advisors? I told you before, we generally attended on His Royal Highness Grand Duke George, not on the Tsarevich himself."

"In that case," Sherlock said quietly, "would you telegram to Paris on my behalf, where Grand Duke George is now vacationing, and inquire as to whether his brother Nicholas has truly docked a warship in Japan so he can negotiate with the King of Siam?"

Chekhov and Anna winced, exchanging nervous glances.

Their reaction settled it. Sherlock had been entertaining several possibilities, but they had suddenly been narrowed down to one.

Confused, Ito turned towards Sherlock, bemused. "Mr. Holmes, what have you discovered?"

Sherlock was silent. He needed some time to organize his thoughts.

The waiter approached with a menu in hand. Chekhov and Anna fussed over it. They held the menu close to their faces before finally ordering only black tea.

The waiter departed with a dubious expression. Sherlock addressed Chekhov. "Tsarevich Nicholas currently resides in the Russian legation. I desire to meet with him. Is there any possibility we could enter the building without drawing the notice of Ambassador Shevich?"

Chekhov's eyes grew wide. Anna stared, too, completely caught off guard.

"Wh…" The blood rushed into the man's cheeks. "What are you saying? Nicholas, in the legation? His Imperial Highness is aboard the *Laskar*…"

Sherlock shook his head impatiently. "I would thank you not to waste our time. I am already aware that the Tsarevich is in the legation. His Highness may be a crown prince, but sneaking ashore in this manner violates international laws of entry. While in the Russian legation, however, he is protected by extraterritorial privilege. He is safe and at his own leisure, so long of course as he is not apprehended while travelling between the two locations."

Chekhov and Anna seemed to reach the same realization at once. Chekhov's shoulders slumped. He spoke timidly. "Your powers of perception are astounding, Mr. Holmes. It is true, Tsarevich Nicholas is at the legation."

Ito's expression clouded. "He entered our country without permission? Without even discussing it with us? How shameful!"

"Yes …" Chekhov appeared thoroughly deflated. "However, that was not originally His Highness' intention."

"The *Laskar* is only a medium-sized ship and is susceptible to the waves," Anna explained, in distress. "It is not so comfortable as the imperial flagship… Tsarevich Nicholas became terribly seasick. That was what caused him to sneak ashore in secret, and take a carriage to the legation."

"I believe I asked for you to be truthful with me," Sherlock reproved quietly. "In fact there were difficulties in getting a certain artisan to Tokyo and aboard that ship. *That* is the truth, is it not?"

Chekhov lowered his gaze in defeat. Anna reacted in a similar manner.

Ito, alone, was confused. "A certain artisan? What do you mean?"

But the truth was out. "Whatever resentment the Tsarevich has formed for Japan, someone must inform His Highness that when a young man in his position runs away from home it can bring great chaos to the world," Sherlock said. "I propose *we* deliver that message immediately."

"Run away?!" Ito exclaimed.

Anna sighed deeply. "You seem to have grasped the situation fully, Mr. Holmes. Everything you say is true. I'm afraid, though, that after everything that has happened, all attempts to reason with His Highness have been in vain…"

"Wait." Ito stared. "You do not mean that Tsarevich Nicholas wishes to defect…"

Only a politician would ask that, Sherlock thought. "No, not defecting. He has run away, that is all, like any wayward boy who is uninterested in his parents' advice and is itching for a fight."

The waiter brought over the tea. Chekhov and Anna appeared to have recovered a modicum of composure. Chekhov stared at the steam rising from the pot for a moment. Eventually he lifted his eyes.

"I would be grateful for anyone who might persuade His Tsarevich," he said. "If that person is you, then I will assist in any way I can."

Sherlock turned his piercing gaze on Anna. Her mind, too, appeared made up.

"At least tell me one thing," Ito begged. He was still in the dark. "When you say he is 'itching for a fight,' do you mean war?"

"Come now," Sherlock dodged. "If I told you now that Nicholas intends war, you would be forced to take immediate action. Humor me until tonight. Then all will be made clear."

24

An exquisitely ornamented table clock announced 6:00 P.M., chiming a barrel organ version of the melody to *Stenka Razin.*

The room was decorated with furniture in the Russian Modern style. The décor would not have been out of place in the salon of a typical aristocratic home. But the Russian legation had different standards. The room was not a social space but a barber's salon: there was a reclining chair, shampooing bowl, and, on the wall, a hanging mirror. The metal mesh hampers were filled with towels, and a wagon in the room held scissors, combs, and other tools of the trade.

The various tools and accouterments implied this was a place of business, but it was no public shop. Not even the legation staff came to have their hair trimmed. The room was reserved for the sole use of the imperial family.

The door opened on schedule. Tsarevich Nicholas entered.

Instead of the overly ornate military uniform he wore for ceremonial events, the Tsarevich was wearing a simple double-collared shirt. In this simple garb, he looked for once his age, a young man of 23. Though short for a Russian, he was slim and fit. His hair was cropped, and his mustache neatly trimmed. He certainly didn't look like he needed a barber. Clearly he was visiting this room for some other purpose—just as Sherlock had expected.

Nicholas approached the reclining chair. He never once glanced in Sherlock's direction; the Romanovs were not in the habit of exchanging pleasantries with the workers they employed. But it was also only natural that Nicholas was feeling dour, considering the unpleasant procedure to come.

He sat down before the mirror and asked a question in Russian. There was a slight tremble in his voice. Most likely he was asking something to the effect of: *Will it hurt? How long will this take?*

Ito had been watching silently, but now slowly approached until he stood directly behind Nicholas. Nicholas did not immediately notice his presence. Ito stared at Nicholas' reflection in the mirror, speaking softly in English.

"Good evening, Your Highness."

Nicholas' expression became startled. He spun around, staring upward at Ito. "Who are you? You're not the tradesman I was expecting."

Sherlock, who had been standing against the wall, walked towards the chair as well. "Please forgive the imposition, Your Highness. This is the Chairman of the Privy Council, Hirobumi Ito."

Nicholas' eyes widened. His eyes ran up and down Ito's clothing.

It was no surprise he had a hard time believing them, Ito thought, considering he was dressed in the same rickshaw driver's uniform as previously, with the livery coat and apron, workman's trousers and tabi. He had no idea what the Nagasaki tradesmen usually wore, but Sherlock had insisted the Russians would never know the difference. The English detective himself had gained entry wearing his usual frock coat, claiming to be Ito's translator.

Getting inside had been that simple. They had kept watch on the legation through binoculars, and confirmed that Ambassador Shevich and Lt. Colonel Kanevsky were confined to a meeting room somewhere else.

Nicholas leapt to his feet and rushed toward the door, shouting something in Russian. Sherlock spun around, blocking Nicholas' path. "A moment, Your Highness. Before your guards throw us out, ask yourself, are you entirely in the right in this situation?"

"What do you mean?" Nicholas stared at him.

"You have entered the country without permission, and without the knowledge of the Japanese government. Inside the legation you are protected by extraterritorial privilege, but in order to return home, at some point you will need to step outside the building. If anyone should spot you, it would provoke an international incident."

"What are you trying to say?"

"Trying to say? Rather, let me ask what you planned to do here today. Why should you come here if you have no need of a barber—which clearly you do not? You were informed, I believe, that the tattooist from Nagasaki had arrived two days early. Your appointment was undoubtedly with him."

Nicholas' face betrayed that he was dumbfounded. He finally glanced around the room and realized the three of them were not alone.

His confusion was instantly replaced with anger. "Chekov! And even Miss Luzhkova! What is the meaning of this!"

In the corner of the barber's room, Chekhov and Anna cowered. "Please forgive us, Your Highness," Chekhov said falteringly. "We lied when we said that the tattooist had arrived early. Only…"

"Your Highness!" Anna's voice was shrill and panicked. "We are prepared for arrest, if it comes to that. But I beg you, please understand. Mr. Holmes already knew everything."

Nicholas turned toward Sherlock in astonishment.

"Would you do us the honor of rolling up your right sleeve?" Sherlock requested quietly. "As you yourself must know, that in itself will be more than ample proof."

Silence descended on the room. Nicholas gave Sherlock a stubborn look, but soon gave in. He unbuttoned his cuff and rolled up his sleeve.

Ito swallowed hard. He could not believe his eyes.

Nicholas' tattoo—the dragon tattoo he had received in early May—was not there!

Of course, Ito had never actually seen the tattoo for himself. When he and the Emperor had visited the Tsarevich in Kyoto, Nicholas had been wearing long sleeves.

Nicholas rolled his sleeve back down with an air of apprehension. "Mr. Holmes, is it? Are you related to the famous Sherlock Holmes?"

"No. I *am* the famous Sherlock Holmes."

"But I heard you were dead."

"Those reports are false," Ito answered. "As a result Ambassador Shevich believes that Mr. Holmes is a spy. On my honor, however, I swear to you that Mr. Holmes and I have come to help you."

Nicholas glanced at Chekhov. "You've betrayed our confidence?"

Chekhov and Anna shrunk into the corner, shaking their heads back and forth frantically.

"Your Highness," Sherlock said softly. "I arrived at the truth quite on my own, I assure you. You did not in fact visit Japan from April to May of this year. It was your brother, Grand Duke George, who visited in your stead."

Ito reeled. "His brother? That cannot be!"

"But it can," Sherlock said implacably. "Grand Duke George was attacked by Sanzo Tsuda, and still remains in critical condition."

Ito could not make sense of it. It was absurd—Grand Duke George was in Paris, resting after an extended campaign of public service. When Nicholas had visited Japan, he'd met with Prince Takehito Arisugawa, interpreter Naohide Madenokoji, Governor Takeaki Nakano of Nagasaki, and even Duke Tadayoshi Shimazu. And above all, he had even met His Grace the Emperor.

In the past, His Grace had met Nicholas during official functions. And Ito had been present with His Grace at the hotel in Kyoto. Surely they should have noticed if Nicholas and his brother had traded places.

Nicholas sighed. "You are an Englishman. I suppose that means the entire world now knows the truth?"

"Hardly. I have yet to inform a soul. I have deduced these facts based on your dealings with Siam and Japan, but I would now like to hear your own account of events, if you might do me that kindness. Though I am capable of discerning how events unfolded, only you may say what your state of mind was at the time."

Nicholas paced in the silence, his expression disconsolate. Then his feet came to a stop. "George is three years younger than me, but he was always tall, unlike me. He is handsome and lively. Mother always fussed over me, so he would cause mischief to get her attention."

"The English newspapers often run stories concerning the Romanov family," Sherlock said. "Perhaps other countries' papers do as well. The papers say that your father is very strict, and has instituted English education for his children. He kept your chambers Spartan, made you sleep in military beds, woke you up at six in the morning, and forced you to take cold baths."

Nicholas frowned with one corner of his mouth. "Mother ran us hot baths from time to time. She was kind. Mother taught us the importance of family."

"And Grand Duke George…"

His voice turned soft. "George was the smartest of us all. Like Mother, he liked society. He and I were very close. We had all the same tutors, we grew up in nurseries next to each other. We both began English lessons at age six, but he improved much more swiftly than I. And we advanced to the program at the Academy of the Russian General Staff together. By then we were fluent in French, and passable at German and Danish. We often went sporting and fishing together as well."

"But your brother's health deteriorated?"

"It did." A shadow crossed over Nicholas' face. "I believe the symptoms were first discovered shortly before he came of age. Tuberculosis. He has struggled ever since."

"Your brother caught cold during your tour of the East and was sent home, out of caution. It was for health reasons."

"Yes. The entire trip was on our parents' suggestion—demand, rather. They wanted us to travel from October of last year to August of this, through all those small regions where the British squabble with us for influence. I had never wanted to go but George was looking forward to the trip. So I decided to make the most of it; at least I'd have him."

"I gather you were not particularly interested in visiting Japan, then, either?"

Nicholas nodded. "None of it suited me. Culture bores me. I detest reading, and find theater and art tedious. The only part I enjoyed was seeing the dancing girls as we travelled down the Nile. I know you are an Englishman, but I found the sight of the British red coats in India to be completely dismaying. And naturally I had no interest in China or Japan. I had heard how barbaric they are."

Ito had a question. "While you were in Egypt and India, did you not say you were looking forward to your visit to Japan?"

But Sherlock only had to gesture at Chekhov and Anna. The two lowered their heads in chagrin.

Of course. That had also been a lie—designed to conceal the fact that Nicholas and George had traded places.

Nicholas snorted. "My brother was the one who wished to visit Japan. He was constantly telling me everything he wanted to see, but I found it impossible to relate. Japan is an uncivilized place. I knew it would be dangerous to visit, I knew it all along!"

Nicholas is remarkably childish for his age, thought Ito. He had all the entitlement one would expect of aristocracy. He highly doubted their father really had been as strict as the rumors said, looking at the result. Besides, it was easy to imagine how much the mother probably doted on him. Nicholas was selfish and ignorant of the ways of the world—unbecoming traits in a crown prince. He was stubborn in his preferences, and chose to run away, rather than change, when faced with anything that displeased him. What he'd said about not even wanting to look at the British officers in India was a perfect case in point—England was Russia's greatest rival, after all.

"When did your brother fall ill?" Sherlock inquired.

"He developed bronchitis around when we got to Bombay. We hoped that the warmer climates would help him, but they had the opposite effect. George left the ship and returned to the Caucasus region with Chekhov and the others. It was a real blow. I had never wanted to go on the trip to begin with. Now there was even less reason to look forward to it."

"Your brother joined you again later, though."

"He did." Nicholas lowered himself to sit on the reclining chair. "He recovered nicely when I was in Singapore. He expressed interest in continuing the trip. Only…"

He glanced at Chekhov. Chekhov nodded and picked up the story. "His Highness Grand Duke George wished to rejoin the envoy, but His Imperial Majesty the Emperor sent a letter instructing him to instead recuperate in the Maldives. His Highness the Grand Duke consulted with Tsarevich Nicholas at this point…"

"Yes, he did." A small smile flickered across Nicholas' face. "When I got George's letter in Singapore, I was overjoyed. I told him to join me and we would keep it a secret from our parents together. George was back aboard the *Pamiat Azova* before we set sail for Siam."

"Naturally I assume you travelled with the Grand Duke?" Sherlock directed to Chekhov and Anna.

"We did," Anna replied. "We were aboard the ship from then on, seeing to His Highness Grand Duke George's health along with the doctor."

"One of the many annoyances during our time in Egypt and India," Nicholas said, "is that wherever we travelled, people constantly confused George and I. He is taller and more sociable, and so many assumed he was the elder brother. This isn't the first time this has happened; people have been confusing us for one another since we were children. So before we arrived in Siam, George and I concocted a plan. I was not enjoying myself at all, whereas my brother very much looked forward to the trip. Why not disembark in my place, and pass himself off as crown prince?"

Ito couldn't believe his ears. "Ridiculous! The Tsarevich and Grand Duke may have some small resemblances in their faces, but they are hardly twins. The difference must be obvious!"

Nicholas turned toward Ito. "Chairman Ito, do you have any brothers?"

"No."

"Of course. Brothers may not look or think alike, but to have a brother is to have a natural conspirator. Siam is a closed country, not a British or Dutch colony. We had no intention of ever returning to Siam, so what was the harm? We had help from my cousin, King George of Greece, as well."

"It isn't the first time they have done this," Chekhov ventured tremulously. "Even in Russia, when visiting the smaller country villages, His Highness Grand Duke George often went in His Tsarevich's place."

Nicholas' face creased in displeasure. "Do not say he 'went in my place.' That reflects poorly on me. George enjoys travelling, but there were few official duties to take him from home. Our interests simply aligned."

"Of course, Your Highness," Chekhov submitted humbly. "If I could be forgiven for saying so, however, while such behavior may have been overlooked in your youth, now that you are an adult... And in recent years, they have made stunning breakthroughs in photographic technology. There is even the Kinetoscope."

It was an unfamiliar term. "The Kinetoscope?" Ito asked.

Anna explained. "It is a moving picture machine invented by Edison. The Tsarevich and his brother resemble each other somewhat in facial features, but it would be as easy to distinguish them through a Kinetoscope, with gestures and facial expressions, as it would be to distinguish them in person."

"We already discussed this at length," Nicholas said impatiently. "With his health as poor as it is, George would never have this opportunity again. He was so looking forward to visiting the Far East. He deserved to go. Besides, it's hardly as if the Kinetoscope has made it over to these backwaters."

"Are you saying that Grand Duke George was sent to attend on the King of Siam in your place?" Ito snapped, exasperated.

"We *told* Tsarevich Nicholas it would be *most* disrespectful." Chekhov's voice cracked. "But Grand Duke George was doing much better, and they promised this would be the last time... We agreed to allow them to swap, but only in Siam and Japan."

"What's that?" Ito was obviously taken aback. "Only Siam and Japan?"

"Those are the only two countries from their trip that are independent nations," Sherlock said quietly, "free from colonial rule."

"And also we assumed they were less advanced," Nicholas added completely indifferently. "For instance, we knew that the Siamese royal family prohibited newspaper correspondents from entering the country."

Ito was beginning to find Nicholas' attitude very provoking. "I imagine Your Highness' opinion had begun to change after seeing our country for yourself."

"True, it is much more modern than I had expected. But we had no way of knowing that before." Nicholas sounded surprisingly contrite. "We did not bring the military photographer ashore in Siam to make sure there wasn't any evidence."

Chekhov sighed. "The entire crew was operating in the utmost secrecy, including the captain. Naturally, not even the palace was informed."

Sherlock stared at the young man. "So you thought if you did not take photographs you would be safe?"

Nicholas' face clouded over. "Unfortunately, we learned later that the Siamese had taken shorthand notes. Things George said contradicted with what I had said earlier in other countries."

"So officially you said you wanted to compare records, but in fact you were hoping to revise the Siamese records to better match your own official views."

"My brother's statements were not the only problem. Some newspaper correspondents had paid local Siamese press to do some reporting for them. George had even been photographed in secret, from afar."

"Luckily for you, the photographs were all unclear," Sherlock filled in. "None of the newspapers realized they actually depicted Grand Duke George. The Russian court has offered a large sum to purchase those negatives, the goal being to remove them from circulation."

"Since the photographs were developed using rudimentary technology, they will likely deteriorate in a number of years. The negatives, however, are a different story. If someone enlarged them they might realize it was George."

Sherlock nodded. "You worried the same situation might occur in Japan, so you didn't inform the reporters of your itinerary. Instead, the Grand Duke snuck out in secret."

"Yes. Of course I'd met the Emperor before all this, so the plan was that *I* would go in person for only the Tokyo portion of the trip. At any rate, Japan agreed with George greatly, and he showed little reserve in his travels. He even visited the homes of commoners. And of course, everyone he met were people he'd never met before. I'm sure he assumed that no one in Asia would be able to tell the difference between him and I. And even the dignitaries were fooled. There were no reporters, everyone bowed their heads on the street, and cameras are not popular here with the public. Photographs were prohibited. I wrote my diary entries based on George's letters, just as I had in Siam."

Ito didn't understand. "But there *were* photographs taken during your visit, I am sure of it. I saw them myself at the newspaper offices. It was clearly you in those photographs, sitting in a rickshaw."

Sherlock held up a hand to stop Ito. "Your Highness, you must have been very shocked when you heard of what occurred in Otsu."

Nicholas groaned. "Shocked! I could hardly believe it. The entire *Pamiat Azova* was in a panic. I was desperate to know if my brother was safe. I could not rest."

"Were you worried for your brother?" Sherlock asked coldly. "Or were you more worried that the Emperor of Japan was on his way to see him? You received notice that he wished to check on your brother's well-being, I believe."

Nicholas closed his eyes and sighed deeply. "And my heart nearly fell out of my chest. I consulted with the officers and other attendants.

We decided I should switch with George before the Emperor arrived. He had been sent to Tokiwa Hotel—if we had admitted him to a hospital there would have been records. We snuck ashore in secret, and travelled to the hotel by carriage."

"Were you able to observe your brother's condition when you arrived?"

"Yes… He was in serious condition, and remained senseless. He still does, today."

The entire conversation had left Ito reeling. They had been notified at first that the injury was serious, and included damage to the skull. During His Grace's visit, however, they were told the injury was quite minor. As confusing as that discrepancy had been, Ito never imagined that the truth would be as strange as this.

Nicholas stared off into space. "I was uninjured, of course, but we wrapped my head in bandages. We arranged our story with the court physician in advance, before the Emperor arrived. George was transferred to the *Pamiat Azova*, then later to another ship, and then to a hospital in Vladivostok."

And this explained why Prince Takehito Arisugawa and the interpreter, Naohide Madenokoji, had not been admitted into the room. Naturally they could not be allowed inside. They still believed Nicholas was the younger brother.

"After the incident," Sherlock said, "the Emperor was not the only person you needed to deceive. There were reporters, as well."

"Yes, precisely. Originally we planned that I would go to Tokyo, and we could take photographs then. It would have looked strange if the military photographers had not taken any photos before the Otsu incident. After Siam, they might have been punished for forgetting their duties again."

Sherlock snorted. "Your Highness is very kind to worry."

Nicholas was offended. "We didn't mean any harm. We assumed the whole matter would remain secret."

"You summoned the two rickshaw drivers to the warship in order to falsify some photographs. That is why you asked them to wear

211

their rickshaw uniforms."

"You have worked it all out, I see. Yes. We paid the drivers a great sum, and awarded them with medals to keep them quiet after. We thought if we had given them a one-time reward they might have had second thoughts afterward. But a lifetime pension meant we could cut off their funds if they should ever let the secret slip."

"Very effective. I suspect your father had a hand in devising such a threat."

"Yes. I had hoped to keep the whole affair a secret from Father, but George was still senseless when we sent him to Vladivostok. We had no choice but to lay the whole thing bare. I had the captain send a wire to ask for Father's orders."

"The medal ceremony was not held until the evening. You invited the drivers aboard at noon. That was so you could sneak them from the ship and take your photographs."

"We lowered the boat from the starboard side in order to avoid detection. Disguising ourselves as commoners, we docked at a small fishing port where we took the photographs using a rickshaw we'd arranged for. I wore the same bowler and blazer that George had when he was in Otsu. We continued taking pictures until the sun dipped and began to set, at which point the photographer said it was too dark to take any more. We returned to the warship by boat, and held the medal ceremony then."

Now it finally makes sense, Ito thought. That must have been when the rickshaw drivers saw Mt. Fuji.

"After spending so much time taking fake photographs, I should think you would have more to show for it," Sherlock said in some astonishment. "You provided only two photographs to the newspapers."

"But if even a single passerby was in frame, someone might work out that the photographs were not taken when we said they were. We had to be sure nothing was behind us that could give away our location, and that the lighting generally matched my brother George's travels. So from all the pictures we took, we were left with only two photographs."

"You expressed gratitude to the Emperor for his visit. Before returning to Russia you also released a similar message in the newspapers, thanking the Japanese people."

"I was nearly moved to tears when I learned of the faith George had inspired in the people of Japan. My brother had truly loved this country. I had to continue expressing those same sentiments to some degree, in his place."

"I assume your true feelings were much less generous."

"Much less," Nicholas replied stiffly.

"Afterward," Sherlock prompted softly, "when the court released your diary…"

"It was Father's idea, to better establish the narrative of my travels in Japan."

"In your diary, however, you stated that none of the Japanese people came to your aid. The statement resulted in controversy."

"That's what my cousin Prince George of Greece said in his report. He insisted quite vehemently that it was he who saved my brother. It was also Prince George who told me that people along the road did not intervene."

"The people standing along the road had their heads bowed," Ito said. "Most of them didn't even see the attack when it happened. Once the commotion had begun and they had finally raised their heads, all they would have seen was a policeman—an officer of the law—running down the street. Of course they only watched. What else would you expect them to do?"

Nicholas raised his eyes to the ceiling. "You mean to tell me that the people did not recognize George because he was wearing ordinary clothes, whereas the familiar policeman projected an air of authority? Is that how the mind of a peasant works? I find that rather unpersuasive."

Sherlock didn't turn his gaze away from the Tsarevich. "The Japanese had hurt your brother. You hated them now more than ever. Correct?"

"Of course I hated them." Nicholas stared at Sherlock defiantly. "Perhaps it is wrong to say this in front of Chairman Ito, but you wanted me to be honest. I knew the Japanese were uncivilized barbarians before we even got here, just like the people in Siam and China. After the Otsu attack, I was still hopeful. I thought George would regain his senses before long. But his condition has grown worse! The doctors say they are unsure how to treat him, and there is no telling if he will ever recover…"

"You referred to the Japanese as monkeys?"

"They are damned monkeys, not even people. How many foreigners were slaughtered in this country, mere decades ago? They are savage yellow monkeys and I will never forgive them."

The hairs on the back of Ito's neck bristled. "Then you take no responsibility for sending your brother in your place? Of making a mockery of our country?"

Nicholas stood up, his eyes flashing with anger. "If my brother hadn't taken my place it would have been me who was attacked. The chauvinism of the Japanese, to protect the man who attacked my brother when you know he should be executed! I detest it!"

"We are not chauvinists! We are a country of laws!"

"Those are empty excuses. Tell me, what were you doing before the Meiji Restoration? Are you going to say you never supported *joui*, not even once? That you never spilled Western blood?"

Ito was silent. Not for lack of a counterargument, however. He knew Nicholas was only trying to change the subject, and he would not allow himself to be provoked. Westerners were quick to bring up *joui* when they wanted to portray themselves as victims and justify their aggression against Japan. However much Japan attempted to develop and progress, their reputation was still shackled to the Bakufu. Was it truly Japan, though, that had been high-handed? No. Rather, wasn't it the Western powers who had resorted to force to interfere in Asia?

Sherlock interceded, raising both hands. "Our only interest now is the truth. Tsarevich Nicholas, you were preoccupied by hatred of the Japanese, and a desire for revenge. The international community, however, has applauded you for your magnanimity. This only caused you further rage."

Nicholas looked down and sighed. "It was *galling*. And Father would not understand at all. He counseled me to be patient. Can you believe it? The ministers and generals all insisted that I abide. They are insane. Russia has been laying the groundwork to crush Japan for ages. Why else would we build the Siberian railway, or Vladivostok port?"

Chekhov shifted in discomfort. "Your Highness, with all due respect, I am afraid you have misunderstood His Imperial Majesty the Emperor's intentions. His Imperial Majesty, the ministers, the generals—all they wish for is peace. They would never pursue any actions they thought would lead to war."

"I don't believe you! I am not the only one who realizes the Japanese are damned monkeys. Important people—in the military, in the government—agree with me. Ever since I was a child, everyone I know has looked down on Japan. The only reason we do not act now is because they have the British backing them. Japan is ours for the taking, if only Father would not fear the Brits. You see, Chairman Ito even came here today with a British lapdog!"

Nicholas' angry voice reverberated. The quiet that ensued almost seemed itself like a sound. The more silent it was, the louder the pulsing in everyone's ears.

"So you demanded revenge against the Japanese," Sherlock said coolly, "but your father refused to lend you an ear. Instead, he ordered that you negotiate with the Siamese. You saw this as an opportunity to take action on your own. You anchored in Japan rather than Siam, and goaded Ambassador Shevich into reigniting disagreement over Tsuda's verdict. You hoped that you could pressure Japan until it broke."

"I wasn't acting alone. The captain of the ship sympathized with me."

"And your father probably predicted what you would do. This

215

explains why he did not allow you to take your imperial flagship. But you requested the largest escort you could, and then led your string of cruisers about like they were toys. You remind me of a boy who has run away from home dreaming of military glory."

Nicholas stepped forward and shouted in Sherlock's face. "You dog! You insolent English dog!"

"Am I as insolent as you were when you deceived the Emperor and King Rama V?" Sherlock said sharply. "Your behavior is not fitting of a crown prince. Protest all you like, but after such behavior I am afraid there are few foreign dignitaries who will find value in your opinion. Even now you flinch at shadows, and you are terrified that unless you get this tattoo upon your arm you will be undone. Your behavior in all this is beneath Japan's dignity."

Nicholas' face turned bright red. He raised his arms in the air, but made no attempt to swing at Sherlock—who towered over the Tsarevich. Instead Nicholas sat down again and cradled his head in his hands.

They heard a commotion from the hallway. Many footsteps approached and the door flew open with enough force to nearly tear it off its hinges.

Lt. Colonel Kanevsky rushed inside, accompanied by three guards. Ambassador Shevich came last.

Shevich glanced first at Ito, and then at Sherlock. Unbridled rage spread across his face. "It is the Queen's mongrel!" he shouted. "How dare you show yourself again! You have broken our agreement. I hope you are prepared now for the consequences!"

Kanevsky and his guards rushed to Nicholas' side. Nicholas remained slumped over in the chair. They seemed to be urging him to escape.

"A moment," Ito said to the ambassador. "You misunderstand."

"Chairman Ito, what on earth are you wearing?"

"Tsarevich Nicholas has confessed everything. Once you learn what he has done, you will realize your own behavior toward our country has been greatly in the wrong."

The Russians paused in confusion. Kanevsky cast a questioning look at Nicholas.

Nicholas rose solemnly to his feet. "I have no idea what they are referring to."

The guards stood at attention, though clearly confused. Nicholas walked past them, and headed for the door.

Shevich turned toward Ito again. "How can you claim Japan is a nation of laws when the Chairman of the Privy Council himself intrudes upon our private property? This is the Russian legation! What could possibly drive you to—"

"Stop!" Chekhov shouted.

Everyone fell silent. All eyes had turned toward Chekhov. There were rivulets of sweat running down his face.

Chekhov stared at Shevich, his face grave. "I heard it all. Unlike in May, it was not His Imperial Majesty the Emperor's will that we come here to call again for Sanzo Tsuda's execution. Tsarevich Nicholas has acted alone. Mr. Holmes laid out the facts just now, and His Highness the Tsarevich admitted they were true."

Shevich's eyes widened. Nicholas was already on his way out of the room, but he stopped, no doubt feeling the stares of disbelief from behind him. He stood motionless, his back turned.

Chekhov continued. "I believe... It seems His Highness the Tsarevich has misunderstood some of Russian policy. The Siberian railway, for instance. Russia has given Japan permission to use it for trade. It was not built to facilitate an invasion."

Anna began to speak as well, her voice high and flustered. "Grand Duke George is still senseless and incapacitated. In his grief, His Highness Tsarevich Nicholas has grown to resent Japan."

"What are you saying?" Shevich was stupefied. "I don't understand. What has happened to Grand Duke George?"

Ito's jaw dropped in amazement. The ambassador didn't know? Was he entirely unaware that Grand Duke George had posed as Nicholas to visit Japan?

It was possible, of course. Tokyo had been the only place Nicholas actually visited in person. He probably only met Ambassador Shevich during that portion of the trip.

And though Shevich undoubtedly rushed to Kyoto as soon as the Otsu incident occurred, by the time he arrived, Nicholas must have already taken George's place in the sickbed.

Chekhov sighed. "The entire crew of the *Pamiat Azova*—the captain, the attendants, even the sailors—were in on this. We were forbidden from telling you the truth, Ambassador. That we travelled with His Highness Grand Duke George on official business for the past four months, that he is resting in Paris… It was all a lie."

The color drained from Shevich's face. "You expect me to believe this?! By the time of the attack His Highness Grand Duke George had already returned home. I was told so by the Emperor himself!"

"We were following His Imperial Majesty the Emperor's orders! And His Highness the Tsarevich's, as well!" Chekhov's voice rose, and his red hair seemed increasingly disordered. "But we were wrong. We shouldn't have!"

The room fell silent again. This time no one broke it. Everyone stared at Nicholas with bated breath.

Finally, Kanevsky drew himself up. He spoke in Russian, but his voice sounded tentative. He seemed to be asking Nicholas a question.

Nicholas continued to face away. His reply was clipped. The guards glanced at each other as he exited to the hallway.

Chekhov turned to Ito with a haggard look. "His Highness asked that they see the guests outside."

Shevich and Kanevsky stared at each other, clearly at a loss.

Sherlock remained calm. "I called at the legation today to help correct your misunderstanding. You are of course welcome to reinstate our previous arrangement until such a time as reports of my death can be confirmed as false. I wish you a good day."

He left the room smoothly.

"Ambassador," Ito addressed Shevich. "My apologies for our sudden visit. I will take my leave now as well. Let us meet again in the coming days."

The other man remained stunned. Chekhov and Anna seemed exhausted, but also clearly relieved. The two had shown true courage. Ito bowed deeply, before turning and walking out the door.

25

The next morning, Sherlock sat at breakfast with the Ito family. He had changed into his morning jacket before joining them at the low table. It was eccentric, but this arrangement was already becoming second nature to him.

"No!" Asako said. "*Obasama* is Japanese for 'aunt.' 'Grandmother' is *Obaasama*."

Sherlock scowled as he worked his chopsticks. "I confess I do not see the difference."

Ito smiled. "It is the length of the vowel, Mr. Holmes. The first vowel sound is held for a beat longer."

Sherlock still could not hear the difference. It was a difficult difference for an English speaker. "How do you say mother?"

"*Okaasama*," Ikuko said.

"Hmph. But don't you call the gentleman across the way as Okasama?"

Asako and Ikuko glanced at each other and burst out laughing. "That's *Oka-san*. Mr. Oka," said Ikuko. "When being polite, you would address him as *Oka-sama*."

"You mean they are the same? Mother and Mr. Oka?"

"No, not the same!" Ito's daughters were still laughing when they were interrupted by a voice from outside, speaking Japanese in a foreign accent.

"Sumimasen!"

One of the servants trotted to the gate. A moment later he returned and approached the veranda. Umeko stood and spoke with him in Japanese.

"A Mr. Chekhov and Ms. Luzhkova are here, from the Russian legation," she said, turning back toward the room.

The air of surprise was palpable. Ito rose to his feet. He and Sherlock put on their shoes at the front door and stepped outside.

Indeed, Chekhov and Anna stood outside the gate. Though they still had a timid air, they seemed calmer now than they had the day before. Ito asked them to enter the garden.

"Will you join us for breakfast?" he invited.

"No thank you," Chekhov said, slowing his steps. "We are only stopping by on our way to work."

"It seems very early. Is something wrong?" Sherlock asked.

The two Russians looked at each other before turning back. "We wanted to tell you our news in person. Once we return to Russia, Ms. Luzhkova and I will be resigning from the Ministry of State Property."

Ito furrowed his brow. "Resigning? Can this be because of yesterday…"

Anna shook her head. "Not at all. Tsarevich Nicholas was angry, but Ambassador Shevich knows we are not to blame. We have chosen to resign of our own volition."

Chekhov nodded. "Chairman Ito, Mr. Holmes, after your visit I feel as if a great weight has been lifted from our shoulders. It has truly been a relief."

Sherlock thought he knew what they meant. Neither had said so much, but they must have felt a deep sense of guilt over their role in Nicholas' deception. The two were sincere and retiring by nature— ill-suited to meet the weight of Nicholas' expectations. But it was fortunate that, as a result, the truth had finally come to light.

"And you truly haven't incurred Ambassador Shevich's displeasure?" Ito wanted to confirm.

They smiled. "Ambassador Shevich says that the scales have fallen from his eyes," Anna said. "He said that even if you *are* here to help establish an intelligence agency for Japan, he is grateful for being given the chance to learn of the truth… He wondered if he ought to express his thanks directly to Ambassador Fraser."

"No need, I assure you," Sherlock said quickly. "Thanks are unnecessary. Please advise Ambassador Shevich to maintain his distance where England is concerned. It is probably for the best that Russia and Britain remain rivals in the Far East, and that our legations stay on their toes when in one another's presence."

Anna looked confused. "Truly? But you seemed so interested in peace…"

"Of course I am." Sherlock cleared his throat. "But I am a realist, that is all."

The Chairman intervened. "What Mr. Holmes means to say is that it is probably best we not force Ambassadors Shevich and Fraser together unnecessarily, as the two are unlikely to get along."

"Oh," Anna said, uncertainly. "If you think that is best then I shall tell the ambassador so."

Sherlock nodded. "Please do. And as Ambassador Fraser is very busy, if there is any information Ambassador Shevich would like to share with the British, I would be happy to make myself available in Ambassador Fraser's place. I know that they are still awaiting confirmation about those reports of my death, but until then, should he have any use for my talents, I am sure that I could be of assistance—well, contingent upon any particulars, of course."

Chekhov fixed his eyes on the English detective. "I'm pleased you say so. In truth, Ambassador Shevich was curious if you knew anything of a man named Olgert Bercerosky?"

"Bercerosky… I'm afraid it is the first time I am hearing that name."

"I see. The Russian police, too, have uncovered very little beside his name. We know that he is an agitator for the Second International, and that he has taken cover in Japan—nothing more."

The Second International—a worldwide socialist organization formed two years prior. Its predecessor, First International, had antagonized the Anarchists, who still exerted a strong influence in France, and been dissolved 15 years earlier as a result.

"The Second International advocates for issues such as 8-hour workdays and the formation of militias," Ito said. "They are hardly extremists. They want May Day to be a public holiday, they organize labor movements...activities on that level. I don't know what you mean by agitator, but he can hardly be dangerous."

Chekhov's eyes fell on Ito. "I can't say for sure, but in addition to being a Marxist it seems this Bercerosky fellow believes in violent revolution. There is a rumor abroad that it was he who commissioned Sanzo Tsuda to assassinate Tsarevich Nicholas, and that he later murdered Tsuda after Tsuda's failure, so as to prevent him from talking... Though in my opinion it all sounds rather fanciful."

Anna smirked too. "Ambassador Shevich heard these rumors through the police, but ignored them. But last night seems to have shaken him. After he learned that Tsarevich Nicholas and His Highness Grand Duke George had switched places, I suppose now anything seems possible."

Ito nodded, his expression composed. "I understand. I will pass the matter on to Police Chief Sonoda."

Sherlock observed that Ito was certainly a skilled politician, with an impressive poker face. But he was likely quite alarmed by what he had just heard.

Tsuda's death had yet to be publicly announced, though naturally the information had already been disclosed to the Russians. If Tsuda really had been assassinated, it was important they investigate this Bercerosky.

"One more thing if I may, while we are here," Chekhov said. "Last night, after Tsarevich Nicholas returned to the *Laskar*, Ambassador Shevich wired to Russia. It was decided... We were hoping... that Japan might keep all this a secret? We would like to keep the fact that Tsarevich Nicholas and the Grand Duke switched places, as well as the Grand Duke's condition, a secret from the world at large."

Ito frowned. "I am surprised the ambassador would ask you two, who are resigning soon, to carry out such negotiations."

"No, no, of course. Please give your answer directly to the

ambassador. Ms. Luzhkova and I only wished to be of further use to our country."

"His Imperial Majesty the Emperor even expressed his desire that Japan might accept some asset from Russia on his behalf," Anna added.

Sherlock chuckled. "You mean to say that His Majesty wishes to inform us that, like the rickshaw drivers, our silence will be handsomely rewarded."

"Yes." Chekhov sounded a little sheepish. "Of course, money or land would prove difficult. I hope you understand."

But Sherlock immediately thought of one thing that wasn't land or money. A laugh escaped his lips.

Ito seemed to be on the same page. "Indeed," he said to Chekhov, a twinkle in his eyes, "I think I know just what to request."

"I'm afraid it won't do very much good to tell us," the other man said shyly. "It would be better if you spoke to Ambassador Shevich directly…"

"No," Ito said, with a satisfied grin. "I believe the Russian Ministry of State Property is precisely the party with whom I need to speak."

26

Two days a later, at a little past noon, there was something of a ceremony held in the Russian Ambassador's office: An official signing, with Lt. Colonel Kanevsky and a number of soldiers in attendance. On the Japanese side there were ten people present, including Chairman Ito, Munemitsu Mutsu (the Minister of Commerce and Agriculture), and Police Chief Sonoda. Nicholas was not there.

Sherlock watched from a corner as Ambassador Shevich and Minister Mutsu signed at a desk in the middle of the room.

Kanevsky looked at Sherlock occasionally, not without a pained expression, but made no attempt to chase him from the room. Under the circumstances, their previous agreement appeared to be moot.

Once the signing was finished, Shevich and Mutsu stood. Chekhov and Anna immediately entered, together carrying a book so large it would have been impossible for one person to handle. The volume was bound in red leather with gold leaf, and the title was embossed in Russian. It was a copy of the latest edition of *The Complete Work on Russian Natural Sciences*.

"I present this book to you as a sign of our good faith, and of the friendship between Russia and Japan," Shevich said to Mutsu, in English.

Two Japanese officials stepped forward and received the book.

"Ambassador Shevich," said Mutsu, obviously pleased, "you have my deepest gratitude. Our country is at a great deficit in regards to the natural sciences. This book shall provide a tremendous boost to our research."

Shevich's own smile was wry. "I am happy to be of use. But you should be thanking Mr. Chekhov and Ms. Luzhkova, who persuaded the Ministry of State Property to agree to the trade."

"If you have difficulty translating any of the passages," Chekhov said, his smile as wide as his face, "collect all the questions together and we'll handle them. I'm delighted we were able to share this book with you."

His emotion was understandable, considering that this was his last official act in government. And it was no small achievement, at that. Anna, too, had been moved to tears.

Afterwards, the room hummed with relaxed conversation. Police Chief Sonoda approached. "Mr. Holmes. You must forgive my rudeness. When we met earlier at the Chairman's house I did not realize that I was meeting *the* Sherlock Holmes. I heard that you had passed away."

Sherlock looked around to see if anyone was listening, and then placed his index finger to his mouth. "Until the article erroneously reporting my death can be corrected, I hope that your police department will refrain from contacting Scotland Yard."

"I assure you I understand. Chairman Ito was quite insistent on that point, as well."

"Chairman Ito appears very concerned over maintaining a separation of powers and modernizing Japan, but I see that he is more than capable of influencing the police force," Sherlock teased lightly.

"Chairman Ito is an exceptional case. His clout is evident in a multitude of areas, and across various branches of government. But he is no dictator. He respects our opinions and does not abuse his power. Chairman Ito and the head of the Supreme Court of Judicature, Judge Kojima, have each grown to appreciate the other's importance."

"Yes, he is a splendid man." Sherlock gave Sonoda a sidelong glance. "Tell me, what cases have occupied the police as of late?"

"There is one very odd case. Lately there's been a rash of burglaries over the country. But only worthless, common household items are stolen."

"Indeed. I myself read an article detailing such thefts. Pottery, dolls, and woodblock prints, I believe."

"Recently, the thefts have largely been of things like paper fans, kimonos, sandals. Looking at the range and frequency of the crimes, we believe they're committed by a single man. The thief strikes a number of houses on a single day, all within walking distance, and then moves onto a different neighborhood the following day. But oddly, he only takes items of little worth."

"Very strange, indeed. Incidentally," Sherlock asked, glancing around carefully and then lowering his voice, "were you able to determine the cause of Sanzo Tsuda's death?"

Sonoda was equally hushed. "The original assessment seems to hold. It was illness."

"Has a funeral been held? I was hoping to view the body."

"I don't see how it could be transported to Tokyo…"

"You misunderstand. I hope to go in person."

"To Kushiro Prison?" Sonoda was aghast. "*Yourself*?"

"I should like to make a thorough inspection of the conditions under which Tsuda expired. Perhaps you might make the arrangements…"

Footsteps drew near and Sherlock broke off. Ito and Shevich approached.

Shevich's expression was complicated and hard to decipher. "Mr. Holmes. Ambassador Fraser has certainly chosen his emissary well. No one from the British legation was invited, but as Chairman Ito's foreign consultant you were of course free to attend this ceremony."

"Indeed," Sherlock bluffed boldly. "If you have any messages for Ambassador Fraser I should be pleased to convey them. And vice versa of course."

"Vice versa?"

"I refer to Ambassador Fraser's own wishes. Britain desires a copy of *The Complete Work on Russian Natural Sciences* as well."

"Britain? Why would Britain wish for a copy?"

"Supplement B. What Russia receives from Japan, Britain shall receive as well."

"That agreement is between Britain and Japan… If you have any claims to make, they should be made with Japan, not with us."

"But your country has asked Japan to protect a secret. Unfortunately, the British royal family has suffered no similar scandal and thus had no need to ask Japan's silence. Instead, Britain should like to request an asset of similar value."

"That is utter sophistry!"

"Japan, of course, will keep its promise. They would never transfer or sell *The Complete Work on Russian Natural Sciences* to another country. Hence why we prefer to receive our copy from Russia, ensuring everything remain above board. Surely you could provide a second copy."

"The presumption! Why should Russia give Britain a copy of the book?"

"Have you forgotten? Japan is not the only country that has been made aware of Tsarevich Nicholas' curious behavior. Britain now knows, as well."

Shevich's face turned sour. "So you are saying if I deliver a copy, your country will also keep this information to themselves?"

"Naturally. I should prefer, however, if we avoid any official ceremonies like the one held just now. Ambassador Fraser does not wish to be publicly involved. I am afraid you must rely on my own good offices."

"The Queen's shrewd and slavish mongrel… You are treacherous indeed, Holmes," Shevich spat, all attempts at politeness gone. He turned on his heel and left.

Ito leaned in close, his expression dubious. "The *Complete Work*? Considering the differences in your natural environments, what use would Britain have for such a book?"

"None. I wish to read it myself," Sherlock muttered. "It includes analyses of soil and rainfall, descriptions of the variety of rocks… Until I learn to analyze natural phenomena here in an appropriately scientific manner, my powers of deduction shall all be for naught."

27

Ito and Sonoda made arrangements for Sherlock to visit Kushiro Prison. He boarded the steam engine at Shinagawa alone, and travelled north via Nippon Railway.

He was riding first class. The carriage's design mimicked that of a British rail car. The seats were wider than those on the train Holmes had taken from Yokohama to Shimbashi; perhaps the designers had anticipated foreigners taking this line. The carriage was brand new, and surprisingly, shook minimally during travel. The ride was much more pleasant than any currently offered by British rail.

The Japanese railway had been extended to Aomori just this month; Ito's tenacious pursuit of modernizing the country, and in particular his fixation with rail transit, was producing results. In the only 24 years since the Meiji Restoration, a major artery already joined Tokyo to northern Japan. Such rapid development was unheard of in any other country. The speed with which the Japanese had adopted these technologies was impressive.

The journey to Aomori would be long—18 hours one way. But Sherlock did not find it at all tedious. He devoted 70 percent of his mental powers to the case before him; he used the remaining 30 percent to analyze and process the various points of visual information. The scenery from the train window was fascinating: Pine trees lined the tracks, and beyond them, sprawling farm lands. When thatched roofs gave way to tiled ones and Sherlock began to see the occasional wagon, the steam engine slowed.

They were approaching a station. The train was making a stop at Shinjuku.

A wide road stretched from the station. There were no Western buildings in sight, only rows of single-story Japanese structures. He saw signs for a blacksmith, a soba restaurant, and a goldfish vendor—with characters he had memorized when he'd been in Ginza. There were not so many people on the streets here as there were in Ginza, and the ones who were were dressed in Japanese clothing. They milled around at a relaxed pace.

Sherlock turned his eyes away from the window and observed his fellow passengers. Intriguingly, he could not form deductions about them as quickly as he might have in London. As first-class passengers, most of them were fastidious with their appearance. Sherlock in particular could not understand why one seated woman, wearing a dress, did not lean back against her chair. Instead she leaned forward, her back stiff.

When they reached Ikebukuro Station, a woman in Japanese garb boarded the train. The broad sash that this woman wore about her waist was tied at her back. At last Sherlock understood. In order to preserve the artful manner in which the sash had been arranged, she had to constantly lean forward as she sat. The women wearing the dress had developed that same habit, and Sherlock concluded that she must generally wear Japanese clothing.

A vendor on the station platform was selling boxed lunches. Sherlock opened his window and called out to the vendor, who quickly approached. "*This-u, is-u, bento*," the vendor said, smiling and repeating himself several times.

He remained in the vicinity of the first-class carriages. As might have been expected, the lunch Sherlock purchased was very high quality. There was steak, as well as several items Sherlock was familiar with from Ito's table: Kyoto-style grilled fish, eel and tofu, grilled and glazed cuttlefish, kamaboko fish cakes… The items varied in shape and amount, but all had been neatly packed into the box so there was no space left to spare. It was all very Japanese. The taste, too, was delicious, as though freshly prepared. When Sherlock had been crossing the Dover Strait to attend on the French government, he had met a Parisian industrialist, who claimed the English had no appreciation for fine cuisine. Sherlock now felt he understood what that man had meant. Though he by no means wished to disparage Mrs. Hudson, he often found himself without appetite in London, and now he wondered if it wasn't the food that might be at fault.

Thus absorbed in deduction and observation, Sherlock passed the time quickly. The sun set and it became night. The female passengers did not hesitate to sleep in their seats—testament to how safe the country had become. Nor did anyone attempt to sneak aboard the first-class carriage without buying a ticket, an inevitable occurrence on British trains. Ito had told him the fine for sneaking onboard was exorbitant, but this was true in England as well; the people of Japan seemed more naturally averse to causing trouble. Of course criminals still existed, but in general there seemed to be a deep-seated appreciation of the group and observance of the rules.

As dawn broke, Sherlock saw a grand mountain range spring into view from beyond the train window. The only signs of human activity were the occasional thatched roof or country ranch. What remained was unspoiled nature, sprawling as far as the eye could see. In contrast with Tokyo, the distance between each station stop was long. The steam engine puffed along at full speed.

Still, Sherlock never felt fatigue when in pursuit for a case, no matter how great the distance travelled. The train passed through Shiruchi Station, before finally arriving at its final stop, Aomori.

He exited the wooden station house and passed through a throng of travellers, before entering an area swarming with livestock and freight wagons. The atmosphere immediately felt more laidback than in Tokyo. Sonoda had arranged for escorts from both the Aomori Prefectural Police Department and Kushiro Police Department to meet him at the station. Included in the group was a Captain Saito, of the Kushiro Police. Captain Saito spoke English. Sherlock was grateful that they'd be able to communicate; he left for Kushiro with them directly, on one of the police ferries.

Though it was only September, it was so cold that a layer of ice had formed across the sea. The cold was a reminder of how close they were to Russia. A misty haze filled the air, through which gradually floated into view a gray mass of land. Hokkaido. Charles Scott Meik, a British engineer working for the prefecture, had recently advanced plans for the construction of a port at Kushiro. The project had only recently gotten underway. At present there was no more than a provisional wharf. There was no modern port town in which they could disembark, but the police had arranged for a carriage. Once they descended on land, they boarded without a moment's delay, heading overland for the nearby town of Shibecha.

The sun was now setting for a second time and they were emerging from a forest, when Sherlock finally caught sight of a massive facility, located beyond the trees. It looked like a small town: Several dozen buildings were arranged at regular intervals. The carriage pulled up alongside one such building, which from the outside looked like a Western-style mansion. It was equipped with sash windows and possessed a protruding arch over the main entrance.

This was Kushiro Prison's administrative building. Inside, Sherlock met with the warden, or director, of the prison. He was a nervous man in his early thirties, named Teruchika Oinoue. For a man in a position of power in such a cold environment, he seemed more naturally solicitous than might have been expected. Apart from basic introductions, however, he spoke no English. A second man, in his late twenties and dressed in what resembled a priest's cassock, was also present. He was the Christian chaplain of the prison, Taneaki Hara, and he did understand English.

Oinoue led the way, and the group was shown to Tsuda's old solitary cell. "Before, it was the same here as at other prisons," Hara explained as they walked. "The prisoners were forced to carry out grueling labor to develop the area. There were many senseless practices, like abandoning prisoners who collapsed to be eaten by wild animals. Since Warden Oinoue's appointment, however, the prison has been remodeling itself in the Western fashion, with respect for the humanity of those incarcerated."

The lone building they arrived at resembled a mountain cabin. The exterior consisted of stacked logs. The door had been left half open. Sherlock stepped inside. There was nobody here. The floor was made of hard concrete and the interior walls were covered in wooden boards that left no gaps exposed. It looked very sturdy.

"Yes, of course," Sherlock murmured. "I see you spoke the truth."

"Pardon?" Hara inquired.

"I said you spoke the truth earlier. In prisons where the inmates are treated poorly, the cells are in an atrocious state. And it's clear you did not clean this room just for my arrival; otherwise, the smell of solvent would still be lingering. There is no smell, therefore the room has been regularly kept clean."

"I see. Well..."

"When did Tsuda arrive?"

"July 2. He was transported from Otsu Prison to Baba Station on May 31. He was then sent by train to Hyogo Karyukan. On June 27 he was transported to Hokkaido with 119 other serious offenders, via a Japan Mail steamer called the *Wakanouchi-maru*."

"Hmm." Sherlock took a look around the cell. "The note, the one that appears to be a will? It was found in this room?"

"That's correct. After Tsuda was transported to the sickroom, Warden Oinoue searched the room and discovered it."

"Where did he find it?"

Hara asked Oinoue a question in Japanese. Oinoue replied, and Hara turned back. "It was hidden in that corner, beneath a blanket."

Sherlock leaned down to inspect the floor. There was a visible stain, probably from when Tsuda had been coughing blood. He lifted his head. "Where is the will, now?"

Captain Saito answered. "Earlier, it was sent to Kushiro Headquarters for keeping as evidence, but they sent it back once it was determined that Tsuda died of illness."

"It is now stored in the sickroom," Hara added. "The one where he was housed."

Sherlock stood up. "Please, show me there now."

The sickroom was even cleaner than the cell had been, and differed very little from patient rooms at any ordinary clinic. The bed, where Tsuda had breathed his last, had been preserved in its final state.

Sherlock had very little interest in the bed, however. The mat was covered with marks as if it had been clutched at and torn. A quick glance at it told him all he needed to know.

The officers gave him Tsuda's will. He glanced at the piece of paper. A few brief lines had been scrawled in Japanese. "Where did he acquire the paper?" he asked Hara.

"It was handed out during English lessons in the chaplain's office. He must have snuck one of the sheets out. Same for the brush and ink. We do not use Western pens. Anything with a point could be used as a weapon."

"This is very interesting," Sherlock said, staring at the note. "I cannot read Japanese, but that allows me to better focus on the penmanship. There are six locations where the characters are particularly disordered. It appears as if he suffered a coughing fit at each. The pressure and tilt of his hand changes several times throughout the note, indicating that he shifted from side to side as he wrote. He would have been searching for a position in which his breathing was more comfortable. This is exactly indicative of acute pneumonia."

Hara nodded. "He had a fever of nearly 40 degrees Celsius and slept poorly. His breathing grew difficult, and his lips turned purple and blue. The doctor said there was no doubt that it was acute pneumonia."

"Where is the body?"

"In the mortuary." Hara glanced to Oinoue. Oinoue ushered them toward the door.

Without heating, the prison would have been freezing. These were excellent conditions for a mortuary.

Tsuda's body was well kept.

It was laid out on a wood slab, as on a bed, with a white kimono draped over it. Uncovering the body was a simple affair. *This is much more efficient than how things were done at the London morgue,* Sherlock thought. He inspected the body thoroughly, his face mere inches from the dead man's skin.

Compared to the photograph he'd seen of Tsuda, his face in death appeared drawn and wasted. The same was true of his body. Sherlock observed bits of string and rusted metal beneath the fingernails. They matched the marks on his bed.

"I see now why you never doubted Tsuda's illness," he murmured. "I am surprised you did not tie him to the bed, considering how much he must have writhed. From the marks and scratches along his body, I assume that his hands were left free."

"To be honest, it was impossible not to sympathize with him toward the end," Hara sighed. "His suffering was difficult to watch."

There was a scar on Tsuda's neck. "What caused this injury?" Sherlock pointed it out.

"That was left by the rickshaw driver, when Tsuda attacked Tsarevich Nicholas. Apparently it was quite painful. He would often double over and press his hand to the scar."

"He wasn't always kept in solitary, was he? Did he interact with the other prisoners?"

"Certainly there was some interaction, but Tsuda spoke very little. And the others seemed to find him off-putting. Warden Oinoue and I took pains to engage him in conversation, and he had just been starting to speak very slightly more. His comments, however, did not differ much from what he wrote in his will. He'd ask us to send his money back to his family, or obsess over the future of Japan."

"There are marks on his neck and ankles, as if from restraints. And there is a hole in his ear."

"Prisoners are required to wear collars and shackles. There are no exceptions, even for simple work such as straw making. The shackles are attached to a round weight. The hole in the ear is connected to the legs via a chain. It is called a *tagane*, and is used to cause pain to prisoners who attempt to escape."

"So is this what you meant earlier, when you said you respect prisoners' humanity?"

"We take pains to treat them humanely, but the prisoners here are serious offenders. Relaxing all of our methods immediately would be difficult."

"Doubtless." Sherlock straightened up. "Tsuda was a simple and unskilled man. Judging from the range of scars along his body he had been involved in several life-threatening battles throughout his career. He was likely proud of his life as a soldier, and I imagine he took it poorly when his Order of Merit was revoked. Judging from the color of his skin his liver was failing. Did he drink?"

Hara shook his head. "Not very much."

"Then it is possible he used sedatives heavily. They would have decreased the functioning of his liver and depressed his immune system, which in turn may have led to acute pneumonia."

Saito nodded. "The Shibecha Prison medical chief kept detailed daily notes. He wrote comments to that same effect. It seems it was a series of unfortunate coincidences."

"We must not be hasty, however," Sherlock said softly. "There is no guarantee his death was accidental. If someone had commissioned the attack on Nicholas, we must allow for the possibility that this person learned that Tsuda's constitution had been weakened through his psychiatric treatment, and took advantage of it."

"How could a third party have learned of such a thing?"

Sherlock's thoughts came together quickly. "Would you wire Police Chief Sonoda?" he requested of Saito. "Tsuda was admitted to the hospital several times for mental illness. Inquiries will need to be made with each of the hospitals he was at. We must look into how their records are kept, and who in the hospitals would have access to them."

Saito took out his notepad and began writing with a pencil. "Of course. Is there anything else?"

"Foreigners residing in Kanto, engaged in private commercial trading. Inform Police Chief Sonoda that I would like a list drawn up. Two young Russian men working together must be particularly suspicious, but it is possible they have falsified their nationality."

"Are you referring to the two Russians who were seen with Tsuda? But why commercial trading?"

"A string of trivial thefts has occurred recently throughout Tokyo prefecture. Until lately the thefts focused on pottery, dolls, and woodblock prints. The culprit has now moved on to paper fans, kimonos, and sandals. These are common household items with no particular value. No particular value, that is, to a Japanese person."

"You believe the thief is a foreigner?"

"As a Westerner, to me it makes immediate sense. Japan has only been open for 20 years, and goods imported from here are the fashion now in Europe. Russia is very close, and smuggling ships could be sent back and forth quite frequently. Such a haul would prove a feast for any commercial trader. Popular demand would likely begin with furnishings and decorations before moving on to personal items and clothing."

"You believe that someone is sourcing goods from Japan in response to Russian demand?"

"The thief strikes repeatedly, moving from location to location throughout Kanto. He would need to lay low somewhere in the country, and support himself with money garnered from his thefts. It is highly possible that one of the young Russians is a man known as Olgert Bercerosky."

Saito's eyes lit up. "I will send a wire immediately."

Sherlock silently looked down at Tsuda's face. It was puckered and drawn, like a dried fish. One act of violence, at Tsuda's hand, had created a network of cracks in the foundation beneath the relationship between Japan and Russia. Thanks to Russia's forbearance, they had averted a serious conflict. But was the danger truly over?

28

Ito and Minister Mutsu walked along the red carpeted floor of the Ministry of Agriculture and Commerce annex. The spacious hall, which faced the corridor along which they walked, was lined with rows of desks at which some 100 professionals were busy at work.

The Complete Work on Russian Natural Sciences had 80 chapters. Each individual chapter had been divided into further sections, with translators assigned to each. In addition to familiarity with the Russian language, the translation also required a range of specialist knowledge. Translators from universities throughout the country had been invited to join the effort.

"With 100 translators on the job," Mutsu reported, "progress is proceeding swimmingly."

Ito nodded. "This large-scale approach is very effective."

"I was inspired by how you handled the railways. At this rate we will soon make up any gaps in our understanding of the natural sciences."

"But I was told you had something specific to tell me?"

"Yes, if you will allow me. Kubo, the project director, should be joining us soon… Ah, here he is!"

A man about 30 years in age, a batch of papers bundled under either arm, scurried towards them. "Minister Mutsu, Chairman Ito," he wheezed. "Welcome. Welcome. This is amazing. The Russians have nearly proven that a mother's breast milk contains immunological properties. In Europe they are only just *beginning* to research this!"

Mutsu held up a hand to calm him. "Slowly, Mr. Kubo. I understand that all this new scientific knowledge is very exciting, but we must prioritize items that most affect the national interest. Do you believe the *Complete Work* will be of use?"

"Without a doubt," Kubo affirmed, smiling broadly. "In Russia they have demonstrated that when the feeding hierarchy in a river or other body of water is disturbed and a single species increases inordinately, that same species will also suddenly die off in great numbers. This explains the recent mass deaths of ayu fish."

Ito smiled. "I see. Has there been anything else?"

"Near certain volcanic chains, trees have been withering in huge patches. The Ministry of Home Affair's Hygienic Bureau has been at a loss to explain it. According to this book, however, the cause appears to be the influence of underground lava activity. The lava robs the soil of the nutrient- and water-retention abilities that such plants require to grow. Seeds can fail to germinate, or, even if they do germinate, they will wither soon after. In Russia, this phenomenon is known as...*vastock*...er ...*vin* ..."

Mutsu frowned. "Never mind what it is called. At any rate, it sounds as if we can expect significant progress to be made in the natural sciences?"

"By leaps and bounds! We also have an indication as to why rice in the paddies near hot spring regions can wither. Spring water with high levels of hydrochloric acid has likely surfaced nearby and contaminated the rice paddies. If we redirect the waterways we can avoid this crop failure. In short, we expect we will now be able to solve many issues we have been struggling with!"

Ito was somewhat overwhelmed by his enthusiasm. "Indeed. Well, thank you for your report."

Kubo bowed deeply, his excitement clearly unabated, and quickly returned to the great hall.

"That is a relief," Mutsu said, a smile teasing at his lips. "After all the money we spent hiring translators, it would have been my head on the chopping block if the book had proven useless."

"Come now," Ito laughed. "Surely the expense was less than we bargained for. After all, we acquired *The Complete Work on Russian Natural Sciences* free of charge."

"That was indeed a surprise. As far as I was aware, our relationship with Russia has grown cold. I wonder what explains this windfall."

Ito didn't say anything. Only a limited number of people knew the truth of the attack against Tsarevich Nicholas. In the cabinet, that included only Prime Minister Matsukata. Mutsu was almost certainly unaware of the truth.

Police Chief Sonoda approached from the opposite end of the corridor and greeted them. "Chairman Ito. Regarding the list of foreign commercial traders…"

Ito had already received word that Sherlock was on his way back to Tokyo. Police headquarters had received the detective's telegraph and were already working to identify anyone in the prefecture who might match his description. Ito glanced at Sonoda. "Do you have a list of names?"

"We do. In fact…" Sonoda's voice brimmed with pride. "We have already narrowed it down to one suspect."

"Come again?!"

Ito was confident that Japan was the equal of other nations when it stubbornly hunted down perpetrators. Of this he had no doubt—and yet, he had feared that they were not as sophisticated with modern investigative techniques as they might be. But the fact that the police had found this suspect without any assistance from Sherlock was very reassuring. Assuming, of course, that they were correct.

Ito sat in one of the meeting rooms at Police Services Kajibashi Secondary Facilities, listening to Sonoda's briefing. A map had been spread out on the table, and the police chief was explaining, with great relish—and considerable showmanship—precisely how they had managed to narrow down their suspects for the Russian thefts.

The room was crammed with top police officials and investigators. Ito, however, was most interested in the reaction of one man. Sherlock Holmes had only just returned from his trip to Hokkaido.

He leaned back in his chair in the corner of the room, puffing away at his pipe. His long legs were crossed, one foot suspended languidly in space.

"I will now ask Captain Minezaki to explain the details," Sonoda said. "Captain, if you please."

Minezaki, standing next to Sonoda, looked to be in his thirties, with a sturdy, florid face. Minezaki pointed to a small scrap of paper that had been folded into four. "This is a ticket for Kirin beer. They are distributed by a drinking house in Kyobashi to customers who want to pay in advance. The ticket has the name and address of the person to whom it was delivered. This particular ticket's owner had hidden it inside a doll's clothing, as he did not wish his family to scold him for his drinking. The doll was stolen mid-month. We determined that this ticket was recently turned in to a police box in Chofu Village. It had been found on the ground in a nearby field. The ink has been smeared—likely from sweat, from being in a man's pocket as he ran away."

Ito walked over to Sherlock. "You must find this boring, unable to understand what they are saying. Shall I translate?"

"Not at all," Sherlock said, remaining seated as he let out a puff of smoke from his pipe. "I can surmise his meaning well enough from his gestures. That ticket was secreted in one of the items that was stolen, and was then later found at some other location."

"You have it precisely." Ito redirected his attention back toward Minezaki.

Minezaki was tracing the tip of a pencil along the map. "The ticket was found in this area. A foreign trader lives not a hundred yards from the spot. Furthermore, the foreigner in question is a young male of Russian origin. Based on other information we have received, it is possible that this is the revolutionary known as Olgert Bercerosky, who may have been involved in the attack perpetrated by Sanzo Tsuda. As this man is suspected of serious crimes, I urge you all to exercise caution…"

"What is he saying?" Sherlock asked.

"A Russian trader lives near where the ticket was found."

Sherlock suddenly stood up, exasperated. He approached the table. Minezaki was in the middle of an animated explanation. He broke off mid-sentence, disconcerted.

"Mr. Holmes," said Sonoda in English. "Is there something you wish to add?"

Ito joined Sherlock, who was staring down at the map. Chofu Village was a mixture of housing and farmland. A mark, which indicated the field where the ticket had been found, was placed on a location a little over a hundred yards from Tama River. The home where the Russian trader lived was not far.

Sherlock picked up one of the pencils and drew a small circle around a point on the opposite shore of the river. "Here. I think you shall find much local gossip about this vicinity, due to the inhabitant's frequent and unusual chemical experiments."

A gasp spread through the room. Sonoda looked puzzled. "Nakabaru Village? There is nothing there but pear orchards and a few farmhouses."

Sherlock was undeterred. "Then if a foreigner is living in the area, he shall certainly stand out all the more."

"Impossible," Minezaki said in Japanese. He frowned sharply. One of his men had been interpreting into his ear while Sherlock spoke. "The Tama River is far too wide, and that location is nowhere near the Maruko Ferry Crossing. After carrying out robberies in Kyobashi, why would he go to the trouble of making a detour through Chofu? Nothing was even stolen from Chofu."

"None of the foreign traders on our list live in Nakabaru," an assistant inspector said, staring down at a bundle of papers.

"It may be a temporary address," Ito said in Japanese. "Or he may have lied about his profession."

Sherlock interrupted. He may not have understood Japanese, but he could guess well enough what they were saying. "I asked you to search for foreign traders residing in Kanto, but I was not suggesting that the culprit could only be a merchant. Though highly probable, it was merely a starting point from which to begin our investigation."

Sonoda hesitated. "I will contact the Kanagawa police force, and ask for their cooperation …"

"Private detectives," muttered Minezaki, disgruntled. "In the end they are all amateurs." He stalked off in a huff.

"Would you like me to translate what he said?" asked Ito.

"Consulting detectives are all amateurs, or something to that effect I assume."

Ito seemed surprised. "You understood his Japanese?"

"Of course not," Sherlock said, chewing his pipe nonchalantly. "I have heard the same often enough before."

29

Ito also insisted on joining the investigation party. Police Chief Sono-da was none too thrilled by this. It was not so much the danger as the fact that Ito's attendance meant that he, too, would be forced to go.

But because Sherlock would be coming with them, Ito wished to ascertain the truth with his own two eyes. They would perform their raid early in the morning, so as not to interfere with the remainder of the day's work—of course, assuming that everything went smoothly.

An early mist hung in the air. Several police carriages travelled along a rutted wagon road that connected the pear orchards beside the Tama River.

Ito was in the rearmost carriage, with Sherlock sitting next to him. The detective's eyes remained closed throughout the entire ride. He showed no signs of tension. Ito glanced at Sherlock's profile and sighed. It almost looked as if he was sleeping. Considering that Sherlock had never been to the area before, Ito would have thought he'd be taking a closer look at the surroundings. What happened to the importance of observation?

The carriage slowly ground to a halt. Sherlock opened his eyes. Ito, likewise, glanced out the window. Several policemen were now disembarking from the lead carriage. Some feet away from where the carriages had stopped, a crude, single-story wooden structure jutted from the earth. Captain Minezaki gave orders to secure the area.

Four days had passed since the meeting at the police headquarters. After several inquiries, the Kanagawa Police Department had learned of a foreigner in the area who was renting the storehouse of a certain farm. Interviewees had spoken of strange smells in the area. The man's name was Yevno Tzybin. Supposedly he was using the storehouse to pursue oil painting. According to the rental agreement, Tzybin lived somewhere else, but the residential address listed proved to be nonsensical. It did not exist.

Though Minezaki had at first been disgruntled, he rose to the occasion without reservation. It did seem unlikely that these circumstances could be mere chance. That said, he had yet to fully warm up to Sherlock.

Not that one could blame him, thought Ito. When Minezaki had asked Sherlock to explain how he had identified the location, so they could get a warrant, Sherlock had offered nothing. He absolutely would not explain what had led him to his conclusions.

In the end they were forced to come without a warrant. This meant they would have to ask Tzybin to speak with them as a witness. They had no other choice.

The raiding party, however, was as large as it would have been were they planning to make an arrest.

Ito exited the carriage. Although it was September, the morning was comparatively warm.

Sonoda approached and whispered in his ear. "We've secured the perimeter. Not a single ant could pass through."

Sherlock had also disembarked from the carriage. He walked swiftly toward the storehouse. "Let us proceed."

Minezaki and several policemen waited in front of the closed sliding door that led into the building. Sherlock joined their party. Though Ito wanted to go to them as well, Sonoda pleaded with his eyes for the chairman to stand further back.

Finally, one of the policemen banged on the door. "Good morning! May we have a word?"

The bar could be heard lifting from the other side.

The door slid open. A man's face peeked out. He had blue eyes, was balding, and past 50. He had a somewhat dazed expression, as though he'd been woken up by the knock. He was dressed in serge

245

fabric, similar to a European factory worker.

For some reason the man stared at Sherlock first. He seemed almost insensible to the presence of the police officers.

"Good morning, Mr. Tzybin," Sherlock said, in English. "Perhaps you will join us at the station?"

Tzybin did a double take. In a panic, he attempted to slide the door shut. The policemen who rushed forward to stop him did not make it in time. The man shut the door; then, he must have lowered the bar again, for as much as the policemen pushed, the door would not budge.

Minezaki pounded on the door in irritation. "If we had a warrant we could just kick the door down. Hoy, Tzybin! Come out, we want to speak with you!"

After a few moments of yelling, a noise could be heard inside. Had the bar been removed again? Minezaki took a step back.

The door flew open, and then Tzybin appeared, waving a towel in the air. The police men flinched, immediately turning their faces.

And then something entered Ito's eyes! Pain! The pain was excruciating! He couldn't see a thing!

This was the opening Tzybin had been hoping for. "He's making a run for it!" Ito heard one of the policemen shouting.

He stumbled aimlessly around in pain. Sherlock, meanwhile, was wiping furiously at his own face. The policemen seemed to be in a similar predicament.

"After him!" Sonoda shouted, blinking furiously. "Don't let him escape!"

Tzybin had broken through the dragnet and was sprinting toward the pear orchards. Several policemen, however, charged after him at full speed. One of them tackled Tzybin from behind, sending the man flying. Soon more policemen caught up with them and joined the pile. The dramatic chase had come to a rapid end.

Finally, Ito managed to open his burning eyes. "What *was* that?" he muttered. "My eyes won't stop watering."

Sherlock's eyes were also bloodshot. "Cayenne pepper in an oil solution, I believe. I have tried my hand at preparing something similar. Tzybin has clearly hit upon a clever formula. It is quite effective."

"Tried your hand? You've made this stuff yourself?"

"Purely in the interests of research, I assure you." Sherlock pointed at the door, which had been left wide open. "Ito, look there."

The storeroom was filled with random objects. It was packed so densely with these items that it was hard to believe that a grown man could actually fit inside. Not a bit of open space remained. There were pots and vases like you might find in any common household, as well as *ichimatsu* dolls and *hina* dolls, woodblock prints encased in frames, round fans and folding fans, kimonos, straw and wooden sandals… The room was simply overflowing. Glass instruments housing cloudy liquids were also scattered about. A gas lamp sat on its side, its fire extinguished.

"It is just as you said," Ito said, delighted.

But Sherlock looked troubled. "This makes no sense. The man is just a common thief."

"What do you mean?"

"He is hoarding the items, he has no plan for how he will sell them. And he has been completely careless in their storage."

"Why has he stolen them, then?"

The policemen had restrained Tzybin and now returned with him in tow. He had interfered with official business; they needed no warrant to arrest him for that. He stood sulking, perhaps realizing that he had dug his own grave.

Sherlock stared at the man. "I gather that you can understand English. If you possess a modicum of intelligence, you should be able to answer my questions. Olgert Bercerosky? No, you are not Olgert Bercerosky, are you? Does the name mean anything to you?"

"What is this bother?" Tzybin spat in English. He had a strong Russian accent. "Call a lawyer. A Russian lawyer! I say nothing!"

"Indeed." Sherlock put up a hand. "As you wish, Mr. Tzybin—so I shall call you, for I do not know your real name. However, I do know that you were forced to go to Vladivostok after your involvement with the Narodnik movement. From there you were hired to travel to Japan. Your employer prepared the papers for your voyage. You have never met the man who rented this storeroom for you, however you were promised a considerable payment for your services. You were directed to gather goods of a typically Japanese nature, and to do so without discrimination. You previously had the means of contacting your employer, and have begged at least once to know when payment for your services might be expected."

Tzybin did a double take. Then he lunged at Sherlock, as though to take a swing. A policeman twisted his arm and kept him from moving. Tzybin's face grew apoplectic. "Bastard, he mocks me! Who is he? Tell me who this is!"

"*I* am the one asking the questions. The truth is I had no prior knowledge of your history. I see an unusual mark upon your hand, as if from a previous bruise. You were struck by a farming instrument, I believe. You went to the villages as a Narodnik, to incite the peasants, but were instead beset by vigilantes. As the son of I assume an at least middle class family, you received formal education in English. After the Narodnik movement failed, however, you were hounded by police and found it impossible to obtain regular employment. You are desperate to receive your payment, thus you opened the door so quickly upon our knock. You froze when you first saw me. Until I spoke you were unaware that I was an Englishman, and as you had never met your employer in person believed I might be him. But you are clearly not very bright—it should be obvious that your employer would not arrive in the company of the police."

Tzybin kicked at the air repeatedly in unconcealed rage. As the police held him firmly, however, none of his kicks reached anywhere near Sherlock. He spewed a stream of Russian invectives.

"But how did you know he had a means of contacting his employer, and had begged for payment?" Ito asked.

"Previously he had stolen only household decorations and furnishings. He later turned to clothing and personal items. Obviously he had asked for payment before, but had been forestalled with a directive to steal different items instead."

"He could have been told to do so in advance."

"No. No long-term plans guided our thief. He thought payment would arrive in a matter of days. If not, he would have lived in less shabby surroundings. Only look at the manner in which he has stored his ill-gotten gains and you will agree."

Tzybin's cursing switched to English. "English pig, you think you are something!"

Minezaki sighed. "We'll question him at the station. Bring him along."

The policemen hauled the man away. He made no attempt to resist, but continued to glare at Sherlock. Minezaki and Sonoda went with them.

Ito remained behind. "He was only hired, then? How can you be sure?"

"Because that is the only possibility," Sherlock said, his tone dejected. "Anyone searching for Olgert Bercerosky would search first for suspicious Russians. Naturally a Russian man holed up in the countryside and supporting himself through a series of thefts would draw particular attention."

"You mean he was only a smokescreen for Bercerosky?"

"Yes, a smokescreen, or perhaps we should say bait, for the police. Once Tzybin had drawn police attention, Bercerosky would realize he too was is in danger. I have just blundered into the criminal's trap."

"You're saying Bercerosky planned this whole thing?!"

"Quite brilliantly, I should say. He even anticipated what we would think about the different items being stolen. He is a clever opponent."

"And the beer ticket? Was that also bait set by Bercerosky?"

"No. The ticket was discovered on the opposite shore. The Japanese police are not capable enough to have identified this location on their own. I'm sure Bercerosky would have realized that."

Ito was not sure whether to take this comment as condescension or conceit. "How did you identify the location, then?" he asked.

Sherlock jerked his head toward the open door. "Do you recognize that piece of rope, lying there?"

Ito blinked in disbelief. There *was* a long piece of rope inside the storeroom, with a flask tied into the middle.

"I see it! It's a sling. Hand-made, but a sling."

"Tzybin discovered a piece of paper, folded in four, in the clothing of one of the dolls he had stolen. A piece of paper that appeared to include a name and address, written in Japanese. How would he have reacted? As a professional thief, he would know better than to travel far to dispose of the paper. He might have been stopped while carrying it, which would have provided evidence of his crimes. Dropping it into the river, meanwhile, would have led investigators upstream."

"So instead he threw it all the way across the river? But how could a piece of folded paper fly so far?"

Sherlock walked through the door. He kicked one of the chemical vials lightly, sending it rolling across the floor. "When saltpeter is dissolved in water it absorbs the surrounding heat, cooling the water. The addition of common table salt creates ice. It is an elementary chemical experiment. All the necessary equipment is here now. The ticket was encased in a clump of ice. Likely a ball of it, to ensure it would fly."

"So that is why the ink on the ticket was smeared."

"He used the sling to throw the ball of ice with the paper inside. Naturally he did so at night. Much better to dispose of the paper this way, though it would take some time to create the ice, than to risk carrying it about with him in order to dispose of it by hand."

"As a foreigner he would have drawn attention. With all the thefts, there was a high risk he might have been stopped by the police for questioning."

"By aiming for those fields he ensured the noise of the ice hitting the ground would remain unnoticed. And with the recent warm weather, the ice would have melted by morning. These beer tickets are as valuable as money. The Japanese are very civic-minded and whoever discovered such a ticket would likely surrender it to the police.

Though far from certain, such a discovery might seriously disrupt the investigation. The opposite shore of the river would appear to be the least likely location for a suspect—it was excellent cover."

"Even still, why go through so much trouble over a single beer ticket..."

"Thieves inspect their items thoroughly. Whenever an item is found that might lead investigators to them, they consider how that item might be used to cover their trail instead. The common thief takes pleasure in such pursuits. We discovered Tzybin's trick with the beer ticket purely by coincidence. He probably had several such ploys."

Ito felt overwhelmed. "This is hard to fathom. What could inspire someone to think of such a thing, using chemistry to create bits of ice?"

"I have attempted the experiment several times myself, as well. You cannot begin to imagine the number of glass instruments I have shattered in pursuit of my hobbies."

Ito had to admit that behavior, while eccentric, was still better than spending his time with cocaine. Besides, an eccentric mind was needed to discern the bizarre habits of the common thief.

Minezaki trotted back toward them, alone. He shook Sherlock's hand, smiling hugely. He spoke rapidly in Japanese, clearly overjoyed. "Mr. Holmes! I don't know how to thank you! Your powers of deduction are every bit as remarkable as the rumors claim. You have my admiration. And my deepest respect! We will take the suspect away, now."

Satisfied, he bowed to Ito and scurried away.

Ito couldn't help but smirk. "Shall I translate, Mr. Holmes?"

"No need," Sherlock said coyly. "I have heard the same often enough before."

30

When the now-Minister of Agriculture and Commerce Munemitsu Mutsu was younger, he had joined Kaientai, the private navy and shipping company founded by Ryoma Sakamoto. At that time he'd already become friends with Hirobumi Ito of the Choshu Domain. After the Meiji Restoration, he was appointed as an official in the Bureau of General Affairs, with the support of Tomomi Iwakura. During the Boshin War, he had negotiated with the Americans to acquire the *CSS Stonewall*. He even managed to convince the merchants of Osaka to shoulder the very hefty bill for the vessel—a significant windfall for the newly created, and very impoverished, government.

At Ito's recommendation Mutsu studied abroad, in London, focusing on England's cabinet system. Later he translated and published an early work by utilitarian philosopher Jeremy Bentham. Additionally, he established Japan's first equal international treaty, with Mexico.

In every position he held, Mutsu strove to overcome international barriers. After rising to the position of Minister of Agriculture and Commerce, *The Complete Work on Russian Natural Sciences* was unsurprisingly his next target.

He received word that the translation was nearly finished only two weeks after the project was begun. He and Kubo visited the Russian legation together.

The Complete Work on Russian Natural Sciences was massive and very heavy. The two men carried it together. When they opened the cover, however, they saw that the individual chapters had in fact been pulled loose from their bindings. In order for the 100 translators to work on the translation simultaneously, the book had had to be divided into parts. It was no longer a single volume, but was essentially now 80 smaller pamphlets, with each chapter bound separately. The pages were also covered with finger smudges and copious handwritten notes.

Shevich met them in one of the legation offices. He looked dismayed at the state of the book. "My word…"

"At least the translation is nearly complete," Kubo said, with some embarrassment. "We only had a few questions…"

Chekhov smiled immediately. "I am happy to help. Since the main translation is complete, allow us to provide you with a new copy. The contents, of course, will be identical."

"Really? You would do that?" Mutsu asked.

"Certainly. Your diligence in translating the book is nothing less than inspiring. Just a moment." Chekhov walked to the door and called out to the next room. "Akhatov! Denikin!"

Anna Luzhkova entered the room through a different door. "Minister Mutsu, Mr. Kubo," she beamed. "Welcome. Oh! The poor book… What happened?"

"We were just telling Mr. Chekhov," Kubo pleaded once again, "with so many people working on the translation…"

Chekhov returned. "No need to apologize, the book was yours. A newly bound copy would be much better for posterity's sake though, don't you agree?"

A brand new copy of *The Complete Work on Russian Natural Sciences* was carried into the room. The effort it took to carry it appeared to be almost too much for the two delicate young men assigned the task. They set it gently on the table and left the room.

"Now," Chekhov opened his notepad. "Your questions, please. Tell me the chapter and page, and I will inquire with our people in Russia."

Kubo lifted up one of the chapters, his eyes shining with excitement. "If we could start on chapter 1, page 17, where it mentions a paper on the Ulugh Beg Observatory…"

Mutsu stroked the pristine red leather cover of the newly provided copy of the *Complete Works*. As the Minister of Agriculture and Commerce, the positive relationship they now enjoyed with Russia was immensely gratifying.

For some reason, he knew, Ito still had misgivings. But why look a gift horse in the mouth? After all, the incident with Sanzo Tsuda had been settled. What was there to worry about?

October. Olgert Bercerosky's whereabouts still remained a mystery.

Whether or not it was Bercerosky who had hired him, Tzybin had never actually met his employer in person. In Vladivostok they had communicated through notices in the newspaper and written letters. In Japan, Tzybin's only means of contact had been through scraps of paper that he slipped into a crack in the archway of a nearby shrine.

Replies would show up in the same crack after some time had passed, but Tzybin had never witnessed the man directly. Once he had hidden in the shadows by the shrine and spied on the archway. He had waited until the sun set, but no one had showed. He claimed that after that incident he had received no further messages from his employer. He also claimed that he had burned all the notes, and that none remained.

The Russians, for their part, did not seem overly concerned with Sanzo Tsuda's death. The *Laskar* remained in Tokyo Bay, and Nicholas remained aboard, but now it seemed his purpose truly was to negotiate with Siam. No further demands were made of Japan.

Tsuda's death had been publicly announced at the end of September. The government feared that old tensions would flare up anew after the announcement, but the Russians largely remained quiet. The state of affairs between the two countries was unchanged. Japanese employees at trading firms travelled to Russia as before, and plans for commercial use of the Trans-Siberian Railway continued to progress.

It seemed as if Nicholas really had been acting on his own in regards to the Tsuda case, and that the danger from Russia had passed in June.

But Ito still had his doubts. What of Emperor Alexander III's demands that Tsuda be executed? Had the Russian court only desired peace from the outset? It seemed unlikely—and they had been given an ideal pretext to attack Japan.

Perhaps the Russian court felt that George's swapping places with Nicholas had put them in the wrong, and undercut their ability to pursue a harder stance. Many of Ito's comrades seemed to believe that to be the case.

But why should a country as strong as Russia feel any compunction when handling a country as small as Japan? Grand Duke George, beloved son of the Emperor, remained in critical condition. And had the brothers not switched places it would have been Nicholas who was injured in his stead. Was Alexander III not angry? Did he not desire revenge?

One evening, Ito returned home to find Sherlock sitting on the veranda alone, legs crossed, poring through several huge stacks of documents.

Surprisingly, these documents were in Japanese. It was a copy of the translation of *The Complete Work on Russian Natural Sciences*, sent to him by the Ministry of Agriculture and Commerce.

Sherlock's copy of the original, in Russian, was also nearby—the volume he had wheedled from Ambassador Shevich and which, strictly speaking, should belong to Britain. The book was heavy enough to require two people to carry, but apparently Sherlock had hauled it there himself.

Ito stood close and stared at his friend. "I thought you were unable to read Japanese and Russian."

"Which makes this all the more intriguing." He presented a sheet of paper to Ito, on which the character for *chou* had been sloppily copied out. "This character means butterfly?"

"Yes it does."

Sherlock was delighted. "I knew it! In the original there is a diagram of a butterfly, and I noticed a certain word appeared several times in the text next to the diagram. It is pronounced *babachika*, I believe, or perhaps *baboochika*? When I turned to the same section in the Japanese version I discovered a character that appeared with that same frequency. The study of language is fascinating. It makes excellent practice for code breaking."

"If you find Russian so captivating," Ito said, half exasperated, "I suppose you know the meaning of Vladivostok?"

"Certainly! It means 'Ruler of the East.'"

"Indeed it does. Russia is desperate for a warm water port. Vladivostok is their gateway to the Far East. It is also a base from which to attack Japan." Ito spoke openly. "Russia is acting far too timidly. I do not like it."

Sherlock turned his eyes back to the Japanese text before him. "Japan was unaware that the brothers had switched places. Do you expect that Russia would have attacked as soon as Grand Duke George was put on the warship? I imagine that was exactly the scenario the Emperor of Japan wished to avoid, when he visited the Russians to apologize in person. Would it have been more in keeping with Russia's character had they absconded with the Emperor while he was aboard the *Pamiat Azova*, as you and your fellows feared?"

"The Russian Emperor's own son lies in a coma. Tell me, why does he not take action against Japan? He must be a man of considerable fortitude if he is not troubled by this. Of the two, I believe I find Tsarevich Nicholas' reaction more understandable than his father's."

"You are tilting at shadows," Sherlock said easily. "Might makes right. If Russia had wanted to, they could have brushed the incident with the brothers entirely under the rug by attacking Japan. You were once a Choshu man. You should understand that."

Ito sulked. "But what do you think? I wish to hear your opinion."

Sherlock lifted his head and stared out at the garden. "The older brother's reaction does seem reasonable. I believe that such familial affection is expected between brothers."

He sounded slightly bitter. Likely he was thinking of his relationship with his own brother, once again. "Are you unhappy you came to Japan?" Ito wanted to know. "Do you still blame Mycroft for choosing your destination?"

"In hindsight I have come to appreciate the kindness of the Japanese people. I find it doubtful, however, that my brother had operated with the same foreknowledge."

"I have no brothers, older or younger, so I am afraid I do not understand you. The members of my clan were like brothers to me, though. We get along so well that we fight, as the expression in Japanese goes."

"Nicholas and George seem to be truly close. I must confess that I am envious."

Ito felt it would be good to change the subject. "So what about parents? I am more concerned with the Emperor's thinking than Nicholas'. Tell me of your parents, Mr. Holmes. Are they doing well?"

Sherlock was silent. His expression was complicated, even fraught.

"I'm sorry, that was a thoughtless question," Ito backpedaled.

"For all intents and purposes, my brother is the only family I have," Sherlock murmured. "Perhaps that is the difference between myself and the Romanovs. It must be parents who prevent brothers from falling out."

"Likely so. If it was only the two of you then it is only natural that you would occasionally fight. It is easier to argue when you are close enough to forgive."

Sherlock did not seem to find any consolation in that thought. "You must find it congenial to be an only child." His expression grew cold.

The man is as perverse on certain subjects as ever, thought Ito. This attitude was typical for him. In this regard he hadn't changed since he'd been a child of ten. "Mr. Holmes. Where do you suppose Olgert Bercerosky is hiding? I am worried he may cause us further problems. Tsarevich Nicholas is still within Japanese waters, after all."

Sherlock's jaw suddenly set. His eyes grew sharp, like a leopard drawing closer to prey.

"Mr. Holmes, what is it?"

Sherlock held up his index finger. "Chairman Ito," he said. "There is someone I would like you to introduce me to tomorrow."

"Whomever it is, I shall make the arrangements. If it is His Grace himself, I shall approach the Ministry of the Imperial Household."

"I doubt it shall require so much effort on your part," Sherlock said, lacing his fingers into a steeple. "You may even be able to summon him here. But not until tomorrow. I need some time to think."

31

In the end, the person Sherlock wanted to see was the last person whom Ito would have expected. The meeting was simple enough to set up, of course, but Ito could see no reason why Sherlock would wish an audience with this person in the first place.

Ito made the arrangements first thing the next morning, and they were on their way to the Ministry of Agriculture and Commerce by noon. The last time they had stepped foot inside this hall, it had been teeming with 100 translators, frantically working to translate the *Complete Work*. Now, not a single desk remained.

Minister Mutsu and Project Director Kubo awaited them in the cavernous empty hall, as had been scheduled. Apparently, it was Kubo, rather than Mutsu, that Sherlock wanted to talk to.

"Are you familiar with rice blight?" Sherlock asked without pre-amble, as soon as they had exchanged hellos.

"Pardon?" asked Kubo, in English. "I'm not sure I understand."

"Please answer my question," Sherlock demanded.

"Yes. I mean, I am aware of it…"

"Naturally you would be, as you work for the Ministry of Agri-culture and Commerce." He inspected Kubo closely. "Are you also aware of the word for rice blight in Russian?"

"In Russian?" The other man appeared even more confused than before. "I'm afraid I couldn't say…"

"Could you look it up now?"

"I could try looking it up in a dictionary, I suppose. I oversaw the translation of *The Complete Work on Russian Natural Sciences*, but I do not speak Russian myself."

"I see. Let me ask you then, what do you know of the effects of a change in the salt density of the tides?"

"In the ocean? Shall I check with one of the specialists?"

"I wish to hear what you know. Let us try another question. Pressure patterns in the vicinity of the North Pole have been changing recently. As a result, winds have been blowing from the North Pole toward the Atlantic Ocean, causing a flow of sea ice. This has decreased the amount of ice in the Arctic Ocean, leading to water shortages in the North American permafrost due to a combination of melting soil and low rainfall."

"Oh?" Kubo's face was dubious. "I have little interest in the Americas, I'm afraid."

"Indeed," Sherlock muttered. "You work for the Ministry of Agriculture and Commerce yet are unaware of such a thing."

Mutsu furrowed his brow. "Mr. Holmes, Mr. Kubo is exemplary in his post. He is not a scientist and cannot be expected to supply such specialized information without notice. The same is true for myself, and I am the *minister* of the department."

"And yet Mr. Kubo was entrusted with a very important job, was he not? To oversee the full translation of *The Complete Work on Russian Natural Sciences*."

"It is completely to be expected that he would not know the answer to every question that you ask."

Kubo lowered his eyes. "I apologize. I have not studied nearly as much as I should. I ought to know more…"

"Nonsense," Mutsu insisted. "You did nothing wrong. Mr. Holmes, why are you inquiring into Mr. Kubo's scientific knowledge? Why these questions?"

"Naturally, I assumed he would know the answers," Sherlock answered, placidly.

Kubo dropped his head dejectedly. "There is no excuse. I promise to apply myself more thoroughly in the future."

Mutsu held up a hand. "Enough, there is no need to apologize.

Mr. Holmes seems to be suffering under a misunderstanding of some sort. You can return to your work now, Kubo. I will speak with Mr. Holmes and ensure that he understands you are one of my most trusted employees."

Kubo hesitated. He bowed again before walking away.

"I see you are a man of distinction, Minister Mutsu," Sherlock said softly, once Kubo's footsteps had grown distant. "Others might have bullied a younger employee but you defended him quite admirably."

Mutsu was angry. "Mr. Holmes! I too have many acquaintances in England. The officials in government offices are not scientists. None could have answered such specialized questions without notice, even as it concerns issues relevant to their own department!"

Even Ito felt Sherlock had gone too far. "Minister Mutsu is correct. What business did you have speaking to Mr. Kubo in that way?"

Sherlock did look a little shame-faced. "I did not mean to cause any pain… Forgive me if I was rude. I will apologize to Mr. Kubo as well, if necessary. But at present there are more urgent matters which I must consider. I will wish you good day."

And with no further explanation, Sherlock began to walk away. Ito glanced at Mutsu in chagrin. The Minister returned his gaze, blinking several times.

Ito chased after Sherlock. "If you have made a discovery, I would like to hear it."

"It is too early for me to stand by any conclusions." Sherlock didn't slow his pace.

"Could I be of some assistance? Mr. Holmes, please, you need not take full responsibility on your own."

"Indeed, there *is* something I would like you to look into. There will be a place where the trees or rice plants are withering. Nearby there will be a river, where a large number of fish have suddenly died. I would appreciate if you could ascertain this location."

"Wait, a place where trees and rice—"

Mutsu's deep voice interrupted them suddenly. "Ashio, in Tochigi," he said.

Sherlock stopped. He turned around slowly. Ito looked at Mutsu, falling silent.

Mutsu approached them, his expression grave. "Representatives from the local governments report problems in their farming villages to the Ministry of Agriculture and Commerce. As minister, I am naturally informed of such issues."

Ito nodded. "I am aware of this issue as well. When I was Prime Minister, the death of the fish was brought up for discussion. But why is this relevant now, Mr. Holmes?"

Sherlock narrowed his eyes. "You two already know? Then the situation is more dire than I had feared!"

32

Though it was part of his duties, Ito found the meeting of the Privy Council that day to be stupefyingly boring. It was four in the afternoon before he was finally freed. He boarded a carriage and raced home. Sherlock had already returned before him. He had surely made progress on the case.

Ito was walking swiftly along the veranda when he spotted Umeko—frozen in place, staring through an open sliding door with a bewildered expression upon her face. "Oh, this is awful!"

What could have happened? Ito hurried over and peeked into the room. He was left speechless.

The tatami room was in a state of total disarray. Every inch of the floor was covered in a sea of loose papers. Each sheet was covered densely in Japanese writing—they were pages from his copy of the translation of *The Complete Work on Russian Natural Sciences*. Sherlock crawled back and forth over them like a dog. He picked up one stack of papers only to toss it aside a moment later and repeat the same action elsewhere.

"Mr. Holmes..." ventured Ito.

"A moment, if you will." Sherlock approached the low table, across which several pages had been flung. He snatched them up, one after the next, and then fanned them out in a semicircle around himself. "The Russian word for cat is *koshka*. Where did I put chapter 47..."

Umeko turned toward her husband, distressed. "How am I supposed to serve dinner?"

Ito groaned. "Set the table in my room."

"Of course," Umeko said, and walked away down the veranda.

He is like a wayward child, thought Ito. "I'd thank you not to treat this place like your lodgings at Baker Street! This space is where I spend time with my family."

Sherlock snorted. "I believe I played at least some part in restoring domestic harmony to the Ito household. Surely that is justification enough for allowing me to borrow the space for a moment as I work on your case."

"And you have my full cooperation. But this hardly seems efficient."

"Watch where you step. It may appear haphazard, but every page has been carefully sorted and placed."

"Really?" Ito stepped gingerly onto a small patch of open floor. "May I at least ask what you are doing? I know you cannot read Japanese. If you are simply practicing code breaking again I admit I will be very disappointed."

"Worry not. I am investigating something of utmost import. Your daughters were most kind and offered to help, but I refused them. I doubt they understand Russian anyway, and looking over so many pages is a daunting task."

"It did take the Ministry of Agriculture and Commerce a hundred men to translate."

"Which is why I am doing it myself."

"It? What is *it* that you are doing?"

Sherlock momentarily stopped and clambered onto his knees. "Exactly what it looks like. First I look at the original Russian text to identify the word that appears most, and from there attempt to determine the subject of that section. I then look at the same section in Japanese to determine if the corresponding kanji or katakana appears with similar frequency. If they match, then that word is the subject. I do not need to know what the word means. If there is a noticeable difference between the two, however, then I look up the meaning of the subject word in a Russian-to-English dictionary."

"You are looking for mistranslations? But the frequency of the subject words won't always match. During translation, subjects and objects can be omitted or even added. Words may be replaced with pronouns, or pronouns with proper nouns."

"That is true. Which is why I narrow the passages down further to those which seem most consequential."

"Consequential?"

"The phonetic subject words I leave for later. Kanji, however, are pictorial in nature. Two trees is a forest, three is a wood. Two fires on top of each other are a blaze. Characters with the *sanzui* element are related to water. If the original meaning is apparent to some degree from the pictography of the characters, the likelihood that it has been correctly translated is high."

"Wouldn't a Japanese-to-English dictionary be more helpful? Shall I bring you one?"

"Asako made the same offer. I declined. Using a dictionary would take far too much time. It is more effective to observe the shapes and strokes with my own unvarnished eyes, rather than through the pre-conceptions of reflected knowledge. Kanji are pictographs that have taken root across multiple cultures. Naturally they can be processed most swiftly through intuition."

"But if the point is to verify, wouldn't it be faster to rely on a Japanese person with knowledge of Russian?"

"Yes, but who can we trust?"

"Does that mean you have discovered something?"

Sherlock cleared a bundle of papers from the floor, revealing the original *The Complete Work on Russian Natural Sciences,* open beneath them. "This is one of the sections where the frequency of what appears to be the subject differs greatly between the original and the translation. It is a section in chapter 56, describing the effect of changes in the salt density of the tides. I attempted a rough translation using a Russian-to-English dictionary, which suggests that when fish are hit by the tide there is a high probability of mass deaths due to the change in salt concentration. The subject word is *ryba*, which means fish. And the Japanese. Let me see… Where is chapter 56…"

"Perhaps you might endeavor to be a *little* less disorderly?"

"Here it is." Sherlock retrieved one of the stacks of paper. The character for fish had been circled. "This character means fish, correct? Judging from its appearance, it is shaped to resemble a single fish on its side."

"Yes. That is correct."

"I am already familiar with the character for 'death,' it appears frequently in the newspapers. That word is also used frequently, though not as often as fish. The word that appears with the next highest frequency in the original is sea, or ocean water."

"*Umi*, in Japanese."

"I do not know the character for *umi*, but I used the same process, searching for a character that would correspond in frequency to sea or ocean water. The word that appeared with the next highest frequency, after fish and death, was this." Sherlock pointed.

Ito didn't understand. "This is the character for *kawa*. It means river, not sea. In fact, this whole sentence…"

"Differs from the original? Judging from the appearance of the character, which consists of only three lines, I too assumed it meant river, waterfall or something to that effect, rather than ocean or sea."

"The word for waterfall is *taki*."

"I took less than a minute to ascertain all of this. Almost entirely by intuition, I was able to deduce that although the Japanese translation concerned the death of fish, the premise involved rivers or waterfalls rather than seawater."

"My god, you are correct." Ito removed his reading glasses, in agitation. "The cause of death is also different. It says that when the feeding hierarchy is disturbed and one of the species increases by too much, that species will die off suddenly in great numbers… Completely different from the original!"

Sherlock flipped through his copy of the original book. "Chapter 38 explains how trees can wither due to changes in Arctic pressure patterns. In the North American permafrost, forests have withered and died due to water shortages brought about by thawing ground and low rainfall. Forests have also been dying off more frequently in Siberia, despite heavy rains, due to the extreme damp. The gist of the article is that forests are dying in Siberia from too much water, and in Alaska from too little. And here, on the other hand, is the Japanese translation."

Ito read the section Sherlock presented to him. "This says that underground lava activity robs soil of the nutrient- and water-retention abilities that plants need to grow, so the trees in volcanic regions simultaneously die off. This is different too!"

"You taught me *furu*, the kanji for old. I deduced that the character combining *furu*, or old, with *ki*, or tree, must mean *wither*. It was clear that the translation also addressed the withering of trees. And yet, although water was involved in the original article, the *sanzui* element was noticeably absent. I noticed that the character for fire was present instead. It appears together with a different character." Sherlock pointed to another spot. "Here."

"That is *yama*. It means mountain."

"As I gathered. The character appears frequently in other sections of the book as well, and by comparing those sections to the original I was able to deduce that this meant mountain. In this section however, fire and mountain always appear together. It seemed probable that this pairing referred either to forest fires or volcanoes. Regardless of which, that meaning did not appear in the original."

Ito was overwhelmed. "And you did this—for all 80 chapters?"

"I am still investigating the remaining entries, but so far I have identified 16 sections that are clearly suspicious." Sherlock rifled through the pages of the original once more. "I am only showing you a few of the most outlandish examples. In chapter 14 there is an entry detailing the mechanism by which rice blight kills rice plants. It is a type of mold, which occurs under conditions of high humidity. Now look at the Japanese translation."

Sherlock held out another document, which Ito now read. "When spring water with high levels of hydrochloric acid contaminates paddies, the rice plants will wither and… Wait! These are the discoveries that Kubo was so excited to report to me the first day we visited."

"Yes, it appears that a great number of unexplained phenomena that have plagued the Ministry of Agriculture and Commerce are included in this book, along with explanations of their causes. And yet in the translation the key points all differ from their original. In the Japanese translation for this entry, as well, the character for 'wither' is present, and judging from its frequency I assume this character—" Sherlock indicated yet another kanji, "—means rice plant. But the original article describes a pathological mechanism. I knew the character for 'disease,' having seen it several times on hospital billboards. I searched for it in the Japanese translation, but it did not appear even once."

"But why? Mere mistranslations could hardly explain such a drastic difference."

"At first I suspected the persons in charge of the translation. I even had my doubts concerning top officials at the Ministry of Agriculture and Commerce. However, when I questioned Mr. Kubo the other day he seemed to lack the vaguest glimmer of information from the original. He was quite modest about his lack of knowledge of Russian, but he seems serious and ardent by nature. I assume he made some attempt to read the original and to compare it to the translation. Doubly so, on those points that had so excited him the day before."

Ito was surprised. "So you believe that the original possessed by the Ministry of Agriculture and Commerce differs from your own? Why? Did the Russians not wish to teach us about rice blight, or dead fish, or arctic winds?"

"Quite the opposite. They wished very much to teach you the *wrong* information. The information in this version claims to be the latest scientific knowledge, but the arguments presented within are quite bizarre. Imbalances do occur in feeding hierarchies, but I have never heard of that leading to the spontaneous death of large schools of fish. And of course trees can wither when a volcano erupts nearby and the lava cools and hardens, but that has nothing to do with underground lava. And here, if enough salt had entered a rice paddy to kill off the plants, that should be obvious just from testing the water. Such knowledge would amount to common sense in the natural sciences. Japan, however, is far behind in this field of study, and displays a willingness to trust in Western science uncritically. The Russians took advantage of that innocence."

"When you put it that way... I have to agree. In hindsight, it seems obvious something is not right about these explanations. In Japan, however, the West seems like a treasure trove of unknown science—and that belief can take precedence over more somber reflection. First we accept, and then we proceed to our own research. That is the Japanese way."

After noticing errors in the original *Anatomische Tabellen*, Genpaku Sugita based his *New Text on Anatomy* on his own corrections, proving that as far back as the Edo Period it was common knowledge that Western science could not be trusted out of hand. Regardless, Western technology had seemed like a miracle in Japan, from firearms to shipbuilding to railways. And like any miracle, it had inspired faith. Having modernized so quickly—with only 24 years since the Meiji Restoration—Japan had lost the habit of distrust of Western technology. The country was impatient. If they were to catch up with the West, they needed to be open to accepting what it had to offer; the "how" and the "why" could come later. Especially when dealing with information that had been formally presented to them by a foreign dignitary.

Ito stared at Sherlock's original copy of *The Complete Work on Russian Natural Sciences*. "The phenomena are similar, but the details have been almost entirely changed..."

"And this ensures that it will be nearly impossible for anyone who is not intimately familiar with both languages to notice a difference at just a glance. That is the ingenuity of the thing. When you only skim, the original and the Japanese translation share many words in common. There appears to be no issue. The first thing people would see is that the topic, dead fish, is the same, before they got around to noticing, for instance, that the 'oceans' had become rivers. And why check any further?"

Naturally, the contents of the original *Complete Work* at the Ministry of Agriculture and Commerce would match the Japanese translation, ensuring a thorough comparison would not reveal the truth. Sherlock had only stumbled upon the changes because of his unaltered copy. Still, were it not for his exemplary powers of observation, the switch would have gone undetected. It was just as Sherlock said— one might attempt to check the entries slowly, using a dictionary, and never notice anything was wrong. The alterations had been inserted into the text too skillfully for the common eye.

But why go to such elaborate ends? Ito did not understand what it all meant. Something dire was unfolding; he could feel it in his bones. He stared. "Ambassador Shevich, perhaps…"

"No," Sherlock said, rising to his feet. "It was Shevich who gave me the unaltered copy. He arranged for a book to be sent from Russia. He must have been unaware that the copy given to the Ministry of Agriculture and Commerce had been altered."

Ito gasped. "Then that leaves only one possibility."

Sherlock gave an enigmatic nod. "The truth was hiding where least expected. Chairman, I believe you have been right after all. Whatever it is that Sanzo Tsuda started, the trouble has yet to end."

33

A twilit sky was visible through the window of the carriage, across which a domed copper-plated roof floated into view. This was the Nikolai Cathedral, just completed in March. The cathedral had no connection to Tsarevich Nicholas, but was rather named after the Orthodox hieromonk of the same name. The brick-and-stone structure had been built on a Greek Cross plan, but its construction had caused no inconsiderable amount of trouble for the area. Agitators had protested the Nikolai Cathedral on grounds that its steeple overlooked the Imperial Palace, and was disrespectful.

Though it pained Ito to admit it, in many ways Japan was still an immature country. He himself was no exception. What difference was there between the protestors who had attempted to block the cathedral's construction, and the passionate youth who had so strongly believed in *joui*? Or even between himself and Sanzo Tsuda, for that matter?

One needed to first know the world to serve their country. Ignorance and idealism were poor weapons to be armed with; knowledge was true power. A nation could only free itself from subservience to the Great Powers through erudition. But in Japan, that work was far from complete. Even now, one of their own government bodies dangled at the mercy of a mere book from Russia.

Yet Ito had not fully grasped the situation. Sherlock still refused to explain the key points. Perhaps he wished to build anticipation, so that when he solved the mystery it would prove all the more dramatic. The detective could be childish in that way. Mostly, however,

Sherlock simply demanded complete confidence. Ito had no choice but to respect that wish.

Sherlock required absolute trust from others. He didn't feel he should have to report on his progress; that inviolable trust was the sole and most important trait he wanted in his relationships. Perhaps the need for such unconditional trust came from support his parents or brother had failed to give him in his formative years. Ito didn't know how Sherlock's family had treated him, but it was undoubtedly true that he seemed to feel it had been lacking. Sherlock now lived the only way he knew how. He was one of the most competent and yet most awkward men Ito had ever known.

The carriage jostled them quietly to and fro, and they arrived at the grounds of the Russian legation. The vehicle followed a private cobbled road to the front entrance before slowing gently. Before it slowed to a full stop, Sherlock jumped out. Impetuous as always! Ito quickly roused himself and followed after.

Sherlock shot up the stairs, waving to the guards with one hand as he passed them. They shouted in Russian and ran inside after him. *As reckless as ever,* thought Ito.

Inside the foyer, employees came running from the back, likely drawn by the guards' shouts. The beautifully adorned hall, with its Byzantine domed roof, was in an uproar. Ambassador Shevich and Lt. Colonel Kanevsky came racing down the spiral staircase.

In a rage, Shevich made a beeline to Sherlock. "Who do you think you are! The records of Sherlock Holmes' death are not confined to the newspapers alone. Scotland Yard believes you dead as well! I spoke with Ambassador Fraser. He knows nothing of your presence here!"

Sherlock froze, genuinely shocked. "You have received an answer already? In less than a month? That is astounding!"

"But Ambassador Shevich," Ito said quickly and slyly, "if Mr. Holmes were a spy surely it is only natural that Scotland Yard and Ambassador Fraser would deny any knowledge of his presence."

"No." Shevich breathed heavily through his nose. "If he were a spy, there would be some evidence of subterfuge. But by all their accounts you truly fell to your death at the Reichenbach Falls. Yet when I made inquiries and examined the photographs that have been taken in secret, it became quite clear to me that you are, in fact, Mr. Sherlock Holmes."

Sherlock snorted. "You have been exceedingly thorough. As I made no attempt to conceal my identity when I first visited your legation, however, naturally I wished you to be aware that I am in fact who I say I am."

"Then you deceived your own country, and came to Japan only pretending to be dead? Why would you do such a thing?"

"Would you believe me, Ambassador, if I told you it was to save your hide?"

"I most certainly would not!"

"No, I suppose not. Removing your neck from the chopping block is only a happy coincidence, and it's true it was never my original objective. But as this is now the situation, I am afraid I must hurry. If you will excuse me."

And Sherlock ran toward a nearby door. It led to the same office used by the Russian Ministry of State Property, as Ito was already aware. Earlier, they had visited the Ministry of Agriculture and Commerce and ascertained its location from Mutsu and Kubo.

Shevich chased him in a panic. Kanevsky, too, attempted to block his way, but Sherlock easily slipped past him and threw the door wide open.

Anna Luzhkova sat inside, alone at a desk. She stood in surprise. "What is this?"

Sherlock stepped in. "There is a very good reason for my visit, I assure you. I have come to ask that you return Japan's copy of *The Complete Work on Russian Natural Sciences*."

Shevich, who was attempting to detain him, stopped short, a curious expression on his face. "Return?"

Anna smiled, but the muscles in her jaw seemed tense. "I have no idea what you mean, Mr. Holmes. The *Complete Work* has already been delivered. There were several witnesses. If you visit the Ministry of Agriculture and Commerce you will find the book is still there, I am sure."

Sherlock stared at Anna. "I came from the ministry now. *A* book was there, but not the book that Japan officially received. Once the translation was completed, Minister Mutsu and Mr. Kubo brought the volume to your office. Mr. Chekhov gave them a new copy in exchange. The original book did not return with them."

"The chapters of the original book had all been removed," Anna said, flustered. "And it was soiled, there were notes over all the pages. We exchanged it for a clean copy."

"I would still like to request the original book. The copy that Russia gave to Japan."

"Yes, well," Anna said, "I'm afraid it has already been disposed of."

Shevich furrowed his forehead. "Disposed of? That book contains national secrets. You do not have permission to dispose of it. Nor to replace it with a different copy. All copies of *The Complete Work on Russian Natural Sciences* are inscribed with a serial number, and the number of the book that was given to Japan has been officially recorded."

Sherlock glanced around the room. "Where is Mr. Chekhov?"

Anna's voice trembled. "He is out. Perhaps this can wait until he returns…"

"You were there, too, when the book was exchanged. As were two young men. According to Mr. Kubo, their names were Akhatov and Denikin."

Shevich looked questioningly over his shoulder at Kanevsky. Kanevsky shook his head. It was clear from their faces that neither was familiar with those names.

"Mr. Chekhov told Minister Mutsu that if he had any questions while translating the book they should speak with him," Sherlock said. "But considering the size of the book, it was only natural that they should have questions. And it follows that they would bring the book with them to ask those questions. With a translation of this scale, you must have foreseen the condition in which the book would be returned. In short, Mr. Chekhov contrived to switch books all along, and replaced the first copy with an original, unaltered version from your homeland."

Anna's voice cracked. "I'm afraid I have no idea what you are talking about."

"I thought you would say as much. Ambassador Shevich, by your leave I will now lay out the facts of this case."

Shevich grimaced and nodded. "Please do."

"So." Sherlock returned his attention to Anna. "The book the Japanese originally received differed from the original in at least a dozen places. Of those differences, three entries dealt with extremely important issues currently under discussion at the Ministry of Agriculture and Commerce. In 1878, large numbers of ayu fish began dying in the Watarase River. On August 12, 1885, the *Choya Newspaper* reported that the cause was unknown. On October 31, the *Shimotsuke Newspaper* ran an article detailing how trees in the Ashio area had begun withering throughout the previous year. Then rice paddies also started to be blasted, both in the countryside fed by the Watarase River and in fields where flooding has washed over the sediment from Ashio."

Anna's face grew stiff. "Those are Japan's problems. We have nothing to do with them."

"But you were aware of them. And you knew their causes. If either situation worsened they would probably be brought up before the Diet. But of course they would consult the Ministry of Agriculture and Commerce. The ministry would then offer an opinion, based on the latest research in natural sciences. Their opinion would be that the situation is not serious."

A shock ran down Ito's spine. "Of course…the Ashio copper mine!"

Sherlock nodded. "Precisely. The phenomena I described are likely Japan's first introduction to public nuisances."

"P-Public…"

"Public nuisances, as they are commonly called. The term pollution, however, would be more accurate."

"Ah, a public nuisance. Yes, of course. Public contamination, inconvenience and injury. We might translate it as *kogai* in Japanese, if need be."

"Pray that phrase becomes common knowledge throughout Japan then, Chairman Ito. So long as people remain unaware of the concept, your entire nation is in danger."

How awful. *Pollution.* The possibility had never even occurred to Ito.

The Ashio copper mine had been operating since the Meiji Era. After the fall of the Bakufu, however, output had slowed and the mine had even been shuttered for a time. But due to recent advances in technology, a number of promising veins had been rediscovered since 1881. Development of the Ashio copper mine—as well as the Hitachi mine, run by the Kuhara conglomerate, and the Beshi copper mine, run by the Sumitomo family—had accelerated drastically, with support from government policies designed to stimulate Japan's economic and military strength.

"The mines likely harvest nearby trees for timber and fuel," Sherlock said. "The factories that refine the mined ore emit smoke, which leads to air pollution."

"Air pollution…?"

"When you visited London, you saw the the thick winter fog. Smoke and soot from burning coal mixes with mist in the air and settles over the ground, resulting in a number of respiratory and health disorders."

"I remember the air being thick, but I do not recall ever hearing that the problem was so grave."

"The government resists admitting there is a problem. The same is true in all the Western nations, and not just England. The newspapers and printing companies receive industrial support and so prefer not to run articles on the matter. As a result, few are aware of the severity of the issue."

"I have read several monographs that suggest emissions from factories could have negative effects... These papers were still at a hypothetical stage, however. I assumed the issue would not yet concern Japan."

"That is where you are wrong. Japan is developing at incredible speed, having achieved in 20 years what took us over a century. But the development has also caused damage at a similarly accelerated pace. In the case of the Ashio copper mine, waste from ore refinement has contaminated water sources in the surrounding mountainside. The extent of the damage was increased by flooding, to the watershed below. You should assume that water and soil in a broad area around the mine is being polluted, even as we speak. Naturally, the same is likely occurring at other mines in Japan."

A chill ran down Ito's back. It was as though he'd learned of a new and as-of-yet-unknown plague rampaging through the country. Factories operated throughout Japan, day in and day out. And no one, not even the managers and workers, had any idea at all of the pollution they were causing. Since the Restoration, Japan had been far too busy to consider such things.

Sherlock cast a hard look at Anna. "The entries were altered in a very clever manner. There were not only theories, but also records and figures, to make it look as though real experiments had been carried out. There were even opinions from supposed specialists. But these figures and quotes were all made up to coincide with whatever was happening around Ashio copper mine. If Japan's scientists were to rely on the information in this book, even should they investigate it is unlikely they would ascertain the true cause of the phenomena. As other scientific branches advanced, they might realize the truth in ten years or so, but by then much of Japan's natural environment would have been poisoned beyond repair."

Anna's expression was alert. "How could a mere book cause so much trouble?"

"A mere book?" Sherlock narrowed his eyes. "The people of Japan have much faith in Western knowledge. They believe it is the key to their future. They are a serious and trusting people, and would never expect that a book gifted to them by Russia would be concealing a trap. It was you who contrived to misuse this knowledge, and abuse their trust."

"But..." muttered Kanevsky. "If the pollution continues, surely the Japanese would realize before ten years had passed."

Shevich didn't agree. "Likely not. In Russia, 30 years have passed since the emancipation of the serfs, but only now is the risk to the peasants' health becoming clear."

"The peasants working in the factories and mines?"

"Yes. In fact, it is concerns over their health that drove Grand Duke George to involve himself in the labor disputes at the coal mines. The government has not released this information publicly, but there is an increasing blacklist of regions where you are not allowed to grow crops, or fish in the rivers."

"But the government has said nothing of this..."

"The workers in our country are lazy enough as it is. If this information got out, they would organize together and abandon their labor. It has all been kept strictly confidential. Russia's rapid industrialization has put a strain on the environment and a strain on the people's health. The same must be true for Japan. But in Japan, they have built a railroad on Honshu clear to the north in but 24 years. They have had even less time to worry about soil, air, and water."

Sherlock rasied his index finger. "Moreover, had the cause of the pollution simply remained unknown, the Japanese would have of course uncovered it in due time. Instead they are being encouraged to believe in lies. Mercury and arsenic poisoning, bronchitis caused by air pollution, changes in the color of seaweed from ocean pollution... The copy Chekhov gave of *The Complete Work on Russian Natural Sciences* is populated with speciously clever fabrications designed to encourage Japan to trust that all these dangerous phenomena require *no immediate action*. From afar, England might suspect that pollution is affecting Japan, but Japan would hardly ask for help from my country to begin with. The Great Powers, meanwhile, are concerned with keeping their own pollution a secret. So there is no hope Japan would receive better advice from another country."

Shevich glared at Anna. "Luzhkova, is this true?"

Anna's face grew cold, like a doll's. "I know nothing. Where is your proof?"

Sherlock snorted, his face revealing no emotion. "You exchanged the books precisely to destroy the evidence. This way, you can claim that any errors in the Japanese translation were absent in the original. You are mistaken, however, if you think that raises you above suspicion."

Ito nodded. "Ms. Luzhkova. The book exchanged between Ambassador Shevich and Minister Mutsu is imprinted with a serial number. It is our right to demand that copy be returned. It does not matter if the chapters have been pulled out or the pages have been smudged. Please return the original copy. And may I also remind you that those pages have been marked by our own translators. We will know if it has been replaced yet again."

Anna sighed. Her expression remained icy. "The book is not here. More precisely, it no longer exists."

"You burned it, then," Sherlock said.

"You had no permission to do that!" Shevich roared.

"Permission?" Anna's voice was low. "Permission from whom?"

The room grew tense. "Who are you!" Kanevsky demanded. "You are clearly no simple bureaucrat."

Anna stood her ground. "Haven't you realized yet, Lt. Colonel Kanevsky? Chekhov and I were sent by the Okhrana."

A ripple spread through the guards. Even Kanevsky seemed to cringe.

"The Okhrana?" Shevich echoed in dismay. "Are you serious?"

Sherlock narrowed his eyes. Ito gasped. The Okhrana were the security force of the Russian Ministry of Internal Affairs—a secret police created in 1866 after the failed attempt on Nicholas II's life.

But Shevich was not cowed. "This is a foreign country. The

Okhrana is charged with overseeing dissidents at home, in order to protect public security and order. What are you conspiring at here?"

"Conspiring?" Anna faced the ambassador coolly. "I can't begin to imagine what you are implying."

"You know exactly what I mean. The Okhrana were originally created as the Department for Protecting the Order and Public Peace, under the Head of St. Petersburg. They may have been created to serve the nation, but are not under the Emperor's direct control."

"As a public security division, we enjoy His Imperial Majesty's complete confidence."

Shevich snorted. "Public security, indeed. You are supposed to oversee dissidents, but instead you cozy up to them so that if a revolution occurs you will still thrive under a Communist government. You vow allegiance to the emperor, but you ally with revolutionaries and support their attempts to overthrow the imperial government. The Okhrana are fork-tongued and a drain on the public coffers, and you have no right to operate in Japan."

"Silence! Who do you think ordered us to join Tsarevich Nicholas on his trip to the East? It was His Imperial Majesty!"

Sherlock started in. "Earlier, when you and Mr. Chekhov were assigned to Grand Duke George, I presume it was to spy on him. His Majesty Alexander III did not like that his younger son supported the laborers?"

"You are correct. But the Okhrana guides our country from a higher ground. Our actions are not governed by the Emperor alone."

Shevich frowned. "Impertinence!"

Her response was quick. "Who is being impertinent? The Tsarevich and Grand Duke switched places like it was some sort of game, and you had no idea at all. You must lead a comfortable life as an ambassador, with your head stuck so far down in the sand. Who is the real drain on public coffers? You have no idea the trouble we have faced. If the international community had learned of what the Tsarevich and his brother had done during their official visits, faith in Russia would have been shattered."

Sherlock was contemptuous. "And when that day comes, the Okhrana will simply side with the revolutionaries."

"It is too early for revolution," Anna said calmly. "The threat in the Far East must be dealt with before the revolution can wrest power from the Emperor. Otherwise internal chaos will create an opportunity for outsiders—the Japanese and their English backers—to advance upon us."

Ito was beginning to lose his temper. "The threat in the Far East?! This is your official policy? To destroy our country through pollution?"

Anna simply nodded. "Naturally. Chekhov and I went to great pains to lay the groundwork for this plan, using our connections in the Ministry of State Property. The book was not our only gambit. Giving Japan permission to use the Trans-Siberian Railway for trade? That too was done to hasten industrialization in the country. If you had not realized the truth, in 20 years' time Japan would have crumbled under its own weight. Sickness would have spread and the nation would have been transformed into a lawless archipelago. An unhealthy environment would also turn foreigners away, and the English would choose not to intervene. Japan would revert to the same state it had been during the fall of the Bakufu."

Ito grew even angrier. "These were the Emperor's orders?"

"Yes, but we were not following the Emperor's orders alone. We were not content to sit by for decades, waiting for Japan to implode. The childish games of the Tsarevich and his brother put all of Russia in danger. So we formed a new plan. What if Tsarevich Nicholas, or rather Grand Duke George, were to be assassinated while in Japan? Then their foolishness, their game of switching places, would be brought to a swift end, and the Emperor and Tsarevich would be so enraged that they would invade Japan immediately."

"So it was your underlings, Akhatov and Denikin, who goaded Sanzo Tsuda into committing the attack," Sherlock said. "They found one man still clinging to his belief in *joui*, a policeman so physically and mentally shattered that it was simple to plant suggestions in his mind and spur him into taking action. They fabricated evidence that Takamori Saigo was alive in Russia, I presume, and showed that to Tsuda."

Anna sneered. "Very impressive, Mr. Holmes. You have it all figured out."

"It was you and Mr. Chekhov who planted the rumors of a man named Olgert Bercerosky. You invented him. He never existed, thus we could find no traces of his activity to uncover."

"We only made up that ridiculous story about dissidents from the Second International after Tsuda failed. Grand Duke George is in a coma, but he is still alive. But originally it looked as if he would recover. The Emperor was not angry enough. He still preferred to wait for Japan to destroy itself with pollution, rather than to invade."

"Nicholas, however," Sherlock said, "was unaware of this fact. The father never revealed his secret plot to the son. At first, Nicholas returned to Russia, sure that his father would seek revenge. When his father failed to take military action or demand compensation, however, he was discouraged. Believing his father to be weak, he sailed to Japan himself."

"The Emperor was aware of this, of course. That is why we were sent with Nicholas. Naturally we had our own separate mission."

"To deliver the altered copy of *The Complete Work on Russian Natural Sciences* into the hands of the Ministry of Agriculture and Commerce. Indeed, this was your primary mission."

Anna shrugged. "It would have seemed suspicious if we had given the book up too readily. Minister Mutsu had been attempting to obtain the book from us for some time. We decided it would appear most natural if it was given as a reward, in recognition of your impressive consulting skills. We knew you would uncover what the brothers had done eventually, if we released the information in stages."

Sherlock's expression remained calm. "That explains why the case was so simple. I was being led."

"Once the translation was complete, we replaced the book with an unaltered copy so that there would be no proof of what we had done. We took great pains to ensure that the staff at the Ministry of Agriculture and Commerce, with their shallow level of expertise, would never notice the discrepancies if they compared the original and the translation. This ensured that if a written stance about pollution were to be presented to the Diet in ten years' time or so, the Ministry of Agriculture and Commerce would dismiss it. Or rather, our plans *should* have ensured it. Mr. Holmes, might I ask how *you* realized the truth? According to our information, you understand neither Russian nor Japanese."

Sherlock snorted and glanced at Shevich.

"I requested another copy be sent from Russia," the ambassador explained.

Anna glared at him contemptuously. "You imbecile. Why would you do such a thing?"

"My reasons were complicated. I wished to avoid British involvement… Regardless, doing so has allowed me to learn the truth. I cannot believe that these were the Emperor's orders. I was told nothing."

"Of course you were told nothing. In the future, if there was a dispute over the content of the *Complete Work,* it was important that you had plausible deniability. Without any evidence, you would feel no responsibility, and Russia's name would remain clean."

"So I was used as a shield…"

"That is what it means to be an ambassador. They are pawns sacrificed to the enemy for the sake of the country. A pawn has no need to see the board."

Ito had still not overcome his shock—not at the sudden change in Anna's personality, nor at the stunning feat of intellect Sherlock had performed to unravel this mystery.

Sherlock had claimed that he only wanted a copy of *The Complete Work on Russian Natural Sciences* to scientifically analyze the natural phenomena of Japan so that his powers of deduction would be put to better use. But it was more likely that he had already foreseen the necessity of confirming the book's contents. His foresight displayed stunning levels of imagination and vigilance.

Sherlock spoke. "Did you think that employing Tzybin would buy you more time? Your plans are over. Now that Japan is aware of pollution, this crisis will be averted. The Japanese are diligent, and will likely find a way to halt or even reverse the spread of environmental damage even before the rest of the world does. The Okhrana's attempts to manipulate both Russia and Japan have now been thwarted."

Anna's expression grew icy. "Are you sure Japan knows all about pollution now? Rather, isn't it only Chairman Ito who is aware?"

The atmosphere in the room suddenly shifted. Anna raised a hand. The curtain by the window split open; a human shadow lurked there. A young man with blond hair, holding a pistol. He raised it in Ito's direction.

Sherlock acted in a flash. He crouched over the chairman, grabbed him by the collar and dragged him down to the floor. A split second later the sound of a gunshot tore through the air. The room was illuminated with a flash of pale blue light. One of the guards groaned and toppled to his knees.

In the next instant, a barrage of gunshots erupted. The bullets must have struck the wall, as a fine rain of woodchips began raining down on them. Soon the room was enveloped in clouds of powder, smoke, and dust.

Sherlock had just saved his life, Ito realized. Even now he continued to shield him from the bullets. At the moment, Ito's only concern was whether or not his friend was safe.

An angry shout broke through the gunfire. The noise ceased, and the voice grew distinct. It was Kanevsky. "Stand down! Stop shooting!"

The few remaining pops trailed off, and the room fell silent. Ito's ears were ringing. As he attempted to sit up, Sherlock crawled to the side and leaned back against the wall with a heavy sigh.

Ito rushed over. "Are you all right?"

"Perfectly fine," Sherlock said, waving him off with one hand. "More importantly, look at this prodigious mess."

Ito glanced around the room and gulped.

The room had been half-destroyed with bullets. The furniture and the decorations were ruined, with pieces scattered across the room. The tattered curtains were caked red with blood, and Anna Luzhkova lay slumped over her desk. Several bullets had apparently pierced her body, and blood was seeping from wounds on her back. Her face lay on its side, eyes wide. Her pupils were dilated and un-blinking. She was clearly dead.

Sherlock approached the window. Ito followed.

There was a pistol on the floor. Sherlock turned over the young man who lay prostrate next to it. His blond hair was stained red. He had been shot in the face.

"Our only witnesses have been killed," Sherlock spat.

Kanevsky rushed to his side. "It was self-defense, it couldn't be helped."

"There was no need to kill the lady as well! There must be a rea-son that Chekhov is not here. It was utter foolishness to allow her to die before we learned what that reason was."

Sherlock rifled through the young man's coat as he spoke and withdrew the man's wallet. There was an identification card inside, impressed with the Russian seal of the double-headed eagle.

Shevich drew close and peered at the card. "Jacob Akhatov, Min-istry of Internal Affairs Security Department. Another member of the Okhrana."

There was nothing else remarkable about the contents of the man's pockets. Sherlock placed his nose near the dead man's temple. "He smells of seawater. He has changed his suit, but before that he may have been swimming in the ocean. There is a depression in his skin where wire was wrapped around his finger. It was not made in one day—he did this every few days. The mud on his shoes is mixed with sand."

The detective withdrew several small paper packets from his own breast pocket. Each was inscribed with a place name, in English. He opened the packet marked "Daiba." There was soil inside. He withdrew a pinch with his fingers, and with his other hand scraped some of the dirt from Akhatov's shoes. He rubbed his fingers together on each hand. "They are the same," he muttered. "This man was walking along the shore at Daiba, no more than an hour ago."

One of the other packets caught Ito's eye. "Hold on, does that say *pleasure quarters?*"

"Consider it insurance, to maintain the domestic bliss of your household." Sherlock stood up. He approached the remnants of the gunfire-decimated desk, and opened each of the drawers. Next he moved to the bookshelf and began rifling through the books, tossing them aside as he searched.

Shevich eyed Akhatov's corpse. "I travel to Daiba frequently and I have never seen this man. Perhaps he was disguised as a sailor."

Sherlock continued upending the contents of the bookshelf. "He has no suntan so he could not have been passing himself off as a sailor. The compression marks on his face indicate that he was wearing a diving suit. Yes, here we are."

He waved a large book in the air and opened the cover. The insides had been carved out into the shape of a cone. He turned to Kanevsky.

"Can you think of any weapons or equipment used by the Russian military that would fit this cavity?"

Kanevsky peered inside the book. His expression grew pinched. "A suction plate for a land mine. It has a waterproof guard so that the mines, usually buried underground, can be used at sea. The plate is attached with wire."

Ito gasped. "You think that this Akhatov was going to sink the warships?!"

"Wait," Sherlock said. "The timing would be too coincidental. We must assume that there have been explosives on the ships all along, and that Akhatov was only checking and replacing them."

Kanevsky nodded. "The waterproof cover is not perfect. If it is left in the water, the cover must be replaced once every two to three days."

Shevich furrowed his brow. "Are you telling me that there have been explosives attached to our ships all this time? To the *Laskar*?"

"They must have taken measures to ensure that Russia would mount an invasion, should their plan to lead Japan down a path of self-destruction flounder at its inception."

"When you say measures…" Shevich's eyes widened. "You mean Tsarevich Nicholas!"

Ito stared at Sherlock. "If Chekhov learns of what has just occurred…"

"He will act immediately. If the warships in port are sunk and Nicholas is killed, it will surely spark a war. Our discovery of the switched books will be for nothing."

"Do you think they are already on the move?"

"I cannot say. But Tokyo is very quiet once the sun goes down. That volley of gunshots earlier was probably audible from a mile in every direction. It's probable that Chekhov and Denikin are in Daiba, but if either one was still nearby and heard the reports, they would be speeding to Daiba by carriage."

Then there was not a moment to spare. "We must mobilize the police immediately," Ito declared.

Shevich cleared his throat. "We shall telegraph the *Laskar*, as well."

Sherlock took charge. "Telegraph Russia first. If the ships in the harbor are sunk, they must know it was the Okhrana's doing, not Japan's. You must notify the Emperor quickly. Otherwise, Chekhov wins."

Then he rushed out the door. Ito chased after him.

They were in the midst of the greatest threat Japan had encountered since the Restoration. Once, Ito had failed to prevent the Battle of Shimonoseki. He would be damned if he failed again, even were it to cost him his own life. If he failed now, modern Japan would meet its demise at the young age of 24.

34

The Daiba port was illuminated with a faint glow. Torches burned, and constellations of lantern light migrated across the area. The sound of hoofbeats was constant. Carriages arrived in droves, assembling at the top of the hill, from which uniformed police officers poured down the narrow path toward the shore.

Ito and Sherlock alighted from one of the carriages and joined the frenzy. The smell of the tide was omnipresent. Cool air blew in from the sea, stealing the heat from their bodies.

Sherlock directed his attention toward the pitch-black sea. The nine warships were still parked in harbor. So far, nothing out of the ordinary had occurred.

Ito rendezvoused with Sonoda. Kanevsky had brought his guards with him and was yelling at the sailors in Russian. Leaving the chaos of the hilltop behind, Sherlock headed for the outlook.

He peered over the balustrade, down at the shoreline, where there were several small boats being gathered. It was a random assortment—everything from steam-powered crafts to rowboats. Policemen crowded around the boats, impatient to board.

"Mr. Holmes," Ito caught up to Sherlock and panted. "Sonoda has gathered over 100 boats. With all these people searching, I am sure we will find the attached explosives."

Sherlock shook his head. "They are not all in diving suits. The ocean is dark, and the explosives are attached to the bottom of the ships. The men will be useless unless they dive."

"The navy is on its way now. They have a great number of divers.

Until then, we must do what we can."

From behind, a voice called, "Ito!"

They turned and were confronted by a Japanese man in a blazer. He approached quickly. Kaoru Inoue! He held his cane in one hand—the one with the hidden blade. "I put a call out to the fishermen as soon as I received your message," he said. "They are all men accustomed to nighttime skin diving."

Sherlock couldn't hide his surprise. "You plan to have them fumble around the bottom of the ships with their hands?"

Inoue nodded. "Of course. With enough men searching, I'm sure we will find the explosives."

"It is dangerous. And the bottoms of the ships are quite deep."

"Japanese fishermen dive naked as far down as the ocean floor. They cannot afford expensive equipment."

Their courage, at least, was commendable. But there were other worries to contend with. Sherlock called: "Lt. Colonel Kanevsky! If the land mines beneath the waterproof covers are tampered with, will they explode?"

"There is no saying how they were set," the lieutenant colonel replied, "but if they need to be replaced on a regular basis I doubt they are so delicate."

"Then how do Chekhov and his man plan to detonate them?"

"Probably they would dive down and attach a wire to the fuse in advance, and pull the wire from some faraway location. That is the only method I can think of. Fishing boats travel between the ships on a regular basis, so I doubt the wires would be constantly tensed."

Sherlock turned back toward Ito. "Excellent. Get the police and fishermen out onto the water, and Chekhov and Denikin will be unable to run the wires."

"According to the sailors, Chekhov set out toward the ships on a steamboat with a young man. They had many sailors aboard with them, so it is unlikely they could dive anywhere along the way. But it's not clear which ship they boarded."

"Not the *Laskar*, surely," Ito murmured.

"Likely not." Kanevsky nodded. "Ambassador Shevich already wired Russia. He also contacted the captain of the *Laskar*. Everyone on board has been directed to remain on standby, and to do nothing prematurely. Naturally that includes Tsarevich Nicholas. All of the sailors on land who have any diving experience are being mobilized to search for and remove the explosives."

Sherlock held up a hand. "No, ask the Russians to stand down. The Japanese police and fishermen are already on their way."

"Stand down?" A look of irritation appeared on Kanevsky's face. "Those are *our* ships out there, and it is our crown prince being targeted. It is the Japanese who should stand down."

"These are Japanese waters," Ito snapped back. "In fact, the boats are still in harbor. Police jurisdiction applies."

Kanevsky ground his teeth. "And what will Japan say if the explosives are detonated first?"

Sherlock replied, "It is less a matter of whose responsibility it is now, as it is of danger. Chekhov is a portly man with red hair—it will be obvious if he attempts to conceal himself among the Japanese soldiers. Denikin, however, is another story. He could get close to the explosives by pretending to be part of the search party, and then pull the fuses in an act of suicide."

"You ask us to stand here biting our nails as we watch from shore?"

"That is precisely what I ask. Any other course would be pointless. You must rely on the industriousness and cleverness of the Japanese now."

"Impossible! As an Imperial Russian military officer, I will not stand idly by while our Tsarevich is in danger—"

Before he could finish, however, a flash like lightning lit up the surrounding sky. A concussive tremor shook the ground. A low roar echoed overhead, followed by a sharp blast of wind.

Sherlock peered into the wind, straining to see. What he beheld took his breath away. Of the three ships moored alongside the pier, the rearmost had sprouted flames. A moment later, a great column of water shot into the air. The ship tilted dangerously to the side before listing toward the pier. The men onboard were thrown overboard like ants. Unable to resist its own weight, the ship began to slither beneath the water's surface.

Kanevsky clutched his head. "No! The *Zaur*!"

The *Zaur*? Sherlock had been almost sure it was the *Arsen* moored in that position. He hardly had time to think that before the aft end of the ship behind the *Zaur* suddenly lurched into the air like a toy. It was the *Yakov*. Soon the ship was enveloped in black smoke, and the bow tipped precariously up. The back of the ship was sinking. The mast broke off and collapsed into the sea. The water's surface churned with frothy waves.

Ito's eyes widened. "What is happening?"

Sherlock watched the disaster unfold with bated breath. He had a bad feeling. He'd discovered that a suction plate had been smuggled in through the hollowed-out book, but there was no guarantee that had been the only one. "It did seem like too much of a coincidence that he had changed the waterproof casing today, when it only needs to be every two to three days," he muttered. "It might be a daily task…because explosives have been placed on eight ships—all of the ships except the *Laskar*."

"Eight?" shouted Kanevsky. "But why—"

Another roar, like thunder, swept the hill. Then a column of water shot up next to the *Kondrat*, also moored at the pier. The ship split in two down its middle, and the halves began sinking separately. Sailors could be seen bobbing on the surface, their heads barely above water, waving their arms desperately in the air.

Sonoda leaned over the balustrade and began shouting in Japanese toward the shore. He was telling them to launch a rescue.

The policemen on the beach leapt into action, joined by the fishermen. One by one small ships began pushing off from the shore, headed for the island pier.

"Police Chief Sonoda, keep your men away from the ships that are still whole," Sherlock cried. "There could be more explosions."

Sonoda nodded. He turned back toward the shore and shouted frantically in Japanese.

Ito glanced at him. "You think the explosives are only on eight ships? Won't they target the *Laskar*, if that is the ship Tsarevich Nicholas is on?"

"Chekhov and Denikin must also be aboard one of the ships, and that is the one that will not sink. It is the *Laskar*."

"But then Tsarevich Nicholas will be safe."

"Once the other eight ships sink, the last ship will also appear to be in danger. Naturally they will evacuate. The Tsarevich will board a lifeboat. That is when the attempt will be made on his life."

"Ridiculous," Kanevsky objected. "Someone would notice at once if anything so large as an explosive were attached to the bottom of a lifeboat. Besides, how would they know which boat His Highness would board?"

"Try to be a little more imaginative, Lieutenant Colonel!" Sherlock chided. "Why would they need to use explosives once they were aboard a lifeboat? They will be alone and isolated upon the water, with few men to contend with. There would be nothing to stop an assassin from taking Nicholas' life."

Ito squinted. "An assassin on the boat? It would have to be someone very close to the Tsarevich. Surely not Chekhov and some unknown young man."

Sherlock was growing impatient at having to explain himself. "Ito," he said, speaking very quickly, "perhaps you have forgotten. Chekhov and Anna Luzhkova were the ones who told us that Chekhov was Grand Duke George's attendant, and not close to Nicholas. Don't you see? That was all a lie. The members of the Russian legation are no more aware of the true arrangements aboard the warships than we are. We must assume that Chekhov is Nicholas' aide."

A look of shock crossed Kanevsky's face. "You think that red-headed hog has earned the Tsarevich's trust?"

"And Denikin as well," Sherlock said. "I never suggested that the *Laskar* would be sunk. Sinking the *Laskar* would offer no guarantee of Nicholas' death. In addition to the destruction of the fleet, he will be assassinated while trying to escape. That will necessitate an invasion on Russia's part."

Another thunderous roar, and another column of water shot into the air. It was the *Kesar*, which had anchored in front of the *Laskar*. She, too, began to sink. The desperate screams of the sailors reached the outlook.

Kanevsky's face flushed red. "Those Okhrana traitors will pay for this."

A sailor rushed toward them. He reported something to Kanevsky, in Russian. Kanevsky nodded and turned toward the detective. "A small steamboat is almost ready. We will be close if the *Laskar* lets down a lifeboat."

"I will go with you," Sherlock said.

"I will tell the guards at the gate. Be at wharf two in ten minutes." Kanevsky turned away and hurried down the narrow path with a group of sailors.

"Mr. Holmes," Ito said. "I will go as well."

That was unthinkable. Sherlock stared. "You can't. Japan cannot afford to lose you."

"But we have come this far together."

"Your courage, enterprise, and authority are not required at this juncture. We are only going to trade a few measly blows with an assassin upon a boat."

"Precisely what I was hoping for. I am a former Choshu retainer. When someone makes an attempt on my life, I must repay them in kind."

"An unbecoming statement from a former prime minister. Mr. Ito, I realized something as I rode that train to Aomori. It is you who is to thank for changing Japan. Its future, likewise, relies on you."

"That is why I wish to settle this in person."

"Please. I understand your sentiments but I do not wish to fight with you again. Our first round was at Baker Street when I was 29, our second was our tussle in the garden at your home. I have already learned my lesson. I hope to never see round three of Sherlock Holmes versus Hirobumi Ito."

"Then give in," Ito urged. "You were only ten when I returned to Choshu. I would have stood in front of the gun barrel myself if it would have stopped those first shots of war. But I was too late. I failed. But if I can prevent war with Russia now, I do not care what should happen thereafter. I will stake my life on this!"

What could Sherlock say? Speechless, he stared at Ito. The chairman returned his gaze, equally silent.

Sherlock recalled what he had told his dearest friend by the banks of Lake Daubensee. *I think that I may go so far as to say, Watson, that I have not lived wholly in vain. If my record were closed tonight I could still survey it with equanimity. The air of London is the sweeter for my presence. In over a thousand cases I am not aware that I have ever used my powers upon the wrong side. Of late I have been tempted to look into the problems furnished by nature rather than those more superficial ones for which our artificial state of society is responsible. Your memoirs will draw to an end, Watson, upon the day that I crown my career by the capture or extinction of the most dangerous and capable criminal in Europe.*

From the moment Sherlock had discovered the existence of that foul villain Moriarty, he knew life was meaningless unless he defeated the man. The achievement of his entire career lay in accomplishing that single feat, or so he had believed. The evil that had beset London must be scourged from the roots. And so Sherlock had found a clear purpose in life.

Undoubtedly, Ito now felt the same. It was a seductive emotion. What use was there in living only at the whims of fate? And yet…

Sherlock sighed. "Ito," he said quietly. "Promise me one thing."

"What is it?"

"You will return home when this is through. Do you swear?"

"Return…home?"

"Japan finds itself in the gravest of dangers. You may believe that to surmount this current predicament is all that matters. So long as there are countries, however, there shall be crises. Who will avert the next, if you are lost? You must return home when this is through, and you must return alive."

He could see the streets of London in his mind: the soft light of the gas lamps in the mist, their reflections in the wet cobblestones. Moriarty might be gone, but even now his brother worked to restore his name. His remaining men still prepared to act. London would never see a day when crime was no more. Perhaps even now, lost souls continued to visit Baker Street, unaware of Sherlock's death. What cases weighed upon their shoulders? What anxieties troubled them?

Sherlock shrugged himself free of his reverie to find Ito looking at him oddly. With a faint smile, the detective said, "Now is not the time for reminiscing."

Ito returned the expression. "I promise we will return. You and I, both."

An ear-splitting explosion filled the air. Water rained down on them, even though they stood as far as the hill. The sky was lit a crimson red. The *Timur*, in the northeastern corner, was now engulfed in flames. Balls of fire rolled across the deck before erupting into columns of flame. Their light was reflected in the sea below, where sailors treaded water, shouting for help. The rescue boats of the police and the fishermen drew closer to them.

"Let us go, Mr. Ito. The hour is afoot."

"Indeed it is."

Inoue called out, "Take this with you, Ito!"

It was his cane, the one with the hidden blade inside. The two Japanese men looked into each other's eyes. Ito gripped it solidly, as if he were receiving a samurai's sword.

Now the ocean wind that blew from the sea carried the heat of the flames. Sherlock and Ito began running. As they descended the hill, a flurry of emotions swept through the detective's mind. In the past he had disparaged Watson's writing. Now, he swore he would write his own memoirs someday. But before one could write his life, one must live it. Life was in the living, not its results.

35

The small Russian steamboat was aerodynamic, shaped like an oversized canoe. Lt. Colonel Kanevsky and four other sailors were aboard. Sherlock and Ito huddled into the back. The boat was larger than the *Aurora,* the steam launch Sherlock had once chased down the Thames, but it was also much faster. They dashed over the black waters as if gliding over pools of ink. The boat's incandescent bulbs illuminated their immediate vicinity, but did not penetrate far beyond that, with the mist and smoke from the multiple explosions. The boat pitched and lurched each time they struck a piece of floating debris.

Another column of water shot into the sky. Flames erupted from the ship to the *Laskar*'s starboard side. The mast tipped over and began to burn.

Kanevsky shouted over his shoulder. "They have got the *Kliment!*"

"Now we finally know where all the ships were located," Ito whispered in Sherlock's ear.

"Indeed. There are only two left now. The *Arsen,* which is behind the *Laskar,* and the *Walery,* to its starboard." Sherlock leaned forward and shouted. "Lt. Colonel Kanevsky, are you sure the explosives are being detonated by pulling wires?"

"Absolutely certain. I spotted a wire stretched beneath the water."

"They must be very long."

Kanevsky nodded. "They are being pulled from the deck of the *Laskar.*"

"The crew wouldn't notice if they pulled the wires from the deck?"

"No. If the wires are wound around the balustrades, Chekhov or

Denikin could loiter on the deck, and would only need to slightly lean over the edge to give the wires a tug. After the first explosion there would be chaos, and no one would be paying them very much attention. Besides, with it so dark, how would anyone see the wires in the first place?"

"The *Arsen* and the *Walery* haven't sunk yet. The wires must be stretched between them and the *Laskar*. You should warn all the boats not to travel between th—"

Another flash lit up the sky. An explosion rang out, and then a huge wave rolled their way. The steamboat tilted hard. Sherlock grabbed the mast. The steamboat nearly capsized before suddenly and violently righting itself. The shaking almost tossed all of them into the water.

Kanevsky peered through his binoculars. "That was the *Arsen*. Only the *Walery* left."

"And the *Laskar*. So long as any other ships are still there Tsarevich Nicholas will remain aboard. It must seem more dangerous to disembark than to stay. The captain of the *Laskar* is likely waiting to see whether or not the *Walery*, too, will fall."

"So their evacuations will begin as soon as the *Walery* sinks."

"Yes. We must close the distance to the *Laskar* before then."

"The crane to lower the lifeboats is on the starboard side."

"Then we should get there posthaste."

Kanevsky shouted at the sailors in Russian. The sailors grew more frantic. They scooped shovelfuls of coal into the stokehold, over and over again. The headwind grew stronger as their steamboat accelerated. *Laskar*'s forward port grew steadily near.

But while the *Laskar*'s silhouette loomed larger and larger amid the darkness, they were still too far away.

Just then, another blast reverberated in the air, with a blinding flash of light. Jagged waves struck their boat, rocking them violently left to right.

Sherlock peered in the direction of the blast. A plume of smoke billowed from the side of the ship anchored to the *Laskar*'s rear starboard. The ship slowly began to tilt to the side.

"The *Walery* is sinking!" Ito shouted. "The *Laskar*'s evacuations have to begin!"

"How much longer?" Sherlock asked Kanevsky.

"Five minutes."

"Hurry. If we are not on time, all our efforts will have been wasted."

The captain would be last to evacuate. The Tsarevich, however, would likely demand he go first. His lifeboat may have even been prepared before the *Walery* was sunk. If so, the boat would be rapidly lowered into the water. But perhaps Nicholas would wait until the boats containing his guards had also been set on the water. No. It was obvious they had to make for land. Nicholas' lifeboat would launch without waiting for the others. Unfortunately, his closest advisors were sure to be aboard as well.

Sherlock clenched his jaw. Watson had once written, of the hour and quarter they spent waiting in an underground bank vault to set an ambush, that it felt *the night must have almost gone, and the dawn be breaking above us.* Sherlock had called this mere exaggeration, but he felt he now understood the expression. Time passed quickly while he was active. Being forced to wait, however, constrained by the physical limitations of the boat's speed, was infuriating. The steamboat represented the collective knowledge of all mankind—surely it could go faster! Even a marlin was faster than this!

The *Laskar*'s silhouette was now so large they had to crane their necks upward to see it. At last their steamboat passed the ship's bow and they circled around to the starboard side. They slowed their speed. Their vicinity was lit up by the boat's incandescent lights. Sherlock looked over the side, shocked.

The water was entirely blanketed with lifeboats. The vessels were manned with a disorderly mix of sailors and men in plain clothes. It was impossible to tell who was aboard which boat. The lifeboat crane, meanwhile, continued to lower yet more boats into the water.

Their steamboat pulled alongside one of the lifeboats. Kanevsky yelled out in Russian. The young sailor who answered them seemed bewildered. The sailors peered about and pointed in various directions. They called out in loud voices to the other boats. The voices from those other boats, however, responded with equal confusion.

Kanevsky cursed. He turned back to Sherlock and explained, "The *Laskar* is only a cruiser, not a flagship. None of these sailors have any experience. Their ranks are totally broken."

"The Tsarevich had run away from home. Likely they were the only men available."

"Can no one tell us where Tsarevich Nicholas has gone?" Ito asked.

"He definitely boarded the first boat and set off immediately, but nobody can say in which direction."

The lights of their steamboat swept over the water like a lighthouse beam, casting the assembled lifeboats into relief. The men aboard the ships worked their oars furiously, heading toward the shore. They seemed mostly terrified. There was no telling when the *Laskar* might also explode.

Sherlock thought carefully. Which direction would the villains have chosen, to best achieve their objectives?

Of course. "Lt. Colonel," he told Kanevsky, "chart a course for ten o'clock. We must travel southeast at full speed."

Kanevsky looked at him uncertainly. "That will take us away from shore. The *Walery* only just sank."

"Hence why we must travel southeast. Chekhov and his men will take Nicholas in the direction in which they expect least interference. Enough time has passed since the ships in the other directions sank, and the Japanese police and fishermen will already have arrived to rescue who they can. The crew of the *Walery*, however, has barely even evacuated."

"So be it." Kanevsky turned toward the sailors and shouted in Russian.

The steamboat began to move once more, gaining speed. The smoke in the air grew denser. The way ahead was thickly shrouded.

The light from their boat was meaninglessly diffused mid-air. They could see no more than a few yards ahead.

But there was something visible in the water. The steamboat altered direction slightly.

Sherlock looked at the object as they passed it. It was a sailor's corpse. He was floating face down in the water, his body motionless and limp. Blood oozed from a gunshot wound in his back.

The steamboat slowed abruptly. There was something else in the water. Unsurprisingly, it was yet another sailor, this one floating face up. His chest was stained red.

"Poor devil," Ito groaned.

The two must have been the guards on Nicholas' lifeboat. They were headed in the right direction. "Lieutenant Colonel, don't slow down. They came this way, there is no doubt about it."

Kanevsky gave the order and their speed increased. The steamboat swiftly hurtled through the dense fog.

"I see them," Ito cried.

Sherlock peered into the murk. A small shadow bobbed into view. It was a boat. Its oars were still. Someone stood inside of it—a young Caucasian man, dressed in a frock coat. His clothes made him appear thin, but judging from his stance he was robust and physically well-conditioned. It had to be Denikin. He was waving a Japanese katana in the air. He gripped the hilt in both hands, staring down, ready to strike.

A man-shaped shadow sprawled at the base of the boat. One arm was thrust forward, and he was clearly begging the other man to stop. He wore a red army coat. He'd probably thrown the coat on in a rush during the evacuation, so that he would be easily recognizable as the crown prince. Nicholas' terrified face came into focus with the light from their ship.

It was obvious why Denikin had chosen a katana. Clearly, he meant to stage the attack to make it seem as if Nicholas had been assassinated by the Japanese.

A third man, sitting in the bow, turned to face Kanevsky's boat.

He was fat, with red hair. He stood up in a panic, pointing in their direction.

No, not pointing. He held a pistol.

There was the crack of a gunshot. The sailors crouched low, taking cover. Several more shots followed before their surroundings suddenly went dark. He'd shot their lights out.

Blast it! A chill ran down Sherlock's spine. How could they return fire with no light? They might hit Nicholas by accident.

Just then he felt something shift behind his back. Then there was a splash in the water. Ito was gone! He had just dived into the water. Inches below the surface, a darker shadow sped, porpoise-like, toward the other boat.

Such recklessness! Sherlock barely had time to register shock before a glaring light flared into existence. He could see again. One of the sailors had lit a torch. The light was bleached and white—made from a mixture of sulfur, saltpeter, and ash, to ensure it would not be extinguished when it touched the sea. The sailor threw the torch onto the waves, between the two boats.

Now they could see their enemy clearly. The sailors began shooting. They aimed their rifles high. With Nicholas held hostage, they could provide cover fire at best.

But Chekhov had no such restraints. He fired, and hit one of the sailors. Kanevsky crouched low behind the balustrade. The other sailors took cover as well. Sherlock, too, was forced to crouch low.

Standing atop the lifeboat, Denikin brandished his katana once more. Nicholas attempted to shrink away, but he was already at the edge of the boat and had nowhere else to go.

Then there was another splash. A shadow rose from the surface, like a fish leaping into the air. Ito boarded the boat, dripping wet, and grabbed Denikin by the leg. He pulled, hard. Denikin lost his balance and fell.

Ito was the first to his feet. The boat rocked violently left and right. Chekhov, bent low, grabbed the boat's edge. Ito's skillful sense of balance, however, allowed him to maintain his own footing.

Denikin stood up. He glared at Ito, eyes wide, and took aim with his sword.

Ito still held the cane. He drew the hidden blade, gripped the hilt in both hands, and squared off against Denikin, his sword brandished high and center. He met Denikin with cold, steady eyes.

The Russian man struck quickly. Ito's sword flicked side-to-side in response. The boat rocked so it was difficult to use footwork, but Denikin had the same limitation. Sparks lit the darkness when their blades clashed. Their struggle seemed intense. The swords crossed and it soon turned to a contest of strength, each attempting to push the other backward. Denikin, who was in better physical shape, seemed to be winning.

The lifeboat began to regain equilibrium. Chekhov resumed firing at the steamboat.

It was no use crouching at the bottom of the boat forever. Sherlock leaned over the edge. "Lieutenant Colonel, your assistance!"

"Wait, Holmes," Kanevsky shouted. "What are you—"

Sherlock did not hear the rest. He was already in the sea.

Underwater, he might as well have been blind. But he had expected this. He could hear the sound of gunshots, muffled by the water. The ocean was frigid, but his clothes helped to keep him buoyant. He followed Ito's example, swimming close to the surface while propelling himself forward with his legs. The current flowed from the side. Sherlock swam quickly, fine-tuning his course as he progressed. There was no time to even take a breath. If he broke water he would surely be shot.

His head bumped against something hard. He stretched his arms out. It was the hull of the boat. He swam around to the other side, reached up, and grabbed onto the edge.

As he broke the water's surface, sight and sound were restored. The first thing he saw was Nicholas, cowering at the foot of the boat. His face was alive with terror. The piercing sound of metal clashing against metal filled the air. Sherlock looked up. Ito and Denikin were still engaged in their fierce swordplay.

Chekhov sat near the bow. He seemed to have regained his composure, realizing that with Nicholas hostage the steamboat was unable to return effective fire. He redirected his pistol, aiming it now at Ito, who stood mere feet away.

Sherlock used all the strength in his arms to pull himself up and roll into the lifeboat. Chekhov appeared startled. The boat shook dramatically, and his aim was thrown off. Sherlock chopped him in the arm. The pistol dropped into the sea.

As the boat continued to rock, Sherlock rose to his feet. Chekhov stood as well, drawing a knife from his pocket. The blade moved threateningly in the air. Sherlock recoiled and the boat nearly capsized.

The footing here was much more precarious than it had been upon the rocks of the Reichenbach Falls. Denikin, too, lost his balance. Ito, however, was much more adept at maintaining his. Completely unfazed by the unevenness of the boat, he swung again. The tables had been turned. Denikin dropped to one knee. Ito struck from above, again and again. It took all of Denikin's strength to defend against the blows.

Chekhov glared. Sweat trickled down his face. "You'd do well not to interfere in Russia's affairs, Mr. Holmes."

"It's over, Chekhov! Anna Luzhkova and Jacob Akhatov are dead. The Okhrana's duplicitous plans end here."

Chekhov gasped, his lips trembling slightly. "You think I will let the British have Japan? I won't allow you to take this foothold in the Far East."

"Japan has chosen its own independence. Your plot to sabotage and destroy the country is a travesty of international law."

"Be quiet!" Chekhov charged, knife-first.

Sherlock grabbed Chekhov by his lapels and, maintaining his balance despite the heaving of the boat, took a step backward. He jammed his elbow tight into Chekhov's side. Remaining close, he twisted his body round quickly and threw Chekhov backward, over his shoulder.

Moriarty's lanky frame had seemed to almost float in the air when Sherlock had executed this throw on him. The portlier Chekhov traced a parabola instead. He landed against the waves with a smack, creating an enormous splash.

Chekhov's body sank, leaving only bubbles before it disappeared from view.

Or so Sherlock thought—but the man resurfaced immediately, his face barely thrust above the surface and both arms gesticulating wildly.

"Help!" he sputtered, barely afloat. "I can't swim, help me!"

Sherlock hesitated. He glanced at the floor of the boat. The sight of Nicholas' terrified face greeted him.

Ito delivered another downward blow, followed by an upward cut. Denikin's katana hurtled into the sea, and he landed heavily on the boards, rump-first. Ito thrust the tip of his sword directly before the man's eyes.

A look of fear crossed Denikin's face. "Kill me then," he cried unsteadily. "Do it quickly!"

Ito did not move. He stared down at the Russian.

Denikin shouted defiantly. "Kill me! Kill me you damned for-eigner-killing monkey savage!"

"Silence!" he roared. "Japan is a nation of laws. You weren't de-feated in the name of *joui* today. You have trespassed against men of all races, and you will be judged under the law. We are not savages and we are not monkeys!"

Denikin trembled and went stiff. A moment later he sighed. He slumped his head in resignation.

Sherlock looked at Nicholas. The Tsarevich seemed half-sense-less, and rolled over. Perhaps he had heard the word "monkey."

Chekov continued to sputter in the water. His voice, as he shout-ed for help, was beginning to grow panicked. "Help! I'll do anything! Dear God, please!"

The image of Moriarty hurtling down the falls flashed now in Sherlock's mind. He had watched as Moriarty grew smaller and smaller, bouncing against the rocks before disappearing into the waters below. His conscience had remained untroubled at the time. Was there any difference, now?

Ito had already sheathed his sword. He stared down at Denikin silently. The Russian seemed to have fully surrendered. He showed no signs of further resistance.

A nation of laws. Even under their current circumstances, faced with the very blackguards who had plotted Japan's downfall, Ito remained dedicated to order.

But it was clear that Ito's was the ethical choice, and undoubtedly the correct one.

Still Sherlock could not help but hesitate. So long as he continued to possess the capacity for thought, such doubts would likely always persist. At some point one must stop thinking and act.

He bent forward. He removed the small life preserver attached to the side of the boat and tossed it to Chekhov.

Chekhov clutched at it desperately. His head continued to bob vigorously in the water, but it remained now above the surface. He seemed to calm down. His breathing grew less frantic. He stared off into the distance, and then sighed, low and deep.

Sherlock couldn't help but snort. He turned back toward Ito. The chairman stared back at him, nodding slightly.

Their steamboat drew near, its sirens blaring. The water was illuminated by the white glow of the torch. As he was rocked back and forth by the turbulent ink-black sea, Sherlock felt he was drifting through nowhere.

36

Nicholas' cabin aboard the *Laskar* was elegant. Without the round port window, it would have passed for a mansion's fine drawing room. But many of the expensive-looking furnishings looked of a different style than the equally expensive upholstery and finishing, and the room felt strangely unbalanced. Nicholas had probably brought in items originally on his flagship—like a child who brings all his precious toys with him when he runs away from home, Sherlock observed.

The detective stood in the middle of the sumptuous room, with a blanket draped over his sodden self. But he did not feel particularly cold. Nicholas sat on the sofa, his face buried in his hands.

No one else was present. Ito and Kanevsky waited above deck. Nicholas wished to hear what had occurred from Sherlock alone.

Sherlock had already finished his debriefing. Nicholas had been lost in silence for some time.

"Your Highness," Sherlock said quietly. "As I explained, Soslan Chekhov and Anna Luzhkova were members of the Okhrana before they ever joined the Ministry of State Property. Although His Majesty the Emperor ordered them to spy on you, they were also conspiring to circumvent his plans."

Nicholas gave a listless groan. "I can't believe it. Father was right all along about the Japanese. But the behavior of those two was outrageous. They tried to kill me!"

Sherlock paused in fury. "I see you still do not understand. It is absurd to say that your father's actions were correct."

"George was a victim of rioting savages, of the Japanese and their beloved *joui*."

"Akhatov and Denikin were the ones who manipulated Sanzo Tsuda into attacking."

"But it was Tsuda who actually attacked," Nicholas snapped pettishly. "He had cruel and barbaric impulses. He was motivated by his naked hatred of the Russian Empire."

"He was mentally ill."

"As are all Japanese, then. On the surface they smile and act politely, but deep down they are violent savages, no different from monkeys."

"Your Highness," Sherlock said cuttingly, "look out that window. A great number of Japanese have congregated on the waters, officials and commoners alike, to rescue your Russian sailors."

"They are only feigning submission to us, as we are a greater power, until they become advanced enough to strike. Once their military and economy might grows stronger, their true natures will be revealed."

"You are next in line to become emperor. Such prejudices will serve you ill."

"Hardly prejudices. When I become emperor I will be hard on the Japanese. It was Father's true intention all along."

"You plan to go to war with Japan?"

"I doubt it shall ever come to that. China will crush a small country like Japan."

"You are mistaken," Sherlock said briskly. "From what I have seen so far, if Japan and China were to go to war I expect Japan to win. And not only over China. If you are to become emperor, I imagine they should crush Russia as well."

Nicholas jumped to his feet in a temper. "You insolent Brit!"

"I urge you to remember, you only stomp and rage in this manner now because Chairman Ito and I risked our own lives to save yours. By all rights you should be lying senseless at the bottom of Tokyo Bay, Your Highness."

"And if I was, Father would have sent the entire army to Japan's shores. I only wish I was dead."

Sherlock snorted. "Do you truly mean that?"

Nicholas glared angrily at him. But Sherlock was unfazed, and met his eyes. After a few moments, the Tsarevich blinked. He lowered his eyes, seemingly less confident than before. He sat down again upon the sofa.

"If the Okhrana have started a rebellion," Nicholas mused absently, "my father will be hard-pressed to suppress it. There will be civil war in Russia."

Sherlock shook his head. "It won't get that far, Your Highness. If the revolutionaries expand their influence, it would be a threat to the court. Right now the Okhrana keep them in check. The moment your father attempts to purge the secret police, the empire would be capsized. Though he knows the Okhrana work with revolutionaries in secret, he can do nothing to stop them. The Romanovs' influence is waning."

"What would you know?"

"You don't believe me? Let me ask you a question. How many of the Russian people would stand up in your defense? Forget the citizens. How many of the soldiers? When you fled the *Laskar* in your lifeboat, not one of the sailors in the water had any idea which way you had gone."

"Those were unusual circumstances. This would never have happened on the *Pamiat Azova*."

"Because your father looks after you and has ordered those men to protect you. But would anyone follow you, without your father? Yet the Japanese people believed it was you who had been attacked, rather than Grand Duke George. They sent letters of concern and prayed for your well-being."

"They knew they would be crushed if a war broke out."

"And what of Russia? Did your own people show any of the same concern?"

"By the time I returned home," Nicholas said despondently, "my safety had already been widely reported. As far as the people of Russia were concerned, my injuries were only minor."

"The Japanese people continued to express concern even after seeing those same reports. Shall I tell you why? They respect their Emperor. It seems only natural to them to show that same respect to the royal family of another country."

"Are you implying that the Russian people don't respect the royal family?"

"The Japanese royal family has existed in harmony with its people for 1,500 years. Even now, the Emperor places trust in Chairman Ito and the other members of his cabinet. But what of the Romanovs? Your family rarely interact with the common people. The citizens are attached to the land, and title in Russia is synonymous with authority. Only those with title may rule. The only relationship is one between the ruling and subjugated classes."

"Father has a close relationship with the government and military."

"Perhaps, but he is unconcerned with the peasants. It is no wonder that the revolutionaries grow in influence."

"No. Father is not mistaken."

"If you do not reexamine these beliefs of yours, the Romanov line will surely end with you."

A tense smile strained the corners of Nicholas' lips. His eyes flashed with anger. "I may become Emperor, and I may lose to Japan, and the royal line may fall. But don't forget, Sherlock Holmes, that we are currently aboard *my* warship, of the Imperial Russian Navy."

"Is that a threat? You mean to suggest that I won't be allowed to leave alive. If you ordered the sailors aboard this ship to kill me, do you believe they would even listen?"

"This is the kind of impertinence one expects from an Englishman. But not even Britain is safe from Russia's might."

"Have you forgotten the Ottoman Empire?"

Nicholas jumped to his feet again. "Who cares about the Ottoman Empire?! It is Japan I won't forgive. And if Britain sides with

Japan then they are just as guilty!"

"Guilty of what?"

"Of what they did to George!" The young man's eyes suddenly welled up with tears. "My brother is in a coma. He is at death's door…"

Nicholas broke off mid-sentence. Sherlock looked at Nicholas quietly. The Tsarevich stroked his face forlornly.

"Your Highness," Sherlock whispered. "In the end this was all about your brother, wasn't it?"

"Don't you have a brother? No one else was born to the same parents, no one else understands me, but George. He is my other self. No one is as thoughtful or full of care for others as he is. Anyone who could attack someone as innocent as George must be dealt the retribution they deserve. It is my duty as an older brother."

Sherlock was unmoved. "Were you aware of Grand Duke George's public service?"

"Public service? Why bring that up?"

"I asked whether or not you were aware of it."

The young man began pacing the room nervously. "If you are speaking of his visits to the coal mines, then yes, I was aware of them. Labor disputes, or some such, are on the rise."

"Russia's rapid industrialization has made its working environments inhospitable. The peasants sent to the mines and factories suffer, while the Russian government levies heavy taxes against them and pushes to raise foreign currency by exporting crops. The peasants are being exploited to the point of starvation. Your brother was concerned for them."

"That is very much like him."

"Yes. But are you at all interested to know why the working conditions of the peasants were so poor?"

"Not in the slightest. My brother's duties and my own are—"

"Pollution. Sickness caused by pollution."

Nicholas froze. He was perhaps overcome by a sense of foreboding. "Pollution…?"

"The peasants suffer from pollution-related diseases. Just as Grand Duke George suffered from them, after having visited coal mines throughout the country."

"Don't be ridiculous. George has been sick ever since he was a child."

"I had Ambassador Shevich telegraph the palace. The court physician denied it at first, but in the end he admitted that pollution was the main cause of the Grand Duke's illness. That is why he developed tuberculosis symptoms last year, and then bronchitis in Bombay. His weak constitution simply made him more perceptible to the polluted air of the coal mines."

Nicholas took a step backward. He staggered against the wall and then collapsed, holding on to the closet to support his weight.

"You have always thought of Grand Duke George as a friend, someone sociable and cheerful. He is the brother who fished and hunted with you. But your brother was aware of his responsibilities to society, as well. You loved your brother for your own sentimental reasons. You never appreciated him for his true worth."

"My brother's public service has nothing to do with this. A complete stranger could never understand the affection we shared. Especially not a stranger such as yourself…"

"*You* are the one who does not understand," Sherlock insisted. "The pollution now hurting the health of the miners is an issue that should have been dealt with by your father, and as the crown prince, by you as well. Your brother listened to the peasants because you and your father refused to. You are the ones responsible for his illness."

"You're lying." Nicholas' eyes grew wide and bloodshot. Tears began to trickle down his face. His voice was shaky. "You're lying. My brother. George…"

"How many times did he try to talk to you about this issue? You remember him broaching the subject, I'm sure. But you were uninterested. You preferred to have fun, not to discuss public nuisances."

"What else could I have done?"

"As his brother, you ought to have shared his burden. You said your brother is your other self. That he is your closest companion in this world. I imagine your brother, however, looked to you not only as a playfellow but also as his best confidante. You would have been stronger together than alone…"

Sherlock trailed off. Nicholas was sobbing. Sherlock had realized several moments ago that the Tsarevich was no longer listening. For whose benefit, then, was he speaking?

The answer, of course, was obvious. For his own. He finally realized the truth. Superficial fellowship was meaningless. It had no worth. The bonds that held brothers together were located elsewhere, at a deeper, more spiritual level.

Nicholas collapsed against the wall. He slid to the floor, cradled his head, and continued to sob.

Perhaps this would motivate a change in the prince. One could only hope.

The Russian palace had informed Shevich that George was not expected to live very long. Perhaps he would never regain consciousness, and his death would be announced in a few years' time. The cause, of course, would be kept secret. How would Nicholas grapple with the truth if and when that time came? What sort of emperor would he become?

But as of now, there was nothing left for Sherlock to say. He opened the door slowly, and left the room.

37

A cool breeze glided over the ocean, creating ripples of shadow and light. The water's gentle blue surface reflected the brittle autumn sunlight, a sparkling and clear deluge.

An enormous, brand-new ship pulled into the harbor at Yokohama Port. Sherlock bent his neck back to see the soaring mast. A far cry from the ship in which he had travelled to Japan, this was a first-class luxury liner headed for Hong Kong. On board, a special-class cabin had been reserved for him.

The night before, Sherlock had asked Ito if there would be any problems with his travel arrangements. Ito had answered with an enigmatic smile. "Leave it all to me," he had said.

The sky, endlessly clear and high, was streaked with feathery white clouds. It was invigorating, but also dizzying. Sherlock lowered his eyes and placed his head in his hands.

"Mr. Holmes," Umeko asked, "is something wrong?"

Sherlock lifted his head. Hirobumi Ito's family had assembled along the pier. Ito was dressed formally in a frock coat. Umeko wore a kimono, and Ikuko and Asako wore dresses. They looked concerned at the possibility he might be sick.

He smiled wryly. "It's nothing. I must still be feeling some of last night's saké."

A look of relief spread across their faces. "Shall I bring another bottle for you to take along?" Ito asked.

"No, I believe I've had enough. You are fortunate to prefer beer. This saké is so easy to drink, that it is easy to overindulge. Particularly when the celebrations last for days."

"One should never stand on ceremony when there is drink available."

"Unacceptable for someone in my position. It is necessary that I keep my intellect sharp."

"Indeed, last night you made a rare error, though you seemed to handle it well."

"That may be the case, but my inebriation is no excuse. What I said was dreadfully rude. Considering how thin and pale he was, coupled with that flamboyant military jacket he wore, I assumed he was just an over-decorated, bureaucratic general."

"His Grace found it amusing."

"It was inexcusable. I have learned my lesson and will henceforth abstain from all drink."

"Truly? That seems to be overdoing things."

"No," Sherlock said exuberantly, "I have drunk enough for a lifetime. From now on, I shall preserve my mind in its natural state, so that my faculties shall be ever ready to serve. If I may be so abstract for a moment, I feel as if I have entered a new stage in my career. I have you and your family to thank for this."

Ito smiled. "As unsentimental as ever, Mr. Holmes, even during farewells. You are a paragon of reason."

"Sentiment?" Sherlock surveyed his surroundings.

The simple, well-apportioned streets around the harbor were quiet—not that he could see them. From a distance, a great number of policemen surrounded the port. Police Chief Sonoda and his men had come out en masse, escorting Ito in uniformed formation. Ordinary passengers glanced over their shoulders uneasily as they approached the wharf.

"Being sent off by someone of your stature leads to too much extravagance. It limits the emotion."

"Mr. Holmes," Ikuko said, drooping her head. "I am sad to see you go."

She said it so simply that he could only assume it was mere

flattery. He thought to answer her with self-deprecating sarcasm, but then Ikuko withdrew a handkerchief to dab at her eyes. He hesitated. The young ladies of Japan were very refined. They were not as apt to display emotion as the ladies of the West. Sentimental or not, Sherlock felt somewhat melancholy as he realized Ikuko's true feelings.

Asako, however, was more open than Ikuko. She beamed at Sherlock, but fat tears welled up in the corners of her eyes. As they broke, they trickled down her face in streams.

"Mr. Holmes," she said shakily, "I guess this is goodbye. I wish you could stay longer."

"Asako," whispered Umeko, her expression pained. "Don't be unreasonable."

She bowed impulsively to Sherlock. She seemed to consider her reproof of her daughter as an indirect rudeness. Her considerate attention was astounding. But beyond that, Sherlock could see how deeply she cared for Asako—even without the bonds of blood.

He withdrew his pipe from his frock coat pocket and placed it in Asako's hand. "Would you do me the honor of setting this upon the table when you take your meals? I hope you will imagine I am still with you as your guest. You must continue to take your meals together as a family, and you and Umeko and Ikuko must all get along. Just the same as when I was here."

Akiko looked up at Sherlock, still crying. She cupped the pipe in both hands, holding it as if it were a priceless treasure. Her pure expression convinced Sherlock she'd keep this promise. He nodded silently.

"Shozo Tanaka, an MP from Tochigi, has begun advocating for a written opinion to be presented on the Ashio Copper Mine conflict," Ito reported quietly. "I suspect Japan will address the issue appropriately and soon change course."

"And how good that the courts judged the sinking of the Russian ships at Daiba was an accident so quickly. And even more fortunate that there were no casualties, thanks to the speed of the rescue."

"It is all thanks to you, Mr. Holmes."

"No, it is thanks to your strength of conviction, Chairman Ito. You know your path. It makes me envious."

"Envious?"

Sherlock brooded. "Even if I manage to get to British Hong Kong, I will likely be arrested in the harbor and extradited immediately to England. And yet there is no other country at which I can legally disembark."

"What then do you plan to do?"

"While in prison, I shall reflect on my past cases and write my memoirs. Watson has often urged me to write for myself."

Ito broke into a smile and drew forth an envelope from his breast pocket. "Mr. Holmes, I hope your memoirs may wait a little while longer."

Surprised, Sherlock took the envelope. It was thick, fine-grained, high-quality paper, sealed in wax with a distinctive coat of arms. A personal letter from Buckingham Palace!

Inside the envelope were several documents in addition to the letterpress. He unfolded the letter first. He gasped. It had been signed by Her Majesty Queen Victoria. *Royal prerogative.* The words at the top of the page made him stare.

"The Queen's authority is immense," said Ito. "All trials in England are carried out under the monarch's name. Justice comes from the sovereign, who provides the right of trial to her subjects."

Sherlock glanced at one of the papers included with the letter. *The prerogative of mercy: nolle prosequi.* A voluntary suspension of prosecution.

He was speechless. He stared at the sky, willing himself to regain his composure, sighed, and glanced down at the papers once more. "When the royal prerogative of *nolle prosequi* is invoked, all legal proceedings against an individual are suspended. The prerogative is not subject to judicial review."

Ito nodded. "Her Majesty did not decide alone. I was told the Minister of the Home Department agreed. The Prime Minister, Third Marquess of Salisbury, had a great hand in it as well. It seems he owes you a favor."

Yes, he had served the Marquess before—a case in which the presence of a second blood stain had proved integral. Sherlock looked at the chairman. "Did you write to Her Majesty?"

"The letter was not from myself so much as it was from the collective people of Japan. After all, no one in this nation would object were they to know the truth of what occurred. The evidence was only circumstantial, but it was enough to convince us that you had faced off against one of London's most dangerous villains and were only forced to kill him in self-defense. Hence our very heartfelt request for *nolle prosequi* by way of royal prerogative. It was a mere request, from a country of laws in the Far East, to the monarch of the British Empire."

The joy Sherlock felt was so great it was almost like grief. He was beset with waves of emotion. He struggled to maintain his composure. His voice sounded shaky in his own ear. "This means then, that I…"

"You are no longer a dead man. Nor are you a suspect in the Moriarty trial."

Sherlock let out a long, deep sigh of relief. He had to close his eyes.

The first time they had travelled to Meiji Palace together, Ito had told Sherlock that he did not desire the death penalty for Sanzo Tsuda. Though he'd been unsure at first, he later resolved his doubts. But Sherlock had never heard why. Ito had also resisted stabbing Denikin, out on the water that night in Tokyo Bay.

Ito seemed so determined that Japan should become a nation of laws. Sherlock finally understood why. The chairman had planned all along to petition the British Royal Family on his behalf. It was vital to show that Japan was a nation with a deep understanding of the law if he was to request a special measure that superseded it. Ito's strength of conviction had been for Sherlock's sake.

And England already knew of Japan's success in avoiding war with Russia. Rather than using this episode to leverage renegotiating an unequal treaty, Ito had chosen to come to Sherlock's aid.

"Mr. Holmes," Ito said. "Scotland Yard is working in secret to round up Moriarty's men. They expect to have the whole gang in two years' time."

Sherlock smirked. "So until then, I take it the London police consider me a nuisance. If Sherlock Holmes were known to have returned, my enemies would take to hiding once again."

"Mr. Holmes," Ito said gently. "Please look at the other documents, as well."

Each document in the envelope used its own kind of paper. Unfolding a thin page folded into four, Sherlock experienced his second shock of the day: the seal of the Qing Dynasty Foreign Office.

"That is permission to enter Tibet. The personal letter underneath is from myself, not Buckingham Palace, requesting an audience with the Dalai Lama. It also secures your entry into the Ottoman Empire, and your personal safety. The Ottoman Empire and Japan are on friendly terms, and our discretion carries weight there. The Caliph, it seems, would like to meet the Englishman responsible for averting war between Japan and Russia."

Sherlock was nearly speechless. "Ito, how…"

"I knew what you wanted to do. It was written in your brother's letter."

Sherlock had no words to describe what he was feeling. But he couldn't help but have some doubts. "I am sure your letter will be taken as authentic, but proving that I am the friend you describe within may prove more difficult."

Ikuko stepped forward. "Perhaps this will be of use."

She held a photograph in her hands.

It showed the Ito family in their garden. Umeko, Ikuko, and Asako, dressed as they were today. With them was Hirobumi Ito, surrounded by his family, a smile on his face. And of course Sherlock, dressed in his usual somewhat genteel fashion.

It felt as though they'd taken that photo eons ago. The memory already felt nostalgic—a sensation of comfort, like the one he had felt on that faraway day, mixed with a longing that tugged tightly at his chest.

"Thank you," Sherlock said to Ikuko. She returned his gaze with wet eyes, but nodded, smiling.

The steam horn sounded a long note. After it trailed off, silence filled the space, leaving only a loneliness like that of falling leaves.

"The ship is ready to depart. This is farewell," Ito said to Sherlock. "Though—I almost forgot. You will keep your stay in Japan a secret between us, I assume."

"I did enter the country on the sly and stay illegally, after all."

"Please keep it a secret from your friend, Dr. Watson, too. Now then, Mr. Holmes. I shall not forget you. Godspeed."

A swirl of emotions filled Sherlock's chest. He extended his hand silently. Ito gripped it in his own. Faint tears welled up in the man's eyes. Sherlock could not help but notice now how much his friend's eyes resembled Ikuko's and Asako's.

At some point, Umeko, too, had begun to cry. She bowed her head deeply, as if she was embarrassed by her tears. Sherlock wondered if all the bowing perhaps served to hide one's face and display of emotions.

He climbed the gangway with the other passengers and stood on the deck. The sky, clear and blue as the sea, drifted past his face. He stared down at the pier, which sparkled under the halcyon light. The policemen bowed together. Ikuko waved her handkerchief. Asako waved with even greater force, and raced after the ship as it began to depart.

Ito and Umeko remained rooted, waving their hands. Even after Sherlock was too far away to see their faces, the Ito family continued to wave, with their hands high in the air.

The sunlight broke over the ocean's surface and reflected back into the air, spreading a soft undulating light over the shore. The clouds above, ephemeral and white, created patches of shadow and light below them as they drifted across the sky.

Sherlock had no doubts that Japan would become a great nation.

He was now leaving behind this doughty archipelago in the magnificent Far East. The nation's people, simple and sublime, grew smaller and smaller as the ship carried him away. The trees along the shore swayed with the wind. Pale autumn leaves fell to the rich brown earth. This peaceful, almost ethereal silence banished the fear and hesitation that had dogged him for so long, and sent them far along their way.

38

Spring of 1894. Since he had last seen it three years ago, the scenery of London had changed slightly. On several of the streets, the old Aberdeen granite cobblestones had been replaced with a smoother macadam pavement. Although the carriages shook less than before, the wheels shaved the roads as they went, and the buildings alongside were stained white with road dust. One could judge how long a door had not been opened for by the amount of dust accumulated on its handle.

It was nearly two in the afternoon. Sherlock disembarked from his carriage onto the long-missed Baker Street. The area remained unchanged, and it was hard to believe that three years had passed. There was the familiar entryway door, crowned with its arched window. There was the number, 221B.

Sherlock opened the door and stepped inside. He faced the back of an old, grey-haired woman. She remained stooped over, polishing the stairway banister with a rag, as she called over her shoulder, "Welcome, come in. Mr. Holmes is waiting on the second floor."

Sherlock felt momentarily disconcerted, but soon realized the situation. His brother must have only told her he was expecting a visitor, but not who it was.

Mrs. Hudson turned around. She stared at him blankly, blinking several times. A violent look of surprise overwhelmed her. She staggered toward him, eyes wide, and gave a strangled cry. "Good Lord! Mr. Holmes!"

Her knees buckled. Sherlock grabbed her to prevent her from

falling. Mrs. Hudson's joy was beyond anything he would have imagined. She cried like a little girl. She must be off her trolley, to greet him in this way.

Mrs. Hudson's voice trembled. "I was sure we had lost you. They all talked of having a gathering, it's near to the day of your passing. Last year Inspector Lestrade sent an entire carriage of white carnations, it was a fine thing."

"Please calm down, Mrs. Hudson. It is very good to see you again. Did my brother tell you nothing?"

"Nothing at all. Oh, that scoundrel, he told me to ready the rooms because a guest was arriving from a laboratory in France!"

"And so I have. He was not wrong. He is upstairs, then?"

"Yes. I am just on my way up with the tea things."

"No need, please rest downstairs. You and I shall have our tea together after I come down."

Mrs. Hudson eagerly invited him to find her in the back room of the first floor. Then Sherlock straightened his collar and climbed the stairs. Trust Mycroft—although he had surely heard the commotion below, he did not step out to greet his brother.

The door had been left ajar. Sherlock stepped inside. The room, which he had not set eyes upon in so long, was organized as though someone had hastily put it in order for visitors. The table and sofa remained in their former position. The laboratory equipment atop the desk also remained untouched. The Persian slipper sat upon the mantelpiece. Likely even the tobacco remained inside, though it would be stale and unusable by now.

Mycroft, who sat in the easy-chair, was thinner than Sherlock remembered, but this made him look younger as well. He stood slowly and extended both arms, a smile creasing his face.

Surely he was not expecting a hug. Sherlock grimaced. "I see everything has been left as it was. It would have appeared less suspicious to Moriarty's ruffians if you'd just cleared the entire place, but I suppose disposing of so many household articles proved too trying. Very like you, Mycroft, to continue to pay the rent simply because it demanded less effort."

"Sherlock, the least you could do is say hello."

"Yes, and you might welcome me back."

He expected a sarcastic rejoinder. Instead, Mycroft said readily, "Welcome home, Sherlock."

The sincerity in his tone left Sherlock momentarily speechless. It took effort for him to say, "It is good to see you…"

Mycroft's expression was not the same as when they had parted at the Port of Livorno. From that day Sherlock remembered only the reproach in Mycroft's face, but now he seemed to be congeniality itself. Perhaps there had been no need to worry so much over their clashing opinions, after all.

Indeed, Sherlock finally understood how much trouble his brother had gone to help him escape. And the difficulties he must have suffered for the three years that followed.

"You look well," Mycroft observed, his face showing subdued joy.

"As do you," Sherlock replied.

"I heard of what unfolded in Japan. There was nearly war with Russia."

Sherlock smiled, and placed his finger to his lips. "I was sworn to secrecy by Chairman Ito. Excuse me, *Prime Minister* Ito."

"Yes, he has been made Prime Minister once again. And the Dalai Lama and Caliph?"

"I was able to gain an audience."

"Ask and you shall receive!"

"Indeed," Sherlock said. At the moment he felt he could speak openly. "It is thanks to you, brother. I am very grateful."

Mycroft seemed a touch embarrassed. "I was not the one who made the trips possible."

"But you provided the opportunity. A chance for a little fish to see the greater pond. I understand now what it means to be brothers."

The bell chimed, announcing the time as two o'clock. Mycroft's expression softened. He hesitated over his words for a moment, then spoke in his usual deflecting manner. "Your decision to return sooner than your original intention has left me rather harried. I thought we would have you pop out from your coffin during the third anniversary of your passing, and scare everyone half to death."

"I heard of the Park Lane incident."

"So you already know. It occurred just as I said it would: after the trial, two of Moriarty's men went free. Your evidence was not enough."

"I still believe what I had gathered was strong enough to make Moriarty desperate."

"We are of different minds."

No matter. "So be it," Sherlock said softly, staring off into space. "Certainly brothers may be of different minds."

So long as they agreed on a deeper level.

Those were Sherlock's genuine feelings. However, it was more than he was capable of putting into words. He hoped that Mycroft understood, even if he did not say as much aloud.

His brother seemed sensitive to his meaning. He smiled and nodded slightly. "Oh, and Sherlock. If you have exhausted your savings during your travels…"

"I have royalties from the record of my Tibet explorations, which I published under the alias Sigerson. It is enough."

"I see." Mycroft approached the table where a bottle of scotch and some glasses had been set out. "A poor showing, but let us drink to your return."

"I must pass. I have given up drink."

"Given it up?" Mycroft's eyes grew wide. "Truly?"

"Yes. I have had enough spirits for a lifetime."

The elder brother had lifted one of the glasses in the air. He returned it to the table. "That is for the best, I suppose. We do not have any soda water anyway. The seltzogene is broken."

"I thought the room had been left exactly as it was, but I see you did not get around to making repairs."

"There is also one other difference."

"An acceptable one. I have already noticed. I do not plan to ever again partake of cocaine."

A faint look of surprise crossed Mycroft's face, but he said nothing. He only nodded silently, with no sarcastic ribbing.

They didn't say anything else for a moment. Then, as though remembering, Mycroft looked apologetic. "Ah, and Sherlock? Perhaps…you hold a grudge against the man atop the cliffs that day, Colonel Sebastian Moran, but I hope you will not do anything so rash as you attempted with Moriarty…"

"Fear not," Sherlock reassured him. "I detest murder."

Mycroft sighed. "You have changed, Sherlock. For the wiser. In a nation of laws, one can get quite far by reading the faces in a jury."

"I shall take your word for that." Sherlock crossed the room and stared down at Baker Street below through the window. He felt as if he'd seen the same view just yesterday.

Across the street, a suspicious man leaned against a gas lamp. Sherlock recognized him: Parker, a small-time strangler and thief. Moriarty's gang was watching him, after all.

"When a person stops trusting in themselves nothing is left," Sherlock murmured. "And when one entrusts everything to the hands of the law, one may also be abdicating direct responsibility. One must always decide for himself how best to act in any given situation."

England's system of laws, though the envy of Japan, was surely not immaculate. At least, Sherlock thought so. What greater proof than that two of Moriarty's men had been acquitted?

He didn't want to take lives—but outside of murder, he would judge the righteousness of a man with his own eyes. He had no intention of trusting in the whims of fate.

Mycroft lingered, but voiced no objections to Sherlock's philosophizing. Eventually he began walking toward the door. "I have changed the lock. You will find the key upon the mantelpiece. I believe you were already in the habit of changing it every few months?"

"Yes."

"Then I shall return these rooms to your keeping. Should you have anything interesting to tell, do come find me at the Diogenes

Club. Do not be a stranger, Sherlock."

In response, Sherlock waved his hand casually. It was enough of a farewell for the time being. They could see each other now at any time they chose.

Mycroft's back disappeared beyond the open door. Sherlock glanced down at the road. Parker had already vanished. Moran would likely soon be hearing of Sherlock's return.

He strode back and opened one of the drawers. Various mementos were inside, just as he remembered. Rummaging through the drawer, his hand suddenly paused on one of his disguises. A white wig and side-whiskers. He was surprised they still remained.

He was struck by a devious thought. A smile tugged at the corner of his lips. This was just what was needed to reunite with an old friend. Though it wouldn't be as dramatic as popping out of a coffin, he hoped his friend would be both shocked and pleased. As a former army surgeon, he ought to have the nerve for it. He would not be so fragile as Mrs. Hudson, at the very least.

39

It was Sherlock's first time visiting Watson's new residence in Kensington, but he displayed no reservations. After all, it was all the same to an old man with grey hair and side-whiskers. If anything, his presumptuous attitude better suited his disguise. The maid at the door had obviously thought of him as an obtrusive old sack, but Sherlock had been counting on her reaction.

He was shown into the study. He hobbled in with a decrepit gait, half a dozen books under each arm, his back hunched. He had included a lower back injury in his performance, purely for his own amusement. He would need to create a clear causal link between his physical state and his movements if he was to fool a doctor's eyes.

Watson stood up from his desk. He looked surprised.

Sherlock was confident in his disguise. Watson would never recognize him. He had already purposely bumped into Watson once, earlier, outside 424 Park Lane, and looked him directly in the face, to receive no immediate reaction other than a vague apology.

At the moment, Watson seemed perplexed, and even pitying.

"You're surprised to see me, sir," Sherlock croaked.

"Yes, I should say I am."

"Well, I've a conscience, sir, and when I chanced to see you go into this house, as I came hobbling after you, I thought to myself, I'll just step in and see that kind gentleman, and tell him that if I was a bit gruff in my manner there was not any harm meant, and that I am much obliged to him for picking up my books."

"You make too much of a trifle… May I ask how you knew who

I was?"

"Well, sir, if it isn't too great a liberty, I am a neighbor of yours, for you'll find my little bookshop at the corner of Church Street, and I'd be very happy to see you, I am sure. Maybe you collect yourself, sir. Here's *British Birds*, and Catullus, and *The Holy War*—a bargain, every one of them. With five volumes you could just fill that gap on that second shelf. It looks a bit untidy, does it not, sir?"

A more guarded man would not have looked. But Watson turned to observe his own bookshelf, never suspecting a thing. He continued to puzzle over the shelf after Sherlock had already removed his wig and false whiskers. Sherlock's heart pounded in impatience and anticipation.

At last Watson turned back around. His eyes searched for the books he expected his elderly guest to be holding. Seeing them on the floor, he looked up queerly.

Sherlock stood straight. He smiled.

Watson stared at him for some seconds. Sherlock had hoped for a cry of joy—such was not Watson's reaction. His eyes opened wide, wide, wider than Mrs. Hudson's had, his mouth gaped—and suddenly he was teetering backward.

Sherlock panicked and rushed forward. He certainly hadn't been expecting Watson to collapse. He'd fainted! Even Mrs. Hudson had shown more fortitude than this.

He almost called for the maid but then thought better of it. The maid would then call for a physician, and what would that do for Watson's reputation and self-respect?

He looked at the cabinet, where there was a small bottle of brandy. Sherlock took it out and crouched over Watson. He loosened his friend's collar and gently poured a touch of the brandy onto his twitching lips.

Watson coughed slightly as he swallowed. Relieved, Sherlock sat down on the nearest chair.

At last Watson's eyes fluttered open. His eyes, still unfocused, swept over the room before eventually coming to rest again on

Sherlock.

"My dear Watson," Sherlock said sincerely. "I owe you a thousand apologies. I had no idea that you would be so affected."

Would he react with anger? Curse him or pull a fit? Sherlock braced himself for both. Instead Watson leapt to his feet and gripped him by the arm as tightly as though for dear life. His eyes twinkled. "Sherlock! Is it really you?"

He seemed almost delirious with happiness. His face flushed red with joy, and his tearful eyes danced with excitement.

Sherlock returned Watson's smile, acutely aware of how unconscionable his own behavior had been. His chest tightened. To have caused such pain to such a dear friend and companion, and then to engage in this trick upon his return? It had been a stupid thought.

Henceforth, he hoped to share every joy and sorrow with Watson. The doctor surely agreed that together, they should overcome any adversity.

40

Time simply flew by—or so it seemed to Watson, who was now 50. It was already the third year of King Edward VII's reign. Edward VII had also been crowned the Emperor of India.

It was early 1903, and the weather in London was colder than usual that year. There was constantly a fire in the stove. Outside the window, snow still fluttered in the air along Queen Anne Street.

And yet today, Watson felt that same thrill in his chest as from his younger days. It was important to remember it all clearly—what he had seen that day, what he had felt.

Since his marriage, Watson was not as close to Sherlock as he had once been. The separation was somewhat painful. Sherlock was still a bachelor, and had turned 49 only yesterday. After so much time, even Sherlock had begun to soften around the edges. Seeing each other as often as they did, Watson sometimes worried he might forget the sharp impression that Sherlock had made in those early days. In his manuscript, he wanted to capture the surprise and excitement he had experienced ten years prior, just as he had felt it then.

He'd only received the go-ahead for his current work a few months previous. Serialization would begin in October. Sherlock Holmes' return from the dead had already been widely reported, and few readers would now be shocked by the revelation. Still, Watson was swept away with joy at the prospect of writing of that April, back in 1894. It had been one of the happiest days of his life—the day he had been reunited with Sherlock.

Watson sat down at his desk. He was in high spirits as his pen moved across the paper. His publisher had urged him repeatedly to use a typewriter, but Watson had long since resolved he would compose all manuscripts by hand. He had his notes on one corner of the desk, but he wrote quickly, without referencing them. He remembered it all vividly, the events as clear as though branded into his mind: The loafers congregating at the Oxford Street end of Park Lane. Bumping into the old man with grey hair and side-whiskers—strictly speaking, that had been their true reunion.

He quickly filled the page. Suddenly, his pen stopped.

He was in the habit of writing down every detail, however trifling, when accompanying Sherlock on his cases. The clients' unusual requests and the splendid manner in which Sherlock solved the cases—Watson could not have forgotten them if he tried. Their adventures had been a series of deep and truly impressive moments.

He had to admit, however, that the details he heard only secondhand were much less clear in his mind. And this meant, naturally, that Sherlock's activities during the three years he'd been missing were still foggy. On the day of their reunion, Watson had not had the presence of mind to take notes; it hardly helped he'd fainted.

When Watson had written of his adventures with Sherlock in the past, he'd always used pseudonyms whenever he'd not been given permission to use real names. For instance, the Marquess of Salisbury had become Lord Bellinger. But in general he endeavored to be as accurate as possible regarding names and places.

Through the open door to the adjoining room, Watson could hear the hiss of the iron. Without rising from the desk, he called out for his wife. "Can you step in a moment?"

"What is it?" she asked.

"How does one spell Lama? Is it with two L's?"

"Yes, I should think so."

As the details came to him, Watson's pen raced across the page. The laboratory in the south of France Sherlock had returned from— it was in Montpelier, surely. Only…

What was that fighting technique Sherlock had used at the

Reichenbach Falls? It was something Japanese, he recalled. But what had it been? If he had been writing this at 221B Baker Street he might have used Sherlock's beloved encyclopedia. Perhaps one of the books in Watson's new lodgings might be of use?

He rose from his desk and began searching, and found the international section of a newspaper that had been stuffed into the bookshelf. The previous year, Britain and Japan had signed a military alliance; all the articles on Japan were largely concerned with that.

Emperor Nicholas II, of Russia, was pursuing a more aggressive stance against Japan in regards to Korea. Emperor Nicholas had ascended to the throne while still young; he had a short temper and seemed to hold Japan in contempt, an attitude that would likely be his own undoing—or so one of the editorials claimed.

Watson continued rifling through the papers, in hopes he might find an article on one of the Eastern boxing tournaments. Unfortunately very few of the articles were concerned with Japan. In March of last year a Japanese politician known as Hirobumi Ito had been anointed Knight Grand Cross of the Order of the Bath. The article mentioned the unequal treaty between Britain and Japan, which had been revised in the last decade or so.

Hirobumi Ito. He had once visited their lodgings at Baker Street, before he grew quite so influential. Afterward, though, there had been no connection. None of these articles had anything at all to do with Sherlock.

Then Watson found an old issue of *Pearson's Magazine*. He seemed to recall a feature on a Japanese fighting technique inside.

Flipping it open, he found it was not about fighting, but rather a form of self-defense that utilized a walking stick, devised by one Edward William Barton-Wright, with a basis in Eastern martial arts. Barton-Wright had lived in Japan until three years prior. He named his technique Bartitsu, after himself. Watson read through the article, but unfortunately it made no mention of the Japanese arts upon which Bartitsu was based.

He groaned reflexively. Ought he to ask Sherlock? No, he was on some case or other and was now at Tuxbury Old Park. Or so Watson had been told. After Watson had announced he would be married, Sherlock had said quite petulantly that thereafter any cases he went on alone, he'd write about on his own as well. And now that Sherlock had resolved to write his own memoirs, it would not do for Watson to be outdone. Asking for help this time was out of the question.

Watson supposed he need rely on memory after all. What was it, then? B… B… Now he had simply gotten "Bartitsu" into his head. But he was sure it started with a B. Something Japanese.

Baritsu. Yes, that was it! Baritsu!

The longer he thought about it, the surer Watson became. He rushed to his desk and resumed writing.

Now that he had overcome that small difficulty, his writing flowed without pause. The cab to Baker Street. The sardonic smile on Sherlock's face. Stepping out into the gloom at the corner of Cavendish Square, and slipping through the alleys to Manchester Street and then Blandford Street. Passing through the wooden gate and into that wild deserted yard. The empty house across from 221B Baker Street.

Watson's face broke irresistibly into a smile. Sherlock was like a tiger stalking his prey: his keen and piercing gaze, constantly roaming. And yet, when those same eyes alighted upon the weak, they were filled with limitless compassion. Though Sherlock Holmes was not one for social graces, he was a fearless defender of justice. His unparalleled intelligence and courage had saved the lives and fortunes of many a client. Surely he would continue to follow that path for many years to come.

My friend Sherlock Holmes, a man of rare courage and conviction.

Watson had perhaps grown a touch sentimental with age. He wiped at his eyes, on the verge of tears. It would be a shame to smudge the manuscript. He regathered his composure and began writing the conclusion to the case.

At that instant Holmes sprang like a tiger on to the marksman's back, and hurled him flat upon his face. He was up again in a moment, and with convulsive strength he seized Holmes by the throat, but I struck him on the head with the butt of my revolver, and he dropped again upon the floor. I fell upon him, and as I held him my comrade blew a shrill call upon a whistle. There was the clatter of running feet upon the pavement, and two policemen in uniform, with one plain-clothes detective, rushed through the front entrance and into the room.

"That you, Lestrade?" said Holmes.

"Yes, Mr. Holmes. I took the job myself. It's good to see you back in London, sir."

"I think you want a little unofficial help. Three undetected murders in one year won't do, Lestrade. But you handled the Molesey Mystery with less than your usual—that's to say, you handled it fairly well."

We had all risen to our feet, our prisoner breathing hard, with a stalwart constable on each side of him. Already a few loiterers had begun to collect in the street. Holmes stepped up to the window, closed it, and dropped the blinds. Lestrade had produced two candles, and the policemen had uncovered their lanterns. I was able at last to have a good look at our prisoner.

It was a tremendously virile and yet sinister face which was turned towards us. With the brow of a philosopher above and the jaw of a sensualist below, the man must have started with great capacities for good or for evil. But one could not look upon his cruel blue eyes, with their drooping, cynical lids, or upon the fierce, aggressive nose and the threatening, deep-lined brow, without reading Nature's plainest danger-signals. He took no heed of any of us, but his eyes were fixed upon Holmes' face with an expression in which hatred and amazement were equally blended. "You fiend!" he kept on muttering. "You clever, clever fiend!"

"Ah, Colonel!" said Holmes, arranging his rumpled collar. "'Journeys end in lovers' meetings,' as the old play says. I don't think I have had the pleasure of seeing you since you favoured me with those attentions as I lay on the ledge above the Reichenbach Fall."

The colonel still stared at my friend like a man in a trance. "You cunning, cunning fiend!" was all that he could say.

"I have not introduced you yet," said Holmes. "This, gentlemen, is Colonel Sebastian Moran, once of Her Majesty's Indian Army, and the best heavy-game shot that our Eastern Empire has ever produced. I believe I am correct, Colonel, in saying that your bag of tigers still remains unrivalled?"

About the Author

Keisuke Matsuoka was born in 1968. A novelist and screenwriter, he sold over a million copies with his 1997 debut psycho-thriller *Saimin* (Hypnosis). In quick succession followed the massively successful *Senrigan* (Clairvoyance) and its sequels, featuring an Air Self-Defense Force fighter pilot turned clinical psychologist. He is also the author of *The Appraisal Case Files of the Omnicompetent Q* series.